"Austin Boyd's fast-paced tale of g[...] world of international politics and [...] impatiently waiting for his next boo[...] novel from a major new talent."

— DAVIS BUNN, best-selling author

"Imbued with a realism that only someone who has served his country can evoke, Austin Boyd has taken us from the inner workings of the government to the emotional roller coasters of military families seized with the uncertainty of whether or not their loved one will return from a dangerous mission. This book has it all—adventure, love, faith, and service."

— JOHN W. MCDONALD, Colonel (retired), U.S. Army, Former Deputy under Secretary of the Army

"Austin Boyd has announced his arrival to the techno-thriller world with a novel that twists around in page-turning drama, heart-stopping thrills, and messages of faith and trust, all of which will capture the breath and heart of any reader. You'll be clamoring for the next installment."

— LYLE BIEN, Vice Admiral US Navy (retired)

"*The Evidence* reflects Austin Boyd's rich experience as a naval officer, aviator, and space engineer and his deep faith in Creator God. Austin has a genius for weaving complex ideas into an enjoyable story that is thought-provoking and encouraging."

— DALE W. SPENCE, Ed.D, Professor Emeritus of Kinesiology, Rice University, Houston, Texas

"From the spine-tingling opening to the cliff-hanging conclusion, Austin Boyd weaves a fascinating story of courage, intrigue, and exploration into the elements of character, calling, and faith. His technical knowledge of the military and space worlds is vast, but even greater is his understanding of the human heart. *The Evidence* kept me engrossed from beginning to end. I can't wait to see how the story unfolds in the next book."

— DAVID W. HULL, Pastor, First Baptist Church, Huntsville, Alabama

2/25/2016
R.L.S.

THE
EVIDENCE

A NOVEL

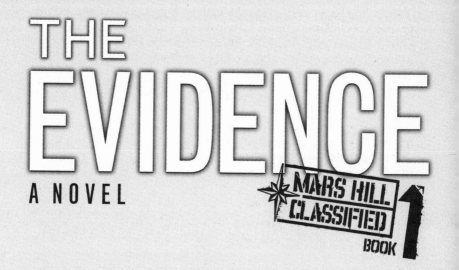

MARS HILL CLASSIFIED

BOOK 1

AUSTIN BOYD

LIVING INK BOOKS

Writing Worth Reading™

The Evidence

© 2006 by Austin Walker Boyd, Jr.

Living Ink Books, an imprint of AMG Publishers
6815 Shallowford Road
Chattanooga, TN 37421

Print Edition:	ISBN 13: 978-0-89957-828-6	ISBN 10: 0-89957-828-4
ePub Edition:	ISBN 13: 978-1-61715-379-2	ISBN 10: 1-61715-379-6
Mobi Edition:	ISBN 13: 978-1-61715-380-8	ISBN 10: 1-61715-380-X
ePDF Edition:	ISBN 13: 978-1-61715-381-5	ISBN 10: 1-61715-381-8

Cover design by Daryle Beam of Brightboy Design, Inc., Chattanooga, TN

This novel is a work of fiction. Names, characters, places, and incidents are either the product of the author's imagination or are used fictitiously. Any resemblance to actual events, locales, organizations, or persons, living or dead, is entirely coincidental and beyond the intent of either the author or publisher.

Previously published by NavPress.

Unless otherwise identified, all Scripture quotations in this publication are taken from the HOLY BIBLE: NEW INTERNATIONAL VERSION® (NIV®). Copyright © 1973, 1978, 1984 by International Bible Society. Used by permission of Zondervan Publishing House. All rights reserved. Other versions include *THE MESSAGE* (MSG), Copyright © 1993, 1994, 1995, 1996, 2000, 2001, 2002. Used by permission of NavPress Publishing Group.

Published in association with the literary agency of Leslie H. Stobbe, 300 Doubleday Road, Tryon, NC 28782.

Printed in the United States of America
1 2 3 4 5 6 7 8 9 10 –B– 17 16 15 14 13 12

To Cindy, my loving and faithful wife and friend.

"This is the woman that you will marry." God laid those special words on my heart in September 1978. Since that day you have been my best friend, my partner facing many trials, and a faithful spouse through decades of activity dominated by the word "astronaut." For all the beautiful years, for all of the hard work you have invested in me, for all the patience you showed and the separation you endured, for all the love you have shared, and for the four wonderful children you have given me, this book is dedicated entirely to you. I love you dearly.

Books by Austin Boyd

It Only Takes A Spark

The Evidence

The Proof

The Return

Nobody's Child

H_2O

SOME OF THE ELEMENTS of this book are true. A few of the people are real, although their names have been changed. Some of the experiences happened as they are recounted, but in different settings. Yet, this book is ultimately a work of fiction. The central themes of this novel could happen, and might. I wrote most of this manuscript long before the devastation of September 11, 2001, and well before the Mars Pathfinder, Spirit, Opportunity, and Curiosity rover missions were launched. So you see, fiction is not always so far from the truth. I encourage you to pray about how you will deal with the events in this novel that have not yet transpired.

With ten years in the formation of this novel, there are many who deserve acknowledgment. I owe great thanks to those who set me on a path to know Jesus Christ as my personal savior: my late grandfather and first mentor, Dr. Dea Bailey Calvin; my first track coach and great friend, Coach Jim McGehee of Hurricane, West Virginia; and my fellow harriers, Jeff Wells and John Lodwick, stellar distance runners for Rice University. Thanks also to my mentors: Dr. Dale Spence of Rice University; Dr. Rudy Panholzer and Dr. Allen Fuhs of the Naval Postgraduate School; Rear Admiral Pat Moneymaker (U.S. Navy, Retired); and Bill Gurley, Marv Price, and Dr. Joe Holmes of SAIC, Inc. I owe particular thanks to Vice Admiral Jerry Tuttle, (U.S. Navy, Retired), who taught me that "great opportunities are often brilliantly disguised as unsolvable problems;" and Captain Don Diaz, (U.S. Navy, Retired), whom God brought into my life that I might pursue my dream of a career in military space.

I owe a special debt of thanks to my father, Walker, and my late mother, Jody Boyd, of Sistersville, West Virginia. They encouraged me every step of the way and provided invaluable guidance in the development of characters and plot. Linda Z. Talley was my first fan, transforming hundreds of pages of handwritten notes into the book outline in 1997. My close friend, Commander David "Choke" Baciocco, (U.S. Navy, Retired), stood by my side for a decade, helping me to bring this book to you through his enthusiasm, plot ideas, and unflagging support. Yet, the manuscript would not be a book without the vision and enthusiasm of my agent, Les Stobbe, and the essential technical genius of many publishing friends, including Heather Szott (Hawkeye Editing, Inc.); Linda Nathan (Logos Word Designs, Inc.); Rachelle Gardner (Books and Such, Inc.); David Lambert (Howard Books); Terry Behimer; Jeff Gerke (Marcher Lord Press); Warren Baker, Trevor Overcash, Rick Steele, and Dale Anderson (AMG Publishers, Inc.), who labored to bring this book back into print.

God laid an intense desire on my heart at age twelve to do something to make a difference. I always interpreted that "make a difference" as selection for astronaut. Through God's direction and support, I came close—incredibly close—to that goal in 1994. Yet, in His perfect plan and timing, I was not selected to join the astronaut corps. God had other things in mind; astronaut selection was part of the journey but not the destination. Perhaps part of His plan was for me to share this story with you, to inspire you to inquire about the Creator who calls you to a personal relationship with Him. I encourage you to ask Jesus Christ into your life today. Ask him to take control of your life, to forgive you, and to lead you. Then share this book and your story with others so that they may know Him, too.

Austin Boyd
304 Broad Armstrong Drive,
Brownsboro, Alabama 35741
www.austinboyd.com

1

JOHN TUMBLED HALF-CONSCIOUS into the night-stand, sending a glass crashing across the cold marble floor.

The pounding that had awakened him still rocked his door. "Launch the alert crew!" the voice shouted again.

Dancing around the jagged glass shards, John sprang into a flight suit before the last knock sounded. Up and down the spartan hallway, shouts and clatter from his groggy combat aircrew shattered the early morning calm.

Seven minutes later, all twelve airmen piled into a cramped European van at the hotel's entrance, flight bags in hand. The smelly diesel-fueled shuttle lurched out of the portico and began a race to Athens airport and the crew's U.S. Navy submarine-hunter aircraft, the P-3C Orion. They had one hour from notification to be airborne.

John glanced at his watch. Nine precious minutes had passed. They caromed down vacant, narrow streets paved with ancient cobbles. Aware that all eyes were on him, John balanced on a tiny, bouncing perch at the front of the van and studied the classified message in his hand. "The Russians just popped up north of Libya. Victor III class," he said.

A low whistle came from a short crewman stuffed in the back. The Victor III was the stealthiest of Russian attack submarines, the quietest of all underwater predators in this, the noisiest water on the planet. No Mediterranean-based crew had ever tracked a Victor III; it was the elite of the Russian fleet. This could be history—if they succeeded.

"I don't just want to track this Ruskie. I want to humiliate him. The U.S. Navy is here to *stay*." John surveyed his experienced crew, a dozen brassy aviators on the verge of a great hunt, every one of them hungry for bear.

MEDITERRANEAN SEA, NORTH OF THE GULF OF SIDRA

Eleven hours later, orbiting over the last known location of the submarine, the crew continued to scan the sea for some sign of their quarry. Patrol Plane Commander John Wells and his copilot shifted in their seats in the cockpit, struggling to stay alert after nearly a half day in the air.

"Any contact, Sonics? I mean *anything*?" John asked on intercom.

"Zero, Flight. Nothin' in this water but fish and freighters."

The tactical coordinator chimed in. "We're almost out of sensors, Hawk. Want to leave early?"

"No way," John said. "Only takes one sonar contact to claim we got him. We stay." He wasn't about to quit what might be his last chance to nail a Russian. In a month, John would be home, his last tactical flying assignment completed. He was almost out of time.

"Only got ten sonar buoys left, Flight. Better drop 'em right on him, or it's all over." John's whiz tactician "Choke" Baciocco sat ten feet behind him in the loud aircraft, planning their next move in this crucial game. The final decision—stay or go—was up to John.

John nodded and double-clicked his microphone switch in silent reply. With a little luck, one of their deep hydrophones would get a "sniff," a brief acoustic trace of the silent craft. Visually scouring the water for any clue to the submerged warship, John strained for a last-minute chance to salvage this historic opportunity.

"Aw, come on, Commander. It's time for Happy Hour," said a voice on the intercom. "Friday night . . . Athens . . ."

"Ouzo!" someone else chimed in.

Not a chance. You never left time on the clock, sensors in your air-craft, or extra fuel in your tanks. Anything could happen—like during the cold war, those glory days when he and Choke flew their first mis-sions together, chasing every variant of Soviet missile submarine that slipped into the frigid North Atlantic. Countless covert missions more than a thousand miles from the nearest land, far from rescue, swearing never to divulge the day's secrets. Those missions were distant memories now, but the lessons were vivid.

"We stay," John said. He snugged his safety harness tighter and rolled into a crisp turn to hit the next computer-predicted drop of another hydrophone. Five thousand flight hours in a dozen models of aircraft guided his smooth control of the airliner-sized plane. Four engines roared as he advanced the throttles, accelerating toward the next sensor waypoint.

John's one consolation in the sunset of his tactical flying career was his return to family. The constant separation from his wife Amy, and his infant son tore at him. He pulled her picture from his sleeve pocket and wedged it under the instrument visor in front of him. As much as he loved to fly, to match wits with the enemy, he was ready to be home, to be a father and a full-time husband.

There was one more benefit to his return: the possibility, however remote, of astronaut selection. "Astronaut" was John's lifelong goal; Amy would say it was his *whole* life. He'd worn his knees out praying about it. Now, after years of work and six NASA applications, he was a *finalist*. Surely God understood that he had to make it this time. Soon he'd be thirty-six. The window for selection was about to close.

He buried his anxiety, pushing it deep to get his head back in the game.

The sun flirted with the horizon in front of him. Somewhere behind his right wing was Crete and beyond it, Greece. To his left, Benghazi and the infamous Gulf of Sidra. The flat Mediterranean shimmered like a golden platter before the brilliant sinking sun. It was an incredible panorama from the cockpit of the P-3C Orion, two miles above the ocean.

Yet the platter had a flaw, pointing straight into the dipping sun, a feather that tore the fabric of perfect gold. It was a wispy submarine periscope wake, unmistakable to his trained eyes, which had found more wakes, or feathers, than any man's in any squadron he'd served in. John had earned his flight call sign, Hawk, by locating submarines the old-fashioned way. With his eyes.

"Tally ho! Periscope. Eleven o'clock!" John called out as he whipped into action. "Radar, get me a fix! Warm up MAD!" The Magnetic Anomaly Detector would sense the slight magnetic field disturbances created by the submarine below, but only if John could get the plane down to two hundred feet, and fast.

"Choke. Set up for active sonar. Might be your last chance."

"Way ahead of you. Active sonar buoy 31, ready to drop. Sonics, d'you copy all that?" Choke said, his voice tight with anticipation.

"Roger that. Goin' active. Ready to pang him."

"Ping."

"Tha's what I said."

"Attack in two minutes, Hawk!" Choke yelled.

"Hang on!" John grinned as he yanked the power levers to idle, dropped the landing gear to increase his drag, and pointed the nose straight down toward the water. He was headed to the surface to slam the Ruskie.

The big plane plunged into a sickening dive. "Yee-haw!" screamed Sonics, their drawling Georgian sonar whiz, as the crew floated weight-less in their seat harnesses. John knew his experienced copilot, flight call-sign Bulldog, had been through this hair-raising maneuver a dozen times, but the color still drained from the face of the young man to his right.

John wrapped the plane into a nauseating sixty-five degree angle of bank until all that could be seen in the windshield was water. The huge craft hurled toward the ocean like a suicidal fighter jet.

Bulldog called out rates of descent and completed checklists as the altimeter wound backward in a wild race toward zero. The flight engi-neer hovered over the power levers and his panorama of dials, switches, and knobs. With one exception, the members of Combat Air Crew Six were a well-choreographed squad. Clutching the radar console behind John, third pilot Phil Armstrong, new to naval aviation, tried to hold down his lunch.

In a flurry of six hands and a dozen levers, the landing gear came up, engines went to full throttle, and the plane leveled in a low-altitude thrill ride just a hair's breadth above the green sea. The surface raced below them at three hundred knots. Surrounded by the piercing whine of four massive turboprops, with a Russian ahead of them and cocked weapon racks below, the adrenaline gushed through twelve modern warriors. This was the stuff of dreams.

"Ready, Choke? Let's waste him."

"Ready, Hawk. Torpedo selected. Get me on top."

The P-3C Orion roared across the water toward the last ripples left by a periscope that had sliced through a flat sea. The sun was half-submerged ahead of them, and the submarine was gone. Ivan was on the run. John shook his head in silence, sure the Russian could hear them. The whine of their engines poured more energy into the sea than a pair of Chinese garbage scows.

No one cared about stealth now. They were about to bang their quarry with everything they had in their peacetime arsenal. Everyone was poised for the magic word: MADMAN—the code word that the airplane's sensitive electronics had plucked a magnetic needle from the saltwater haystack. In the middle of a million square miles of water, they had to fly directly over the Russian to find him.

Had it been wartime, the open bomb bay and its loaded weapon racks would be ready to release a deadly accurate high-speed torpedo to chase down even the fastest quarry. Today, however, their torpedoes were simulated. If they caught him, their quarry would live to see another day—but not before a dreaded active sonar buoy would ping the Victor III into submission, ripping away any veil of stealth. In this high-stakes peacetime game, locating the enemy with an active sonar buoy was as good as a kill.

John leveled his wings and flew toward the invisible submarine, armed with a sixth sense. The Russian was below him. He was sure of it.

"MADMAN! MADMAN!" The sensor operator alerted the crew as the sensitive stylus flailed in a bloody frenzy across his data recorder. "Pen banger!"

"Weapon away! Smoke away! Active buoy away!" Choke yelled into his microphone as he punched a dozen buttons on the tactical panel. A smoke buoy fell to the water, igniting to mark the sub's location, and the sonar buoy began to unreel its acoustic gear seconds after water impact. The bomb bay weapon rack clicked open, releasing an imaginary torpedo to find its prey.

Most eyes were on the tactical computer scopes, but John craned his neck to the left, searching for a sign of white smoke on the water as he counted to himself. He trusted his eyes. John knew that many of his crewmen dreaded what came next. It took a perfect gut-wrenching three-G turn to make the maneuver work. He counted down the final seconds out loud. ". . . Two, one, now!"

John concentrated on the altimeter as he hauled the big airplane into a sixty-degree turn to the left and pulled hard on the yoke. Any slip in his airmanship at this point and the plane would dive headlong into the ocean below. They were either seconds from death or a minute from the next simulated kill. The force of three gravities drained blood from his head in the tight turn. Over the intercom, Choke let out a piercing war-whoop.

The plane never dipped. The altimeter looked like it was stuck on two hundred feet as they whipped in a tight circle to capture the escaping Russian. There was nothing to see outside but a watery grave as the plane shuddered in the tight turn. In his peripheral vision, John saw Bulldog shake his head in wonder. His copilot had never succeeded at flying the perfect high-G turn.

"Hydrophone's deployed. Ping it!" Choke commanded over the intercom in the back of the noisy bucking plane.

"Fixin' to pang him . . . now!" The Georgian's next move blasted a wall of acoustic energy into the sea that could be heard by whales a thousand miles away. The ear-splitting *poing* jolted the warm waters as it located the submarine with astounding precision and reverberated through the enemy's soundproofed black hull. *Poing! Poing!* The Georgian boiled the water with sound.

"Got him! Forty-three yards, bearin' 280 degrees off buoy 31."

"MADMAN! MADMAN!"

"He turned left!" Choke called out orders as John, anticipating the Russian, counted quietly and rolled into a tight right turn. Another three G's of churning guts and head-numbing joy. Behind him, John could hear Phil puke a chunky puddle on the cockpit floor. John's nose wrinkled as he remembered his own days of barfing in hot cockpits where there was no up or down.

"Sorry, buddy. We're not done yet." John's eyes were fixed on the instruments, his lips moving in a silent prayer. He snapped the plane to wings level, bearing down on the invisible prey.

Again, the sub made a radical course correction. But it was too late.

"MADMAN!"

The open bomb bay doors roared in the airstream as Choke simulated the release of a second torpedo. "Weapon away!"

John high-fived his flight engineer as they closed a virtual coffin on the unseen Russian submariners, then wrapped the plane into a third hair-raising turn.

"Time to go," Choke announced moments later, grunting under the G-load. "Relief aircraft above us . . . want some of Ivan . . . before it's too late . . . lots of pukin' back here."

John nodded, clicking the mike twice to confirm his friend's request, then leveled the wings and advanced the throttles. The aircraft leapt forward as John pointed the nose into the sky and headed for home base. The placid emerald waters quickly faded into a blue grey sea far below them.

Half an hour later, on the return to Athens, John turned the pilot seat over to Phil and sauntered to the back through the cockpit's blackout curtains. Choke and the navigator met him at their station sporting wicked grins.

"Message from Naples, sir." The navigator pointed to the printer.

"Guess they got our news, eh?" John said with a smile. "'Saw sub. Sank same.'"

"Seems so." The grins got bigger.

John's smile faded as he eyed his crew warily, sure of a prank. Choke was full of them. "Okay. Hand it over."

The navigator tore off a sheet from the line printer and passed it with a reverential bow to John.

Something was amiss. John yelled at the pilots beyond the black-out curtain. "You guys okay up there? I think I'm about to get had."

"I'm sure you deserve it," Bulldog yelled back. "Be sure to read it on intercom."

Now John was sure he was being set up. Bulldog, a quiet young man with no sense of humor, was somehow in on this, too.

John read the terse tactical message aloud. "One-eight December. Well done, crew six. First active sonar contact on Victor III in Med. Admiral Tuttle sends personal congratulations. Additional news for Mission Commander—" John blanched, then coughed, unable to continue.

"Go on, John," Choke urged, his smile widening. "We all want to hear."

John felt light-headed as he scanned down the message. He leaned his tall frame into the white bulkhead and continued. "Skip—" He took a breath and continued. "Skipper advises that NASA requests you report to Houston, Texas, February 1999. New assignment: Astronaut Candidate. Congratulations, Hawk. You finally made it."

MONASTIRAKI SQUARE, ATHENS, GREECE

"No more for me!" John waved off the offer of another souvlaki sandwich and the bottle of cheap yellow wine.

"Come on, Commander. *Retsina!* Celebrate the kill!"

John shook his head and toasted his happy crew with the dregs of a lukewarm Coke.

"I've really enjoyed this, fellas. Now go home. And don't let the Ouzo loosen you up, got it?" He smiled, sure that at least one of his airmen would drink his way into trouble.

"Where'll we find your skinny body tomorrow?" Choke kidded as they stood up.

"The Parthenon." John slapped his best friend on the back as they parted ways on the crowded sidewalk. "Get 'em to bed, Choke. And sleep in." Combat Aircrew Six, the "Sons of Thunder" from Patrol Squadron Eight, flowed downhill toward their hotel, cheering their commander as they sang off-key on their way to the next bar.

Alone at last, John soaked in the night air and the old market district. He loved Athens. He closed his eyes and drank in the odors—roasting lamb, souvlaki spits, coffee shops, olive oil, spices, and that unmistakable but elusive odor of oldness—the ancient city smell.

John climbed through the cobblestone alleys of the Agora toward the Acropolis, heart pounding with expectation. He was on a quest for closure. Beyond the tall cedars and clay tile rooftops, the Acropolis dominated the skyline. Athens' crown jewel, the Parthenon, adorned the top of the mount, bathed in a spectacular white light. It was his beacon, the Sacred Rock.

The years of toil that had brought him to this hour were now behind him like the sidewalks and cafés in his wake. He had reached the final ascent of his personal Everest: selection for the astronaut program.

Today's news confirmed the unwavering sense he had received years ago—a sense that he was called to make a difference. He'd endured years of ridicule for his insistence that he was destined to be an astronaut, but tonight all the jibes were forgotten. The Acropolis and its sister mount to the west, Areopagus, rose before him in the distance. One of countless pilgrims across forgotten centuries who had followed the apostle Paul to this place, John was here for closure and to give thanks.

He climbed past old women in black shawls and scarves, old men arguing politics, and groups of nubile Greek girls trolling the sidewalks arm in arm with their girlfriends. A late-night sea of shoppers parted as he pressed upstream, past the three-thousand-year-old walls of the city. History and its monuments towered over him.

Ahead, the path scaled the Acropolis on marble steps carved by long-forgotten hands. John climbed with care up the well-worn marble, once the site of the ancient court of Athens. The slick, bare, rounded rock of Areopagus rose like an ancient lectern above the ruins and the city below. On this rock, the apostle Paul once stood in the midst of Athenian nobles and orators, preaching with confidence about the Unknown God.

He scaled the rounded outcropping, alone at the peak. A small, red New Testament waited in his pocket for this very moment. Only Amy knew the story of the precious old book, a fifth-grade gift from the Gideon Society. It flew with him on every flight, wrapped in a waterproof bag and stored in his survival vest. He opened the brittle pages to the story of Paul's witness to the Greeks in Athens. As he did, he connected with history, reaching out across the millennia.

> *From one man he made every nation of men, that they should inhabit the whole earth; and he determined the times set for them and the exact places where they should live. God did this so that men would seek him and perhaps reach out for him and find him, though he is not far from each one of us. 'For in him we live and move and have our being.'*

✦

Few people, except perhaps his wife, fully understood what compelled John so powerfully toward space. Amy had been so upbeat when he shared the news with her tonight by phone, but he also felt her angst, her deep longing for him to be home. That separation was his lone regret about his chosen career.

I will provide.

The promise flooded over him, a quiet assurance that he and Amy would not be tested beyond their ability to cope. He could see a clear handprint on all the open doors and vanquished challenges that stretched out behind him. God had brought him this far—had brought him here—for a purpose.

Areopagus. The Mars Hill of Athens. John sank to his knees on the cool polished rock, a lone pilgrim late at night, overflowing with thanks. As he prayed, he looked up, probing the few stars that weren't washed out by Athens' lights. A fuzzy red dot in the washed-out sky twinkled as it beckoned him.

Mars.

BRUNSWICK NAVAL AIR STATION, MAINE

Amy Wells stood motionless at the bay window of her old duplex on Brunswick Naval Air Station. The winter sun was at the apex of its low arc to the south, beyond massive fir trees that encircled the senior officer housing. She stared at the cul-de-sac, invisible below a perfect blanket of fresh snow and bordered by four-foot-tall frozen ridges of dirty white stuff. She was in awe of the handiwork of nature poured out before her.

Powder drifted down from the giant hemlock in the front yard, showering the house in a mini-storm. Gems danced before her in the noon light as she longed for what she had not yet lost. She twirled long hair in her fingers as she watched the frozen wonderland. There would be no snow in Texas, no cold, no sledding or L.L. Bean, no clam chowder, no lobsters or Bar Harbor. Only concrete, stucco, and heat. Oppressive mind-numbing heat.

And a husband? Would her one love be lost to the complete immersion that John would require as he fulfilled his dream, training for dangerous missions that would take him away? She wished silently for more time with him, and for peace—reminding herself that the anxiety tugging at her was the enemy. She smiled sadly as she marveled at the snowy images dancing before her. Texas would have its own magic, she tried to convince herself, but her shoulders sagged.

John's distant voice still echoed in her ears, so full of joy from far away in Greece. She could imagine him standing before her, his face alive with emotion. He would be cheering their achievement of a lifetime. She smiled again, wishing with all her soul she could be celebrating with him. She bent over, distracted by an errant sock on the floor, one of Abe's many articles discarded about the house.

Deep within her spirit was a painful tug, a strain in her heart, some sense that in John's calling she would have her own ministry and suffer dark trials. As John was sure of his call to space, she was certain of something else: There would be sacrifice and loss. Doubt crept in, and she drove it out, again forcing a smile—yet never completely freeing herself from that nagging dread, that sense that this life mission of her husband's would test her to the limit. And a sense of defeat that, despite her best efforts at the daily control of her life, it was coming unraveled at the worst possible time. She wanted to stay. In Maine. With John.

Sunlight danced across her round face through the glitter of falling snow as she sank to her knees beside the couch.

The reassuring "tick-tick-tick" of her baby's wind-up swing had stopped.

Amy rolled to her side and sat on the floor, her knees numb. A damp spot on the couch marked where she'd buried her head an hour ago to pour out her heart. She chided herself—she had forgotten to wind the swing. She checked the clock. She had eighty-seven minutes left until her next insulin bolus.

Seven-month-old Abe was immobile, his head tilted back in slumber. The peace would be short-lived, but the silence was sweet. The old house snuggled her in its familiar oil-fired warmth.

Chaos.

A tumult raged inside her, a desperation for order and control amidst a life whose well-planned structure was unraveling by the second. She marveled at sleeping Abe, his tiny face at peace with the world.

Change.

She sat down by her son and rested an arm on the damp cushion, struggling to clear her mind of all her tasks and schedules, to free herself of images of mountains of boxes and the carnage of burly movers. Reminders of new messes that she must clean, a new home that she must build. Without John—because her husband would be immersed in yet another challenge, with more training, more trips . . . more accomplishments . . . that would leave her alone. Again.

She fought the tears, scolding herself for slipping into self pity, for losing control. For separating herself from the other women who tried to reach out to her. She would endure this, too. Like all the other lonely times—just one more solitary Navy wife.

A new stream of tears pulled her head down in defeat as Abe rested quietly beside her.

2

thirteen years later

A CLOUD OF WHITE dust rose behind a tractor-trailer as it cut across the sagebrush plains of Nevada's high desert. The truck moved slower than the narrow dirt road demanded but fast enough for the nervous driver, picking his way down the private ranch lane. Ahead, foothills rose from the desert floor and swallowed the road in the distance. The truck and its occupants, anxious for dusk, chased a retreating sun.

The sun began to settle as the driver reached the foothills and eased the rig back into a dry canyon. He climbed out of the cab and checked the road behind him. He was alone.

Five minutes after his arrival, the trailer was disconnected, and he was on his way. Behind him, the unmanned refrigeration trailer remained hidden between steep rock walls. By the time he joined the main highway, the last remnants of the sun had disappeared beyond the foothills, shrouding the trailer in darkness.

Five hours later, a light plane approached from the south. Flying low, a twin-engine Beechcraft circled southeast of the canyon. Two passengers maintained surveillance of the canyon mouth with night-vision equipment and telephoto cameras.

"Trailer's in sight," said the passenger in the rear seat, dressed in camouflage and armed with a nightscope to pick out the trailer against the backdrop of rock. His face was nondescript in the eerie green glow of the night-vision device.

The pilot nodded and made a quick radio call. "Lima 42 has traffic in sight. Ready for vectors."

The reply was immediate. "Roger, Lima 42. Stand by, fifteen seconds."

A quarter of a minute later, the sky northwest of the aircraft erupted in a searing, white-orange flash. As if hit by a shock wave, the nightscope observer fell backward across the plane's rear seat, cursing and grabbing his eyes. An inferno one hundred meters across exploded into the night sky and transformed into a mushroom-like cloud at its zenith. The intense blast pulverized the canyon into a pall of orange dust and rock. The cockpit, seconds before illuminated only by the red glow of the instrument panel, was now bright as day.

The pilot struggled hard to focus on the flight instruments. His night-vision was shot. As the last of the fireball faded, no canyon remained in sight, only a ragged rubble-filled pockmark in the side of the arid Nevada hill. The passengers deafened each other with a succession of war whoops as the Beechcraft banked to the east, twenty meters off the desert floor, flying below the watchful eyes of radar.

Darkness was their ally.

INTERNATIONAL SPACE STATION ALPHA

The intercom speakers chimed eight bells, reminiscent of the brass ding of a ship's clock. Twelve midnight, Houston time. Every star in the sky shone on the brilliant white International Space Station as it sped past the California coastline toward a sunrise over Scotland. The half dozen Tinkertoy cylinders connected to mirror-like solar wings created the brightest light in the night sky.

Twelve years after his selection as an astronaut candidate, Navy Captain John Wells, age forty-seven, pulled himself closer to the massive viewing window in the Destiny laboratory module of the International Space Station. Floating weightless with his face close to the optical glass, he marveled at the incredible night scene below. He'd just finished his watch as the duty pilot and drifted to the laboratory to catch a sunrise. He never tired of watching the sun peek over the rim of Earth every ninety-five minutes as they emerged from the dark side of an orbit.

After twelve years with NASA, John was on his third space flight, but his first in the space station, or "Alpha," as they called it. The recent addition of a habitation module made the outpost more spacious than a four-bedroom home—and four times as large as its Russian predecessor, Mir. He was honored to be part of the first-ever four-person crew. But this flight might also be his last. After four months in orbit, he already dreaded that day two months away when he would have to leave. His space career . . . a good one . . . was nearing its end. Younger astronauts would take his place. Retirement, from NASA—and the Navy—would come too soon.

As the glow of Los Angeles passed behind the station, a huge orange beam burned through the blackness, creating a brilliant point of light easily visible three hundred and fifty kilometers above. The intense color riveted him.

"What *was* that?" a voice asked.

John flinched and looked back. Mission Specialist Astronaut Dr. Michelle Stevens had floated up behind him, her hair encircling her head in a perfect wreath—a pleasant characteristic of weightlessness. "Don't know," John replied, "but it lit up like a nuke—about five hundred kilometers east of LA."

Both astronauts watched in silence. John hoped for a repeat performance, but the orbiting station moved out of range.

"Got to call that one in," John commented as he pushed away from the glass and headed for the station's operations module, Zarya.

"Hurry back, or you'll miss the sunrise," she reminded him.

John pulled himself through the hatch. "Plenty more yet to come," he said over his shoulder as he squeezed past the "wall of water," a dozen thirty-liter bags of life-giving fluid lashed to the bulkhead.

"It was beautiful, John." Michelle turned a shoulder toward him as he returned. She moved aside only slightly, and John had to nudge in close to get a look, grabbing one of the portal handholds to slow his approach. A bright yellow morning swept over the emerald isle in the midst of a brilliant blue Irish sea. "Get the message through?" she asked.

"Houston will call the Air Force in Colorado. They'll look into it."

She stared at John as he peered through the glass. The bright light gleamed off his forehead and washed through the graying stubble of his flattop. Earthlight illuminated his face, throwing shadows across high prominent cheekbones, traces of Cherokee blood somewhere in his past.

John turned his head and caught her gaze. She blushed and quickly looked back out the window toward Earth.

"You okay, Mich?"

"Me? . . . Yeah. Great view," she said.

"Sure," John replied, his eyebrows bunched and deep furrows creasing his forehead.

Michelle put on her best pearly smile as she looked back down at him. "Relax, Hawk. You're safe here." She winked as she spun around and pushed away.

ANDALUSIA, ALABAMA

Bright lights streamed out the windows of a long recreational vehicle parked near the banks of the Conecuh River. Except for the hum of generators, nothing disturbed the warm March night in this abandoned deer camp deep in the pinewoods of south Alabama.

Inside, Tex Fister, a lanky man dressed in his usual straight-legged jeans, oyster button shirt, and pointed boots, was hunched over a radio control panel. Watching his four men from the far end of the cramped RV, Tex's boss waited for news of their mission.

"Plane's off the area, Nick," Tex reported. "Huge success."

Their leader nodded assent. Nick's eyes gleamed from the glare of the array of flat-panel screens that bedecked the control consoles of the mobile command post and its satellite communication equipment.

"A toast," Nick said, picking up a bottle of Cabernet, his trademark beverage. Glasses were passed around the van as his crew shared in the revelry. Nick watched the others as he swirled the red liquid in a tall snifter, occasionally sampling the contents. In stark contrast to the larger and heavier well-tanned men in his employ, he was a small, well-muscled man, pasty white.

Nick basked in the dark mystique of his private covert operation. His team's actions, and their ultimate escape, had been planned—and financed—for years. There would be no careless mistakes, no trailer parts with traceable serial numbers or explosive taggants, to give his team away. The forensics on this explosion would be fruitless. He could have launched his inaugural bomb anywhere. Somehow, it had seemed most fitting to take the daring approach. He had exploded it where everyone could watch.

Expertise in space operations, learned through long years in the Air Force, was the technical niche that Nick brought to this mission. He could just imagine the evening watch at the 14th Air Force Space Operations Center at Vandenberg Air Force Base in California. At this very moment, response teams would be scrambling to confirm a cue from distant space systems that had detected the huge fireball over the Nevada desert. A blast that large would be clearly visible to the remarkable military satellite systems stationed forty thousand kilometers above the equator.

Space Station Alpha would have been over Nevada at the time of the burst, and someone on board might have reported the intense flash. United Airlines Flight 52 would be into the first hour of its red-eye flight from Los Angeles to Washington DC. The bored pilots wouldn't hesitate to tell FAA of the fireball that lit up the Nevada desert. Someone, probably at Northern Command in Colorado, would inform Washington, the Joint Chiefs of Staff, and surely the media.

Explosives experts from the Department of Homeland Defense would model the blast and calculate that a forty-foot trailer, filled with a twelve-thousand-kilogram mix of diesel oil and nitrate fertilizer, had been remotely detonated under a night sky. Intelligence analysts and explosive experts would rush to discover who had made the bomb and why. Nick's team had been careful to feed all the false leads they needed to preserve their anonymity.

Covert operations, especially on the scale of this one, were expensive. None of the men knew the identity of their mysterious and wealthy benefactor. Nick knew only that it was a woman, older, presumably rich, with a deep sophisticated voice. Likely well-connected and influential. But names didn't matter. They shared a common philosophy—and a common enemy. Using Nick's ingenious Internet communications, the two spoke every Saturday morning, and the money flowed whenever and wherever it was needed. Nick operated around the law with slow meticulous planning, flawless execution—and no trail.

"Pack up! On the road in thirty minutes," Nick barked. The wine disappeared in an instant.

The team pulled down a satellite communications antenna, rolled up power cords, and packed generators. Twenty-seven minutes later, a caravan rolled out of the deep pinewoods southwest of Andalusia, one man sweeping away all remnants of their passage in the loose sand. Only a few hours after they'd arrived at the deer camp, they were gone, not even a tire track left to mark their brief stay.

MONDAY, MARCH 21, 2011: SOUTH OF COAL CREEK, COLORADO

Ten days after their sweaty night in Alabama, the caravan was parked at an abandoned airstrip and mining operation in southwestern Colorado. Shadows of fallen buildings, piles of mine tailings, and a disheveled hangar were their lonely hosts at this forgotten site. In the old hangar, ten single-engine aircraft waited in their tie-downs. The last four-wheel-drive pickup pulled into the old Colorado mining camp under a clear night sky long after midnight.

"Wake up, Boss," Tex said from his seat in a swivel chair near the front of the RV. "Billy just pulled in."

Nick snapped upright in a narrow bunk. "What time is it?"

"After midnight. He's late."

Nick swore aloud, crawled out of his bed, and made a beeline for the pickup and their tardy partner. He walked up to the Ford and caressed the dusty red metal of the fender. When he caught Billy's eye he slammed the hood with his fist, creasing the new truck.

"Ease off, Nick," a large man said. "The front tire blew and the spare was flat. Had to hitch a ride, buy a tire, and mount it. That takes time." Billy was no pushover at twice the weight of his boss, and a foot taller.

"Migrant family gave me a ride. I took a cab back to the truck," Billy said, looking away.

Nick tensed, aware of the vulnerability Billy's bad fortune had thrust upon them. He shook his head, narrowing his eyes as he looked the big man up and down. "All right. Get going. Make up the lost time."

Billy unloaded his generators and lights. Once the area was lit, the team began to install radios and global positioning receivers into the aircraft equipment bays. With practiced precision, Red and Cliff, the team's avionics and engine experts, configured the ten light planes and towed them out to the short runway. Cliff began to test satellite communication control links between the aircraft and Tex, who was at the RV's remote controls.

"D'you think Billy gave us away?" Red asked, looking back at Billy where he worked in the hangar. Red was a heavy gray-haired man, sweating in the cold air as he willed old muscles to pull harder while he maneuvered the last plane into position.

His partner, Cliff, didn't answer right away, but followed Red's gaze back toward the vehicles. "Not on purpose. But who knows what those Mexicans saw when they picked him up?"

At precisely 4:00 a.m., Nick jogged out of the RV and headed for the aircraft. "Comms check perfect," he said. "Button 'em up. Launch in fifteen minutes."

"They're ready." Red patted a Cessna 152 on the wing. "Three hundred kilos each of high explosive. Remote control, autonomous navigation, radar altimeter fuses. These babies can do it all."

Nick made a point of stroking the propeller of each plane, fascinated with this weaponry's ingenuity and power. Years of careful planning and practice had built to this crucial moment. "Get Flight One ready for takeoff," he said. He spun and headed back to the RV.

Inside the RV, Nick paced as he watched the final preparations, a Coke in hand. Displays on five consoles, complete with joysticks, provided Nick and Tex a readout of all the aircraft instruments and airplane locations transmitted covertly over military satellite communications. A large plasma display on the wall at the end of the RV provided digital maps of Colorado and the United States. Whether parked or driving down the highway, the team could direct the flights of all ten aircraft. When necessary, they could also provide remote voice communications, lest air traffic controllers realize the aircraft were unmanned. Nick and Tex had prepared four of these mobile control centers, now deployed around the country. They had reached the defining moment in their long preparation. They could not fail.

Nick watched as Cliff held onto a custom-built control handle at the rear of the first aircraft, Cliff's unique contraption to steady the airplane on the runway with one hand while the engine was running. Nick signaled the men with a flashlight, and Red started the engine of the first plane from a remote panel in the tail avionics compartment. The plane's prop wash buffeted the men in the dim light as Red and Cliff held the plane, waiting for Nick to give the command and send the Cessna to the sky.

"Launch Flight One," Nick said at last.

At the first console, Tex took remote control of the flight system, and with the click of a button, he powered the aircraft out of the old man's grasp on the runway. Nick watched the aircraft roll smoothly down the runway and lift into the chill predawn air. He nodded silently, his eyes on the monitors and a digital clock on the wall of the van.

"Climbing to two hundred feet, en route waypoint one," Tex said as he engaged the autopilot and allowed the onboard computer to do the rest of the work.

One by one, Tex launched ten aircraft and flew them east at separate departure vectors well below radar. When they finally popped up on Air Traffic Control, with flight plans filed to Colorado Springs, the aircraft would look to the FAA like unrelated general aviation contacts.

Forty-five minutes later, Tex slapped a console and pointed to the big screen video that showed the ten aircraft tracks flying north along the foothills in the general direction of Colorado Springs. "All birds are nominal, Nick. We're ready to roll. Impact in an hour."

"Okay. Put the birds on auto." Nick leaned out the RV door and called the rest of the team in to join Tex at the consoles. Minutes later, each man seated at a console, Nick was ready to begin.

"Point Bravo checkpoint south of the Springs at 0530. Computers should drop 'em down low at 0545 and plow into home base promptly at 0600." He paused, looking around the assembled group, making eye contact with each man. "Flawless execution, gentlemen. No mistakes."

They nodded. Two years of training were paying off.

"Check on the other crews, Tex." Elsewhere, aircraft launched in just the way these ten had been converged on their targets in northern Virginia, Maryland, and Washington DC. Four control vans, four teams, forty aircraft. Twenty handpicked experts.

"Picture looks good. All forty aircraft are airborne," Tex said, motioning to the U.S. map and forty separate tracks. "Links are also up to the fixed sites. Good reports from everyone."

Nick settled down in a captain's chair at the rear of the compartment, popping open a fresh can of macadamia nuts as he spoke in a quiet firm voice. "Let the games begin."

3

"GOOD MORNING, ADMIRAL. WELCOME back from Saudi."

"Thanks, Petty Officer Nathan. It's good to be home. Snow, mountains . . . and no more sand fleas."

The young petty officer stood at her desk when he entered, her uniform perfect and posture ramrod straight. She had coffee prepared every day by 5:30 a.m. The drip had just finished.

"The morning brief is ready when you are, sir."

"In a minute. I'd like some private time."

"Yes, sir."

The admiral passed through the executive assistant's office into his own and closed the door. Behind him, the daily activity of Northern Command, or NORTHCOM, shifted into high gear. Watch standers spent the night mining data from around the world and gathering intelligence assessments to prepare their bosses for the decisions of the coming day. The day shift presented the material and developed the responses. Petty Officer Nathan was one cog in this massive machine called Homeland Defense. Near the top of that chain sat Rear Admiral Victor Hayes, the NORTHCOM director of operations.

Inside his office, Rear Admiral Hayes pondered a strange sense of foreboding. He couldn't explain it, but something was very wrong. He stared out the expansive window at the snow-covered slopes of Pikes Peak to the west and the single light at the top of the rugged mountain. Sunrise was in full swing, and the snow took on a pastel hue as the rays painted it pink, red, and orange. Within an hour, the snow would be blinding white.

He imagined the new workday beginning deep within the impenetrable snow-capped Cheyenne Mountain, south of Pikes Peak, as Strategic Command watch standers soon would change shifts at 0600 hours. Today's new crew would consume terabytes of data from satellite surveillance systems, ship radars, ground cameras, and the super-cooled optic eyes of the Defense Support Program, each sensor combining to give them the eye on any missile launch around the globe. He knew the rigors of their often tedious job, defending against a possible missile salvo and nuclear holocaust. A job for which surveillance of space junk was also a critical part of their mission, preventing potential ultra-high-speed impacts that could disable critical national space intelligence systems, the shuttle orbiter, or the International Space Station.

All the operational capabilities of the United States military were at his disposal. He could reach the president, the secretary of defense, even the NATO secretary general from his phone if he wanted to—yet all the power of his position could not quell the uneasiness that gnawed at him.

Turning from the window, the admiral sat on the corner of his desk and thumbed through a well-worn leather-bound Bible, not searching for any particular passage, but open for insights. Then he heard a plane.

He looked up abruptly—a flash on the side of Cheyenne Mountain, to the left of Pikes Peak, illuminated the predawn murk. As he strained to see where the explosion had occurred, a second fireball erupted. It was the Cheyenne Mountain entrance, he was sure. Rear Admiral Hayes was reaching for his red phone, the classified direct line to the operations center in the hardened core of the building, when a Cessna 185 flew by low—much too low—headed toward the high-security antenna farm adjacent to NORTHCOM. Those antennas were his eyes and ears and his command link for the defense of the country. He was momentarily frozen—then his training kicked in as he screamed for Petty Officer Nathan, picked up the red phone and threw the Bible on his desk.

He'd only spoken half a word into the receiver when a thunderous clap slammed him violently from the back. Glass shards sliced the air like hundreds of razor-sharp shotgun pellets. Pierced with glass, a blast wave flung him across twenty feet of red carpet into the flinching body of Petty Officer Nathan in the doorway. Intense heat melted their polyester uniforms and charred their flesh. The admiral's face slammed into the doorjamb. Furniture, books, and a storm of glass flew around them as they careened through the doorway.

The lifeless admiral and petty officer and a massive walnut desk caught a surprised Navy captain squarely in the back, crushing them all through the next wall toward the center of the building. The anti-terrorist blast protection for the exterior of the complex was insufficient to contain the power of this explosion.

NORTHCOM lay ripped open. After two successive aircraft bombs, a ragged smoking gash lined with twisted girders and shredded concrete led from demolished outer walls to the hardened core of NORTHCOM—the Operations Center—the only part of the building that remained unbreached.

But not for long. Minutes later, a massive detonation razed even that hardened core. A tall green Air Force pumper truck, the first to arrive and parked adjacent to NORTHCOM, erupted along with ten thousand-kilograms of embedded explosives. The cleverly disguised fire truck weapon pulverized the headquarters for America's homeland defense. NORTHCOM and the brains of America's space surveillance system collapsed in a pall of dust, concrete, and twisted girders.

SOUTH OF COAL CREEK, COLORADO

As the telemetry links from each aircraft fell silent, Nick silently tallied the impacts, his lips moving slightly.

He knew that the watch floor at Cheyenne Mountain would be pandemonium by now. His little gift wouldn't slow down operations, but it would have obliterated the command's primary entrance. The huge blast doors would be sealed under a temporary wall of rocky rubble. Nick smiled as he remembered the narrow emergency tunnel, now the crew's only access. It would be days, perhaps weeks, before the operational capability of the mountain's watch teams was fully restored. A tiny smile played at the corner of his mouth.

Nick and his crew watched the satellite transmissions as telemetry links failed when flights drove their deadly payloads into satellite ground control sites, antenna farms, and mission control buildings at Peterson Air Force Base to the northeast. Inside of three minutes, the aircraft destroyed the entire ground-control infrastructure of the national network of infrared space sensors, along with key offices of the Northern Command Headquarters.

"All seven primary targets are destroyed. The mountain and NORTHCOM are blind—for now."

"What about the mobile missile defense control vans overseas?" Nick asked.

"Verified that they were out of commission an hour ago. Just like you planned," Tex replied as he manipulated the controls for an aircraft on final approach to its target.

"Beautiful," Nick said, setting the empty macadamia nut can aside to make an entry in a notebook that he carried in his back pocket. "Place the call, Tex, and continue to the secondary targets."

Tex nodded and hit "speaker" on a phone to his left. He dialed and the line rang once, then answered.

"Status?" asked a cultured feminine voice.

"All clear. You have a window of twenty-four to thirty-six hours," Nick said as he crossed his arms. "No more than that. I'll keep you informed."

"Very well." The line went dead.

Video imagery from each attacking plane provided a bird's-eye view as each craft struck its target. "This is a rush," Billy said, as his own aircraft homed in on its target.

"Front-row seat," Nick said. "Enjoy it."

As a group, the men watched the terrorist aircraft fly to within centimeters of their designated impact points. Billy's aircraft flew through the yawning glass mouth of Air Force Space Command, a block west of the decimated NORTHCOM. The camera continued to transmit interior images of the office complex as the wings ripped free, spewing a cloud of gasoline throughout the modern alcove. The explosive payload in the fuselage careened through the center of the glass-and-metal structure. With no interior walls to cushion the blast, three hundred kilos of high explosives eviscerated the facility moments after the gasoline ignited.

Like the Twin Towers ten years earlier, the top of the shiny modern building came crashing in upon itself. It would never reopen.

The last two aircraft flew north to Buckley Air National Guard Base near Denver, where they hammered home into space antenna farms and a fortified building. Inside of ten minutes, Nick and his crew rained one-and-a-half metric tons of high explosive on the northern Colorado military space complex, snuffing out the eyes and ears of the nation's space surveillance and missile defense.

Back east, it was a typical morning commute, 8:00 a.m., March 21, 2011. Traffic snarled in the wet Monday morning weather.

One by one, thirty light aircraft on legal, prefiled instrument flight plans transited the metropolitan Washington DC airspace from every compass point. Once cleared by the FAA through the terminal radar area, the planes dropped out of sight, descending to treetop level at thirty preplanned waypoints to foil radar and antiaircraft defenses. Fighter aircraft, notified by desperate FAA controllers, scrambled too late from nearby Andrews Air Force Base in Maryland. The military had disbanded its combat air patrols over Washington a year earlier, citing the lack of credible intelligence on airborne terrorist threats against the capital. In truth, their cancellation was a cost-saving measure.

Nick's deadly darts sliced through America's air defenses. Three aircraft were lined up on filed instrument approaches to Ronald Reagan National Airport, while another eight screamed downriver skimming above the Potomac and its bridges. Eight more came upriver from Mount Vernon, and another six flew at low altitude off the wooded banks of the Maryland side of the Potomac. Five penetrated from the north down the Anacostia River. Covertly placed Army air defense systems went into full alert, but they were overwhelmed by the multiple threats skimming low above the water and trees. Even if they had been ready for this onslaught, the hidden missiles could not home in on such low-altitude targets.

The first Washington telemetry link failed at 0805. This was the lead bird, a twin-engine aircraft on a flight plan to a landing at Ronald Reagan National Airport at 8:07 a.m. Just as it was supposed to bank right abreast the Lincoln Memorial, the aircraft dove left and low over the Ellipse. Moments before impact at the White House, a shoulder-fired Stinger missile dispatched the attacking Beechcraft twin-engine Baron and its monster five-hundred-kilogram warhead, raining a hailstorm of fiery debris on the Rose Garden.

The explosion shattered all the windows on the exposed face of the White House, raining glass on the presidential staff and hurling President Manchester and his staffers into the curved walls of the Oval Office. They were being whisked, too late, from a meeting to the hardened basement of the mansion following notification of a possible attack.

The second aircraft on approach to Reagan Airport deviated to the right, before the National Capital Region emergency response system could react to the White House attack. With only a slight change of course, the twin-engine aircraft plummeted into the heart of the Pentagon. Perfectly timed, the airplane detonated moments before impact, setting off a shock wave five meters above the ground within the inner courtyard of the Pentagon, affectionately known to its workers as "ground zero." The five-hundred-kilogram blast sent jagged glass shards ripping through the "A" ring of the world's largest office building, at the height of commuter activity, killing hundreds. Three minutes later, a second twin-engine bomb found the same mark. The inner ring of the Pentagon disintegrated as Nick's team drove two successive stakes into the soft underbelly of America's military power.

Air defense artillery picked off a few flights from the north as they tried to come in low over the Anacostia and turn west into the city. Two crippled craft and a thousand kilograms of high explosive fell on the low-income neighborhoods northeast of Washington DC in a hail of burning gasoline and exploding ordnance.

Tower controllers at Reagan Airport saw an aircraft approaching low from the south—just before it decapitated the control center in a single fiery explosion. Another plane, coming downriver above the Potomac, was narrowly missed by air defense artillery and bored in on the Reagan Airport concourse, flying through the tall glass walls at the city end of the terminal. A different weapon load, three hundred kilos of jellied gasoline, sprayed flaming hell on hundreds of passengers and employees. Few were able to escape as glass and flames erupted out of the disintegrating crystal terminal along its entire length.

Elsewhere around the district, the Bethesda Naval Hospital and the vice president's residence at the Naval Observatory were each destroyed by surprise attacks. The National Security Agency north of Washington was also a target, but the attacking aircraft was shot down on its approach to the ultra-secret facility.

In only five minutes, thirty aircraft and ten thousand kilograms of explosive terror overwhelmed the world's center of democratic government. Washington ceased to function.

In their mobile command post in southern Colorado, Nick switched his attention from the telemetry monitors to CNN and Fox news broadcasts, which began to capture the devastation in the first moments after the attack.

"How long?" asked Tex, anxious to execute the next phase of their operation.

"Wait till traffic's deadlocked. Where's that report?" Nick paced slowly behind his men and their computers.

Tex nodded and selected a speaker for a live TV helicopter transmission from Washington. He also selected webcams of traffic at critical nodes throughout the capital. Emergency vehicles tried in vain to reach Washington from Virginia and Maryland; the district's streets were gridlocked by escaping motorists and fires from planes shot down over the city.

"Traffic's snarled."

"Make it happen." Nick licked his lips. Less than five seconds later, Tex's remote command ignited charges planted on the pylons of every bridge in the metropolitan Washington DC area.

Near Dahlgren, Virginia, the towering Route 301 bridge, weakened at two critical pylons, collapsed in the center and plummeted a hundred meters to the Potomac River below. Two hundred metric tons of concrete and steel pressed dozens of motorists forever into the bottom of the broad waterway.

In quick succession, the George Washington, Memorial, 14th Street, Key, Roosevelt Island, and Chain Bridge structures all collapsed at their centers. Hundreds of cars were demolished as they plummeted into the rivers, the drivers trapped in frigid murky water, unable to escape through inoperative electric windows. Each of the Anacostia River bridges plunged into the polluted northern tributary. The center of the new Woodrow Wilson Bridge near Alexandria disappeared into the Potomac, severing the last artery to Maryland.

Near McLean, Virginia, a gasoline delivery truck barely missed diving over the edge of the pavement when the Cabin John Bridge disappeared on Interstate 495. As the driver struggled to stop the rig, it was gored and upended on the bridge's concrete side rails. The driver had no time to react when the punctured diesel tanks spewed fuel on hot brakes and set the entire rig ablaze. Traffic helicopters captured the graphic event on video, showing the truck swerve and turn the southbound lanes of I-495 into an unquenchable inferno.

The Metro and Amtrak river crossings were detonated near their centers, severing the last possible link into the city from the south and east and blocking any future river traffic. The Yellow Line Metro, headed from the Pentagon to downtown, jolted as the bridge heaved in the middle, then tumbled and fell twenty meters into the Potomac. Many of the riders woke from a commuter nap to a neck-snapping impact as the train plunged headlong into the river. Television cameras on a traffic helicopter captured the sickening image as the Potomac swallowed the Metro.

Nick raised his arms in a two-armed weight-lifter cheer, fists clenched. He slapped Tex on the back, intoxicated with the remarkable success of his complex operation. The grisly horror on the news channels fanned his passion in this moment of triumph and revenge. He made another note in his pocket notebook, then placed a second call on the speakerphone.

"Phase two complete," he said when the erudite woman answered.

"Very well. Continue," was the only response, followed by the purr of a dial tone.

"Pack it up! We're done here," Nick ordered. "On the road in fifteen minutes."

Three minutes ahead of schedule, the Colorado team was gone, headed in two different directions. As the RV pulled out with Nick at the wheel, he turned toward the back of the van and issued his final order of the attack: "Tex?"

"Yeah, Nick."

"It's time. Light up the others."

"Just waiting for your word," Tex said, as he hit the 'Enter' button on his keyboard.

A Red Cross blood van was parked in front of Washington's beautifully restored Union Station terminal, a strategic area to seek donations from commuters. Tex's command ignited the explosive-laden van and destroyed the only remaining transportation hub in the district. Ten thousand kilograms of fuel oil and fertilizer emasculated the historic structure, decades of history collapsing upon hundreds of travelers.

Outside Washington, a Dulles Airport bus, which had been parked at the baggage level all morning, disintegrated in another ten-thousand-kilogram explosion. It took half of the terminal with it, bringing the swooping new addition crashing down on the baggage-handling level. The explosion decapitated the northern Virginia air terminal and crushed the capital's last ability to function effectively as a transportation hub. With both airports gone and no routes open across any river, Washington was cut off from the nation.

A thousand kilometers to the south, Tex's signal ignited the most potent weapon of all. A small version of Hiroshima razed a commercial space propulsion research facility in Huntsville, Alabama. Multiple trailer bombs identical to the Nevada test obliterated a rocket research industrial park in a series of blasts and secondary fires that leveled every building within a quarter-mile radius. More than two hundred employees in the secret rocket development plant died in the blink of an eye.

A half hour after the first aircraft impact in Colorado, the nation looked over its shoulder expecting more carnage, but none came. The attack was complete.

4

"ALPHA, HOUSTON. DID YOU copy my last?" The speaker barked a second time as John pushed hard to reach the microphone at the main communication panel.

"Keep your pants on," John said out loud, to no one in particular, as he reached for a portable mike. He wrapped the headset over his ear and clicked the transmit button.

"Houston, Alpha. We're up. Sorry about that."

"Called you twice, John. This is Jake at CAPCOM. Where is everyone?"

"Michelle's asleep; Sergei and I were arms deep in the Soyuz stowing material. Don't know about Frank. He's off duty too — probably in the sack. We left our portable mikes back in Comm. What's up?"

"Gonna need to wake the crew, John. We've got trouble, and we need all our eyes on this one."

John stiffened. He knew Jake Cook well, and despite his friend's proclivity for practical jokes, this was not his fool-around voice. "Talk to me, Jake. What's happening?"

"Terrorist attack probably, could be worse. Perhaps war related. Just too early to tell. You guys have your CNN feed on?"

John shook his head. "No. Like I said, Sergei and I were up to our keisters in water bags and trash 'til you started yelling at us." He looked up at a camera above him. Somehow he was sure that Houston was watching him on video. The shrinks would be loving this, as sick as that sounded. They lived for stress situations.

"Got it. Here's the short story, and then you'll know as much as we do. Major attack on Colorado Springs, with kamikaze attacks on Cheyenne Mountain, some buildings on the base, and up north, around Denver. Washington took it the worst, though. Big explosion in the middle of the Pentagon, tried to hit the White House, blew up most every bridge in the district and northern Virginia. It's bad. Even hit Huntsville. No one can see any pattern in it, and damage assessments keep coming in." Jake paused. "You get all that?"

John floated in a daze, staring blankly at a flashing light on the communication panel.

"John?"

"Uh . . . yeah. I got it. We'll turn on the news up here. But what about our families, Jake? What about Houston?"

"Everything's okay here. Of course, NASA's locked down right now—probably all over the country too. But we're fine."

"Understand. I'll go get Sergei, and we'll pull the crew together."

"See you back here in five," he said. "You guys are looking good, Hawk," Jake added in a subdued voice after a short delay.

John nodded in silence. Jake confirmed it. Mission Control was watching him—all of them—on video. The shrinks were at it again. Space voyeurism.

John's heart raced as he peeked a second time into Michelle's private sleeping area in the habitation module, or "hab." She hadn't replied to the intercom or stirred in response to his first tap on the aluminum bulkhead. Floating in a fetal position, she was deep in sleep, zipped up to her waist in a cocoon that was tethered in her tiny personal compartment. The loose tail of her polo shirt had ridden up on her torso—to a level higher than Mich would be comfortable with, John was sure. He started to reach in and shake her, then pulled back, self-conscious.

He watched her breathe for a long moment, then knocked again on the bulkhead, hard this time, and stole one more glance at her before he averted his eyes. "Michelle!"

She caught her breath, and as she startled, John glanced back. She opened her eyes to meet his, her trademark dimple disappearing as her mouth formed an "O" in surprise.

"I'm sorry, Mich. We've got some serious trouble. Need you in Comm."

She opened her eyes fully, began to struggle with the zipper on the sleeping sack, then blushed and tugged her shirttail back down. He turned away again.

"What is it?" she said.

"There've been some massive bombings in the States . . ." His voice trailed off as he looked back at her.

Michelle managed to unzip the cocoon with one hand and grasp a handhold with the other as she scrambled out of the bag fully dressed in a pair of skin-tight shorts and her crew polo. "What else?" she asked, her voice garbled, as she rubbed her face.

"It's 9/11 all over again, according to Jake. That's all I know. Houston's fine, but Mission Control wants us for a quick briefing. So hustle up."

John's eyes followed her hands as she bent at the waist to tug down the legs of her shorts. She looked up and caught his eyes, canting her head as she watched him follow her every move. Feeling his face heat up, John turned quickly, fumbling for a handhold to pull himself out of the compartment.

"Wait up, okay?" she called after him. "I'm coming."

"Gotta go," he blurted, looking over his shoulder at her. "See you in Comm."

Michelle adjusted her polo shirt and pulled down her shorts once more, stretching the fabric tight. Unlike most of the women before her on Alpha, she preferred black lycra to the loose khaki kangaroo shorts that the other astronauts wore. She hated the way the baggy material floated up around her thighs. But lycra had its drawbacks, too. You couldn't easily tuck in a shirt, and there were no pockets. Her solution worked like a charm; she buckled her trademark pink fanny pack around her waist, cinching down her loose shirt in the process. She shoved a brush, a hair clasp, and two Chiclets in the pack before pushing off after John.

Michelle's heart began to beat harder as she thought of the carnage of 9/11 and what that day had meant to her. She'd been on a plane landing in Houston for astronaut candidate training. A day she would never forget. She wondered about John as she passed through the hatch in his wake. She knew he'd lost friends in 9/11.

She froze as she floated past the viewing portal in the Unity node. Her home planet revolved peacefully below her, beyond the thick optical glass, across the deadly vacuum of space. The view transfixed her. Untold scores of Americans may be perishing below, yet she realized in that moment that, whatever was happening on Earth, there were few for her to grieve.

Her father left her decades ago. Her mother was dead. There was no other family that she knew. She'd cut friends out of her life for so long, in favor of school or work, that besides her NASA associates, she was completely alone. She fought the pain that welled up inside her, the same pain she'd felt ten years ago, standing agape near a TV in Houston's airport, watching the Twin Towers collapse upon themselves. Raw pain, a deep void inside her that she couldn't reach, or even fully describe. Stark utter emptiness.

Work now, weep later, she reminded herself. She reached for a handhold to move on, but suddenly fought an unseen vise that began to squeeze her chest, taking away her breath. Then the realization hit her without warning: Despite her successes, her accolades, and her shallow friendships, she was truly forlorn, a one-woman island in an infinite ocean of space.

John rounded the intersection at the Unity node and floated into the communication area of Zarya, their control hub. Sergei Nickolaiev, the commander of this mission and a colonel in the Russian Air Force, greeted him with a hand on John's shoulder. "I am very sorry, John. Bad attack in your country. Much worse than 9/11."

"What have you heard? Did Jake call back?" His commander was a man of few words, a trait that often paid dividends during crises. But right now, John wanted to hear it all.

"Couple minutes ago. Only talked for a minute, much going on there. And news feed is working." Sergei pointed to the monitor, with CNN tickers carrying snippets of the graphic horror. "No damage in Houston. Just DC and Colorado."

A lump rose in John's throat as memories of friends raced through his head. John prayed silently that his mentor and friend, Rear Admiral Vic Hayes, was stuck somewhere in Saudi Arabia and not headed home. He pushed aside the thought of all his buddies who were stationed in Colorado, Washington, or the Pentagon.

"Our eyes are gone," Sergei continued. "Jake said NORTHCOM is 'blind as bat,' I think you say. Attacks destroyed space surveillance system. No one is tracking debris. We must."

"Colorado's blind? What about the Mountain?" John asked.

"Only know what I heard," Sergei replied, pointing at his own portable headset, then to John's. "Make sure yours is on."

John checked the volume on his earpiece. It was turned off. He'd missed the call because he'd been watching—ogling—Michelle. He scolded himself mentally for the lapse—one of many, he was ashamed to admit, in the past months. Lapses when his natural self won over what he knew was right. He tried to shake off the mental images of a sleeping Michelle. Alluring images that plagued him. He hated himself for his weakness.

Frank Peters floated into the module. "I was in the galley. Heard John come to get Mich. How bad is it?" The climatologist shoved his way between John and Sergei to get closer to the monitor and the news.

John shook his head and frowned. "If NORTHCOM's blind, I'll need to get started on a quick debris prediction. Gotta get my laptop from the lab." He pointed at his headset. "Frank, you guys make sure I'm on the comm circuit when you talk to Houston. If I'm not, call me on the intercom."

Frank flipped up a hand in assent, staring ahead at the macabre news.

John knew that, right now, his best medicine would be work, and lots of it. Work that took his mind off things he didn't need to be thinking about. He needed to stay *busy*. The bombings had threatened the space station and their lives. Without space surveillance, they were flying blind in an orbital storm of deadly space junk. They had a lot to do. "I uploaded a new space debris catalog last night, Sergei. It was huge, but it'll meet our needs for a week. After that—" John shrugged.

Sergei nodded and waved him on.

John pushed away, headed for the lab. "I'll get started after I phone Amy," he called back over his shoulder. "You guys should call home, too."

The thought of Amy began to calm him as he headed for his compartment, a mental image forming of her, waiting on him with the children, standing on the runway in the Florida sun eight weeks from now. He longed for his wife and forced pleasing thoughts of her to the front of his conscience.

CLEAR LAKE CITY, TEXAS

Amy held her six-year-old daughter in her lap while she cradled the phone, using a free hand to smooth the wrinkles in her child's sundress. The fabric didn't need adjusting, but Amy needed to be a mother more than anything right now. With Albert and Arthur in elementary school, Abe a teenager in middle school, and John up in space, Amy had only her daughter to lean on. Little Alice hugged her mom as images of wrecked buildings, smashed cars, fractured bridges, and smoke—every scene with smoke—filled the screen of the muted LCD television.

"Why are you shaking, Mommy?" Alice's hand rested on her mother's chest, eyes wide in wonder. The mysterious pounding deep within Amy pulsed them both.

Amy's smile was weak as she caressed her daughter's hair. She nodded in response to John's words on the phone, her shoulders slumped under the stress and the receiver.

"Are you in any danger, John?" She didn't expect an honest answer but hoped for good news.

"We're fine, Amy. But I wish we had more information. You know more than we do."

"That doesn't help much," she said, swallowing hard and wiping puffy eyes as she reached for a sheet of paper near the couch. "I made a list . . ." she began.

"Of what?" he asked.

"People," she said, choking. "Friends we know . . . who were . . . I used the Christmas list."

Amy was the card queen. She had addresses reaching back to their first days in the Navy, and she had followed every family they had bonded with during that time. She never missed a birthday or an anniversary. Networking with friends and family was her passion.

"I counted more than a dozen in Washington, and half that many in Colorado. You know some folks in Huntsville, too—they told you about Alabama, right?"

"A minute or so before I called. It's horrible there."

Neither spoke for a moment. The appalling images on her plasma screen said it all. She was glad John couldn't see them; at least she *hoped* he couldn't. She didn't want to know what his military role was on the space station though he claimed there was none. She would only worry more.

"The phone lines are tied up, John. It's useless. I tried everyone. I just hate not knowing." She choked back the emotion she'd struggled to contain all morning. Images and memories consumed her—those of friends and of times past. In particular, she thought of Sudy, her best friend. Sudy who'd served as her first birth coach when John was deployed, Sudy who'd shared painful days with her while Amy came to grips with the move from Maine to NASA. She prayed silently for her spiritual sister in Washington as John spoke.

"Amy, I want you to go home to Pensacola. Leave tonight."

John's tone had changed, she thought. He wasn't consoling.

"There's no panic, but let's play it safe. Go be with family . . . just in case."

She nodded as he spoke, fear welling up in her throat. "We'll go—I'll pack before the boys come home. We all need to escape some of this." She paused. "John? If—if you'd never been selected for astronaut, where would we be today?"

The line to the space station was silent. She knew the answer, but she had to ask.

"Would you be . . . I mean . . . still in the Navy? In the *Pentagon*?" she asked, pressing for a response.

"Probably."

Alice laid her head on her mother's chest, as though listening to the erratic drumbeat. Amy held the telephone with reverence, her only palpable link to John for weeks to come. She stroked Alice's blond curls with her left hand.

"I was afraid you'd say that. I'll call when we get to Mom's."

She sniffled as she pulled Alice closer, the realization hitting her that there was no safe place for anyone. Whatever this horror was, it could reach her wherever she ran. No matter what she did.

"How's your diet, honey?" John asked. "Keeping everything under control without me to cook for?"

He was changing the subject, trying to take her mind off the countless obsessions that overwhelmed her when crises struck. "I'm fine. It's harder to cook for five, but we manage."

"I miss it. I miss being with you in the kitchen, working in the flower beds, talking in the mornings before the kids wake. I need you so—" John's voice seemed to stop in mid-sentence.

She paused, so many questions on her lips, fears she wanted to share with John, her closest friend.

"I love you," she said, but her final words were met by static, the link broken at the worst possible time.

Terror flashed again across the screen in front of her. Muted by her remote, she imagined death reaching a smoky hand out of the plasma panel, trying to seize her family in its bony grip.

She snapped the television off and pulled Alice closer, burying her face in her daughter's fragrant blonde curls.

5

"YOU'VE BEEN HUNKERED OVER that laptop for six hours. Give it a rest," Michelle said as she darted through the lab module headed to yet another high-priority task.

Engrossed in his work on the debris conjunction analysis, John jerked upright. He'd been so busy since his call to Amy that he'd managed to tune out the seething mix of grief and anger over the attacks. And his maddening focus on other things. Michelle's interruption brought it all back.

"Oh, boy! Nothing like a gourmet meal, Hawk." She grabbed the tray of thawed space lasagna floating nearby, the top clearly crusted over. "This stuff's rank when it's not hot."

John glanced at his congealed dinner and made a face. "Guess I got pretty focused. Haven't eaten for hours." He set the laptop adrift and grabbed the cold lasagna. "Thanks for handling my assignments today. Everything okay?"

She nodded her head as she turned to make an entry on a remote data terminal. Half a dozen laptops were strapped to the walls around her. The module was a crazy array of lockers, computers, wires, and posted papers. John forced away thoughts of reorganizing the controlled mess.

As he changed his focus from the lab's disarray to old food, the news began to tear at him again. He tried to block it, his pilot training working overtime: *Don't let a personal problem become a professional liability.* News four hours ago from NASA had confirmed his worst fears. Vic Hayes was dead.

Michelle hooked her feet under a rail across the compartment from John.

He looked up at her watching him eat, her frown deepening as the silence continued.

"I've seen you twice since you called home," she said, "but you haven't said a thing about the attack—or Vic. I'm sorry. I know you two were close."

John shrugged and forced another bite.

"I'm trying to show you I care, Hawk," she said as she floated closer to him, her eyes meeting his. "Don't let something horrible happen in your life and then shove it into a little box. Okay?"

Her voice seemed to mellow with every syllable. Listening to her made him feel good.

She wrapped her left hand around her right fist. "The psychiatrists call that compartmentalization." She shook the cloven hands in his direction. "You listen to Dr. Stevens, Hawk. Don't do that to yourself."

John shrugged, looking back at the pasta. "Maybe," he said. He'd lost four buddies in the 9/11 attacks, and now Vic. But this was no time to dwell on the problem. He had an assignment to complete.

He chewed the same bite over and over, speaking through a half-full mouth. "You might not like it, but my approach is a reasonable defense,

Mich. People depend on us to carry out our jobs, pain or no pain."

Her hair bobbed as she nodded. "I know that." She came closer and put a hand on his shoulder. "Please, tell me about Vic."

"Don't care to, thanks." He moved slightly to the left so that her hand fell off his right shoulder. "Got work to do."

She floated closer, leaving a waiting experiment beeping loudly in the background. "When you want to talk, I'll be ready."

She placed a hand on his forearm, holding it there for a long moment. John flinched, and he was sure she could feel it under her warm embrace. Her touch felt good, and he tried not to dwell on that. He didn't pull his arm back, but his heart and head screamed for him to run. He needed the physical contact more than he wanted to admit—but not from her.

"Later, Mich. Thanks," he said, breaking the physical connection as he pointed toward the source of a chirping experiment alert. He let go of the cold dinner.

Michelle shrugged and pushed away, trailing a light scent of something fragrant he'd never noticed before. He looked up as she passed, staring at her much longer than he should have.

Shaking his head, John hit his forehead with his fist and turned away, taking the laptop with him as he pushed to a new module to continue his work. He didn't say good-bye.

Fifteen minutes later, her next assignment finished, Michelle retrieved the rubber pasta and John's fork. She floated to the galley in the hab module and warmed the meal, then took a new juice packet from the pantry and went in search of her friend. She found him in Zarya, uploading a new space debris data file from Houston.

"You need this, John," she said as she traded him the meal for his laptop. "Our lives depend on that collision prediction. So eat."

He turned stiffly, his jaw twitching. "Thanks," he said as he took the meal.

He finished the lasagna in silence while she completed his data retrieval. For some reason, she felt like he had one eye on her and one on the dinner.

John broke the silence minutes later. "For the record, Mich, this is a really bad time for me—for all of us. But to answer your question about dealing with pain, there's more than one way to skin a cat."

Michelle didn't turn around, speaking louder as she disconnected the laptop from the communication port. "That's a challenge that I've never tackled, Captain Wells, but I'm up to it. You ever skin a cat?"

"A few," he said. "And it's no fun."

She thought she detected a hint of sarcasm. *At last.* Michelle turned, sporting her first smile of the day. She caught his eye.

"Some folks talk about their problems," John said, forcing down the last bite of food, as he pointed the fork at her. "And some folks," he added, turning the fork toward himself, "well—we just deal with 'em."

"Go on," she said, waving her hand in his direction.

John shrugged as she watched. "It works."

Michelle remained quiet. She remembered a fellow astronaut's comment from ten years ago during the 9/11 attacks. "Do we have to go back?" had been the station commander's way of saying it was hard to assimilate America's grief when isolated from the country up in space. Despite all their computer and communication connectivity, they were completely alone. The isolation during this attack tore at her, and she desperately needed someone to share it with. But John didn't. She decided to push it one more time, then let him be.

"I've seen the same news today that you have," she said after a lengthy silence. "Why won't you talk to me?"

He looked up from the empty tray, playing with his fork as if searching for the right words. He swallowed hard, then spoke slowly.

"Because it hurts, Mich. And talking about them won't bring any of my friends back."

6

TEX PULLED THE RV off the empty Colorado highway onto a gravel road that led into a remote mountainous area of the San Isabel National Forest. Negotiating tight curves, he was headed to a little-known campground west of Trinidad, Colorado, and Cordova Pass. Miles from the prying eyes of law enforcement, Tex pulled the mobile command center into a deserted campsite.

"This is it, Nick. The place is empty."

Tex moved out of the driver's seat to join his boss in the back of the RV. He poured his boss a glass of Cabernet and popped open a Corona for himself. He selected Nick's favorite woodwind ensemble CD to play in the background as they fell into their captain's chairs. Immersed in the darkness and the blue-green glow of a large satellite-TV plasma screen, they soaked up the classical music and latest "man on the street" CNN summary from the Pentagon.

"Jack Spritzer reporting live from the Virginia bank of the Potomac River. In the distance behind me you can make out the colossal rescue effort underway where only hours ago two aircraft rained terror on the Pentagon. Helicopters are moving dead and injured out of the Washington area to hospitals all over the East Coast. Every medical bed from Portland, Maine, to Charleston, South Carolina, has been filled. The magnitude of this rescue effort rivals that of any disaster response this country has ever experienced."

The reporter paused as another Air Force medical jet roared overhead. Flashing lights were everywhere.

"Washington is in gridlock. Only helicopters can supply emergency support. Thousands of Americans have died in their cars in the cold river waters, or in the Metro, unreached by rescuers. There simply aren't enough divers . . . or enough time.

"Secret Service personnel and the National Capital Police have set up a perimeter around the White House and Capitol and what little remains of the vice president's residence and Bethesda Naval Hospital. Federal officials have authorized deadly force to maintain security and tonight's curfew, a strong warning to potential looters.

"Communications here are strained to the limit. Cellular coverage is nonexistent, and landlines, for the most part, are inoperative. At the bottom of your screen is a Web address and phone number where you can obtain more information about identified victims, their medical status and location. This is Jack Spritzer, reporting live for CNN from Washington, DC."

"D'you get that?" Nick asked, pointing a lazy finger at the screen.

"Roger that." Tex was already at work on a computer terminal. "Should have the site down in less than five minutes." He tapped the last key with flair, putting the finishing touches on a computer worm he had prepared in advance. "Eat this!"

"Bon appetit," Nick said, hoisting his glass. "Any other news?"

"Roads are shut down as far west as West Virginia . . . just like we'd planned. The I-81 bridges that we torched closed the last north-south route in Virginia. It's utter chaos."

Nick switched to Fox News for a different perspective. Tex was right. Like a fast-spreading cancer, critical northbound traffic feeding New York, Philadelphia, and Boston was piling up in the Virginia area, and then deviating at glacial speed west into the Mountain State. West Virginia and Pennsylvania, desperate to keep their own transportation arteries from collapsing, had begun to divert the glut further west. Traffic jams led to stalled cars and gas shortages, and within only eight hours, fuel was nearly exhausted along the major arteries. Nick had crushed one of the weakest links in American transportation. With no way north or south for train or truck, commerce on the East Coast would soon grind to a halt. It was only a matter of time.

"Ready for phase two, Tex?" Nick asked with flair.

"Ready as ever. Just a button away."

"Make it good."

"FBI hotline. Please state your name."

"Abdullah al Salah." The thick Arabic accent triggered alarms among listeners at the FBI operations center at Quantico. The computer traced the call to a residential telephone in a middle-Eastern immigrant community of south Los Angeles.

"What is your phone number, sir, for verification?"

"Do you want to speak to me, or do you want number?"

"Your number, please, sir, and then we would like to hear what you have to report."

"I will give you number, and you can do with what you wish. Open box 321 in Falls Church, Virginia, post office. I claim this attack in the name of my brothers and their cause. My name is Abdullah al Salah. We are many, yet we are one." The telephone connection went dead.

Abdullah patted the computer and his synthesized Internet voice connection, put his boots up on the counter and hooted like the cowboy he was. Tex's Arabic language training in the Army had come in handy once again.

Within the hour, through a network of covert webcams, Nick and Tex had the visual confirmation they needed. From Falls Church, they watched through a camera hidden in the post office ceiling as their box was opened by federal agents and gave up its fake manifesto, setting the great chase in motion. An hour later, they watched from special cameras disguised as fire detectors as agents burst into an immigrant residence in Los Angeles, finding no occupants but plenty of warm hummus and pita, dozens of prints, and stacks of inflammatory rhetoric in Arabic, all pointing to Abdullah al Salah and his disenchanted band of legal jihadist immigrants.

For the next three hours, with strains of classical music in the background, Tex and Nick clandestinely watched agents scour the apartment for planted computer files, credit card charges, explosive taggants, stolen aircraft rental records, hotel billings, radio purchases, and telephone records that would cement the case against a radical, but heretofore unknown, fundamentalist Muslim sect. The evidence would ultimately lead to more apartments and safe houses, more records, and damning confirmation of subversive Iranian activity funding a credible Arab plot that sought the destruction of the United States and its way of life.

Nick turned off the music, pouring the two of them one last drink. Together they toasted their imaginary Iranian and Arabic comrades.

"To truth!" Tex exclaimed, his glass raised.

"And to its glorious consequences," replied Nick.

"You've got to be kidding."

"This is no joke, sir." The suited men led their reluctant charge down a set of steep stone steps, guns at the ready, speaking regularly into their cuff mikes.

"Excuse me, gentlemen, but hiding the vice president of the United States in a crypt below the National Cathedral strikes me as a far cry from 'spirited away to an undisclosed location for reasons of national security.' Or am I the only one who doesn't get this joke?"

Five Secret Service agents hustled him along silently. When he didn't get the response he expected, the veep turned on his entourage, just missing sight of one who rolled his eyes in response to the constant whining of the second most powerful man in the free world.

The lead agent spoke as the others stood in stony silence. "Sir, I understand your frustration. This location is quite secure. We control all of the approaches."

This wasn't the techno-whiz bunker he was used to beneath the White House or at the Pentagon. But the location was the best he could manage with no open streets or ability to escape the city. He was lucky to be here at all; it had taken hours to reach the National Cathedral from the White House, negotiating a frantic burning gridlock of panic. For now, it wasn't safe to fly.

"Okay, stupid. You don't mind if I call you 'stupid,' do you? Because stupid is what you are. We're at the highest point in the district, underneath a huge stationary target, and with no avenue of escape. We're just fine as long as we stay right here, snuggled up with the mummies. But we have a nation to run, and I need some connectivity. So show me that, Agent Stupid."

Moments later, the vice president was red-faced as Agent Larson led the contingent into the crypt-like vault, through a door labeled as the tomb of the Bishop of Washington, 1895. Bright lights flooded the dank corridor, exposing a modern control room with walls ringed with plasma displays, imagery, television feeds, and banks of phones and radios.

"Your TOMB, sir," Agent Larson said, drawing out the double entendre as he swept his arm around the Temporary Operations and Management Base. "TOMB" was emblazoned above the ornate executive table, already manned with military personnel amid the buzz of an active operations center.

"That's better. You're dismissed, Agent—what *was* your name?"

"Larson, sir. I'll be at the door."

"Right. You do that."

The veep turned his attention to the watch team at work in the expansive facility beneath the historic National Cathedral of the Episcopal Church of America. It was impressive, though he'd never admit it.

A steward approached him with directions to his personal quarters. The veep brightened at the prospect of a bath and fresh clothes. His last shower had been in the early morning, before the fateful attack that he and his family had only narrowly missed. Most of his household staff was dead by now. He tried to remember their names but couldn't. He let the thought go.

Half an hour later, refreshed and ready for action, Vice President Lance Ryan convened the special high-security TOMB staff. His regular office staff had no idea where he was.

"Has Manchester held any briefings since I left the White House?" he demanded.

"No, sir. But we have a direct connection to his operations center—"

"Why didn't you say so? Get him on the line!"

An hour later, Vice President Ryan groaned as he shifted his bulk in the chair. President Manchester was being indecisive, as usual. Today, injured and in mild shock from the attack, the president's vague nature was hampering the national recovery.

"Just *do it*, Mr. President. Make the decision, and let's move on. CNN and Fox will fry you if you don't," Vice President Ryan said as he shook his head in disgust.

The president wavered, every pore of his face visible in the teleconference image. "I trust your judgment, Lance." He turned to the White House chief of staff, forehead still bandaged from the morning's attack. "Announce a press conference. I'll address the nation at 8:00 p.m. eastern. No joint session of Congress and no move to the bunker in West Virginia. We need people to feel that we have this one under control, even if we don't."

"Good decision, Mr. President. We don't need to look like we're on the run."

"Thanks, Lance. By the way, how're Bunny and the kids?"

"Safe and sound in the Australian Embassy. Probably dining on blue Queensland champagne and roast kangaroo, if I know her."

"Good." The president took a note from an aide, nodding to someone the vice president couldn't see off screen. "Seems there've been some intelligence developments, Lance. I'm shipping this over to you."

"And?"

"FBI has a credible claim from a splinter group. Agents raided an apartment in LA and a post box in Falls Church. Looks like we might have a jihadist terror cell operating right under our nose."

"I vote for early action, sir. If we have plausible indicators, let's track back to the source and kill them. The longer we wait, the weaker we look."

"Too soon. But I hear you." The president paused. "It'll be a while before you and I can move above ground. The Marines will fly some decoy missions to draw fire before we use the helos to fly us out. Keep them in your prayers."

"Yeah. Sure," the veep said. "So we just sit here and wait?"

"I'm open to other suggestions, but the cabinet sees it the same way. What cabinet I have."

"We'll wait, Mr. President. But you've heard the press. If I have to listen to another 'how could this happen?' interview, I'll puke."

"It's a valid question, Lance. We didn't see this one coming. Maybe we should have."

"I don't give a flip if it's a valid question. You can't protect the nation against every contingency."

"And that's the point we need to make over and over when we get out of these holes."

"Count on it. But I'm not taking the fall on this one—I mean *we're* not taking the fall." The vice president's face reddened.

"I know what you meant, Lance. I'll call you later."

7

NICK, LYING MOTION-SICK on a bunk in the RV, gagged as Tex cut the big vehicle in a sharp turn off the main highway onto a slag-covered road. They'd been homogenized by rough West Virginia back roads all afternoon, on the final leg of a well-planned odyssey — but Nick was too ill to rejoice. They plunged headlong into the rattling, dusty dark.

Nick's stomach churned. In his misery, he imagined he was surrounded by deafening sirens, spotlights, and surveillance helicopters with FBI agents rappelling down to spirit him to death row. Amid waves of nausea, he drifted into yet another nightmare of a long-ago, late-night drive, the cause and the justification for the complex plan Nick had now set in motion.

*

Nick had once been a decorated military man, on the fast track in the enlisted ranks of the United States Air Force. He was Elias Ulrich by birth, the youngest Senior Master Sergeant on active duty, famed for his talents and decisive leadership. The son of German WWII immigrants, Ulrich was a scrapper, athletic and energetic. He took top honors in every job he tackled — every job but one. He'd begun his enlistment as a naval ordnance technician where he'd earned the hallowed warfare insignia of the U.S. Navy SEAL, but a ruptured inner ear as a result of a diving accident and extreme vertigo in small black rubber boats bobbing in rough seas had ultimately been his undoing. The intense motion sickness that crippled him now, due to the hypersensitive inner ear, had forced him out of the Navy and into a different military specialty.

Ulrich rose fast in his new service, the 14th Air Force, excelling in space operations as a watch stander. He caught the eye of ambitious officers and pinned his advancement to the "fast movers," the leaders who depended on good people to help them climb. Ulrich was such a man.

It was seven or eight o'clock on a February evening in 1998. Ulrich was the Command Duty Officer — the CDO — for the 30th Space Operations Group on a two-week temporary assignment in Colorado. His men were off for the night and Senior Master Sergeant Ulrich watched television in the duty office to pass the hours. His men deserved a break.

Colonel "Boomer" Fredericks was in town for the week — their stellar commander at 30th Space Wing, another fast climber, a golden boy. Ulrich was his top man. Fredericks's mistakes, including a proclivity for many women, were safe with this loyal senior master sergeant.

"Ulrich! What're you doing here so late? Get a life!" the colonel said, swaggering in tipsy from a prolonged afternoon at the Officer's Club.

"Duty Officer, sir. Need anything?"

"Yeah. A driver." He stumbled into a chair along the wall. "Hurry up. Grab some keys and let's go."

"Where to, Colonel?"

"Cripple Creek. Some action. Just you and me."

"I can't leave the base, sir. I'm on duty. It'd be fun to hit the slots with you some other time, though." The Senior Master Sergeant couldn't desert his post.

"Maybe you didn't hear me, mister," Fredericks slurred. He tripped over another chair. "I wanna go to Cripple, and you're goin' with me. Nobody cares about this stupid job. Grab the keys . . . now!" He fell toward the wall.

"Sir, I—"

The colonel released a string of profanities. "Your evaluation's only a couple of weeks away, Sarge. Be a shame to screw that up. Know what an order is?"

"I do, sir."

"Then shut up." He stumbled back toward the door of the office, leaving the stench of whiskey in his wake, and thrust his finger into the air. "Cripple Creek waits for no one!"

Seven hours, too much liquor, and too many wild women later, the car and its two occupants careened across an icy curve, smashing into a piñon pine that saved them from plummeting to their deaths in a deep mountain ravine. Ulrich's head slammed into the steering wheel, and he slipped into blackness. For untold hours of dreadful cold and pain, he lay pinned, bleeding, and broken in the car. Alone.

Ulrich's next memory was racing through Woodland Park in an ambulance, medics tending to his broken arm and fractured back, blood oozing from the gash that left him with a plate in his forehead. His blood alcohol was off the chart, his pockets were full of Cripple Creek chips and ATM receipts, and the blue Air Force sedan hanging on the edge of the cliff was a total loss.

No one Ulrich talked to in the Colorado Springs hospital knew who or where his passenger was.

But two days later, Boomer Fredericks stood crisp and tall in Ulrich's hospital room, shaking his head. The two men were alone. "Why'd you do it, Sergeant?"

"You were there, sir. It was a direct order—" He winced from the pain of turning to see his boss.

"You're hallucinating, mister. I left the club, came to the duty office to check on the men, and you took me home. After that, you were on your own." The colonel paced the room, hands on his hips. "How could you do this? Gambling and drinking on duty, off base during duty hours in an official vehicle, driving under the influence, using a government credit card for gambling ATMs . . ." He shook his head. "I thought I could depend on you."

Ulrich tried to rise from the hospital bed to rip out the throat of this man he had trusted, to stop his lies. But there was a rush of pain from his broken back, and he fainted. When he awoke, the colonel was gone.

Months later, slogging through the Air Force legal system and burdened by a maladroit defense attorney who had once served with Colonel Fredericks, Ulrich had no witnesses and, in the end, no escape from a mountain of damning evidence. Even though half-a-dozen waitresses at Cripple Creek had served him, somehow each of them had lost all memory of the colonel, but remembered Ulrich with absolute clarity. Senior Master Sergeant Ulrich fought his case all the way to the Secretary of the Air Force, never giving up. But he failed. Ultimately, Ulrich left the Air Force in disgrace. And Boomer Fredericks was legend, a storied colonel easily able to withstand the accusations of a vindictive enlisted man addicted to lies, gambling, and booze. Fredericks was also the compassionate colonel who showed Ulrich mercy in his last days in the military and spared him a near-certain trip to military prison. Ultimately, the system promoted its own. Brigadier General Boomer Fredericks moved on to greatness.

Tex swerved violently, and Nick was thrown out of the bunk, sure they were plunging off the road into the Colorado ravine and his death. But the RV stopped, still upright, and the interior lights came on.

"Sorry, boss," Tex said. "A deer jumped in front of us. You all right?"

Nick didn't respond. The nightmare was over, along with the nausea. Fully awake, he realized that after thirteen years he'd finally won. Against incredible odds, he'd beaten Fredericks and the system. Reality freshened him.

An hour later, Nick and Tex maneuvered the RV deep into a narrow coal shaft of an abandoned mine with a dozen other vehicles, parked nose-to-tail. They walked out of the dank corridor into a cold West Virginia night, drinking in the fresh air. Billy and Red waited for them to clear the shaft entrance. They shut a large, rusted door, setting the lock.

"Over there." Nick pointed across the loading yard to a trailer-sized industrial trash receptacle. Leading his men single file, Nick strode up to the dented container and beat three times on the side. The top of the trash pile parted to reveal a hidden door. Without a word, the crew climbed in, the last one sweeping coal dust behind them with a limb. The sweeper threw the limb on the pile of debris and shut the door. It was the last time the men would be seen in the United States.

Inside the padded, electrified, and food-stocked dumpster, they slapped each other on the backs and whooped with abandon. Nick pulled a chilled bottle of vintage champagne from a cooler and popped the cork, sending the missile bouncing off the sides of their small temporary home.

"To freedom!" he said, swigging the bottle's overflow, then serving up crystal goblets for his entire crew.

"To freedom!" they echoed in a raucous chorus.

Nick motioned to the team to take their seats, twenty plush captain's chairs built into the wall of a twelve-by-three meter receptacle. Double bunks above the chairs ringed a lavish interior and a narrow central table that rose up from a recess in the floor.

"Risk is a beautiful thing, gentlemen. It is the greatest of competitors, and the most loyal of allies. It is more complex than a woman, more cherished than fine gold. It keeps us alive, makes our blood pump. Risk is the foundation of reward. And we have beaten risk today. We have used her to our great advantage." Nick sipped. "We took the ultimate risk—and we prevailed."

"Now, gentlemen, we enter phase three of our operation. Our new homes await, just to the south. Well-stocked homes, sumptuous homes, and plenty of compensation for us all. We will not all be together. To do so would be to give risk the upper hand. We will separate, and I will show you the details of our plan as we transit to the south."

Nick lowered his glass, setting it down on the lectern at the front of the room.

"But know this. I will defeat risk at every turn. I will not tolerate failure, loose lips, or stupid mistakes. We depend on detailed planning and flawless execution. Those are the essential elements of success. If you fail, I have a plan. But you will not live to see it carried out. Do your part, keep to yourselves, spend your money, and enjoy your life, and all will be fine. But cross me, or those who support me, and your blood will run. I'm sure we're all in agreement, yes?"

Nineteen men raised their crystal goblets in silence and clinked them in the affirmative.

"Very well. We understand each other. Now, enjoy yourselves. We have a long ride ahead of us. This is your night."

Nick took his own goblet and swigged the contents, raising the empty glass high. "Well done!"

By sunup the party was over, and even Nick slept well.

Shortly before noon the next day, a large truck pulled into the mine site and coupled to the large trash trailer. Inside, the movement jolted Nick awake and signaled the next leg of their journey from the law. Their plan was complete. They were in for a long ride across the border on a trash train to freedom. Wheeler Waste Company, with twenty terrorists in tow, rolled out of the rutted coal yard, headed for the railhead, Mexico, and anonymity.

8

"SPECIAL AGENT TERRANCE KERRY, FBI." The trim African-American lawyer handed his business card and badge to the commanding general of Northern Command and waited, erect. The agent fit the federal mold, a sharp contrast to the large pudgy man before him.

"Wish this were under different circumstances," the general said as he towered over Kerry, teeth clenched and arms crossed. He wouldn't shake the agent's offered hand.

"So do I, sir. I'm sorry for your family's loss." Kerry dropped his proffered greeting.

"These have been difficult days. I lost my only child in that attack; she was on a path to a successful career. She could have been great . . ." The general stopped mid-sentence, his tone changing. "It is the bitterest of ironies, Agent Kerry."

"Sir?"

"I have the power to wage war, command weapons that can destroy millions of people I will never see, with armies at my disposal to defend the entire homeland. But these four stars on my shoulders can do nothing to bring back one innocent girl who happened to be reporting for duty at Cheyenne Mountain at the worst possible time." General Fredericks coughed and turned to face the window of his temporary office, staring at the shredded NORTHCOM headquarters two hundred meters away, beyond the perimeter fence. "After her mother died, Mary was all I had. Now she's gone—and so is my command." He pointed at the pile of rubble.

Special Agent Kerry moved deftly to his right to maintain eye contact.

"Sir, we're evaluating possible motives for the attack on the mountain and antenna sites."

"I can get you in. You won't find any significant data. But give it a try. I'm sure you have a job to do." The general's shoulders relaxed slightly, but his eyes retained their faraway gaze.

"Thank you, sir," Kerry said. He paused a moment, watching the general fidget with his watch, checking and rechecking it, as though he couldn't remember the time. "Why 6:00 a.m., General? Why attack so early?" he asked.

After twenty seconds of stiff silence, Kerry probed again: "Sir?"

At last the general turned to face him. "I have no idea. Nearly everyone knows the mountain is impervious to nuclear attack. So why bother?"

"NORTHCOM wasn't impervious, sir, and they attacked here. But why 6:00 a.m.? The building was largely unmanned, except for your operations center, and Admiral Hayes' office."

The general shrugged his shoulders. "Who knows? Some twisted sense of preserving life? It's beyond me."

Kerry watched him pick up the picture of a young female Air Force officer.

"One more question, before I go?"

Fredericks waved in assent, a deep frown gathering on his plump sweating face.

"I understand that the watch standers in the mountain rotate out at 6:00 a.m.," Kerry said, moving close to the general, watching his face and hands. "Isn't that correct, sir? So, could this be a motive to strike the mountain during a time of vulnerability?"

The general exploded, his fascination with his daughter's picture forgotten. "I don't know. Do your job. Find them. And leave me alone."

The agent kept his cool. "We have a suspect, an unknown terror cell led by someone named al Salah. They seemed to know where our weaknesses were."

"Are you so sure?" the general hissed. "They killed my operations officer, along with a hundred of my staff, and razed my space campus, but never tried to get to me. Why? Riddle me that, Colombo."

Kerry bristled. "We can't be absolutely sure of anything, sir. There's no motive . . . yet," he said.

General Fredericks slammed his fist into the wall, shaking the paintings that lined one side of his temporary office. "Of course there's a motive, Mr. Kerry. You just haven't figured it out yet."

"Perhaps. Your intelligence staff reported that there was a great deal of unauthorized satellite communications use during the past six months." Kerry stopped for a moment to watch for a reaction. "Apparently they were instructed—by you, sir—that the interference was a low-priority problem . . . not to worry about it."

The general stood more erect, still facing the wall. He crossed his arms. "Are you done?"

"I can be," Kerry said, staying in front of the general as he moved.

"Then go." With a rude flip of the hand, he waved the agent toward the door. As Kerry turned, he saw the general wipe beads of sweat from his forehead with the sleeve of his blue uniform coat.

Kerry memorized that snapshot of desperation, and quietly let himself out.

General Fredericks crossed the room moments after the agent left, closing it in the face of a surprised aide, and punched the lock shut. Wiping more sweat from his forehead, he moved to his computer, calling up e-mail folders.

It was there. Again. He'd deleted the folder three times this morning, but it came back, time and again. Like pesky spyware or a gag birthday candle, he couldn't rid himself of the menace.

A special folder was filled with e-mails, messages he had deleted dozens of times in the past two days—and the folder kept returning, each time with a new missive, a new threat to leave the folder intact, "or else."

One line of bold type heralded the latest message. He opened it, wishing this was some sick joke from a system administrator. But he knew better. His pulse pounded as he opened the mail, its capitalization screaming at him in the digital silence.

Subject: "WHY DID YOU DO IT?"

The body of the note was equally terse: *"This mess has your fingerprints all over it, Boomer. You may fool them, but you won't fool me."*

Kerry wished he could be free of the case for a few days to clear his head, get some rest, and spend some time on a trail in the nearby mountain wilderness. His legs ached to conquer a peak, to push hard, to burn the news out of his head with blistering exercise. He needed to get away and see the big picture. Many in Washington were certain that the evidence pointed directly to Muslim extremists, with some bloodthirsty motive grounded in Islam. But after Kerry's morning with the general, he wondered. . . .

Kerry strode into the makeshift FBI command post on nearby Fort Carson, taking quick note of the agents and analysts buzzing around him. He absentmindedly fondled his pocket watch, a gift nearly ten years ago from his late wife. "It's only a matter of time," she used to tell him. He pulled it out, looking at her worn picture on the inside of the ornate old timepiece. Jet black hair cascaded over tiny brown shoulders above a red corsage. For a long moment, he was far away from this madness.

"Special Agent Kerry? You have a call. From the International Space Station. Captain Wells, sir." A sharp young Air Force officer stood at the door of the interrogation office, pointing to Kerry's desk. The agent slipped the precious watch back into his pocket and picked up the line.

"Captain Wells! Good morning. Not every day I get to hear from space."

"Good morning to you, Agent Kerry." The connection sounded like the station was in the next office. "This is John Wells. I reported the explosion a couple of weeks ago. You wanted to talk to me?"

"Yes. Thank you for calling, sir," Kerry said. "I'm the lead agent investigating the Colorado attacks, and the Nevada evidence. Can I ask you about that explosion?"

"I'm all yours," John said.

Together, the two men moved through the story of the brilliant orange burst as the space station passed over Nevada, and John's notification call to NASA.

"How about the attack on NORTHCOM and the mountain, Captain—have you been briefed on that yet?"

The link was silent for a moment. Kerry thought the line might have gone dead. "Captain?"

"I'm still here. I lost a close friend in that attack. And yes, I've been briefed. Naval intelligence spoke with me yesterday. How can I help?"

"Motive, Captain. I'm looking for one."

John was silent for a time, then replied. "You and I both know what was found in Los Angeles."

"Come again, Captain?"

"Al Salah. I've been filled in on all the details. Arabic jihadists funded covertly by Iran. But what was their motive?"

"I have my theories. I'd like to hear yours."

"You don't have to look much further than your own backyard, Kerry. Don't know if your people have much space expertise at the Bureau, but what happened in Colorado Springs was a coordinated attack on the space surveillance infrastructure of the United States. A deliberate and well-executed attack."

"Help me there, Captain. Military, civilian, Rockies, DC, bridges, bases, launch contractors . . . a pretty wide spread of action. Why do you think it was meant to take out space surveillance?"

"What if the attacks on DC and Colorado *aren't* all related?" John asked, the stress rising in his voice. "Suppose they destroyed one target to disguise the motive for another."

"A cover? That's a stretch."

"Not necessarily. It would be sort of like shutting down Washington at the same time you sank the fleet in Pearl Harbor. Makes responding to a national security issue that much harder. D'you follow?"

Kerry chewed a yellow No. 2 pencil out of habit as he pondered the theory. "Like shutting the system down when you need it most?" Kerry asked.

"Exactly," John said, his voice drifting in and out as the S-band satellite communication system transferred downlinks. "The bridges, the civilians, the White House, all had nothing to do with Colorado. So don't tie them together." He paused. "And don't discount DC as a possible diversion."

"Diversion?" Kerry dropped the pencil as he got up from his seat on the office desk. "What's so special about Colorado Springs? They nearly killed the president of the United States, Wells. Now *there's* a primary target."

"We used to call that a 'target of opportunity.' I'd bet they only threw a plane at the White House for effect. Icing on the cake, so to speak."

"Did you surmise all this from the news broadcasts?" Kerry asked.

"No need to get flip, Agent Kerry. I told you I lost friends in this attack. I don't think there's anything about this disaster worthy of sarcasm." John's voice was stern. "By the way, didn't you meet with General Fredericks?"

"Sorry, Captain. And yes. I did meet with him. About an hour ago. Didn't learn much, though." Kerry's voice trailed off. He hoped that perhaps John would fill in the blanks.

"Can't speak for the general, but I can explain my theory. Got a piece of paper or a white board?"

"I do."

"Then draw a circle inside another one, and put little satellites on the outside circle at twelve, three, six, and nine o'clock. Those are our missile launch detection satellites."

Kerry put his phone on "speaker" and went to the white board.

John continued. "The U.S. and Russia have—or *had*—a capability to detect the launch of nuclear missiles . . . or any missiles, for that matter. An early warning of impending nuclear attack. Our satellites are ancient, but they work pretty good. We're waiting to launch the replenishment constellation, but the new program's way over budget and behind schedule. It's pretty bad. With me so far?"

"Keep going," Kerry said, standing at the board, pen in hand, with his phone on speaker.

"Okay. All of the birds sit about forty thousand kilometers over the equator. The satellites can see from pole to pole, but there's a catch. There's no coverage, even on a good day, in an arc that goes all the way from the North Pole down the middle of America. You could shoot a missile at us from the south any day of the week, and we'd miss it. And over the entire East Pacific, for a dangerous forty-five minutes a day, the sunrise blinds the spacecraft. You could fire a flare into the satellite and no one would even know it. With me so far?"

Transfixed, Kerry renewed his chomp on the pencil as he tried to draw the orange peel-shaped voids described by John. "I'm with you. Big hole over the central U.S. Major gaps in the East Pacific when the sun's in the way. Right?"

"Perfect," John said. "These satellites can see infrared signatures—from the flames of rocket exhaust. They can pinpoint a launch, a forest fire, or even a jet in afterburner. With them, our watch team can provide us the exact location of a missile launch and precisely predict where the missile will hit. Depending on the missile origin, you only have fifteen to forty-five minutes from launch to impact. Not much time to identify the missile and make a decision."

"Got it." Kerry waved him on, forgetting that John couldn't see him.

"Good. This is the essence of space-based missile detection. The Russians had a similar capability—"

Kerry interrupted. "Had?"

"Yes. Had. The Russian economic crisis is so bad that they've sold every available launch to bring cash into the economy. Like us, they haven't replenished their own constellation." He paused. "But theirs finally failed."

"Go on," said Kerry.

"The Russians are completely blind to missile attack and have been for the last year. One of the great intelligence secrets of the decade."

Kerry whistled and set down the marker. "I'd bet that both countries have been careful not to publicize that vulnerability."

"You're a fast study, Agent Kerry. But it gets worse," John said. "This attack hit us in every location that has a role in the data feed, telemetry and control, or back-up, for our own missile launch detection system. They hit us hard and wiped out the entire ground segment for space surveillance. The satellites were working fine. But for two critical days we couldn't talk to them. We were blind."

"You're sure?"

"Positive. Confirmed it with Naval intelligence today. The ground search radars for missile defense were all functional, but for a critical forty-eight hours all space-based missile plume detection was gone. Any country on earth could have attacked us. I worked my tail off for two days here on Space Station until they got most of the space surveillance piece back on line again. Even our mobile satellite downlink vans were mysteriously out of commission—all three of them, on the same day, in Korea, Bahrain, and Germany. I'll bet the general didn't share that little tidbit with you, did he?"

"No. He didn't. In fact, he didn't share any of this," Kerry said, pacing the office.

"Probably because his tail was in a sling for forty-eight hours, and he'd just as soon forget that little nightmare."

Kerry's countenance tightened, the crinkly lines by his brown eyes matching the grim set of his mouth as his scowl deepened. He remembered the general's flippant summary all too well.

"They couldn't possibly affect our operations . . ."

Kerry walked to the board again, tracing the orbits of imaginary satellites on the slick white surface. He fondled the watch with his left hand, deep in thought. "Are you sure about all of this, Captain? The remote sites were all shut down? Every one of them? You had no contact with the satellites?"

"Positive. Thus it stands to reason that the attacker had detailed knowledge of our system and meant to shut it down."

"If that were true—" Kerry began, stopping short as he considered the implications.

"The general never briefed you on any of this?" Kerry could hear the anger in John's voice.

"No. So much for national missile defense . . ." Kerry said, turning back toward his desk.

"We still haven't established a motive for the attacks," John said. "We've assumed these Muslim extremists had some fanatically religious agenda. But what if they attacked us for the Russians? Or for someone else who intended to exploit the missile launch vulnerability? What if they did it just to see how long they could shut us down? Or suppose they launched something into orbit that's sitting there now ready to plow down your throat and incinerate the Springs? What then?"

"You don't feel strongly about this, do you?" Kerry asked, staring at the phone.

"Does it show? I lost one of my best friends in the attack a few miles from you. And it could happen again. Worse, the entire country is vulnerable. The space station is vulnerable, too—we could get creamed any minute because there's still not anyone watching for the small debris up here. That part of the system's still not operational. All I can do is work with old debris data and predict what big stuff might be drifting around in orbit. See where I'm going with this?"

"I do," Kerry said slowly, walking toward his desk.

"I'm saying—" John began.

"—that there's someone working for them—whoever 'them' is—who knew exactly which vulnerabilities to exploit." Kerry said, finishing his sentence.

"Very good!" John said. "We're communicating now. Time's a wastin', Agent Kerry. If I were in your shoes, I'd start turning over lots of rocks in Colorado and inside the United States Air Force. And I'd start with that general's office as soon as you can get in."

9

THE EBONY FACE OF Earth rolled by in the dark below, gloomy and foreboding. A series of flashes from the top of a thunderstorm caught his eye. John marveled at the fury of the weather over the Indian Ocean. Bolts flashed like fireflies deep within the heavy gray cotton that covered the sea.

Michelle floated up behind him. "Watching storms again?" She shoved at him to gain some space for herself. Together they watched as lightning popped and crackled like immense flashbulbs far below.

"Can we talk . . . for a minute?" she asked later as she watched Hong Kong's brilliant lights burn through the cloud cover.

He turned away from Earth-gazing to watch Michelle's distinctive face. Her pixie nose swept up like a tiny ski ramp, framed by hazel eyes and round cheeks. She hated that Bob Hope nose, but he thought it added to her distinctive and gentle profile. Her softness in the midst of the station realities was refreshing. The aroma of her hair reminded him of Amy.

"What's on your mind?"

She didn't hesitate. "You are." She turned to face him, her face covered with smile.

John blushed and edged back a little. "Ah . . ."

"You're on my mind, but not as you might like to imagine." She flashed a smile. "Something you said has been bugging me."

He shook his head. "Like I said, after forty, memory's the first thing to go."

"Then let me refresh it for you," she said. "About six months ago. At the dive tank. How you got into this business."

"Yeah. I remember. We were talking about a sense of destiny."

"Uh-huh," she nodded. "Something about voices, too. I'm still having a hard time with that." She paused. "So, enlighten me."

Her hair floated above her, small diamond earring studs glittering in the brilliant station lights. He stared at her for a long time in the silence.

John finally looked away and rubbed his chin, making a faint washboard sound in the silence. "I was twelve, growing up on a farm near Sistersville, West Virginia. We ran a dairy. I was feeding calves one morning in the summer, and it hit me—"

"The calf?" Her dimples dotted both ends of her grin.

"No . . . this was a *feeling*, Mich. Everything around me got quiet. I had this incredible sense of destiny—maybe a calling. It's kind of hard to describe. In a way, it felt like a warm blanket wrapped around me. But something seemed to speak to my heart in that old barn—a longing—or a direction—that I would somehow 'make a difference.'" John fixated on the white bulkhead, reliving the moment of thirty-five years ago. "In that direction—to make a difference—I felt an incredible pull toward 'astronaut.' Don't ask me why a farm boy gets ideas like that in his head. But I did."

Michelle shook her head. "Just like that? From dairy hand to Captain Kirk?"

"It's a little more complex than that. But, yes, the great chase started there."

He watched her drift free of the foot restraint, lips drawn into a smile, head cocked. It reminded him of his daughter Alice's rapt attention when he read to her at bedtime. Some of that little girl in Michelle slipped through on rare occasions.

"You're a romantic, John. One minute you're a farm boy, the next minute you're Moses by a burning bush." She tilted her head quizzically. "Do you really think God—or whoever it was—spoke to you in a *barn*?"

"It's not so hard to believe." He turned away, moving to the optical glass. "Moses was a sheepherder, and he was called away to save a nation. I'm no Moses, but what I experienced was as real as this moment is to you."

✳

RAISIN, TEXAS

"The border patrol scans the empty containers coming into the country—to keep out illegals. But no one scans trash on the way out."

Nick watched the mesquite roll by on a large screen display at the front of their living container, now two days transit south of West Virginia and five days after the attacks. Digital versions of windows, their hidden cameras gave the crew an outside feel while they rode in their special luxury-configured conveyance toward Mexico.

Tex crossed his legs, feet up on the central table. "We crossin' at Brownsville?"

Nick pointed a remote control at the screen, and it changed to a map of Texas with a GPS location for their train, moving south near US 59. "No. Here." He pointed at a city south of the bend in the Rio Grande. "At Eagle Pass. The train is headed to Morelos . . . here, to the southwest. But we aren't. A new engine will pick us up in Piedras Negras, and we'll scoot down south as part of a Mexican freight load—all the way to Tecoman on the Pacific, south of Guadalajara. Then Route 200 to Guatemala. From there to our new homes."

The rest of the crew watched the discussion with Nick, some nodding in agreement, others nodding off.

"How much longer?" asked Red. "Two days?"

Nick shrugged. "Eagle Pass sometime tomorrow for sure. After that, we're on Mexican time. But no more than three more days in here. Then it's the open air."

SPACE STATION ALPHA

Ventilation fans hummed in the background as John and Michelle floated in place, the east Pacific rolling by below. John turned away momentarily to dim the bright lights in the laboratory.

After a long moment, Michelle turned from the window to face him. "I'm sorry about that Moses remark. I'm sure you heard . . . something. I mean, to you it was real. That's good enough for me." She placed her hand on his forearm. "Forgive me?"

He flinched as she touched him.

"Why do you always do that?" she said as she pushed away, her voice hurt.

"I'm sorry," he said. "It's—it's my problem. I didn't mean anything by it."

She moved toward him, and he backed up again, unconsciously.

"You see? What is *wrong* with you? What do you think I am? Some love-starved space bimbo?" The red in her face subsided for a moment. "Wait a minute—what kind of problem?"

John shook his head. "Just call it a thorn in my side. Let's leave it at that."

"No. I won't just leave it there. I noticed this in Houston, but shrugged it off. Figured you were some kind of prude. But I've got to live with you for two more months, Blue Eyes. So come clean. What's your hang-up?"

John's frown was deep. He ran his hands through his short hair. "Trust."

As soon as he said it he shook his head. *Why can't I just keep my mouth shut?*

"Trust? You don't trust yourself—or you don't trust me?" she demanded.

"Both—I guess."

Her eyes flamed again. "You don't trust *me*?"

"I said 'both.' I don't trust myself, *or you*, when it comes to defending my marriage. We're human, Michelle. And we're in a very difficult situation."

"Enlighten me, Hawk. Surely I'm missing something."

"You're a beautiful and intelligent woman. . . ."

"And?" she asked, moving closer toward him, her face creased with a fierce scowl.

"And we're stranded up here, away from family and friends at a time when we're both desperate for comfort. Torn over the attack and the isolation. Looking for someone to reach out to. If we aren't careful, whether we planned it or not, we could become too familiar. We depend on each other for strength." John hung his head. "And to be honest, I'm not all that—I mean—I haven't always been all that strong."

Michelle was silent for a long moment, her mouth agape. In the lull he looked up at her, offering both hands, upraised. "Sorry, Michelle. What you see is what you get."

She closed her mouth as she shook her head. "Yeah, you're right there, bucko. Go on. As the crew medical officer, I command you. Tell me more about your 'female phobia.'"

"It's certainly not a *phobia*," he said as he took a deep breath. "Just the *opposite*."

The red flashed in her face. "What *is* it with you men?" Michelle said as she made a beeline for the hatch, pulling at her hair with both hands. "Aaahhh!" she exclaimed. "It really is true! Men are such animals. All they ever think about is sex."

ENCINAL, TEXAS

"The border's close," Tex said, flipping between the outdoor view, a Texas map, and two hundred channels of satellite television.

"Grab some news, Tex," Nick said from his chair. He threw a Macadamia nut into the air and caught it on the way down between his front teeth.

"Left or right?" Tex asked, pointing the remote.

"Fox."

"—for a balanced view. Now with us in Washington, Darren Maxwell reporting from the new Fourteenth Street ferry that will start tomorrow, less than a week after the attacks. Darren?"

"Darla, it's been nearly fifty years since the last ferry ran in the nation's capital, but tomorrow, government-funded ferry services will commence at each of the downed bridge spans. The Corps of Engineers assured us we'll have temporary military crossings late next week. It's been a harrowing six days, with the city cut off from the south, but commerce and commuters will begin to flow again on Monday morning. The Metro from Rosslyn through Foggy Bottom has been the only way in or out of the city from Virginia, and that link will lighten up soon as cars begin to roll."

"Hey, Tex?" Red asked. "Didn't we have a plan for that contingency? For the ferries and all?" Red wiped his mouth with his sleeve as he finished yet another slice of pie.

"We did," Nick answered as he pitched another Macadamia into the air. "But we're saving it for a surprise," he said quickly, and caught yet another nut with his teeth.

✦

SPACE STATION ALPHA

"It was fun talking to the kids tonight. I needed that—today more than ever."

"It was a fight for the phone down here, John. Your calls are the highlight of their day, even after all these months," Amy said, her voice lilting.

"So. How about you? How're you taking it?" John asked, floating in his tiny personal cabin with a remote microphone. Amy's voice seemed so distant. He needed her to be close.

"I'm okay. We're okay," Amy said, hesitating. "We're coping."

John could hear her sniffle on the other end of the connection.

"But it's tough," she continued. "The body count keeps on climb-ing, the two political parties cut each other up assigning blame, and nothing's getting done. I hate that."

"Me too," he said slowly. "New subject. How are your folks?"

"They're fine. They said 3/21 reminds them of hurricanes. Long lines, no gas, devastation everywhere. They've lived what the folks in Washington are dealing with—a different kind of problem, but they can relate." She paused. "We're going home to Clear Lake tomorrow. Life seems to be getting back to normal—I hope."

John could hear the kids playing in the background, a loud televi-sion in the distance, and some heated argument over a remote control.

"Some things never change," he said. "Who's winning?"

Amy laughed. "I am. What they don't know yet is that I took the batteries out of the remote. We're going to study a fifty-year-old art—how to get off the couch to change channels. Maybe that way I won't have to watch three hyperactive boys flip through cable all day."

"They're just bored," John said with a chuckle. "Don't sell 'em short. They'll figure it out."

"We'll see." She paused. "You have that sound in your voice. What's up?"

John shook his head, glad that she couldn't see him. She knew him too well.

"Nothing much. A little conflict. I hate it."

"With who?"

"Mich."

"Let me guess—"

"I'd rather you didn't, thank you."

"Now *there's* an answer. John, I don't know why God wired you—wired men—the way He did, but I've got an opinion on this. Sometimes God left out the critical wiring about relationships. I'm sure there's a reason, of course." She chuckled as she said it, but John knew that the subject was more serious than she was making it sound—and that it had caused her more pain than she was showing. "Maybe that's why God brought us together—I'm the other half of your circuit."

Her voice took on a more serious tone. "You told me once that you go out of your way to avoid temptation, even if it makes you look stupid to other people. Do you remember that?"

He nodded. "I do."

"So, I just wanted you to understand that—even if you are wired wrong from a woman's point of view—I do appreciate your honesty. And your effort to confront your weaknesses. It makes me warm inside to know you'd put your reputation and your image at risk for me . . . you know, put a hedge around our relationship."

"I would—and I did."

She was quiet for a long moment. "Is everything . . . okay? With you, I mean?"

"I'm fine, Amy. And I know it's tough to talk about this kind of stuff . . . when we're so far apart. I came off judgmental with Michelle today. I'll admit I'm probably overcompensating for my—as you call it—wiring problem. But I can promise you that there's only one electrical connection in this body of mine—and it runs directly to you."

"Thank you, John. I needed to hear that."

"And I needed to say it. Everything up here is dandy, but I can't wait to be home with all of you."

"Same here. I love you. Bunches. Guess I need to go now. Got to get the kids to bed."

"Me too. I love you, Amy. More than I can express on a telephone.

Tell the kids good night, okay?"

He heard a sniffle, then another. Her voice seemed to crack as she tried to say good-bye.

"Thank you . . . again," she said.

"For?"

"For trying so hard—and sometimes making a fool of yourself—for me."

10

A SQUARE JAW, A graying flattop, and penetrating blue eyes gave Rex Edwards a fearsome appearance. His short, muscular body filled out the twenty-inch neck of a crisp button-down shirt and reinforced his powerful image. Only his trademark red bow tie softened the otherwise massive and forceful presence of the man. Articulate, well dressed, and a genius in rocket design as well as business, Rex Edwards was a force to be reckoned with. He scaled the stairs to the stage and the podium, two steps at a time.

Little more than a month after the annihilation of his rocket research facility in Huntsville, Alabama, preparations for his big announcement had reached their climax at the world headquarters of Delta-V Corporation in Palmdale, California. More than two hundred VIPs and press representatives filled the auditorium, many of them coming simply for the industrialist's famous reception feasts. Now standing alone on the dais of his lavish conference center, Rex Edwards surveyed his audience as he enjoyed the fruits of thirty years of labor. Fifty-three years old and a billionaire twice over, he was a giant in the aerospace industry. No company had the unique corner on space propulsion that he held, and no competitor could match the technology card that he was about to play. He was in total command of his destiny.

Yet his command was bittersweet; Rex's empire was under attack. More than two hundred loyal employees of Delta-V had died in an instant forty-two days ago in the unprovoked attack on his Advanced Propulsion Systems aerospace plant in Huntsville, Alabama. Fifty thousand kilograms of high explosives had leveled the windowless buildings of his classified engineering complex with a crushing shock wave that converged from all four sides. The heart of his classified military space propulsion business had been obliterated in a moment. The plant was his crown jewel, developing a risky but extraordinary rocket propulsion process, essential for highly classified antisatellite weapons and a looming future war in space.

Rex grasped both sides of the podium, and his voice boomed. "Six weeks ago, as we prepared for this day, life was much simpler—and safer. On March 21, a day that will now live in infamy, my company launched and flew a space mission that changed history. With no control or support from the ground, one of my specially-configured space tugs located, grappled, and returned to Earth the abandoned military communications satellite you see on the dais behind me." He gestured to a glittering box-shaped gold and black spacecraft dangling above the stage, rotating under spotlights like a multimillion-dollar bauble. "History is made at those junctions in time where policy, technology, and adversity collide. Today represents such a nexus.

"We all thought this spacecraft was a lost cause—stranded in a useless orbit. Expensive debris that, but for lack of a proper orbit, could have been a valuable military asset. I brought it home without permission.

Why? Because someone had to take the bold move to prove the feasibility of the process of automated rendezvous, refuel, and retrieval—what we call the 'A-Triple R' maneuver—and now we've done it. Policy, technology—yes, and adversity—collide today in a remarkable way. This is history!"

Rex pointed to an admiral in the front row. "Admiral Enterline, I relinquish all salvage claims. I believe this satellite is yours!"

The admiral responded with a slow nod.

"I know that a dream like mine burns somewhere within *all* of you. It's a dream to conquer and subdue space travel, not just to loft a payload or a man into low Earth orbit. Delta-V Corporation can enable your vision today, with our endothermic fuels, proprietary reactive nozzle technologies, and our proven equatorial launch complex on Baker Island—where we produce fuel on site and launch payloads for a fraction of the cost of conventional systems." He paused, sweeping his hands in a wide arc, gathering in the audience.

"Seven years ago, President Bush challenged us to go to the Moon, and then on to Mars. For a grand moment, while mired in Iraq, fighting a rancorous war on terror, and dealing with the devastation of multiple hurricanes, it seemed we might yet embark on a new course, grasping for new horizons. But true to form, budgets have come and gone, and the vision for manned space exploration is dying." Rex slammed the wood of the podium with a ham fist.

"I am here to arouse you, to rekindle your passions and dreams. With my advanced lift and propulsion systems, we have the ability to literally pump fuel to orbit. This is the dawn of low-cost access to space. Delta-V Corporation opens the heavens at last—to every man. We can go—and we will!"

He swept his hands again across the panorama of his audience.

"Will you join me?"

11

"FEDERAL OFFICIALS ANNOUNCED TODAY, six weeks after the attacks of 3/21, that a fully functioning bridge across the Potomac River would open near Dahlgren, Virginia, allowing traffic to move up and down the East Coast. Virginia and Maryland officials cut the ribbon on the Army Corps of Engineers temporary span, and traffic was queued up on Route 301 for thirty miles north and south of Dahlgren as truckers and travelers sought a way across the Mason-Dixon line."

Sergei, Frank, and John watched in silence, munching on space dinners around the communal table, absorbing the news from 350 kilometers below.

An interview rolled by with an irate trucker, unable to make his costs due to the slow travel and the expensive fuel. Still another angry commuter in a Mini Cooper blamed long traffic lines on the government, yet another on poor highways. Eventually, the reporter asked a federal official for comment. "Blame the Arabs," a tall redheaded woman said on camera. Or the Iranians. Or *both*. "They blew it up. Not us."

"When did *that* get out?" asked John, wide-eyed as he watched his first television report in four days.

"Yesterday." Frank Peters, the crew scientist, didn't look up — he just kept shoveling in tonight's pasta primavera, talking around a mouthful. "Didn't you hear us yapping about it at supper last night? Big press announcement. Some yokel in the state department spilled some critical intel and the press picked it up. Iranian money. Arab bombs."

"That was a mistake," John said, fork in midair, staring at the monitor.

"Why?" asked Sergei. "What difference does it make?"

"A lot of difference," John said. "Now everyone will spend all their time talking about Iran . . . not acting on the potential for Islamic fanaticism. A shred of intelligence leaked to the press suddenly becomes fact, then that supposed fact becomes the subject of op-eds and political debate, and eventually people scream for action against Muslims . . . or Iran . . . or whomever . . . when all along, it was just a leak, and maybe a bad one at that. Whether it's urban legend on the Net, or weapons of mass destruction in Iraq, fiction has a way of cleverly weaving itself in with fact in a world that shares information at the speed of light."

"Nice speech, Hawk. What's it mean?" Frank said.

"The Iranian connection," John said, narrowing his eyes at Frank. "It's just a shred of intelligence. And I don't believe anything's ever as simple as it first appears."

Michelle darted into the command module, scooting up to the table, a warm tray of pasta in tow. "Still soaking up the news, I see?"

Frank nodded, his mouth too full to talk.

"Sorry to hear that," she quipped, raising an eyebrow.

"Why?" asked Sergei.

"Didn't you catch the press conference?" Michelle's eyes were wide with excitement.

"You mean old man Edwards and the space tug stunt? 'Ladies and gentlemen, the father of all time, the grand master of liquid hydrogen, his great preeminence, Rex the King.'" John's parody elicited a rare chuckle from Sergei as they floated around the communal table for an evening meal.

"So, how about Mars, eh?" Michelle asked. "We can get there cheap, if you believe him."

"How about it?" John asked as he gave Sergei a playful punch in the arm. "Coming with us? Chance of a lifetime, Boris."

Sergei's scowl softened. "I would gladly burn capitalist fuel, but must bring Communist women. Need *strong* crew."

All three of his comrades doubled in laughter. Sergei's Soviet parodies were a welcome contribution to the crew's limited humor portfolio.

"Count me in. When would we go?" Frank wondered aloud.

"To Mars? Decades. None of *us*, for sure," John said as he forced down another bite of space chicken. "But we'll all live to see better barbecue. My back porch. Hot moist smoky brisket and spicy sauce, with a tall glass of ice-cold sweet tea and a double slice of lemon."

"Shut up, Hawk. I can smell it already," Michelle said, fanning the air as if to bring some of the imaginary aroma over her way. "But seriously, what if we could go? To Mars." Michelle directed the question to the three of them.

"Absolutely!" was Frank's immediate reply. "First in line."

"Yes." Sergei said no more, but John knew he lusted for yet another great space adventure.

"And you, John?" Michelle asked as she smiled.

John toyed with the pasta as he sipped on a juice packet. "I might," he said after a long delay. He squinted at the food, deep in thought.

"Might? Not that gung-ho Roger Ramjet anymore, eh?" Frank asked.

The sarcasm penetrated deep under John's skin. He liked Frank less each day, and he fought the urge to spit words back at his crewmate.

"It's a valid answer, Frank. Being away for two years is a big commitment if you *care* about your wife and four kids. I want to go—and I would . . . if I felt it was in God's plan." John's voice drifted off.

"Enough God-talk," Frank said with a frown. "I'm outta here." He left a fork in midair, spun about, and shot for the hatch.

Sergei shook his head as Frank sped out of the dining area. "He's been on edgy all week."

Michelle smiled. "On *edge*. And it didn't start this week. More like when he was born."

Sergei smiled and nodded as he bid good-bye, then followed Frank to their next task. In a moment, the meal area was the silent domain of John and Michelle, whose twelve hours on duty were at a close.

Michelle shook her head. "So, do you want to go to Mars or not?"

"I do," John mumbled, struggling to talk with a full mouth.

"Then what's with this 'God's plan' stuff?" she asked.

He swallowed and gave her a long look before he answered. "You sure you want to talk about this?" he asked, with a smile.

"Uh-huh. Lay it on me."

"You remember what I shared with you about my sense of a calling . . . a destiny?"

She nodded.

"I meant what I said. I pursue major decisions with an eye on what I feel I'm called to do. Where God's leading me."

"Fair enough," Michelle replied. "So what if you feel a spirit force or something—like your experience in the barn—is telling you in no uncertain terms to go to Mars, but Amy pitches a hissy and tells you to stay home? What then, Mr. Man of God?"

John grinned. "The great dilemma, eh? I don't know. I'm sure that decision would be difficult, but so was the choice to come here. Amy's never been settled on this astronaut thing. She hates the risks, despises the weather in Texas, and dreads the constant separation. But she followed me because she loves me and trusts me, and because she trusts Him to care for the details."

"You make it sound like God is some kind of Geppetto." Michelle's frown seemed to deepen the more they talked. She helped John put away the last of the dinner materials.

"No. We're not puppets, but like Pinocchio, we do have the free will to make our own decisions . . . and the free will to accept or reject His plan for our lives."

Michelle squirmed. "Enough," she said, waving her hand dismissively. "You're starting to sound like a televangelist."

"Thank you . . . I think," he said with a chuckle. "We'll talk later."

FRIDAY, MAY 13, 2011: PASADENA, CALIFORNIA

Dr. Robert Kanewski ignored the Los Angeles traffic report on his desk radio, still working in the office past sunset, as had been his custom for twenty-five years with NASA at the Jet Propulsion Laboratory near Los Angeles. There was no one waiting for him at his small apartment in the San Fernando Valley. *This* was home. NASA's center for planetary exploration. And the years of hard work had paid off; The name Kanewski was as closely associated with Mars as Opportunity, Spirit, Pathfinder, Viking, Zubrin, and red dust.

At peace with the late hour and his avocation, he hunkered over the cheap door that served as his second desk in the cluttered famous corner office of his laboratory building. He pushed long thinning hair back over his bald spot and rubbed a red chubby face. He was only months away from launching a groundbreaking rover mission to the red planet. There was still so much to do.

The sound of running feet broke the usual evening calm. "Robert! Robert!" shouted an elderly man hurrying down the hallway. White-haired and red-faced, Dr. Alexander Watrick burst in.

"Alex! What's wrong?" Robert headed for the door just as Alex rounded the corner and careened into him, sliding across the newly polished tile floors, white hair flying. He upended a stack of Edgar Rice Boroughs novels on the floor near the desk as both men went down like trees.

Robert laughed at the look of surprise on Alex's face, the important news lost for the moment in their headlong collision. "Custodians always wax on Thursdays, Alex. You okay?" Alex was seventy-two; the last thing he needed was a broken hip. Alex nodded, still dazed. Long white shocks sprang from his head, ears, and nose like wild grass.

Robert pushed himself up from the floor, a short, plump, barrel-chested man teetering atop skinny legs. "So, what's the rush?"

The flush returned to Alex's face. "A signal from Mars!" he whispered as he stood up. "Viking 1 is on the air."

"What are you talking about, Alex? Viking 1 died in 1982. She's gone."

Alex slowed down and put a hand on his friend's shoulder. They'd been research collaborators on a dozen deep space missions. "The Deep Space Network antenna at Arecibo, Puerto Rico, picked up a strong signal almost two hours ago. They were doing a general sweep and found it by luck. Arecibo ran a signal match, hoping that they had a possible extraterrestrial or something. It was an exact frequency match with our deep-space exploration channel assignments."

Alex caught his breath for a moment, still panting heavily. "We tried to call you, but your phone's off the hook . . . as usual." He cast a glance at the old desk phone, the black receiver dangling on a dirty white cord.

"It gets better. They got a perfect fit with the Viking 1 imagery waveform. The mission director at Arecibo in Puerto Rico called our operations center about twenty minutes ago. We pulled a Viking file, transmitted it back to them, and they sent us their file data for independent analysis. We both came up with the same results." He paused, barely able to form the words. "Viking 1. No doubt about it."

"This isn't a prank, Alex? Tell me it's not one of your elaborate hoaxes."

"No jokes tonight, friend. Our old baby's back on the air. Or its clone—and at the same landing site. The location was confirmed by Arecibo." He looked Robert squarely in the eye. "This is the real McCoy."

Robert sank into his chair. "You said it was an imagery file?"

"Didn't say so . . . the computer match did," Alex said. "The signal's live right now. Arecibo's feeding it to us as long as they can see Mars. Remember, Viking's data feed was slow as a tortoise."

"Some things I don't miss," Robert said, his mind drifting back to the days of adding machines, batch processing, and eight-track tapes.

"Want to watch?" Alex grinned.

Robert grabbed his engineering notebook and was out of the office before Alex could regain his composure. "In the ops center!" he yelled back at his friend as he raced down the hallway. Despite his extra thirty pounds, he bounded like a youngster through the laboratory building and into California's cool evening air.

In a flash he was through the front door of the Mission Operations Control Center, where his staff was gathered around a bank of signal monitors. Robert slowed his pace as he caught sight of the team and the spectral displays. His knees buckled as he fought to regain his breath. Alex rushed up behind him moments later, panting like an old dog.

"Do you remember . . . the date?" Alex asked breathlessly.

"Viking 1?" Robert asked. "Couldn't ever forget it. Landed July 20, 1976. What a day! First to land, and last to die. Final signal November, 1982. Those were six glorious years, weren't they?"

Alex placed a quivering hand on his friend's shoulder and they both regained their breath. "Those *were* great times," Alex said. "I think part of me died as they faded away."

Robert nodded, unable to form the words. His memory raced to those heady days when he'd cut his teeth on Mars exploration in this very building as a whiz-kid PhD at the age of twenty-two.

"What's next, boss?" Alex prodded his friend in the back.

Robert moved forward to the display, and his team parted like water before the bow. With a sense of reverence, he gently touched the large plasma screen as if to reconnect with a long-lost child. Like touching a live wire, the connection energized him, and he spun toward his team.

"Harlin! Pull the Viking 1 files. Get with Goddard Space Flight Center. Shake 'em out of bed if you have to. But break this signal and do it now! Pam, build me up a separate data feed for the lab. Get more antenna coverage with the Deep Space Network. Promise them anything. We need dual antenna coverage. Scott! Give me a bank of monitors, data feeds, and a working control terminal. I want this place humming with pictures by *dawn*. Let's go!"

The team scurried off, leaving Dr. Robert Kanewski alone with the mysterious display. Somewhere, hidden inside this fuzzy squiggle of a signal, there were probably critical data from Mars. A squiggle that reminded him of an erratic heartbeat on a hospital monitor. Yet, this was a heartbeat—maybe Viking—from another planet. The frenzy of preparation surrounded him, but the sounds and sights were distant. He was lost in thought. His stubby fingers tipped with chewed fingernails returned to the squishy soft face of the plasma screen, as if to somehow touch the untouchable.

One hundred fifty million kilometers away, yet at his fingertips, Viking 1 was alive.

12

JOHN AND MICHELLE WERE intent on their latest repair, troubleshooting a fuel meter malfunction in the Zarya module. Armed with an ohm meter and pliers, and speaking with two ground engineers in Huntsville by portable headset, John was crammed in the tight Russian-built spaces, floating face-to-face with the Russian Orbital Segment Motion Control System. Michelle manned the checklists outside the equipment bay at John's feet. Fuel, air, water, and electricity were the stock of life here, and survival depended on the Russian equipment suite in Zarya, the oldest module in orbit.

As he fished into the labyrinth behind the metering panel, Michelle asked, "Did you figure out where our gas went?" He felt her nudge his foot with her own.

"Absolutely. That asteroid destruction mission sucked us dry."

She didn't respond.

"Surely you remember, Mich," John continued as he squirmed in zero-G, his arms deep in the tight cabinet. "A giant space shuttle stopped here to get fuel on the way to destroy an asteroid that threatened to smash Earth." John laughed at the comment from ground engineers as he craned his neck back toward Michelle.

"Okay." She put a finger to her temple, like the *Wizard of Oz* scarecrow. "*Armageddon*, 1998. Entertaining but totally unrealistic."

"Can't stump her!" John announced into the headset microphone. "Good memory, Mich."

"Thanks, John. So how's *yours*?"

John pushed up to his shoulder in the cavern of wires and tubing. "Pretty good," he grunted, trying to hold on to the bulkhead with one hand while his contortions in the small space forced him to float in another direction.

"Great!" Michelle said, then hesitated. "So . . . I've been thinking about your lecture the other day."

John grunted again as he reached even deeper into the compartment and adjusted a valve behind the panel at the limit of his reach. "Lecture?"

A bank of lights above him switched at once to green from their red "warning" glow.

"That did it, Hawk. We're green across the board," she said.

He pulled his arm back and patted the control box. "Fixed it, Huntsville!"

Michelle completed the checklist, coordinated the final quality assurance checks, and signed off the communication link for the two of them. She touched the green lights on the fuel panel. "Another one for manned space flight! Can't do *that* with a robot."

She helped him clean up the last of the checklist and paperwork as they listened to "Sweet Home, Alabama" piped in from Houston, today's tune to wake their crewmates for the next watch. Her attempt of a country two-step in zero-G was a miserable failure.

"For the record, Michelle, that music was *not* country," John said as he wiped his eyes, recovering from a fit of laughter. "So . . . what unfinished business do we have tonight?"

"Roadmaps, John. Curiosity got the best of me."

He tried to figure out what she meant, then shrugged.

"In our little talk last week you said something that I've been unable to shake, something about God's plan. We've been so busy that we haven't had ten minutes to talk in private in the past ten days."

"It *has* been busy."

Michelle's auburn hair floated in a donut and framed flashing hazel eyes full of questions. She drifted closer to him, shaking his shoulders as she smiled. "Our work's finished. How about it? Talk to Dr. Mich." She winked at him, waving him toward her.

"You should have been a shrink," John said, wiping his hands on his shorts and shaking his head.

"I tried," she said, with a faint grin.

"About this plan for your life. Has God ever spoken to you?" she asked five minutes later, half of her hoping he'd say "yes," the other half sure she'd found a vulnerability to exploit in his spiritual shell. She was anxious to know more but felt as if she had to pry every word out of John.

"Yes," he replied bluntly.

Her mouth hung open. "Like you're talking with me right now?"

John shifted in his foothold as he drew in a deep breath. "Yes—sort of . . . I can't describe the voice exactly. I know that when I've heard Him, the experience was unforgettable."

"Tell me what you heard. I really want to know." Her face lit up.

"Fair enough. This is a story about Amy," he said, raising a brow.

"Even better!"

"I met her during flight school. I was an ensign in the Navy and she was the choirmaster at a tiny country church, She asked me out to dinner one Saturday night. I came up with reasons not to go, but she was persistent. I finally succumbed."

Michelle let out a belly laugh. "Succumbed?"

"I'm serious. I'd proposed a month earlier to my high school sweetheart. Melody was struggling with the decision, and I was waiting for an answer."

Michelle wagged her finger.

"Not so fast, Mich," John protested. "I went into that dinner lonely, but my intentions were pure. Anyway . . . after dinner we were walking in the host's garden. One moment I was talking to her and the next, every fiber in my body was aware that someone—but not Amy—was talking to *me*."

John paused, seeming to stare off beyond her. "Everything around me went silent . . . again, like that time in the barn I told you about. And I heard these words loud and clear: 'This is the woman that you will marry.'"

Michelle concentrated on not smiling, but failed.

"This is no joke, Michelle. I was madly in love with Melody for seven years. I was convinced that she was the woman I should marry, and I was waiting patiently for her decision. But out of the blue, this powerful call to shift course, to jettison everything—to marry a woman I hadn't spent an hour with." He paused again. "There was no doubt in my mind—or heart—that this was His voice."

Michelle drifted out of her foot restraint, hanging on every word.

"I promise . . . if you ever hear it . . . you'll *know*."

Michelle slowly drew in a breath. "What about the fiancée? How did you *deal* with her?"

"It's a long story of prayer and counsel. It ripped my heart apart."

Michelle exhaled audibly. They both drifted without a word in the Zarya module. "You walked away from your first love and a seven-year relationship, at the threshold of marriage, to follow this Voice and marry Amy?" She stated it like a question, but she already knew the answer.

"Best decision I ever made. I fell in love with Amy while I said good-bye to the only woman I'd ever loved. You get through times like that only with a firm grip on God's promises."

Michelle felt her eyes begin to mist. Something about his story grabbed her and rooted in her heart.

"We're each called in different ways and at different times. Usually through a quiet whisper, or a tug on our conscience. No words, just a strong sense," John said. "I call it my little Voice."

She stared blankly, looking through him.

"God tries to speak to all of us, Michelle. Trouble is, we usually don't listen." He hesitated, and she immediately locked eyes with him. "God's wisdom is perfect, but His way isn't always easy. You need faith that's tough as nails to live out the answers you get to some of your prayers."

Michelle was subdued as John's last words hung in the air.

"You've experienced the same thing, haven't you — the quiet whisper?" he asked, his eyes never breaking her deliberate gaze.

Her silence framed his question, no words on her lips but volumes aching to break free of her chest.

Her reply was raspy as she nodded. "Yes — I've heard it." Then she fled through the node behind them as the mist in her eyes overflowed as tears.

13

"WE'RE READY, DR. KANEWSKI," Scott McGrady said as he gestured with pride toward a bank of computer equipment shoehorned into Rover Mission Control. The team of scientists and technicians was now three times its normal size. At three in the morning, dozens of sleep-deprived engineers and technicians were pumped with adrenaline and caffeine. They had just finished rigging the equipment and software to decode the mystery data stream from Mars.

"Engage!" Robert Kanewski said with a nervous laugh, wishing that he was at the terminal typing the commands. Yet this discovery might be the highlight of Scott's career. The moment belonged to his protégé.

"Here we go . . . but no promises," Scott said, his fingers crossed. "This application's not debugged. But there's no time for perfection." He hit the "Enter" key with the flair of a concert pianist.

Instantly an image sprang onto the screen. The entire data stream was decoded, smoothed, and displayed faster than a supercomputer could have done the same job in 1976, when Viking 1 landed. Thirty-five years ago those first landers, squatting spider-like in the red dust, had excavated and analyzed soil, photographed stunning sunrises and sunsets, and revealed more about Mars than all the study missions before them. Now more than three decades later, before the astonished NASA team, the computer screen displayed an image that defied imagination. Wide-eyed, the forty explorers gaped, their silence broken only by a few audible gasps.

Highlighted against the rugged red Martian landscape was a scene no person had ever observed—only imagined. A white Viking Lander stood alone, the U.S. flag prominent on the side of the soiled thirty-five-year-old explorer. Pictures from Viking years ago had shown the control crews a panorama of rocks and low ridges around the spacecraft, but never Viking itself.

This view was no panorama. The perspective was of the entire lander, as seen from perhaps ten meters away. Thirty years after the last signal had died out from this landing site, today's remarkable transmission revealed a solitary and dirty-white, frozen sentinel against a blue Martian sunset amidst a backdrop of ruddy red dust and rock. Yet, Viking 1—even if it were alive—couldn't possibly photograph itself.

Someone else—or something else—was on Mars. Transmitting pictures of a robot explorer silenced long ago.

CLEAR LAKE CITY, TEXAS

Amy Wells was not a morning person. The one consolation for children growing out of their cute and adorable years as toddlers was that they chose to sleep in on Saturdays. Once a week Amy and the family were blessed to let eight o'clock slip by unnoticed, and today was that one opportunity. If John were home, he'd be up at six, even on a weekend. As much as she missed him, her situation with growing children and a space-bound husband had its advantages at least one morning a week.

Victoria, the family's calico cat, stretched on top of the car in her morning ritual as Amy passed through the garage. Amy was late with the cat feast and her morning trip to grab the paper. Victoria ran ahead of Amy to the end of the white concrete drive in the warm spring morning sun. The odor of the sea blew in from the bay, moist and fishy. Amy squinted at the brightness, and waved to an early neighbor already starting a lawnmower. When she bent over the paper, Amy knew that the news inside was special from the sight of the wrapper. Color headlines on a Saturday were rare for the *Houston Post*. News in hand, she and Victoria made their way toward breakfast.

Back in the kitchen, the toaster and coffeemaker dinged and hissed their ready sounds as CNN cycled through advertisements. Her morning fuels were ready: A cold boiled egg, one Eggo with diet syrup, caffeine, and printed news, each with its distinctive aroma. Amy tossed the paper open onto the antique family table, its top an encyclopedia of stains from meals, homework, and school projects. With a forkful of waffle in one hand and the paper in the other, she stopped in shock at the full-page color photo and the headline's amazing news. Highlighted against red soil and a blue sunset stood a striking white image of Viking 1, America's historic lander on Mars. As she read the headline with a dripping waffle in midair, the television news broadcast chimed in.

"The mystery is, who took the picture, is it real, and, if it is, why did they send it to us? NASA, as well as the Russian, European, Japanese, and Chinese space agencies, all deny the existence of a secret Martian mission. More on this breaking story from—"

Amy's heart sped up, fluttering in her chest. "It's stress, not a heart attack," her internist had assured her. Right now, it felt like a full-blown myocardial infarction. Sweat began to form on her forehead and on the back of her neck. She found that she had already set down the fork and newspaper; her hand immediately went to her heart.

Why did her body always do this? She willed the fear that gripped her to leave her alone. It didn't. She reached, unconsciously, for her blood sugar tester and fought to remember how many times she had punched her insulin pump this morning. Once? Twice? Her heart leapt again as her eyes fell once more on the paper and its one-word headline.

Transfixed by the photograph, largely ignoring the television, her mind raced through a dozen possibilities related to alien life on Mars. Just last weekend, in her Sunday school class, someone had forced a discussion of the possibility of life on other planets. She'd ignored the discussion, trying not to think about problems that would affect her husband, the space program, or his return home.

Now, despite her best efforts, the distraction that she sought to exclude from her life, the anxiety about space flight, her fears of the unknown, grabbed her by the throat. She trembled as she realized that her carefully controlled environment, the tenuous world of patient astronaut wife waiting out a boring space station mission, was about to slip from her control. UFO aficionados, news reporters, and thrill seekers would seek her out. After all, of the three Americans in orbit, only John had a spouse—and she was it. She grasped the paper with two shaking hands as the picture of Viking 1 burned itself into her memory.

Amy pushed the tips of the glucose meter into her fingertip. Tests. Control. She would regain her composure. Order.

A tingle ran up her spine—an effect, she thought, of her blood sugar that must surely be tanking. Then another tingle. Suddenly, she was aware that this was all about more than just news. Her heart fluttered yet again, but at last she was at peace. She knew this feeling.

This must be what John felt, she thought, shivering in the kitchen. She looked down at the blood tester. *Good.* Her sugar level was normal.

In that moment she knew, without question, that she was now somehow part of this strange news, a player in a great drama. She felt called somehow, and prepared, like a runner setting out at last on a long-anticipated and difficult race.

✳

PASADENA, CALIFORNIA

"Who released it, Robert? I want names. Not excuses." Her temples flared, swollen and sweaty. Jet black hair that was frazzled from her dash to the office flew in all directions early on a Saturday morning.

"Answers, Robert!" she screamed as she slammed her desk. A heavy walnut nameplate dislodged and fell to the floor: Dr. Felicia Bondurant, Center Director, NASA Jet Propulsion Laboratory. Her delicate first name stood in stark contrast to her shrewish temper.

"Names!" She shrieked as she threw a copy of the *Los Angeles Times* across the room at Robert. The bold red, white, and blue of a Viking on Mars fell at his feet. "Aliens?" was emblazoned as the headline.

"Felicia, I have no names — and no way to know."

She let loose a string of profanities. He stood straight, arms crossed, unmoving.

"It's a matter of only a few mouse clicks and the image is on the Web, Felicia. You know that."

"No trace? I don't believe it!" The usual sparkle in her eyes was gone, replaced by bloodshot whites.

"The Ops Center was a zoo last night. Anyone could've done it. After all—you were there."

"Shut up!" she screamed as she whirled hard on a cheap sandal. The strap broke and sent her tumbling tail first onto the floor, legs askew, and her black hair flying up to expose a tiny white skunk stripe down the middle of her scalp. "Get out!" she yelled, flat on her back.

He picked up the *Los Angeles Times,* folding it slowly and placing it with care on her desk.

"Treat this as an opportunity, Felicia," he said. "You at least know how to do that."

Robert paced the floor of the Operations Control Center, every member of his staff present as he mustered all of the venom his calm nature could produce. "Early this morning, we witnessed what might be one of the most historic moments in space exploration. Or it might be a colossal hoax. In either event, it was big news. But one of you is an idiot bent on the ruination of careers and a critical Mars rover mission. Exciting or not, we are scientists and engineers, and we always test data before we publish it. Sending that image to the Web was the epitome of stupidity."

His throat tightened as he thought of his life's work perishing. "One of you . . ." he said, raising his voice as he waved his hand at the twenty-six explorers in his midst, "took it upon him or herself to release an image, without my consent. You destroyed our credibility and created a national hysteria."

He stopped pacing and glared at his loyal but mystified team. "You may have meant well, but you really blew it." His head drooped. The silence was heavy.

"It was me."

An exclamation of surprise rippled through the room. Robert knew the voice but didn't look up, stabbed by the startling admission from a trusted friend. "Why, Scott?"

"The rush of the moment. I posted it on my website—and someone picked right up. It was dumb—I've ruined this for all of you."

The room parted around Scott McGrady, a pariah. Robert was silent, head bowed.

Scott approached him, stooped in shame. "I'm really sorry, Doc."

Robert turned to greet his star protégé, a younger version of himself. His scowl deepened. "Of all people." He gazed around the room. "Why not just stab me? I know Felicia will," he said as he remembered too well the pay of a junior research assistant. Scott would have to go, and he would surely be demoted into Scott's position. The thought humiliated him.

Robert waved the rest of the staff away. "I was counting on you."

"I know," Scott said, head bowed.

"Get back to your terminal," Robert commanded. "I'll decide what to do after this shift. But no more stupid stunts, understand? Your job's already on the line. And the rest of our jobs too, if I know Felicia."

Scott nodded and then turned in surprise as another of the engineers called out, "Come to the phone! The director's on the line!"

"Put it on speaker, Jill." Robert said, with resignation. "Felicia, this is Robert. What can we do for you?"

"I want names, Robert."

All eyes focused on Scott. No one spoke.

Robert broke the silence. "It was me. My decision."

Scott looked at the floor, and other members of the team fell into their chairs. Yet no one spoke.

"You're either a seasoned liar or a perfect genius." She hesitated, then continued, "Anyway, I've just talked to the vice president, who I'm sure you're aware serves as the head of the National Space Council. He called to congratulate me on our gutsy move . . . our brilliant decision to release the photos of the Viking. It would seem, Dr. Kanewski, that the person you're covering for is something of a folk hero as of this morning. For whatever reason—" she paused—"the White House loves you."

**SUNDAY, MAY 15, 2011:
LOS ANGELES, CALIFORNIA**

"We are poised on the edge of history, Foster. Mankind is at a critical juncture, and we have a great role to play in this cosmos."

Foster Williams, talk-show anchor for the Sunday morning edition of *Foster's World* was a plastic face, with not a tooth or a hair out of place. His role was selling current news with unusual but well-connected guests. Today, it was Dr. Malcolm Raines. The tall guest's black hair was straightened and greased into a wavy part that gave him the look of a conservative business analyst, complemented by expensive round gold-rimmed glasses and a perfectly tailored suit.

"Reverend Raines, you're a vocal proponent of the resurgence of our manned space flight program. Why does a man of the cloth preach on this subject? After all, wouldn't our tax dollars be better spent here on Earth? Like recovering from 3/21?"

Malcolm Raines, spokesman and principal cleric for the World Inclusive Faith Church, crossed his legs as he settled into the deep plush studio chair. He spoke slowly, with deliberation, as though affecting a genteel British upbringing with the barest hint of a backwater Louisiana accent.

"No, Foster. There are better uses for our resources than to plow them right back into the ground you take them out of. We have a good start on the rebuilding, but we can't take our eyes off the future. Some of what this nation produces needs to be invested in a world yet to come. We need to help those less fortunate than ourselves by developing our universe, not simply reconstructing a small part of it. We're called to a broad vision as a human race. A vision for great exploration. The universe is infinite, and it requires us to stretch our imagination, to get outside our comfort zones."

"You've certainly put your own talents to work, Reverend. After a great basketball career, your eight years in Phoenix have seen a huge growth in your spiritual following. I've heard you say often that you preach 'good news for all men who venture forth and reach beyond their grasp.' If this were your hour to share your message with the world, what would it be?"

"Quite simple really. A grand opportunity awaits us. We will soon witness absolute proof that we are not alone in this universe."

"You're referring to yesterday's images from NASA of the Viking lander?"

"In part. Our scientists say they can't explain the signal from Mars or its striking image. But we certainly can't ignore it, can we? So . . . what if it *is* from an intelligent race? Shouldn't we reach out to those beings and embrace their message? I have prophesied of this for two years, and it has come true this week. This revelation won't be the only one. Greater unveilings are on the horizon. Let's just stay tuned, shall we?"

Raines flashed a brilliant toothy smile that Foster thought dovetailed perfectly with his guest's king-sized ego.

"That we will, Reverend Raines. Apt words for times such as these." Foster turned to the camera. "And you stay tuned. We'll be watching Reverend Malcolm Raines, a man for our times—and it seems—a man with an unusual vision for what's to come."

CLEAR LAKE CITY, TEXAS

"What a charlatan!" Amy turned the television off in disgust as she tried to get the children out the door for church.

"What's a charlatan, Mom?" Alice asked, ignoring her untied sundress.

"It's a lizard that changes colors. Everyone knows that," Albert said with confidence.

"Good try, honey, but that's a 'chameleon'—although your word fits Malcolm Raines pretty well, too." Amy patted them both on the back, prodding them toward the door. "A charlatan's a fake, or a deceiver. I just don't like that man." She was in a Sunday rush, cajoling the boys as she brushed Alice's hair.

"Why don't you like him?" Abe, her teenager, waded into the conversation as they all piled into the family minivan. Backing out to the street, Amy almost forgot to lower the garage door, confounded by the rush out of the house and Abe's penetrating way of asking a question. She stopped, punched the remote four times to make the dying battery do its job, and left when the first panel started down.

"Raines. What is it you don't like?" Abe asked again. "He's got a huge following in Arizona. He graduated from Georgetown, played basketball for the Hoyas and for the Orlando Magic. He's a college hall-of-famer, got a doctorate from Oxford, and coaches high school ball for disadvantaged kids. Seems like Mr. All American, if you ask me."

Amy didn't answer for a while. She turned and smiled at Abe to let him know that the comment registered while she navigated the streets, a dozen thoughts competing for her attention. At last, she breathed deeply and took on her son's challenge.

"It isn't fame that makes good people, Abe. Integrity and character make a man . . . and his heart. Raines is . . . charismatic. Suave. A smooth speaker. But his heart is in the wrong place."

"He's a chameleon!" Alice said, then squealed when Albert punched her in the side for stealing his word.

"Charlatan. Yes, that's it, Alice. He talks a great line, but his ministry isn't to people, it's just to make himself look better. Full of fame and full of himself."

"You're judging him, Mom. We're not supposed to do that," Abe said as he crossed his arms in the back of the van.

Amy cast a quick glance at him in the mirror, pensive in his seat. No one talked the rest of the short ride to church, waiting, she presumed, for Mom to take the upper hand with Abe. She pulled under the portico at the youth center to let her family out. She motioned her oldest son aside as he exited.

"You're right, Abe. I *was* judging him. That's wrong. But what I'm telling you about his ministry is factual, not judgmental. I want you to look into the man. See where he stores up his treasure. If he's all words and no action, and doesn't practice what he's preaching, then that's not the kind of man you want to emulate. Don't focus on his basketball skills. Look at his heart."

Abe nodded silently and left his ball cap in the van, pushing Alice along to her class. He turned as the rest of the Wells clan dashed inside the church. She waited as he looked back at her.

"Mom?"

"Yes, Abe?" she answered, a hand on the wheel, about to pull her door shut.

"He might be right, you know."

"Who?" Amy asked.

"Raines and the alien thing," Abe said. "They might be out there. And what then?"

14

"I'VE ALREADY ANSWERED THAT question. Six weeks ago, if I recall correctly." General Fredericks pushed back from his desk, his eyes shifting about the room.

Special Agent Kerry watched him in silence. He would let the silence hang for a while and see what happened. The general stood up and paced near his window.

"You have no idea what this is like, Kerry. To lose your daughter." The officer's gaze bored in on Kerry, then he turned to look out the window of his rented office space, facing toward the construction cranes on the base, razing his old building.

"I might."

General Fredericks turned around, head cocked to the side a bit. "Might?"

"I lost my wife a few years ago, sir. She was pregnant with our first child."

"Oh. Perhaps you do understand."

"I carry it with me every day. I completely relate to your pain. And I know from experience that you have to carry on. The pain never leaves. It just hides."

Fredericks nodded. "So. Since we have more in common than I realized, let's get to the bottom of this issue *now*, shall we? You asked me earlier about the tactical impact of the attacks. You realize, of course, that the intelligence regarding the Iranian terror cell was air-tight, correct?"

Kerry nodded.

"And if you've been briefed, as I am sure you have, you know that we have strike options in work to respond to the attack. On a classified timeline, of course."

"Of course."

"The attacks on 3/21 had no tactical impact other than major damage and a temporary disruption in operations, Kerry. If there had been an impact, it would have been all over the media. We don't understand completely why the Iranians targeted Colorado. Perhaps it was the iconic monument of missile defense. Like crashing into the Twin Towers, but this time Cheyenne Mountain. But I must reemphasize: America was—and is—safe."

"Fine. Let's leave it there, general. After one last question." Kerry stood up, his eyes below the general's level, following him from across the room. "I've consulted the maintenance records for the mobile mission ground sites of the infrared space sensors. Your backup downlink sites, as it were. Remarkably, they have nearly a 100 percent availability rating over a twelve-year period. Yet, on that day, March 21, all three sites were out of commission. At the same time. Beginning just as the attack happened. For relatively minor problems that were resolved in forty-eight hours. Think about it. For the first time in the history of space-based sensing, there were no operational downlink sites, precisely at that moment when Colorado was hit."

General Fredericks's face began to redden and he shook his head. "There must be some mistake. I'm sure I would have been informed. But as you said, 'we can leave it there.' No impact."

"But you *were* informed, General. In your daily reports. And by e-mail from your field commanders in those regions. I'm sure you have a record on your computer if you don't recall the briefings. I've found the information on my own. I don't understand why you, of all people, would work so hard to insist that what is public knowledge simply didn't happen."

"I've heard enough, Kerry. You asked me if there was a tactical impact. I told you there was none. Now you're just trying to use your badge to goad me. Maybe they were down. I probably forgot. But no missiles were launched. America was and is safe from missile attack. No tactical impact. End of story." The general stood at his desk, leaning over the back of his tall leather swivel chair. He pointed toward the door. "You may leave now."

"Thank you sir, I will. But I want you to help me with one more thing . . . as a fellow American and a patriot." Kerry held his hands palms up, waiting on a response.

"What? I thought I asked you to leave."

"Help me understand how terrorists funded by Iran managed to castrate our missile defense system for forty-eight hours with a targeted strike, and during that time, *nothing* happened. If you worked so hard to accomplish something of that magnitude, wouldn't you at least leverage your success in some way?"

"Like I said, good-bye, Agent Kerry. Don't presume to do my job for me. Maybe the sites *were* down. It doesn't matter. If there *had* been any launches, any missile attacks, we'd surely know by now, wouldn't we?" He pointed Kerry toward the door.

The agent headed out, and stopped with one hand on the doorknob. "Would we? For the past six weeks you've claimed to know nothing about the maintenance status of your own forces. I wonder. . . ."

"Get out!"

General Fredericks's hands shook violently over the keyboard. He tried three times to enter his password for the screen lock and failed, then pushed away from the desk in disgust, exhaling a cloud of Tennessee Whiskey across the room as he swore at the recalcitrant computer. After two deep breaths, he tried again, forcing himself to calm down and work through the fog of liquor and lost sleep that clouded his brain. The computer complied at 2:46 a.m.

There it was again. The e-mail folder, with one unread message, just like the time before and the times before that. Each e-mail had been read and the folder discarded, yet it always came back, with all the previously read e-mails and a brand new one for the week, each time with a new horrific message. Pain shot through his left temple. His left arm was numb. He fought on through the pain to open the e-mail. A searingly hot spike was driving itself deep into his left eye socket, he was sure. Somehow, he had to ignore the pain and press on.

"'INCREDIBLE.' What kind of subject is that?" he mumbled, as he selected the latest missive. The mail opened, with only two lines.

Incredible claims require incredible proof. Don't you agree, General?
Arab attacks? Incredible claim. Have you shared the incredible proof about your role in this tragedy?

He slammed the keyboard, breaking the black plastic and scattering keys across his desktop. General Fredericks swore again, cursing nonstop as he tried in vain to cancel the e-mail and delete the folder with a broken keyboard, forgetting the able mouse at his right. After a few minutes, he swam through the booze and found the delete function with the mouse, sending the dreaded e-mail to temporary oblivion. He breathed a sigh of relief, unable to face the reality that next week it would be back, a new message that would draw him tighter into the noose, with no apparent hope of escape.

The pain in his eye socket stabbed him again, and he staggered back from his desk, hands to his head. He fell over his chair, landing on his back, his head hitting the edge of the window sill with a loud thud.

He lay on the floor, dazed, trying to think, swimming in the stupor of too much liquor and a mild concussion.

"Get rid of the computer. That'll do it," he said to himself, shaking his head to clear it, half of him not quite sure how throwing away his machine would help. "Throw it away!" he reassured himself, looking for something . . . anything . . . he could do to make things better. He had to rid himself of the e-mail trail and his personal files. "Good idea," he mumbled as he struggled up from the floor and fell over his desk.

An hour later, having undocked the laptop from his office port, General Boomer Fredericks flung his notebook computer, wrapped in a black plastic trash bag, into a dumpster on Bijou Street near the Interstate 25 interchange.

"Gone. Now try to find me," he said with a slur, spitting on the trash bin. He slammed the lid of the receptacle behind the Clarion Hotel and teetered back to his car, driving away unseen in the early morning hours, headlamps forgotten, as he headed home to bed. Alone.

✳

Inside the green metal bin, an older man awoke him from a deep snooze and nursed a pain in his side where something had smacked him. Homeless and cold, never wandering far from the river and downtown, this was his billet for the night. Ripping open the black plastic bag he found on top of him, he uttered a short prayer of thanksgiving as he found the future pawn for his next week, or perhaps a month, of hot meals. He pulled it close and fell back to sleep, dreaming of a full stomach.

SUNDAY, MAY 22, 2011: SPACE STATION ALPHA

"John. You were right. There's more to this than meets the eye. Learned today that all the mobile mission processor sites were down for forty-eight hours beginning at the time of the attack. Give your concepts some more thought and contact me next week. Kerry."

John stared at the e-mail for a moment, wondering what Special Agent Kerry meant.

In a flash, he could see it. He pushed away from the monitor to find his laptop. There was much to do.

MONDAY, MAY 23, 2011: SPACE STATION ALPHA

Nine days after the first images of Viking 1 were released in Pasadena, a new Sun peeked from behind a black Earth as the Space Station orbited into a new day. Below, the Caribbean Sea shimmered in the stillness of the early morning. John craned his neck to make out the coastline of Central America in the darkness, imagining the coast of Honduras where he'd spent memorable college summers working as a commercial diver off the reefs of Roatan and in the Miskito Keys. The Sun broke over the limb of Earth in full force.

"Good sunrise, John?" The Russian floated past him in the lab on his way toward the Zvezda module and some last tasks on his watch.

"They're all good. I'm going to miss this the most when we go back."

Sergei stopped a moment in the cupola. "Yes."

John knew that, after two Soyuz missions and assignment to the station, this would be Sergei's last space flight. Younger cosmonauts and Russia's economic collapse assured him of no future missions.

Together they watched the South Atlantic shimmer every color of the spectrum in the reflected light of a new day. Bermuda sparkled at the northern edge of their view, a pink sand gem suspended in a vat of brilliant blue. John smiled at the irony, looking down on what was once a hotbed of antisubmarine warfare, where he had flown clandestine missions tailing Soviet nuclear missile platforms. Today he and his close Russian friend looked back at the same ocean with a wholly different perspective.

"I'll miss it too, John. You heard latest news about Viking?" Sergei shook his head slowly. "Nine days, same picture, every day. Why are people so excited?"

"Got a point there," John said. "One picture of an old lander is not enough to convince me there are aliens. By the way, rumor has it that Russia sent a secret mission to Mars. Any truth to that, Colonel Nickolaiev?" John tried hard to squelch a laugh.

Sergei slapped him on the back. "Yes! Russian cosmonauts land on Mars and transmit pictures of your robot landers. This month Russians invent perpetual motion machine and cold fusion to solve world energy problem. I read this today on Internet." With a chuckle, Sergei pushed off to his next assignment.

John stayed at the window a moment longer to catch the last of the sunrise and then followed the station commander. There was no more time for stargazing. He found Sergei concentrated on a status screen on the Portable Computer System.

"Why the long face?"

Sergei's frown broke with a small, almost imperceptible grin. "Power reserves are in decline. I tracked charge cycles of Photovoltaic Module last two days. Slight reduction in output current. Houston confirms. Problem with Beta Gimbal Assembly on port solar wing. Does not point correct. Sooner or later we must fix."

John studied the display, impressed that Sergei had isolated the electrical fault. Each man attempted to best the other on systems knowledge; often the winner succeeded on nothing but gut instinct. Sergei was a remarkable pilot with a sixth sense for what made the station tick. Yet ten days from now they'd be on the ground, and Sergei would eventually be assigned to a key space post at the Cosmodrome in Tyuratam or Kapustin Yar. Their paths might never cross again.

"Good catch, Sergei. What does Houston say?"

Sergei shook his head. "'Standby.' Maybe another one of your famous study teams to recommend a course of action in three months."

John grinned, sharing his friend's view of NASA's tortuous bureaucracy. "And you, Skipper?"

Sergei brightened up. "We go fix, of course!"

John nodded. "No better way to trace a problem's source than to go to the failure and inspect it. But you're right. The EVA and safety committees will study this one for days." The contrast of NASA's storied safety processes, and their two lost orbiters, was ironic.

"Did you recommend an EVA?" John asked, pushing the safety issue aside.

"Yes!" Sergei shot back.

"Give 'em a day or two. They'll come around." John patted Sergei on the shoulder and moved to the communication terminal to send another message about his latest repair of the ever-troublesome space toilet.

"Mr. Plumber," Sergei joked a few minutes later. "Come see this."

John joined Sergei at the power management control station, bristling at his new nickname.

"Watch. Power output is dropping slowly." Together, they observed the data flow in from the failing solar panel wing motor, filtering the inputs with their years of practical experience.

"The Beta Gimbal Assembly's busted, Sergei. I'll bet NASA calls you inside five minutes."

It wasn't that long. Moments later the radio crackled. "Station, this is Houston. Are you and Sergei on the Electrical Control Unit screen?"

"Affirmative. We've got a problem in the rotation of the port Photovoltaic Module. The incident radiation on the solar panels is reduced, and our power generation is declining every orbit."

"We concur. Sergei, we got your e-mail and agree on EVA. We'll need to move fast on this before you start to dip into power reserves. We'll manifest a new gimbal motor on the next flight."

Sergei closed with a quick Russian good-bye. He smiled as the two men gave each other a high five that sent them both spinning across the module.

"One more EVA, Boris! Go tune up your suit!"

"Kerry."

"This is John Wells. You asked me to give you a ring."

"Yeah, John. Thanks. Hope everything's okay topside. You doing all right?"

"Some maintenance issues. We're doing an EVA this week. This place is a mess with all the garbage stowed for the replenishment flight.

Otherwise, ops normal." John paused. "I think I found something you might like to know."

"I'm all ears," Kerry said. "In a car on the 405 in LA though. If I lose you, dial me back."

"It's pretty simple . . . answers your e-mail about possible motives, but it'll take some explaining."

"Ready as ever. But no white boards, okay?"

"Got it. I looked at the missile defense vulnerability window we had in the first hours after the attack. I plugged in all of the National Missile Defense systems, the ships we knew were deployed as pickets, and the ground radars in the Pacific. It's a pretty complex model."

"I'm starting to lose you," Kerry said, "and I don't mean the signal."

"I'll send you some stuff on e-mail that you can see," John said, searching for another explanation. "But think of it this way. I'm recreating the times that the sentries were watching the city walls. In this case, all of the sentries were blind, or dead."

"Check. So what'd you learn?"

"Same thing you should have learned in Colorado Springs, so tell me if I'm repeating something you already know. If you'd launched a missile in any of the typical profiles, like the Russians shooting at us, then we'd have seen it with something other than a space asset. No question. The radars at Kwajelin atoll and in Hawaii were working just fine. Aegis cruisers in the Pacific would have picked up any missiles from that region as well."

"Duplicate information. Go on."

"The sensor stare for space-based sentries that day was predominantly to the north—for support of national missile defense—with a focus on the Middle East. When Colorado Springs went down, with no downlink capability at the remote mobile vans, there would have been an opportunity for a midlatitude launch toward the south, into a polar orbit, and it wouldn't be caught."

John took a breath, amazed he was having this conversation. "The organization that attacked us knew our system very well. They knew just how to take down a global surveillance system with complex interconnects but not prevent our homeland nuclear defense. That's probably why the Department of Defense claims that the attack had no impact. They're right . . . from a continental missile attack perspective."

"That's what they're all saying," Kerry replied.

"I think there's another possible motive, though," John said. "Much less obvious, and harder if not impossible to prove."

"Enlighten me."

"What if there was no intention to attack us with a missile? What if the bad guys just wanted to loft a payload, or many payloads, into a covert orbit? With the space surveillance and missile detection systems down, no one could have seen the launch. No attack, therefore no tactical impact. Nothing to fear."

"How about the rest of the surveillance system you told me about? Wouldn't the orbits of whatever went up there get noticed?" Kerry asked.

"Eventually. It might take two or three revolutions for a polar orbit to register with the Air Force space surveillance systems. But of course . . ."

"They were dead."

"Yep. For two days. In all that confusion, and with all the lost data, it would have taken days to sort out the changes and pick up on a new satellite. If the bad guys keep changing their orbital parameters once per orbit, you'll never find them. The system is only designed to identify predictable orbits."

"You're kidding."

"I wish I was. If no one sees you launch, and if you change your parameters every orbit, you could, in theory, create a plan to hide forever—especially over the equator. That is, unless one of the Hawaii deep-space cameras picked you up by accident. That happens on rare occasion."

"That's scary. The hidden orbit part. But why would someone want to do that?"

"I've been thinking about it," John said, picking his words carefully. "Maybe some country—Iran's a pretty good candidate right now—wants to put a nuclear weapon in orbit, hide it, and rain it down later. Maybe dozens of nukes, spread all around the globe. Or nuclear space mines. Perhaps they want to launch a fleet of antisatellite weapons, just waiting for the first space war. Or maybe . . . " He paused. "Maybe some rich terrorist bought himself a missile and a nuclear payload from a cash-strapped Russia, and now an Islamic megaton maniac has a payload in orbit ready to strike—with no notice. We'd never see it coming. No defense. Very ugly."

"John. No one I am talking to, or that the Bureau has spoken to, has been this blunt. There's got to be a reason."

"Two reasons," John interjected.

"Two?" Kerry asked.

"Either the administration has already figured it out, which I would bet is true and you just haven't been informed, or—"

"Yeah?"

"Or they're stupid. Don't ever discount that option. This much I do know. Anyone could have launched a missile over the South Pole or into some limited equatorial orbit for up to two days after the attack, and they'd have never been caught. They could've hidden whatever they sent up—it could still be up there . . . up *here*. The system simply isn't set up to find stuff if we didn't anticipate the launch. Low Earth orbit is a big place. We look for missile launch plumes, not nukes posing as space debris."

"You're confirming what I've been running up against at every turn," Kerry said. "This was perfectly timed—a little too perfect. And we're working against someone with insider knowledge—if in fact the three mobile mission processor sites were all busted at the same time."

"The Iranians are smarter than we're giving them credit for," John said with a half laugh. "They've funded Islamic terror all over the globe. They're in bed with the Russians, and they might have nukes." He paused, then added, "Better not underestimate 'em."

15

"I'M CLEAR, HOUSTON," JOHN said into the microphone of his white Extravehicular Mobility Unit. The panorama of space enthralled him as he floated in his suit, the whisper of his air supply the only sound in the incredible vacuum that surrounded him. Free of the confines of the cylindrical habitat, he was suspended above a perfect blue Earth, with the huge space station spread out before him. For a brief moment, the giant solar wings and depth of space took his breath away. He'd been bottled up in the station's modules for three months since his last EVA; life had taken on much smaller dimensions. He stared into the expanse above him, a bright sun filling his gold visor. *Short of dying*, he thought, *this is heaven.*

John pulled his way along the external handholds of the station toward Sergei, who waited on him to exit the Quest joint airlock module. After four hours of prebreathing pure oxygen while they camped out in the equipment lock, then another couple of hours donning the EMU and the Russian ORLAN spacesuits, and the half hour to pump down the crew lock, they were on their way at last.

"Are you ready *yet*, John?" Sergei kidded as his fellow pilot approached.

"Ready, Sergei. It always grabs me the first time I step outside. Let's get our hands on those gimbals."

Together they pulled from handhold to handhold along the airlock, chatting with each other and Houston as they worked their way over to the truss segment and up to the mobile transporter unit. The camera on the Canadian Space Arm followed them as the transporter crawled slowly along the station's backbone. Each man was a miniature spacecraft. Protected against the vacuum of space, they were self-contained units of oxygen, water, pressurization, cooling, filters, power, and communication.

Every few handholds, John would pause and look down at Earth turning slowly below him. Of all the facets of space flight, this was the activity that John liked most, hanging alone hundreds of kilometers above the surface of his planet, whipping along at thirty thousand kilometers per hour. He and Sergei were part of an intricate space ballet, moving effortlessly along the huge truss in bulky white suits, framed against the backdrop of their blue-and-white terrestrial home.

They moved from tether point to tether point, clipping and pulling along in a slow but safe pace out to the end of the port photovoltaic arrays. After more than forty minutes, they finally arrived at the base of the big solar wings. The huge solar field dwarfed the men who stood out brilliant white in their suits against the backdrop of a raw unfiltered sun. Like ten thousand bathroom mirrors arrayed about them, the eighty-meter-wide solar cells bathed the astronauts with an intense reflected light.

From her perch at the cupola window in the Unity node, John knew Michelle would back them up as the human eye of the watch team. Even with sunglasses, she would have to occasionally shield her eyes. The newly installed cupola, built like a miniature control tower would give Michelle a panoramic view of the station and their work.

"Looks good from here," she reported. "You guys okay?"

"Just fine, Mich," John said. "Ten minutes till eclipse."

The two veteran space walkers reached the base of the port solar wing and worked with precision to set up their tools before the Sun hid behind Earth.

"We'd better find a way to fix this thing today, Sergei, or we'll have to take cold showers for a while."

"Shower, John? Has been so long, I've forgotten," Sergei joked.

This last EVA was a dream for both of them, so close to the end of a memorable six-month mission. Yet John and the entire team were attentive to the potential for electrical disaster today. The Photovoltaic Modules, as the solar wings were called, produced 160 volts using the near-continuous solar radiation. A wrong move, or a failure to disconnect the station electrical load from the power of the solar wings, could spell their end, turning John or Sergei into human fuses. Like a giant grounding plug, the station spewed an invisible electron stream of xenon gas into the vacuum to produce a long tail that grounded them, and the station, to the space environment. There could be no mistakes.

"What do you see, Sergei? We've got your chest camera video, but we can't make out any obvious trouble." Jake Cook was the voice of Houston for this operation, a familiar astronaut at the Capsule Communicator position, or CAPCOM.

"No external damage," replied Sergei.

"Looks like the textbook from the outside, Houston," replied John. "We'll open it up to see what's wrong. Rotate it one more time, Frank."

Frank Peters, their climatologist in a pinch role as a space station electrical contractor, commanded another rotation of the solar wing with the same negative result. It was jammed.

As the astronauts and their space station glided through night and into the dawn of a new orbit, they unbuttoned the insulation on the Beta Gimbal Assembly with painstaking attention to checklists. Thermal blankets were pulled back. Power and control connectors were removed and inspected. Harnesses, cables, and power junctions were reconnected and certified. Through two orbits and three hours of EVA, every aspect of the gimbaling actuator was evaluated and rebuilt.

"Tired yet, guys?" Michelle asked as the next sunrise passed.

"I never get tired of this," John said, waving toward Michelle in the cupola, "but lunch would be nice. Okay, Frank, we're ready. We've reset every connector. If that didn't do it, we'll need a new gimbal motor on the next flight."

"It's already manifested, just in case," Jake responded from Houston. "The crew's in the dive tank practicing the installation right now. But time's getting short, fellas. Sergei's suit's only good for five hours. We need you to wrap this up and be out of there in no more than half an hour."

"Concur," Michelle said, chiming in.

"Roger that. I'm ready to rotate the wing when you are, Frank."

"Check. Step 48. Rotate," Frank said as John and Sergei floated back from the large bulbous gimbal actuator. "But we've gotta wait for some sunlight so that we can test the tracker mechanism."

Sergei waved at John. "Take five!"

John took advantage of the momentary break to watch the stars above him in the midst of an orbital eclipse. No one on Earth could ever see the stars he saw, free of atmosphere and background light, the whole array of the southern hemisphere's heavens spread out before him. He was a human Hubble telescope, scanning the brilliant heavens and the

Southern Cross, in awe of the majesty of creation.

Moments later, the sun began to rise, rays peeking over the limb of the Earth as they completed yet another orbit. The warmth of the solar radiation broke the chill of the past fifteen minutes in the dark cold. He watched in wonder, listening to his beating heart in the perfect silence.

"Here goes," Frank said once the Sun was half exposed. On cue, the Beta Gimbal Assembly began to spin, slowly turning the wing in a one-hundred-and-eighty-degree rotation, then reversing to the opposite detent, and returning the solar wings to point at the Sun. The unit tracked the new Sun with subtle changes as the station orbited Earth below. John raised a hand in a high-five greeting with Sergei, who returned the congratulations with a soft glove impact.

"Guess we got it, Houston." John pointed playfully at his Russian teammate. "You da man, Boris."

"You are as good electrician as you are toilet repair man," replied Sergei.

"You guys may need to leave that for another trip," Michelle said, her voice suddenly tense.

"What's up?" John asked.

"Sergei, your CO_2 just spiked," she said. "O_2 suddenly dropped 20 percent. Acknowledge?"

"Houston concurs. EVA officer shows a sudden loss of all O_2. Confirm?" Jake replied, the calm gone from his voice.

There was no cheerful EVA banter in Sergei's next transmission. "Confirm. Caution and Warning Light. Primary O_2 supply is dead. Attempting backup. We're aborting." Sergei waved at John, drew his gloved hand slowly across his throat, and then pointed to the distant airlock.

John knew the look, the sign language, and the deadly impact of Sergei's situation. Sergei's suit had only a thirty-minute emergency oxygen backup. They were at least that far from the crew lock if they left now. This wasn't Russia's first ORLAN suit failure in the history of EVAs on station. But it might be the worst.

What should have been a jovial celebration of a critical space repair and last EVA for Sergei and John at once became a desperate and potentially fatal race against time. In a flash, without the need for cues from Houston or Sergei, the crew of the International Space Station went into emergency response mode.

Sergei's life hung in the balance.

Michelle darted from the cupola to confirm the readiness of the joint airlock, her pulse pounding in her ears. She or Frank could be suited up and outside in as little as an hour, but they didn't have the luxury of that much time. Sergei had only minutes, if that long. She raced back to her viewing perch, grabbing an essential medical kit on the way, and then strained for some sight of John.

Below on Earth, hundreds of NASA, Russian, and contract personnel were scrambling for terminals, running to vehicles, manning ground sites, fueling aircraft, and forming emergency teams, all for the express purpose of meeting an emergency on the International Space Station and perhaps recovering the emergency lifeboat — the Soyuz capsule. If Sergei's oxygen would hold until he returned to the crew lock, there would be no need for this preparation. But if medical support were required, he could be on the ground on the steppes of Russia in as little as two hours. The intended space station lifeboat, an emergency glider craft that could have flown the astronauts home fast and in one piece to a runway landing, had never been funded.

"Talk to me, Sergei. What's your O_2 tellin' you?" John said. Michelle could see that he kept a hand on Sergei's suit as they clipped and unclipped their tethers and hastened their long trip back toward the airlock.

"Reserve O_2 is down, John. Level dropping. I'm okay."

"Understand, buddy. Breathe slowly. I've got a hand on you."

"We'll send this suit to burn up in next Progress trash shipment, yes?"

Despite the incredible gravity of the moment, Michelle was amazed that Sergei found the time to make a joke. Progress vehicles brought supplies to the station from Russia and carried away their waste, including Russian ORLAN suits that had accumulated ten EVAs. Sent on a short ride toward Earth, they incinerated in the atmosphere along with the unwanted vestiges of life in space.

Michelle listened to their banter, and Sergei's heavy breathing, on the intercom and medical display at her optical station. As she pressed close to the window she could make out John's suit in the distance far down the giant truss. Her heart quickened as she flashed back to memories of their many talks at this window and in the lab.

"Headed your way, Mich. I can see you," John said.

"Copy that. What are you feeling, Sergei?" She tried to sound calm as she monitored the carbon dioxide rising toward a deadly concentration in the Russian's suit.

"Dizzy," the Russian replied, his speech slurred.

"Hustle up, fellas," she said, crossing her fingers.

They reached the Solar Alpha Rotary Joint as they crossed the inner port solar wing, still twenty minutes of fast progress away from the hatch and perhaps thirty from a vented lock. The airlock was on the opposite side from Michelle. Precious meters farther to go once they reached her panoramic window.

Not enough time!

She watched Sergei fumble with his tether clip. The carbon dioxide was affecting him, and his failed oxygen backup was providing none of the precious gas that he needed to function, or survive.

"Sergei, talk to me!" John said, as Michelle watched him pulling and pushing his partner along in the clumsy ORLAN suit.

The Russian's response was unintelligible Ukrainian gibberish. Sergei appeared to go limp.

"He's spiking, John. Hustle up!" Michelle's voice rang in John's helmet.

"Heart rate erratic," Jake added. "Get to that lock, John. Fast."

"We're too far!"

They were still forty meters from the cupola. Another ten to the crew lock on the opposite side from their direction of travel. Michelle watched in disbelief as John unclipped his harness, pulled it to the extent of the spring load, and wrapped the safety line twice around Sergei's limp waist. He clipped the tether back on his tool belt, lassoing himself to the lifeless Russian.

"What are you doing?" Michelle's voice was shrill. From her clear view in the cupola, she could see John tied to Sergei's suit.

"Vent the lock, Mich. We're comin' in."

"The lock's on the other side!" she screamed.

"Got any better ideas? We're cuttin' loose," John said, panting.

In that instant, Michelle remembered John's comment to her months earlier, that he'd always rather ask forgiveness than seek permission. This was one time she was glad he waited on no one. She craned her neck in the small window to see her friend, rocketing toward her in a fearful free-fall toward safety. His brass in this dire moment was Sergei's only hope.

John unclipped Sergei's harness, their only remaining connection to the station, and released his handhold on his unconscious friend. Tied to Sergei, the two began to fall away from their space home. John looked down at Earth, speeding by four hundred kilometers below, his stomach churning.

He reached down behind him to Sergei's thigh and unclipped his friend's SAFER, the Simplified Aid For EVA Rescue. Quickly estimating a trajectory, he prayed for wisdom as he pointed and fired the gun-like gas jet mechanism. They were committed. He might not get a second chance.

"John's going free, Houston!" screamed Frank. "Mich, crack the lock. He's coming over!"

"It's *been* open!" she snapped.

Controllers at Johnson Space Center leapt from their seats as they saw the station drift away in the video transmission from John's chest camera. "John! Confirm you have Sergei!" Jake screamed from his console in Mission Control.

"Roger! Makin' a beeline for the lock!" He yearned to wipe his face behind the helmet visor as he tried to shake burning sweat from his eyes.

Towing Sergei, John was now a two-man satellite. It was the only way to save his friend—but a dangerous move if he failed to compensate for the doubled mass. The hairpin turn that faced him in thirty meters made his heart race all the more.

"John, this is Houston! Use short bursts! Don't overcompensate!"

"Copy," he replied, trying hard to cover the terror in his own voice. "Talk to me, Boris. Come on. We're in this together now."

Sergei's limp body trailed behind John, a white Gumby doll undulating on the tether as John fired controlled pulses to refine their trajectory. There was no response from his friend.

"His heart rate's dropping fast. Can you see him?" Jake asked from half a world away in Houston.

"Can't. He's limp. And this SAFER's out of gas." John's heart pounded violently. He was committed in the worst way, speeding now

across the vacuum toward safety, with no more pressure remaining in
Sergei's emergency jet unit. He scrambled to clip the spent thruster to
his tool belt, flying across the truss segments much too fast and unable
to do anything about it. Panic gripped him. He fumbled in the stiff
EMU gloves for his own SAFER, clipped to his left thigh.

Where is it?

John could see Michelle plastered to the glass in the cupola. He was
headed straight for her. The crew lock was behind her. Somehow, he had
to make a U-turn to enter her back door.

It's in your hands, Lord.

Sweat beads floated in front of his face, fouling his view as they
stuck to the inside of his visor.

"You're coming in too fast!"

John found the precious propulsion gun, fouled by his tether to
Sergei, and freed it. He was out of control now, plunging like a car
across glazed ice toward a chasm. He jerked the thruster free of the clip,
directed it by instinct, and fired a huge pulse to prevent a fly-by into the
abyss of deep space. He fought a wave of nausea as he realized how fast
they were flying past Michelle and fired yet another pulse just as he
passed out of her view, headed for oblivion.

I only get one chance at this, Lord. Make it good.

In less than sixty seconds, John had raced, too fast, across the void
toward the crew lock and life-giving air for his friend. He fired another
blast of his SAFER, halting their trajectory and reversing their course.
He deftly pitched back, maneuvering the two of them into a rapid
descent feet-first toward the open door on the back side of the module.
He tried to break their closure rate with a counter pulse, but the second
SAFER was spent. He swallowed hard and his legs tensed, preparing for
the impact.

"Stand by, Michelle!" John screamed. The two men shot straight down into the crew airlock, slamming into the floor with a painful jolt. Sergei was unconscious and probably felt nothing. John was not so fortunate.

"Close and pressurize!" John cried, ignoring the searing pain in his right knee. He looked up as he called for the pressure and saw Michelle outside the hatch, calm and controlling the repressurization.

"He's in!" Jake yelled in Houston as controllers cheered and slapped each other.

The lock door closed slowly. Sergei was immobile, strapped behind the EMU. John struggled in the tight compartment against the limitations of his inflated suit, zero G, and the bulk of two men. Somehow he managed to unhook Sergei and spin him around. As he maneuvered his friend he caught sight of Michelle again through the viewing hole in the lock door, hair flinging wildly as she pulled medical equipment toward the bay.

"Five PSI, John. Standby leak check!" she cried out over the radio.

"Forget that! Pump it up!" John was ready to unzip the back of Sergei's clumsy ORLAN. Pulling his limp friend out of this disposable space suit was going to be hard, and he had no time for frills.

"Ten point six PSI! Go!" she cried, moments later.

Working against the clumsy EMU gloves, John unsnapped the last of the ORLAN backpack from the hard upper torso. The crew lock was equalized to the station atmosphere, and they could finally open the hatch.

"Sergei!" John yelled, forgetting that he still had his helmet on.

The airlock door into the station module opened. There was no time for procedures. John held the ORLAN unit with both of his feet wedged against the hatch. Four hands reached in and slipped Sergei out of the back of the ORLAN's rear access like meat popping free of a lobster tail.

✦

Working against the vagaries of zero gravity, Michelle and Frank struggled to pull Sergei's limp body free of a tangle of suit communication cords and his liquid cooling garment. There wasn't time for them to strap Sergei into the Crew Medical Restraint System, the space version of a litter.

"He's got a pulse but no respiration!" Michelle's portable microphone was live, and her words were heard around the globe as she sprang into action in her role as the crew medical officer. With two hands on the shoulder pads of his thermal suit and her two feet planted firmly between bags of equipment lashed to the bulkhead, she pulled Sergei to her as easily as she might a doll, forcing him up close to her face. She cradled her right arm around his neck and pulled his head back by his hair in a sleeper hold so quickly that John could only watch, amazed. With her left hand she pinched off his nose, and then she forced her mouth over the Russian's grizzled face, breathing life into him. It had been more than four minutes since Sergei had air. NASA's Respiratory Support Pack remained clipped to the bulkhead. Her way was faster.

With the practiced skill of an emergency medical technician, Michelle breathed and counted, her right hand deftly monitoring the pulse at his neck, an eye on the defibrillator in case she should need it. She hoped not. Without the space litter, they couldn't insulate the shock of the paddles from themselves or the station.

The Russian coughed. Floating sputum caught Michelle squarely in the mouth as she inhaled to begin another breath. She didn't gag but turned her head to see if the cough would follow with a breath. When it didn't, she breathed life into him again and again. Then he coughed a second time, and his engine started, wheezing deeply and gasping for air. At last, he caught his breath with a deep gurgling snort, and he opened his eyes.

Still locked in her arms, Sergei regained consciousness. She watched his eyes dart around the cluttered module, and then connect with her own. In his eyes, she could see her own round face framed by tousled auburn hair.

Michelle blushed at the sudden attention of Sergei and Frank as she realized her hold was no longer required. She removed her arm from around Sergei's neck and kissed him on the cheek. "Welcome back, Dorothy. Shave next time." Out of breath, dizzy, and heart pounding, she pushed back toward the wall of the Unity node. Michelle smiled and pointed at John, floating in the lock, fully suited, his helmet off. "You took the express!"

Sergei followed Michelle's eyes to John and his fast ride home. Without a handhold for leverage, Sergei could only bend in zero gravity as he tried to sit up in the cramped spaces. Sergei garbled a short "thank you," panting as he continued to catch his breath and cough up more phlegm. He looked around the node packed with bags of clothes and water, and now home to an assortment of drifting medical equipment, the ORLAN suit, and EVA paraphernalia.

"Module is mess," Sergei said, thick-tongued and shaking his head from dizziness. "Clean up it and back get to work."

16

"IT'S HARD TO BELIEVE we're going home," Michelle said, watching the peach-sized globule of juice that wobbled in front of her. She prodded it gently with a pair of chopsticks then plucked her drink out of the air and slurped it free of the tongs. "Strange how a place like this can come to feel like home in just six months."

John grunted something she couldn't understand. She cupped a hand over her ear.

He swallowed his food and repeated himself. "I'm torn about it. I want to be home with my family. I also want to be here."

John's carrots spun in midair, three of them rotating in synch, a new meal record for the grown boy who always played with his food.

Michelle was fascinated with John's three-ring food circus. "I'd rather stay," she said. "There's no one to go home to."

John nodded in silence.

Michelle squirted out another juice globule and pierced it slowly with a chopstick as she pondered her next words. "John, before we leave, I wanted to thank you."

"For what?" he asked, adding a record fourth carrot to the spinning vegetable menagerie.

"For being a good friend . . . who listens . . . someone to talk to . . . to work with and learn from." Her heart leapt. "I'm going to miss you, Hawk."

John grinned. "You're welcome. For what it's worth you helped me too . . . to break the mold."

"What mold?"

"The pilot thing. You forced me to express myself." He grinned. "I had to talk about something other than flying or space. A very un-pilot thing, you know."

"Uh-huh."

The ship's clock chimed seven bells in the background, framing their silence as they watched the carrots spin.

Michelle tired of the food fair. "Hey, can I ask you a favor?"

"Sure." He set the dinner adrift.

"I've heard you praying. In the cupola, when you watch the sunrise."

John's ears reddened. "I thought I was quiet."

"The acoustics aren't great . . . but I've got good ears." She toyed with her hair until he looked up at her. "Besides, your eyes were closed, so you never saw me. I was very touched."

John rubbed his face with both hands, his eyes avoiding her stare.

"It's not a side of you I'd ever noticed." Michelle leaned a little closer to him over the small table. She finally caught his eye. "My head tells me that what I'm about to ask is completely illogical, but here goes. Would you pray . . . for *me*?"

A smile lit John's long, craggy face. "I'd be honored . . . and I have been." He narrowed his eyes and matched her gaze. "I'm surprised you didn't hear, you eavesdropper."

"Wow. I mean—thanks."

He smiled again, nodding in silence.

"There's one more thing . . . ," Michelle said, her voice trailing off as she shifted her position in a foot restraint.

"And that is?"

"The other day—during the rescue—you and Sergei were just about out of time. Before you cut loose and flew across the gap—"

"That's a moment I won't soon forget."

"Or me. I can't explain it exactly, but at that moment when all seemed lost, part of me just opened up and cried out for you. Not out loud or anything, but like—in my heart. I guess it's what you call 'prayer.' I'd never experienced that, you know?"

He nodded, undulating up and down as he held his position with his feet in a toe hold.

"But that's not all. Just as soon as I let out this virtual cry, I had this déjà vu kind of feeling. It was weird like that warm blanket feeling you talked about a long time ago, something wrapped around me, giving me this peace that everything would be all right."

"What do you think that feeling was, Michelle?" John asked, his eyes holding her gaze as she struggled to share her story.

"I don't know. I was hoping you could tell me."

John smiled. "I don't have an explanation for déjà vu, Michelle, but I do understand when God is trying to get through to me. I think you were at a point of extreme need; you got over all those science hang-ups and asked Him for help. He answered you."

"Wow."

John nodded again. "'Wow' is apropos. It's incredible to hear from the Creator, and to know He heard you. He loves you so much, you cannot imagine."

"That simple? Just say something in your heart and—poof—it wings its way to heaven and finds His mailbox?"

"That simple. If you *trust* that it's so. Most people can't reach out to Him except when they're in a point of extreme need. You were. I was. He heard us both."

John moved to a new position—a little closer to her, she noticed.

"Thank you for praying for me," he said. "For interceding on my behalf."

"You just said 'trust.' You told me once before that you have to have 'faith.' What's the difference?"

John looked up at the floor above him, as if searching for an answer. "Trust is the same as faith. I have faith in my wife that she will keep her marriage vows. So I trust her. I trust in God—like on the dollar bill—and I have faith that He will care for and direct me. Same thing."

She pushed her hair back out of her eyes where the long bangs were floating in her face. "I don't know . . . maybe you've got this whole faith thing figured out—but it's got me baffled. However—trust—now that's something I understand." She looked down for a moment. "Can't say there were very many people I've ever trusted in my life. But it's a concept that I value." She reached across the table to place her hand on his. "I trust *you*. Above all people."

John didn't flinch.

"Thank you," she said slowly, squeezing his hand and pulling hers back.

"For trust?"

"Not just for that. For talking to me . . . and for not freaking out when we connected."

WASHINGTON, DC

Terrance Kerry stood on the steps of the Ronald Reagan Building in Washington, DC. Tourists and workers hurried by, headed to appointments or sightseeing, everyone sweating in the oppressive humidity of a hot late spring. June was only days away. Customs agents, federal servants, and government contractors filed in and out of the cool air of the building in a steady stream. No one ever made eye contact.

For a long time, Special Agent Kerry watched the people and wondered about their private lives. Any one of them could be his conspirator. He had a mountain of seemingly incontrovertible material that pointed directly to Islamic fundamentalist terror cells in Iran, but somehow, it didn't make any sense. It was too easy.

His phone warbled. Kerry stepped aside to take the call away from the crowd and the noise.

"Today? When?" he asked, shielding his ears to be able to hear above the din of the traffic and passersby.

"Don't know when it was pawned, but we got it today. Seems a techie at the base bought the laptop off a gun-and-jewelry shop two days ago. He hacked the password—don't ask me how—and was checking out the files when he realized what he had. He works at Peterson Air Force Base. Knows he was playing with fire."

"What'd he find?"

"Laptop belonged to the big guy. General Fredericks. Fellow you were railing about the other day after he threw you out. And his e-mail files have some pretty ugly stuff, Kerry. We've got the techie here in the office. We can't let him leave and go shooting off his mouth. The e-mail implicates Fredericks in the attack, if you can believe it. But the techie could have planted 'em, too, for all we know."

Kerry whistled, startling a tourist on the sidewalk. He turned and moved further toward the building.

"Somehow I don't think the laptop was a plant. But hold your man until I get out there, if you can. Tell him it's the witness protection program. Book him. Anything. I'll be in the Springs by tomorrow morning. If you can send files, get the techie to help you zip the worst of the e-mails and send them to me right away. I want to read 'em on my way out."

"Done," the voice on the phone said. "Anything else?"

"Yeah. Find out who pawned the computer. And put a tail on Fredericks—right now."

17

"I, FOR ONE, BELIEVE that there *are* Martians." Stone-faced and perfectly coifed, Rex Edwards, America's preeminent space tycoon, sat across from Foster Williams on a late May edition of *Foster's World.* While Foster hyped his show, Rex played his host like a master plays the violin, creating a harmony all his own.

"They're sending us pictures from Mars, and the scenes match the Viking location to a tee. You could perhaps make a conspiracy case that this is the ultimate Internet hoax, done with smoke, mirrors, and Adobe Photoshop. Or that the Russians are faking us into thinking there are aliens. I don't buy either of those options. I believe in intelligent alien life, and right now that life is imitating us to perfection. Look at the evidence. It's mounting up by the day."

"Martians, Rex? Do you mean little green men—or people like us?"

"Little green men don't fit my mental model of sentient alien life,

Foster. I've always been partial to Ray Bradbury's image of lithe copper bodies with slender limbs and yellow coin eyes. But from a probability point of view, they're as likely to look like us as anything else—after all, we are the only intelligent life any of us has ever encountered, so why *not* look like us?"

Rex Edwards paused a moment. "That wasn't a hypothetical question, Foster. Why *not* look like us?"

Foster shook his head, seemingly unable to form an answer.

"Consider this," Edwards said, gesticulating with his hands as he spoke. "There are centuries of history where people, the French in particular, maintain that we were visited centuries ago by angels—or aliens. Have you heard of Saint Michael's Remnant?"

Foster shook his head again.

"A curious bunch, with an engaging theory. They maintain that several thousand years ago, an alien force seeded human life on this planet, and that the Father Race, as they call them, will return one day when we have the capability to do the same." Rex waited to see if his host would respond.

"You mean, to also seed life on another planet?"

"Yes. Modern adherents of that sect say that capability requires, of course, space flight, and the ability to genetically manipulate life, such as through cloning and transgenics. Which we can clearly do. And they say that the Father Race will return to see us when that day comes. The Remnant, literally a 'hold out,' worships on Mont St. Michel off the coast in France. That's where they say we will see the return—on top of that little mount."

"Fascinating," Foster intoned as he shifted his position and consulted his notes. "Should we go find out, Rex? I mean, is it time to mount a mission to the Red Planet?"

Foster's trademark double question focused the steely-eyed Rex

Edwards. He put his hands together, finger to finger, and flexed them twice before answering.

"Absolutely! It was time thirty-nine years ago after the last Moon mission. Now is better than ever. We have all the necessary propulsion and technologies, cheaper in current-year dollars than ever before. In fact, with my propulsion systems, I can put a man on the moon for a fourth of what we spent the last time."

Rex scowled as he ignored the host's next attempt to interject. "It's simply an issue of national will, Foster. You can fund *anything* if the people want it. We found more than two hundred billion dollars to fight a war in Iraq. Another two or three hundred billion to rebuild after the hurricanes. And a fat lot of good it did us, too. We're still vulnerable to terrorists and calamities. It's time for action, not military studies and mountains of plans."

Rex shoved back from the table, his chair scraping loud enough for the microphone to pick it up. "There's plenty of money, Foster. But it's not a money issue. It's all a matter of will. We aren't on Mars because we don't *want* to go, because we don't have the national *will* to explore beyond our borders. Yet we're willing to spend obscene amounts of money fighting terrorist and natural problems that we can't seem to beat."

He coughed and moved back up to the table. "My competitors might not like to hear this, but here's the naked truth. The manned space program that President Bush started years ago, to return to the Moon and go on to Mars, has cost us another hundred billion dollars, yet the major contractors have yet to produce a flyable vehicle. The shuttle is still the only way to the space station, but it was supposed to be out of service last year. There's no other launch option in sight for at least another five years. NASA and their contractor minions have squandered our money—along with a marvelous opportunity."

"Then what's the solution? How do we reach out to—whatever—

is sending us the pictures of Viking?" Foster asked, leaning forward over the interview table toward his guest.

"We go on my rockets, of course!" Rex said, thrusting a finger into the air. "Launch a wave of inexpensive propellant tankers into orbit from my space complex in the Pacific. Build a craft in equatorial orbit, using existing station and orbiter technology and whatever NASA's actually proven with this new crew exploration vehicle—the one the prime contractors can't seem to finish. Use the verified stuff—no new tricks—and fly a low-budget mission to Mars. It can be done *today*, but only if you have the will—and 'will' includes an acceptance of a certain level of risk. Somebody might die, just like they do in war. We lost thousands in Iraq, and spent hundreds of billions. Shouldn't we be willing to lose three people, and spend a fraction of that amount, to reach Mars?"

Rex's passion was intimidating. He knew he wasn't the usual Sunday morning fare of Congressional windbags, self-absorbed movie stars, and media airheads.

"Do you really think it's achievable?" Foster asked, leaning further into the table.

Foster's question brought Rex out of his seat, nostrils flared and sweat beading on his TV pancake makeup. Foster gulped and pushed back as the muscle-bound tycoon leaned over the table, one finger stuck in Foster's face, the other hand clenched in a fist.

"Achievable? You give me the green light—tell NASA to stay out of my way—and I'll have three men headed to Mars in three hundred days for thirty billion dollars. On schedule, fixed price. Guaranteed. I'll get 'em there, or your money back."

Foster whistled in disbelief and was about to speak when Rex cut him off in a rage.

"What's the matter? Don't you believe me?" He turned left and pointed into the camera in fierce defiance. A young cameraman recoiled backward.

"Hear this, America. I saw this opportunity coming. I invested two billion dollars—of my own money—in my Ghost Works in Palmdale, California, and I have a working prototype of a manned planetary exploration vehicle. It's ready to go. I *will* put three men in Martian orbit, put a man on the surface of the planet, and then get all three of them back to Earth, for half of what you spent on the space station. Mark my words—I never fail. Thirty billion dollars. Launched in three hundred days. Fixed price."

As Foster tried to recapture the spotlight, the producer cut him off and replayed the stark image of the fierce multi-billionaire pointing straight into the camera, red-faced below a perfectly cropped flat top, with neck veins and muscles bulging above a bright red bow tie. The short caption enthralled the world.

"3 men to Mars. $30B. Launch in 300 days. Fixed price. Guaranteed."

SPACE STATION ALPHA

"I never thought of you as the *Foster's World* type!" John said, catching Amy on her cell phone as she and the children waited in Florida for the launch of Atlantis—and John's return flight home.

"I'm not. But he seems to be talking a lot about things that affect you. Have to be well informed, you know." Her voice was scratchy in the bad cellular connection, but familiar. It warmed his heart.

"I'll be home in seventy-two hours. So, old man Edwards put his credibility on the line, eh?"

"He did. Surprised a lot of people that he had a secret program to develop a spaceship to go to the Moon and Mars. *I'm* not surprised, though. He's a risk taker. It's got everyone in Houston excited, talking about getting the manned space program back on track," she said. "Just don't get any bright ideas."

"I'd be lying if I told you it didn't fire me up a little," he said, suppressing a smile that she could not see. "Mars and all."

"Shut up and get home, John. We need you."

"Agreed. Heard anything new on the DC front?" he asked, trying to change the subject.

"Ferries are running, and people are getting to work. Transit is slow, but commerce is moving. You don't dare wear an Arab headdress anywhere unless you want to get shot. The United Nations is trying to avert a war between us and Iran. Just a typical day in America."

John chuckled a little at the irony of the litany of difficult news that Amy and others had become so accustomed to in the past months.

"You at the Hampton Inn again?" he asked, tickled by his news-junkie wife.

"And ready as ever. Hurry home. We'll be praying for you. I love you."

John wiped his eyes, so anxious to be close to her after six months in orbit. "Love you too. Hug the kids and eat a fish taco for me."

MONDAY, MAY 30, 2011: SPACE STATION ALPHA

"Stand by to dock!"

Atlantis approached the station in slow motion as she nosed into the docking mechanism at a final closure rate of three centimeters per second. Air Force Lieutenant Colonel Melanie Knox guided the craft with flawless precision to a gentle bump as the orbiter contacted the massive outpost. The latches on the pressurized mating adaptor were thrown automatically, and Atlantis was now one with Alpha.

"Hello, Station. Your chariot awaits!"

Everyone cheered except Sergei.

The orbiter would be leaving early to meet his medical needs, and for that reason, the whole world watched. This was a medical evacuation, so to speak, and Sergei had already made it clear that he didn't care for the notoriety of shortening his friends' stay in space. Until today, he and two other Russians with his name held the three longest career space records—Sergei Krikalev and Sergei Avdeyev, each with more than two years in space—and now he'd be remembered as the Russian who ran out of oxygen, not the space professional with more than 17,000 hours in orbit. His frown grew deeper.

John patted his friend on the shoulder. "Not so glum! We had to go home sometime. You know as well as I do that you've still got some lung problems to deal with."

Sergei nodded but didn't smile.

Atlantis would stay coupled with Alpha for only two days, and then return on an abbreviated seventy-two hour trip, far less than the original plan of twelve days. Important space station repairs and final construction efforts would be delayed. Many people would lose time on orbit because of Sergei's tenuous medical situation. John could tell it was all weighing on his friend.

"Hey, look at it this way, Sergei. They'll recycle Atlantis back into the lineup, and the crew will get an immediate second mission. Two for one," he said. "Just don't remind the taxpayers," John added, with a whisper.

"It could be worse, Sergei," Michelle chimed in. "All that mouth-to-mouth might not have worked."

Sergei's scowl melted. "You are good kisser, Dr. Stevens. Good lungs, too, for American woman. You should go to Mars." Sergei's grimace returned. And he began to cough.

"D'you hear about the latest with Rex Edwards?" Michelle asked them both. "Mars launch in less than a year? He's crazy."

John winked. Sergei had heard. "Perhaps. Maybe somebody will take him up on the offer, and we'll fly an international crew. We can all go together! Back home for a year, cycle back into the lineup, blast off for Mars and some more great food!"

They all laughed. John's smile faded to a slight frown.

"I think we're a long way from a Mars program," John said wistfully. "A very long way."

Two days later, and with a double crew on board, the station was crowded. The logistics payload module had been hoisted from the cargo bay, and a used module, packed with five months of waste, was back in the orbiter ready to return home. John took advantage of the break to finish cleaning his tiny stateroom before his last nap in space.

He was gliding through the long cylindrical station past walls lined with fresh supplies when a globule of blood hit him square in the mouth.

"What?" he exclaimed, reflexively spitting out the blood, his first thoughts of a malfunction in the Waste Management Facility on the eve of his return home. That would be a fitting end to this mission, for the astronaut/repairman now known as Mr. Plumber. But this wasn't waste. More blood struck him, smearing across his nose and into an eye. Then he heard a cry of pain. Someone was moaning in the crew's toilet.

John pushed ahead faster. Red globules filled the air. He'd once bled in orbit, after nicking his ear with a razor, but nothing like this. He gagged as another blood ball found its way into his mouth, unseen until he felt the warm copper ooze on his tongue. He spat again.

"Who's in there?" John yelled as he neared the toilet, bright red raindrops littering the approach to the door. He grabbed the flimsy covering and ripped it aside, exposing Chuck Baker, flight call sign CB. His friend was wedged between the toilet hand-holds, pants down, bent at the waist, vomiting a stream of crimson blood and chunky yellow bile.

John dashed to his left and a communication terminal. "Emergency in the Hab module! Get Mich and the Doc down here fast!" he announced on the public address, and then turned to a medical closet for the ambulatory medical pack, or AMP, and a crew contamination protection kit. Armed with a mask, gloves, and a red biohazard bag, he pushed back to the toilet and to CB, who could barely compose himself between the violent waves of nausea. His friend was pallid, his eyes bloodshot from the exertion of dry heaves, head weaving.

John never heard the siren of an emergency Claxton that sounded throughout the station. He thrust the biohazard bag in front of CB and cradled him in his arms as the man doubled over again in a bloody heave. CB's belly was as hard as a board, and he began to slump in John's arms, nearly unconscious.

Darting toward the cramped node like a hummingbird through a pipe, Michelle shot through the hatch and gagged as she smacked into a large dollop of blood that smeared across her face, and another blood ball entered her mouth as she gasped.

"Bright red, Mich!" John yelled as he held CB. "Bleeding internally. Get Doc Lynn!"

"On his way," she said, quickly pulling another mask and gloves from the AMP along with a blood pressure cuff, stethoscope, a bag of Ringers lactate and an IV kit.

CB suddenly went limp in John's arms, still wedged in the toilet. Together the two astronauts pulled him free, pulling up his pants in the process.

"He's perforated!" Michelle blurted out as she regained a hand-hold and pulled him loose from the tiny compartment. "His stomach has severed. Probably busted an artery and he's also got stomach contents in his abdominal cavity." As she said it, she pulled a towelette free from her pink fanny pack and began to scrub CB's forearm near the elbow for an IV. She slapped the cuff on his upper arm, pumping it up, wedging herself into him with a stethoscope over his bicep.

Dr. Martin Lynn, the newly arrived astronaut-pilot-internist-flight surgeon, was only meters behind Michelle, with a classic black medical bag in tow, as she began to get a pulse and a pressure. He pushed around her and joined John near the cramped toilet, moving with amazing ease in the weightless environment. He dove through the splatter of numerous blood and vomit bombs but never gagged.

"Passing blood, some bile. Bright red, arterial," she recited while nodding gently, completing her count of his pulse. Doc Lynn pulled his own stethoscope free and found a heartbeat under CB's bloody polo shirt. The new engineer didn't respond to the probing or questions directed to him. He was out cold.

"Stiff belly, Doc. Tachycardia, pulse one-twenty, BP seventy over thirty. He's fading fast." She pulled her own stethoscope free and ripped the IV kit open with a free hand and her teeth, locking down his right arm with her left while John took the bag of fluid and held it aside. At best, John was an orderly in the service of two medical professionals. Or one doctor and one very savvy biochemist geologist. Before John could squint, Michelle had shoved a needle with a quick prick into CB's right arm, then pulled it and tried again. And again.

"Flat veins," Doc Lynn said as Michelle squeezed CB's arm hard and threaded the IV on the fourth attempt. She had the IV portal taped before Doc Lynn finished palpating CB's belly.

"Probably perf'ed an ulcer," Doc Lynn said with amazing calm. "We'll lose him if we can't stabilize him fast and get home in minutes." He looked at John as he ripped tape with his teeth for Michelle's IV. "How fast . . . can we be . . . on the ground?" he asked between mouthfuls of sticky gauze.

"Minutes—like sixty, if we set a world record," John blurted out, already releasing his hold on CB.

"Cut that in half if you want to save him," Doc Lynn said, looking back to Michelle as she cinched the Ringers lactate to the IV portal and began squeezing the bag gently to get critical fluids into CB. Without gravity, she had to milk the lifesaving liquid into his veins.

John let go and pushed away, stained head to toe with CB's bright blood. Doc Lynn called after him as he sped for the communication station. "Perforated peptic ulcer. Brisk bleeding, possibly arterial. BP seventy over thirty, pulse one-twenty."

"Got it. Get him to the orbiter," John yelled back as he disappeared through the hatch.

Sergei met John at the communication station, nodding toward the radios and the emergency checklist as he dashed through the narrow corridor, direction John had come. Sergei was still station commander until properly relieved, and he sped to join the doctor and Michelle.

"Houston, Alpha," John called, shaking as he held the weightless microphone. "We've got a class one medical. Baker's in serious condition. Immediate bingo." He recited the litany of deadly symptoms like a medical recorder.

"Houston copies. Is this John?"

"Yes."

"This is Jake. What are your plans?"

"Get out of here as fast as we can, recover on the closest runway, or CB dies. It's a bloody mess up here."

"Roger. We'll spin up the plan. Can you get Blaster on line?"

"Standby." John keyed the public address to call Colonel "Blaster" Allison, commander of Atlantis, to the communication panel.

"Blaster's up, Houston. I'm already in the orbiter. We can be out of here in less than ten minutes, emergency breakaway. Running the orbital projections now."

"Roger that, Atlantis," Jake replied from Houston. "We'll calculate bingo for you. Initiate emergency recovery." He paused. "Station, Houston. Patch us through to Doc Lynn."

John directed the video teleconference link with NASA's best physicians directly into the Habitation module. He grabbed his right hand, trying to force it to be still. Chuck Baker, his replacement and crew engineer, was bleeding to death. Atlantis was packed with his personal gear for the return home. They were ready to leave—and now *this*.

John's mind raced as he completed the emergency checklist. The call from Doc Lynn moments later broke his concentration.

"How fast, John? We gotta go *now*, or we'll lose him."

"Shove off emergency recovery in eight minutes. Houston's setting up the reception. At the Cape in less than an hour."

"Roger that. Tell Blaster we're headed his way. Mich, Frank, and I will ride with him in the lower deck. Tell Houston we'll need to do a full decon up here."

"Houston copies." Jake was listening in real-time from the ground. "John, you still there?"

"Affirmative."

"Director Church needs you."

"Go ahead." The head of NASA's Johnson Space Center came on the line. "John, there's no time for debate. You've got to stay. Can you pull your gear off Atlantis?"

John froze. Suddenly, the threat to CB's life was replaced by images of Amy and the kids, already in Florida for the orbiter's arrival at the Cape tomorrow night. He could imagine her face when she learned that he wasn't coming home. Yet he had to stay.

But, no! He needed Amy and his children, to hold her, to listen to them run around the house, to wrestle on the family room carpet, to go to lunch, to soccer and hockey games, to a movie, to Galveston beach. He dreamed of embracing Amy as he walked feebly off Atlantis, the once-in-a-lifetime welcome home with Sergei, Michelle, and Frank. He looked at the crimson stains on his sleeve and fought the urge to vomit, his head spinning.

"Alpha, Houston. This is the flight director! Did you copy my last?"

John's heart raced, his palms began to sweat, and his chest was bound like a barrel. He couldn't inhale. The world closed in on him, and his eyes told him he was tumbling. John's dreams of home were dashed—after all the stresses Amy had endured, through all the terror of the past months, after the craziness of the alien news, a possible Mars mission, and his growing kids who desperately needed a dad—he couldn't get to any of them now if he wanted to. This was out of his control. The irony of it all consumed him.

"John? This is Blaster! We gotta go!"

Another frantic call from Houston.

"Answer me, John!"

All this in half a minute.

Then that quiet, familiar Voice began to sing to his heart, unmistakable, powerful, yet soothing. John never had been in control—but God always had. None of these developments caught God by surprise.

Verses came to him from memory, refreshing as a cool wind. *I can do everything through him who gives me strength . . . In all these things we are more than conquerors through him who loved us . . . If God is for us, who can be against us?*

He recognized the Voice as his breath came back, his hand steadied, and the vertigo disappeared. He closed his eyes and claimed the promises that he felt welling up in his heart. In a strange mixture of pain and calm, John keyed the microphone. "I copy, Houston. I haven't checked out yet."

John left the microphone adrift and pushed hard toward the docking port. His stomach churned as he sped to the orbiter, determined to retrieve his personal belongings in the next three minutes. Clothes and his laptop weren't at the top of his priority list. He needed those family photos, his Bible, and his books, before the orbiter departed without him on an emergency return to Earth.

18

AMY WELLS ROASTED BY the pool in the wilting glare of the early June Florida sun. Albert and Alice, her two youngest children, cycled through the line at the diving board at the Cocoa Beach Hampton Inn in their quest for the perfect mother-soaking cannonball. The aggressive splashes missed her, but not by much. Amy rarely wore a bathing suit in public, but, anonymous here in Florida, the petite brunette indulged herself today. She adjusted the suit where it hid her insulin pump, then pushed her long brown hair out of her eyes, gathered it into a long ponytail, and wrapped it into a bun.

Amy kept an experienced eye on the water as she completed, for the fourth time, Jim Dobson's book *The Strong-Willed Child*. She and John had been blessed with four healthy and independent children. Dobson's wisdom helped guide Amy while John was gone. But soon her husband would be home.

"Mrs. Wells?"

Amy looked up. A young desk clerk hovered over her.

"Yes?"

"I'm sorry to bother you. People from NASA have been calling your room nonstop for the last hour. I thought you might want to know."

"NASA?" Amy blurted out, automatically reaching for her purse. But her cell phone was locked in the room.

"Yes, ma'am," the girl replied. "Would you like to take their call at the desk?"

A thousand memories flooded Amy at once. Calls from distant wars, from squadron duty offices, from secretaries at John's office — they were all the same. The recollections brought an ominous rush of fear as she anticipated the worst. This one was different. She could feel it. This was *bad news*.

She knew the worst kind of news came in a visit from a captain and a chaplain in a black Navy limousine. She'd seen them up close during the cold war. Two somber men had come in stony silence, arriving in a shiny car to bring news of the death of her neighbor's husband, another pilot. Amy had cried inside for a week, realizing that it could as easily have been her who met the Death Angel in a crisp Navy uniform.

Or, this could be the "I won't make it home tonight" call. Those were aggravating, but they meant only a delay in the homecoming, not a cancellation. She'd had dozens of those calls from John, stranded somewhere exotic and unable to come home to Brunswick, Maine, because of snow, or Jacksonville, Florida, because of storms. He always managed to be stuck in garden spots like Bermuda whenever she had a blizzard, tornado, or hurricane to deal with. *Who was stranded?*

Amy couldn't make herself get up. One hundred seventy-four days of praying John would return safely. One hundred seventy-four days of wondering, fearful of the worst, dreading the notification that there'd been a problem. Terrified of reliving the horror that too many of her friends had faced, friends whose spouses had died eight years before on Columbia, while they'd waited with expectant smiles in the stands at Cape Kennedy. John's previous shuttle missions had each meant only days of wracked nerves. This had been nearly six months—months fraught with terrorism, death, Martian mysteries, and space rescues. Yet, in the midst of the stress and raising four children, she'd patiently endured, day by day. One step at a time, struggling to give up control—to let go and let God.

"Mrs. Wells? Are you okay?"

Amy looked up, her face wracked with shock as she imagined the worst. She nodded. "I . . . I'm all right. Thanks." Like rising out of bed with morning sickness during each of her pregnancies, Amy struggled up. She had to take the call, yet she dreaded it. Every step to the front desk, followed by her dripping youngsters, passed in slow motion. She kept her focus on three words: *God will provide.*

She took the phone from the clerk and held it as though it would bite her.

"Amy? This is Jake," the voice said. "Are you there?"

"I'm here, Jake. Please, tell me everything is okay." Images of Columbia, as it streaked in flames over Texas, replayed over and over in her mind.

"John is fine. I promise," Jake said. His voice sounded sure.

"Then tell me why you called. Don't sugarcoat it."

"I'm sorry, Amy. There's been a sudden change of plans. CB is very sick. Atlantis is inbound on emergency at the Cape as we speak. It's serious."

"What about John?"

Jake hesitated, a sure sign of trouble.

"He couldn't make the flight, Amy. We'd be without an engineer.

He had to stay another cycle . . . at least until the next replenishment mission."

Amy stared through the "You are a valued customer" sign behind the desk as if she could see all the way to Miami. Then she nodded and stooped, her tiny shoulders sinking under the burden of another five months of life alone. Her bun unraveled; vaguely, she felt long brown locks cascade over her shoulder.

"How . . . soon?" She forced every word, knowing the children would read her mood immediately.

Amy nodded at Jake's final response and hung up. Albert and Alice shivered on the cold marble tile, focused on Mom. She turned, eyes brimming with tears, her full lips pulled tightly into a flat line.

"Is Daddy okay?" asked Alice, the youngest, who'd been born after John's first mission and had always known Dad as the astronaut. She drew close to Amy and repeated the question, pulling at her mother's terrycloth cover-up.

"Yes. He is. But he can't come back this week."

"When, Mom?" Art moaned. "Why?"

As they tugged at her, the *whump-whump* of a double sonic boom rumbled through the motel lobby. Atlantis was back, much too soon, and Dad wasn't on it. Minutes from an emergency landing, with a critically sick crewman aboard, the orbiter was on the Heading Alignment Circle for a touchdown at the Cape. For everyone else in the city, this emergency would be exciting. But not for the Wells family. Or CB's family.

Her two youngest children looked at Amy with saucer eyes. Amy stared out the front window of the hotel, as if to locate the returning orbiter, falling like a rock somewhere above them. She knew that the crew would land in only minutes, but her soul mate was not onboard. The words were so hard to form.

"Four or five more months, kids." She knelt, gathering her shivering wet son and daughter close to her.

"Pray for your dad. He's going to miss us. Let's go tell your brothers and give Dad a call."

FRIDAY, JUNE 3, 2011:

SPACE STATION ALPHA

"Sorry about the change in plans, John. Really. That's got to be hard."

"More than you know, Agent Kerry," John said, straining to be positive. He'd endured two dozen "Golly, I'm sorry" calls. He hoped this wasn't another. "How's the investigation moving along?"

"Funny you ask. We've got an interesting development in Colorado Springs. Can't say just what, but your idea about someone inside the system might just play out."

"I don't like to hear that," John said, frowning.

"And . . . the Iranian connection gets stronger. We've traced the money to Tehran. You probably heard that the United Nations is pushing hard to prevent the U.S. from striking back at Iran."

"I did. I doubt that anyone really cares what the U.N. thinks."

Kerry cleared his throat. "Actually, President Manchester's showing lots of restraint, in my opinion. It's the veep who needs Valium."

They both laughed.

"Any more luck on the 'weapons hidden in orbit' theory?" Kerry asked.

"None. I pulsed the system from here, claiming when I called Cheyenne Mountain that we needed information for debris deconfliction. There's nothing up here, they claim . . . nothing that's not supposed to be here. So I got me a copy of the entire space catalog . . . several hundred thousand elements of debris and about five hundred satellites.

Nothing out of the ordinary. But I told you that might happen—"

"Right," Kerry continued. "If they keep changing orbits, no one will see anything unless a stray camera gets lucky."

"Exactly. We put in a request for a full-camera survey of low Earth orbit. Takes a month of pictures running all day and night from Hawaii, but it might show something. We'll have some early indications in three weeks." John covered the microphone a little and continued. "I had to pull some strings to get STRATCOM to do that one. You owe me."

"More than you know, John," Kerry replied. "More than you know."

| **FRIDAY, JUNE 24, 2011:**
| **PASADENA, CALIFORNIA**

"How?" Dr. Robert Kanewski asked out loud, alone in his office.

He hunched over the plasma screen, late in the evening, staring at the lone Viking in the image from Mars displayed on his computer monitor at NASA's Jet Propulsion Laboratory.

The speaker on his desk chimed, announcing yet another e-mail. More information overload. But the author and subject line intrigued him, drawing him away from the strange picture of Viking 1.

He opened the message immediately.

"*Robert. Canberra Deep Space Communication Complex, Station 43 Radio Telescope, got a sniff of a constant source signal yesterday for twenty seconds. The eighty-meter dish was doing sweeps in the direction of Mars. They confirmed at 9:46 EST tonight the existence of an emission, unknown origin, transmitting low data rate on 381 megahertz, the standard NASA deep space radio astronomer tracking beacon frequency. They've pinpointed the location and orbit of the transmission. Something is headed our way—fast—in an orbit that appears to begin at Mars. Estimate passage near Earth in six weeks. This is HOT. Call me at home. Jim."*

Robert knocked over a half-finished cola as he scrambled for the phone. The call reached Dr. Diamond late at night, pacing next to his computer.

"Jim! Just got your mail. What is this?"

"Man, I'm glad you called. Answer your phone or get a cell or something. Honestly, Robert—"

"I'm sorry, okay? What's happening?"

"It's not a gag. The signal's on 381 megahertz. Deep Space Network picked it up two days ago and passed it over to the SETI folks once they had the exact orbital parameters. It's headed straight for us, and it's coming in fast. We've done some extensive research throughout NASA, and contacted every foreign space agency as discreetly as possible—there's nothing out there that's supposed to be on an orbit headed this way. That's why I called you. I really need help from inside NASA."

"Jim, there have *never* been any probes coming back to Earth. What's at Mars always stays there. And we certainly wouldn't waste the fuel it takes to blast home on a fast-transfer profile. That's twice the propellant load of a minimum energy mission. This is either a huge government cover-up, or we've just stumbled on the news of the millennium."

Robert felt his lips widen into a broad grin as his mind raced through dozens of possibilities, his imagination stretched by the implications of this news—for science, and for his career.

"Let's sleep on this—if we can, Jim—and try to make heads or tails of it in the morning. I don't want to be the guy who starts a panic. But I darn sure want to be there if we announce the real McCoy."

Jim exhaled so loudly it carried over the phone. "This could be the evidence we've been waiting for."

"Alpha, this is Houston, over."

"Go ahead, Houston. This is John."

"You guys aren't going to believe this. Then again—after all the problems these past few weeks—you might. Big announcement in fifteen minutes on the news. Hush-hush. If you can believe it, the Deep Space Network has confirmed another unknown transmission. This one's on a fast-transfer orbit leaving Mars and heading straight for Earth."

"You've gotta be kidding. It's not April Fool's for nine months," he said.

"If what I heard's correct, we're going to get a visit from whatever it is lots sooner than that. August probably. Now you know everything I do, so pull up the broadcast. And be prepared. This thing might impact the next launch."

"Everything impacts the launch. But thanks for the warning. Alpha out."

John had come to grips with tough news in the past month. First it had been the unexpected double cycle on the station when CB got sick. His friend had nearly died of a perforated ulcer, a byproduct of CB's popping so many aspirin to cover the pain of a back problem that he'd never confessed. The sudden decision to get him home had saved his life. If nothing else, John's delayed return home was worth that—his friend's survival.

But the bad news didn't end there. On the turnaround flight inspection, technicians discovered that the aging shuttle's speed brake deployment gears had been replaced backward—*again*. The gears were corroded and cracked in every orbiter in the fleet, and it would probably be months before Atlantis or any other orbiter could come to relieve

John and the station crew. Good news was hard to come by. The shuttle was supposed to have retired nine months ago. The replacement program, a capsule on a rocket, was two years behind schedule. The Russian Soyuz was the only ride to orbit.

Amy and John had resigned themselves to the realization that he would be in space for a while, at least until an October Soyuz mission could bring him home. They tried not to think about the missed summer and lost family time. As luck would have it, though, the Russian financial crisis reached its zenith—the planned October backup Soyuz mission was cancelled. Russia couldn't fund a flight, and no amount of NASA money could get all the unpaid, disparaged Russian workers back to work in time to make Soyuz ready. The best choice was Atlantis's hoped-for return flight near Christmas. With all the delays, John would probably break the U.S. space endurance record. Amy said she worried about all of it—aging broken space shuttles, no emergency backup transportation, long-duration space flight . . .

The stress and delay weighed on John, too, but he covered it daily in prayer, usually on the phone with his wife and children. Special times of prayer as a family, even if it was by speakerphone. NASA psychiatrists, he was told, worried about something they called his "fragile mental makeup," their codeword for "faith." John was unfazed; he was in good hands with his Creator.

Elena Alibekov, the new chief scientist for this crew cycle, threaded through the tunnel-like Unity module into Zarya while he daydreamed about the past seven months. "What is funny?" she asked.

John wanted to say, "Your silly haircut," but held his tongue. The middle-aged Russian chemist had trimmed her own hair that morning to keep it a manageable length. She wouldn't let her fellow male crewmates help with the job, and it showed.

"Hi, Elena. Did you listen to that last broadcast from the center?"

"Nyet."

"Well, hold onto your borscht."

She grinned. "It's hot. Cannot hold long."

"No it's not. Borscht is served cold."

"Correct! So what is news?"

"More signals from Mars. Headed our way."

"Yes. I do not believe this, but I am interest. Are there more image?"

"Better than that, Elena. SETI says—"

"What is 'set-hee '?"

"Search for Extra-Terrestrial Intelligence . . . SETI."

She nodded. "Yes, I know this. I did not understand your—how you say?—twang. Continue."

"The Deep Space Network found the signal of a possible craft and it's headed our way, due near Earth in August. There's a special report about to break. We'd better call Al and let him know."

"This is another of your joke?"

He ran his fingers through his flattop and grimaced. "Going to have to convince you, I see. But it's probably a hoax."

"Agreed, human. I watch broadcast. You find Al and JJ." Elena sat transfixed at the monitor as John darted off to find Colonel Al Rogers, the station commander and long-time Air Force astronaut, and Jimmy Johnson, Frank's replacement.

A few minutes later, the four were wrapped into foot restraints for the big announcement. Surprises had become the daily diet here, and this was yet another course.

"Alien Summer?" was emblazoned on the news ticker as CNN joined Drs. Jim Diamond and Robert Kanewski live at the podium in SETI headquarters. Alpha, the only space habitation of the human race, was silent as the astronauts tuned into the press conference, already underway.

"The signal has us stumped." A man labeled "Dr. Diamond, SETI" spoke in a quiet, mousy voice, and stooped over a podium like he had a spine problem. "No one has ever seen this kind of signal encoding. It's quite an elegant bit of communications."

"Dr. Robert Kanewski, NASA Jet Propulsion Laboratory" spoke up next. "This is unusual news, to be sure, in light of the recent images from Mars. Up to this point, the evidence confirms that a transmitter we cannot decode, its signal riding on a NASA beacon frequency, is headed our way, and much faster than we would ever fly on a trans-Earth trajectory. A typical mission profile return would be at least 210 days. This one appears to be coming in about a quarter of that. Whatever it is, and it's not a U.S. or foreign payload as far as we know, we need to be ready when it arrives in about five weeks."

Five minutes later it was over, and the crew was abuzz. After half an hour of conjecture, professional speculation, and a few conspiracy theories tied to 3/21, the crew laughed and broke up to return to work.

"Is not Russian plot," Elena insisted as she pushed away, a broad smile on her face. "Would not waste precious fuel to fly back so fast."

"Sure, Elena. Sure," Al said as he patted her on the back and gave her a shove toward the hatch.

As his crewmates dispersed, John glanced up at a collection of DVDs pinned near the video monitor, including the complete collection of *Alien* movies so popular with the crew and occasional visiting millionaire demi-astronauts. Scanning the collection, he felt that familiar tug again, pulling at his spirit, the little Voice hinting that this crazy news was all part of the Plan. His call—the sense of direction—was once again unmistakable. As Al, JJ, and Elena drifted out of sight, he focused on the unwavering sense of revelation, as he stared, transfixed, at the movie locker.

He closed his ears to the drone of the news network in the background and listened, with all of his strength, to his heart and God's Word.

19

"I'M ON MY WAY."

Malcolm Raines flipped his cell phone shut, pulled a ball cap low over his trademark greasy wave, and dashed out the revolving door of the Hilton Hotel on Century Boulevard near the Los Angeles airport. "Live! Girls!" flashed in buzzing neon beyond him, flooding the Hilton parking lot with an eerie blue tint in the late evening. As he sped out of the parking lot, he barely missed two drunken vagrants panhandling clientele of the hotel who were headed to the strip club down the street. Raines pushed hard through the traffic until he reached a shopping plaza twenty blocks away in a depressed part of town adjacent to the I-405. Despite his height and face, he was unknown here. This was a Latino part of town.

"Welcome to Wal-Mart!"

Raines ignored the older Hispanic man at the door and headed straight for the book section of the store. Thirty minutes later a muted voice to Raines' right, far down the aisle near the magazines, asked "Are you absolutely sure?"

He looked up at the voice, the male patron hidden behind a gardening periodical.

"I'm taking a big risk—at the last minute," the voice continued, the face covered by the magazine. They were alone in the aisle.

"I'm sure you are," Raines said in a low voice, pretending to be immersed in his own material, as he inched closer to the other shopper. "But my risk is far greater. My reputation's on the line. I assure you, they talk to me in a voice I can hear. A *clear* voice." He took a deep breath. "Trust me and you'll be on top of the Nielsen ratings."

Raines closed his book and dropped it in a red plastic hand basket on the floor, never looking again in the direction of the mysterious voice.

As Raines slipped away around the corner, the other reader retrieved Raines' science-fiction novel from the basket, pulling out a small envelope labeled *The Alien Message*. The anonymous patron tucked the missive away, and drifted out of the store by a side entrance, hurrying past boxes of broken plastic chairs, cheap lawnmowers, and a bored young woman checking receipts.

"Thank you for shopping Wal-Mart," she droned as he moved past her, head down. When he was halfway out the door, she snapped to and called after him, excitedly.

"Hey, aren't you on TV?"

MONDAY, JULY 4, 2011:
LOS ANGELES, CALIFORNIA

"Happy Independence Day, and thanks for tuning in! With us today on this special edition of *Foster's World* is the Reverend Malcolm Raines, pastor of the World Inclusive Faith Church in Phoenix, Arizona. Reverend Raines has been a guest with us before and has some fascinating revelations for today's holiday segment. Live from Burbank, California, this is Foster Williams . . . with news that could change your life."

"Thank you, Foster. A point of clarification. In our faith I am referred to as 'Father Raines.' It's my great pleasure to join you on today's show."

"Yes! And thank *you,* Reverend. I understand that you've had some unusual insight into recent news of a possible visitor from outer space. What's all this about?"

Raines was silent for a moment, knowing that Foster hated dead time as much as Raines despised that "Reverend" title.

"As NASA proclaimed last week, an object is headed our way through space and will fly by Earth in about five weeks. I don't want to alarm you, Mr. Williams, but I must be direct. That object is an alien spaceship. I can promise you that, as the months go by, NASA will work hard to cover this up, to minimize the news of this alien life force headed our way. Many people will call you to say that I'm a fake, a nutcase—even a false prophet. Nevertheless, I can substantiate that we're about to be visited by an alien probe sent from Mars—bringing an advance message from a race of intelligent beings who are very much like us. This spaceship is proof of their existence and evidence that they understand our civilization and our technology. This contact is offered to us as a message of peace." He folded his hands, staring straight into the camera. Studio lights gleamed off his gold-rimmed round glasses, framing Raines' iconic chiseled face and trusting smile.

Foster's face contorted as Raines watched him try in vain to suppress a laugh. "Alien messages? How can you be so sure?"

"This insight is a direct revelation from God," Raines replied, setting his jaw, his lips drawn. "And I can prove it."

"Proof, Reverend? What proof?"

Raines turned from his host and faced a camera. "I can be very precise, Foster. In precision we find truth. At the point of closest approach to Earth—and NASA told us exactly when and where that will occur—we will discover that this is a vehicle unlike any we've ever seen before. A golden messenger, I am told. When it reaches that closest point, the probe will reveal its remarkable message. The spacecraft will not enter orbit around our planet."

"*God* told you this? That the signal comes from a probe sent by an alien race to deliver a message to Earth?"

"No. What God audibly revealed to me multiple times is 'Voyager will return. The Father Race is coming.' He told me to proclaim this message from every corner of the globe as long as I have the resources to do so." He gestured to Foster and the camera. "As you know, I have significant resources. So here I am."

"But Voyager left the solar system something like . . . twenty years ago."

"True, it passed into interstellar space in 1993 and can never return, at least not in our limited thinking. But God audibly told me that 'Voyager will return.' Therefore, I have no doubt that God will reveal his meaning in time. Do you doubt, Foster?"

"Perhaps, Reverend Raines," Foster said, a slight smile pushing up his cheeks. "Are we in any kind of danger?"

"Only the danger of disbelief. If we don't believe, we'll miss God's amazing message. A foreign intelligence has traveled for centuries across the galaxies to reach us. Through these new peoples, we'll find new faith in ourselves and in our accomplishments. Ultimately, we will transcend our limited understanding and find faith in our faith."

He leaned forward to grip Foster by the forearm, his strong hands causing the host to wince. "In basketball, I learned an important lesson. When the coach tells you that he has a plan, and he warns you that your behavior or performance will hurt the team, you listen. In this case, we have another coach, and he's giving us plenty of warning. I'd listen to the coach if I were you."

Foster coughed as he tried to pull his arm free of Raines' viselike grip while appearing in control. "Thank you, *Father* Raines—a priest for our time."

Raines released his hold on Foster.

"Your prophecies will certainly be the source of great debate in the coming months. Of this we can be certain: something is coming our way, and we've been told tonight that it will be here next month to herald a grand message to humanity. I'm Foster Williams, reminding you that this is a sign of the new times. You heard it here first, live from Burbank, California . . . with news that could change your life."

SATURDAY, JULY 9, 2011: SPACE STATION ALPHA

"Alpha, this is Houston."

John took the call while he worked on propulsion maneuvers to keep the station in its proper orbit. The solar wing, toilet, fuel system, gyros, and ventilation were all humming along these days. Food was in good supply, he and Elena had tidied up the outpost, and he'd completed all the repairs, for the moment. The persistent air leak, the station's fourth, had stopped at last, and the oxygen generators were working for the first time in a year. There was an advantage in keeping the same crew engineer on the station for a year: stuff got fixed.

"Go ahead, Houston."

"John, this is the flight director. The media is spewing lots of wind about Malcolm Raines' predictions, but I just got a message from the NASA Administrator. I'll read you the important part: 'In light of the continuing discussions about the meaning and intent of the signal headed toward Earth, and in consideration of NASA's role as an exploration and science agency for the American people, please refrain from any public comment about the incoming signal or about NASA plans to evaluate the possible probe vehicle.' That's about it."

"Understand. What about that planning meeting we had yesterday, boss?" John asked. "For the 'probe response,' I think we called it. Didn't you think that session failed to address a couple of key issues?"

"No. Don't think so. This could all be a big hoax, although it's being built up as the real thing. You guys take pictures, record any transmissions, be our eyes and ears wherever you can. Nothing less. Nothing more."

John thought the flight director sounded a little testy, but pushed ahead with his next question anyway.

"And what if it tries to dock with Alpha?" John asked, his voice lower and grating.

"I'm not going there, John."

"I know you aren't, and that's just the problem. Sorry if this sounds hardheaded, but NASA leadership is dodging a significant issue—as usual. Not that it changes anything up here. We're fresh out of proton torpedoes, and our shields have been down since I got here."

"If this is your idea of a joke, I'm not laughing."

"I'm *not* joking. We haven't planned for all the contingencies. We really do need to cover all the bases, and that includes the improbable ones. Even if doing so creates a bit of a stir with the public. I'm just kidding about the proton torpedoes, though. We have a full load, and our phaser bank is fully charged."

John let that last comment sink in for a moment and continued. "Sarcasm aside, I'm betting that this 'probe' is just a piece of forgotten space junk. Probably missed Mars because of a programming error and came whizzing back our way with a garbled transmission queue. But what do I know? I'm just an old farmer from West Virginia."

"That's more like it, Hawk. Thought for a minute you needed a shrink. Your concerns have been duly registered. Pass the word to the crew about the new policy."

"Roger that, Houston. Impulse speed, shields up, and phasers locked on. You can have that crazy holographic doctor come up to see me anytime." With his eyebrows scrunched down and jaw jutting out, John pointed two fingers toward the video monitor and commanded an unseen crew. "Engage!"

MONDAY, JULY 11, 2011: SPACE STATION ALPHA

"What do you make of it?" Michelle asked, her voice warbling in the shaky phone connection from the station to Houston.

"It's funny you should ask," John replied, speaking into a portable microphone while he drifted in front of the Destiny lab window, watching Africa drift by. "The idea of intelligent alien life had never really crossed my mind. I've always set my sights much lower . . . like water on Mars, or fossilized bugs in rocks from other planets . . . that sort of thing."

"Me, too," she said. "Especially the fossil part. I assumed most of this was a hoax at first. Now—I'm not so sure. No . . . let me rephrase that. I'm more *open* to other possibilities."

"Agreed. I can find an alternative explanation for most UFO phenomena, Michelle. But what has me puzzled—willing to consider the alien option—are two data points. The images are, without question, coming from Mars. You can't take your own picture, at least Viking can't."

"And the other?"

"It's coming toward us way too fast. We've never shot a mission out at that speed—much less brought one back. So—like you—I'm more open to other possibilities than I was a month ago."

"You said it better than I could have," Michelle replied.

"So how's terrestrial life treating you? It's been eight months since we blasted off together," he said, staring off at a picture of Sergei, Michelle, and Frank taped on the bulkhead to his right.

"I envy you," Michelle replied. "The extra time in orbit, that is, but not the separation from your family." She paused a moment. "Speaking of separation, you're still praying for me, aren't you?"

John's heart warmed. She hadn't forgotten. "I am. Praying for you to listen to that little Voice that's calling you . . . and for someone special in your life."

John heard her sniffle in the next pause.

"Thank you," she said, speaking slowly. "You're the first person who listened and cared but got nothing out of it. So . . . I have some great news. There *is* a man in my life. You surprised?"

He smiled and nodded. "Not in the least. It was bound to happen."

"He's a pilot. Flies for Global West."

"A pilot? Well, you could do lots worse," John said with a laugh.

Her voice was bubbly and full of excitement. "I can't shake the feeling that meeting Keith was no accident. It's weird, you know. I'm thirty-six years old, and I've been trying to fall for someone since I was twelve, but until I met Keith, I never realized that I was the cause of my own loneliness. I'd never let anyone in close enough to stay there. I know meeting Keith . . . and waking up to my own problem . . . was no coincidence." She paused. "I'd never admit that to anyone other than you."

"God's at work, Mich. Your Keith — and your insights — may be a direct answer to our prayers."

"Yeah . . . I guess," she said, her voice seeming to drift away for a moment. "You really buy into this, don't you? I mean, it's so real for you — prayer, and God, and all that."

"It is. Do me a favor. Next time you're in a hotel, pull a Bible out of the dresser drawer and read the book of John. Better yet, I'll have Amy bring a Bible over. Or you guys could get together for lunch. Read it and simply ask God to show you more about who He is. I promise you, He will. Now — tell me about Keith."

They talked for half an hour about how she had met her pilot and how their relationship had grown in the past month. Michelle did almost all of the talking.

"There's something I've wanted to ask you for a few days, John. About the probe." Michelle was silent as he formed a response.

"Yeah? Well, Houston says we're ready for whatever happens. Elena thinks it's hilarious."

"*She's* hilarious. I saw her haircut on the monitor yesterday. It's a gas. So, Mr. Bible Man, what's the good book say about all this alien stuff?"

He paused. "It doesn't."

"That's all? 'It doesn't?' Then what do *you* say — from a Bible point of view?" Michelle asked.

"The Bible says nothing about aliens, but that doesn't mean they are a biblical impossibility, any more than airplanes and computers are impossible. They don't show up in Scripture, either. What we do know is this — we're called to love God and to love people. If aliens fall in that mix, I'm ready for 'em."

John hesitated to see if she'd resist. The line was silent. "Like I said earlier, I'm more open than ever to the possibility of other life, after all this news. But the engineer in me says that we've missed something, perhaps a small essential clue. Tell you what, though . . . even if a little green man *does* come knocking on the crew lock, I won't be shaken in my faith—my absolute conviction—that Jesus Christ lived and died for me."

"And them?"

"Them?" John asked, puzzled.

"The aliens. If they *are* real, did Jesus die for their sins, too?"

20

"I HOPE THAT YOU don't feel uncomfortable, us meeting like this." Michelle adjusted her skirt as she settled into the deeply padded wicker chair at a beachside restaurant on the seawall boulevard in Galveston.

"No. I don't," Amy said, tilting her head. "Why would I?"

"I mean . . . I'd understand if—well, you know—me sharing time with John for six months. That sort of thing."

Michelle seemed on the verge of stuttering. *She's nervous*, Amy thought. She waved at a young woman waiting tables, and ordered soft drinks for both of them.

"My concern is always for John's safety, Michelle. Nothing more. He knows his frailties, and he's honest about them. I think that's healthy, and I trust him completely."

"You should. He's a straight arrow—a little distant, sometimes too rigorous—but the kind of man that a woman can trust." Michelle played with her napkin, her left hand settling on the rattan table. The sun sparkled through her diamond ring.

Amy pointed at the ring. "It's very pretty. Beautiful setting."

Michelle nodded. "Thanks. Keith gave this to me on Saturday. I'm amazed at how fast all of this has happened. We met a month ago."

"John and I only dated for two months before he proposed. We met in church."

"He told me. A wonderful story, about how he really felt led to you after proposing to someone else."

"John's prone to stretch the truth a little when it suits his purposes, Michelle. But that's one story that's never changed. He didn't tell me until we were married."

Michelle showed a thin smile. "He's a storyteller, that's for sure. Probably didn't want to scare you off." She looked away, eyes misty. "How do you do it, Amy?" she asked, pushing her bangs back.

Amy cocked her head, searching her companion's countenance for some sign of what was bothering her. Michelle continued to stare off into the distance, toward the surf and the beachcombers. Amy shivered in the extreme cool of the air conditioning while she waited for the next words. She'd let Michelle lead.

"I mean, how do you handle the separation?" She looked back at Amy, her eyes brimming wet. "For years? When Keith and I finally tie the knot, he'll have his job, and I'll have mine. We're setting ourselves up for a long-distance marriage—and that scares me."

Amy smiled slightly, nodding her head as she took a deep breath. "You know I'm a diabetic, right?"

"Yes."

"Ever since I was young, I've been sticking myself. Finger pricks, blood tests, and insulin doses—every four hours. Waking up every night at three in the morning, slogging my way to the bathroom to check my numbers. Every day for thirty-five years." Amy folded her hands in front of her. "Handling separation is like that. Some people deal with it in four-hour blocks, one step at a time. If you dwell on the enormity of days, weeks, or months of separation, you won't be able to handle it. If you don't break it up, you'll fall into some form of destructive behavior—or reach out for someone else." She reached across the table to Michelle's left hand. "You just need to take it one day at a time."

Michelle gripped her hand, holding it for a long time. Amy returned the soft pressure.

"John says you're quite the disciplined woman."

Amy raised her eyebrows. "Did he talk about me?"

Michelle laughed, and then stifled her response. "Oh, did he! He claims to want to keep to himself, but when it comes to family, flying, or faith . . . he's a talker." Both women chuckled, bonding in the union of knowing some aspects of the same man so well.

"What did he say about me? I'd like to know." Amy let go of Michelle's hand for a moment. "I mean, if you don't mind sharing . . . "

"Oh, no. Not a problem. He talked about you guys all the time. Seems like he increased the frequency of it as we got closer to the return, like he was spinning all the tales about his family so he'd remember them better. As though he's locking it all in memory or something. He's funny like that."

Michelle's smile broadened. "You should have been in the simulator with us once, before the mission. It was classic. We were practicing a boom operation. Sergei was a little off on the capture of a package with the grapple. Just a little . . . nothing significant. He blew it off and continued, but John got on the intercom and chided him for the error. 'Amy wouldn't let you get away with that,' he said. 'Make your numbers.

Our lives depend on it.' He was quoting you, apparently. Something about you weighing your food every day. But he said it like he was *really* proud of you." Michelle stopped, and then put her hand on Amy's.

"Not just proud, Amy. He's in *awe* of you. You are so in control, you know? I mean, with a family, raising four kids, handling your diabetes, teaching piano to what—twenty students?—all without him here to help. *I'm* in awe."

Michelle squeezed Amy's hand with both of her own. "We have nicknames for you guys at the center, you know. John's probably never heard 'em, but they fit."

Amy released her grip and wiped her eyes. "Really? I mean—me? A nickname? I hope it's not 'Mrs. Plumber,'" she said with a grin.

"Not a chance. The other girls in the astronaut corps talked about giving you an honorary cape when John comes home. He gets a Swiss Army knife. 'Space MacGyver and Superwoman,'" she said, poking at Amy's forearm and laughing.

Amy shook her head, wiping away a tear. "Superwoman. Wow. Is that what *you* think?"

"It is. I don't know how you do it." Michelle wiped at her own eyes. "That's why I wanted to do lunch. And to talk about—you know—the Bible stuff."

Amy nodded in silence. They both sipped at their Diet Cokes, fidgeting with the menus for something to do in the uncomfortable lull.

Amy exhaled deeply and pushed her drink to the side. "I'm not Superwoman, Michelle. But I'm honored that you think so."

"You've got us all fooled, lady."

Amy grinned, daubing at her eyes with her napkin. "Maybe. But it's not me."

"If not, then what? I really want to know."

"'I can do everything through him who gives me strength.' That's a verse from the Bible. I tried to be strong, on my own. But I failed."

Michelle rested her chin on her hands, waiting, Amy thought, for more.

"I was the controlling type for a long time, Michelle. I guess you've got to be sort of compulsive about details if you're diabetic. When I met John, I was the consummate detail freak. I still measure my food, but I used to obsess over it. I mean, obsessive-compulsive disorder kind of obsession. Over the food, my weight, my blood sugar, my diet, over my house and dust and gas mileage and bugs and the checkbook balance and how many jars of baby food I had in stock. Everything." She stopped, taking a few breaths to collect her thoughts. "And I still slip into that mode, every so often. It's hard not to."

Amy was glad that Michelle was happy just to listen. It felt good to talk about her problem.

"John went on his last deployment and I went nuts . . . for details, that is. Without him around to buffer me, and with only one child to care for, I was relentless. I held poor Abe and myself to a schedule that would drive anyone else crazy, and we endured those seven months in four-hour increments. It worked, but I remember none of it as fun. I completely lost sight of living."

"But you seem so in control, Amy," Michelle interjected.

"What you see here is not 'four steps to an ordered life,'" Amy said, pointing at her heart. "It's not me, but He who is *in* me. I quoted Scripture a minute ago. That's my key now."

Michelle tilted her head, raising an eyebrow. "John spent lots of time talking to me about that kind of stuff."

"He really cares about you. As a friend."

Michelle blushed. "I could always see that." She looked away for a long moment.

"It's not about control any more, at least not for me," Amy continued, looking down at the tablecloth. "I almost went over the edge with obsessive-compulsive behavior during that deployment. And I was so obsessive . . . so focused on beating my life into submission . . . that I never sought help for what I've learned is a treatable condition."

Amy looked up, lacing the fingers of her hands together. "We moved to Houston, and the disorder almost broke me, with the move . . . the new location . . . John gone for training. We had three more children—high-risk pregnancies because of my diabetes—in our first eight years at NASA. The more kids we had—the more I had to monitor every facet of my life and diet—and the more I *had* to let go. Or go crazy." She shook her head and let out a long breath.

"I came to realize that I'm not *in* control, Michelle. Not in the least. But God *is*. I had to let go and put my total trust in Him. I learned to walk through each day—each hard pregnancy—the best I could, with His help." She reached out and touched her companion's arm. "In the end, I didn't need a doctor's help with my obsessive behavior as much as I needed God's help. Does any of this make sense?"

"I've heard it before, if that's what you mean," Michelle said with a grin. "From 'you know who.'"

They both laughed.

COLORADO SPRINGS, COLORADO

"I'm beginning to think we've got the wrong guy." The agent spoke quietly as they sat in a Denny's restaurant across the street from General Fredericks's condominium, watching for his early morning departure for a planned flight to Washington. "We've been on him how long? Six weeks? In all that time, not one e-mail out of place, not an action we couldn't explain. I think that techie set us up, laptop and all."

Kerry watched the front door of the condominium in silence.

"You listenin' to me?" the agent asked.

Kerry nodded as he scanned the front of the dark building. He watched a particular window, where the lights were on low. A figure crossed the glass. The apartment was occupied. "He's up there. Or someone's in his apartment," Kerry said.

"So we watch for him to head to the airport, and then we can take a breather."

"Maybe," Kerry said.

"I say we shut this down now. We need the resources to follow up other leads." The partner huffed. "*Real* leads. Arabs, for example."

Kerry finally turned toward his companion. "The Arabs just pulled the trigger. And we've already got an army of agents chasing the money trail to Iran. But no one else is working this angle. So keep the tail on him. Sooner or later he'll slip up. Until then, maybe he can teach us something."

21

"HERE IT COMES," JOHN said, scanning the Hawaiian telescope images broadcast from Houston to Alpha. "Looks like a gold dot. It's a long way out yet."

Elena nodded, pouring over the image on the monitor and enlarging the picture. "No detail. Very smooth."

"Or we aren't seeing something. We'll know in twelve hours."

Elena barely smiled. "You believe in UFO, John?"

He let out a belly laugh, shaking his head. "It's not what I believe about UFOs that matters, Elena. Right now, it's what we observe. If this really is some alien craft, it'll shake me up as much as the rest of humanity."

"That is strange."

"Why?" he asked, pushing back from the monitor.

"Because you say to me other day about your church—that you

believe in savior even if you cannot see him. Yes?" She turned away from the monitor, and gave John a wink. "So I ask again. Do you *believe* in UFO?"

John blushed and shrugged his shoulders. "You've got me there. Okay. At this point, after everything that's happened since I came to the station, I'm open to any possibility."

"This is good. Me too." She turned back to the computer and called up another image, another gold dot.

"Try tracking it again with our scope," John suggested. During their passes on the dark side of Earth, the telescope on Alpha could pick out a distant fuzzy reflection from the craft. Originally meant for long-range imaging of distant satellites, the station's telescope was good for stunning presentations of star fields and picking out cracks in tiny shuttle tiles. Now, it would be pressed into its most important mission ever. When the arriving craft passed Earth, only the telescope on Alpha would be able to slew fast enough to follow the passage . . . if the mysterious craft passed and didn't enter orbit.

Elena switched image feeds to the scope while they were still in eclipse. The craft was there but seemed to be a featureless gold circle.

By this time tomorrow, John thought, it will be here and gone.

Until last week, no one had been able to decipher what the incoming probe was saying. Beeping away with a waveform never before seen in communication theory, the mysterious craft had scientists stumped for a month. After weeks of intense study, SETI had at last deciphered the waveform and modulation scheme for the probe's beacon signal. News reports highlighted SETI's cooperation with experts at the National Security Agency, NSA, in Maryland. With the spy agency's unusual assistance, the cipher team learned that the probe provided an hourly translation of the "alien" waveform.

The probe's cipher key was an elegant communications innovation, translating between Earth computers' binary data and the probe's encoded alien data impressed on a radical new waveform that no electrical engineer had ever considered. This complex explanation from NSA helped a little; at least, SETI could see the alien data now, although no one understood it. On Friday, five days ago, the spy agency came through again, supplying a second key that mapped the alien data stream to a series of twenty-one perfect audio tones in whole steps.

Three octaves, twenty-one notes.

NASA and SETI scientists wondered at the complexity of it all. The "aliens" could have simply modulated the tones on their waveform just as music was impressed on an FM band. After all, that's the way they would have done it. No one could understand this curious close encounters-like focus on sound instead of digital data, but it didn't matter: NASA was out of time.

Through all the hubbub of signal analysis and the frantic preparations for its arrival, the probe kept up its simple message, embedded in an unknown alien code on a cryptic alien waveform. From low to high, cycling without end through three octaves, twenty-one clear tones with one note every second resonated day and night from the mysterious object as it raced toward Earth and a planetful of humans seeking answers.

THURSDAY, AUGUST 11, 2011: SPACE STATION ALPHA

"We have a lock on the probe, Houston. Are you getting this?"

John's transmission went unanswered for several seconds as the astounded Mission Control teams in Houston and Huntsville were transfixed by the astonishing images from Alpha. As the probe flew in an elliptical arc ten thousand kilometers above the station, in view of the Sun, the astronauts were still in eclipse on the dark side of Earth. With their onboard telescope, John and the crew imaged a brilliant golden sphere more than five meters in diameter. The smooth surface of the probe was broken only by a pair of what appeared to be dish antennas inset into the surface, like small craters on the surface of a miniature golden moon.

"Image quality is excellent. Whatever it is, it's not like anything we've ever seen."

"Roger that. And the probe's silent."

"SETI confirms: no more background signals. It's almost like the spacecraft knows we're here—or it knows we know that it's here," John said. "This is freaky."

Just as the first images were released by NASA to news networks around the globe, the alien sphere began to rotate. Polished surfaces reflected the sun in shimmers of gold, and the probe spun until a dish antenna, inset into the surface of the perfect sphere, was pointed directly at the space station. Some would say the sphere resembled a small but brilliant gold version of the *Star Wars* Death Star—before Luke Skywalker blew it up.

"It's turning, Houston. Some sort of antenna is tracking us," John said, his voice quavering slightly as his words were transmitted around the world on live television.

"Transmissions!" Elena blurted out, moments later. "Strong signals." She shouted out the spectra as fast as she observed them, using a signal-processing station in the lab module where she could monitor the electromagnetic spectrum in the direction of the passing craft. "Five discrete frequencies. Signals every decade . . . 3 megahertz to 33 gigahertz. Signal-to-noise ratio is strong. Craft is *talking* to us."

"We copy, Alpha. Very little side lobe, definitely not harmonics. We're applying the NSA cipher to the data now. Stand by."

"It gets better, Houston," John said. "There's a blue light emanating from the middle of the dish antenna."

"Houston copies. Could be laser comms, Hawk. We've cut off the audio feed to the networks. JPL confirms this is *not* an Earth vehicle." He continued, with a more somber tone. "We're in uncharted territory here, fellas."

"Roger that," John replied. "But there's no place to go if we have to leave."

The dot in the center of the screen continued to intensify for the next half-minute, and then changed color.

"Red laser now, Houston!"

"We copy. Positive match on the waveforms. SETI says that the probe — or whatever — is transmitting the same message on all frequencies. It's tonal again, like the earlier stuff. But here's the strange part . . ."

John, Al, Elena, and JJ waited in silence on the other end of the link for Houston's next words. The next transmission was from the flight director himself.

"Alpha, this is Houston. SETI advises that the satellite is transmitting multiple repetitions of the same message. We have initial indications that the repeated file is a *sound* track — an exact copy of the Golden Record greetings to extraterrestrials in fifty-five languages, launched thirty-five years ago with Voyager 1. We've terminated live network audio until we get a handle on exactly how to announce this. Stand by for further instructions and be prepared for a possible emergency return on Soyuz. Houston, out."

A checklist drifted, forgotten, as the crew stared at the computer image of the sphere, a green laser dot in the center of the screen, cycling every twenty-one seconds through three distinct colors. The crew was silent, the hum of equipment and cooling fans the only sounds for more than a minute.

"Alpha, this is Houston. SETI and independent analysis now confirm the transmission is an exact copy of Voyager's Golden Record data. Continue to monitor the probe. We have no idea what comes next. Houston, out."

The laser dot disappeared the moment Mission Control in Houston said "out." The astronauts and NASA watched in fascination as the sphere, apparently aware its message had now been understood, rotated back to its original orientation. Instantly, every one of the five transmissions also ceased.

Less than an hour later, the perfectly spherical golden craft had passed around the backside of Earth, departing on a trajectory back toward Mars. After weeks of national preparation to meet the fleeting visitor, the brief few minutes of historic contact were past, forever changing the way the human race would view the possibility of intelligent life beyond Earth.

FRIDAY, AUGUST 12, 2011: FREDERICKSBURG, VIRGINIA

"I SEND GREETINGS" leapt off the headline of the special-edition *Washington Times* on display at the train station. Special Agent Kerry halted, gaping at the giant words in red, until Amtrak gave its final whistle. The deep bass "toot" echoed off the old buildings in Fredericksburg's historic downtown, many of them vacant this morning. In a hurry, he shoved money into the newsstand, grabbed the paper, and stepped aboard the near-empty train for the ride north to Quantico. Kerry took a seat near the door, groaning as he dropped the loud headline on his seat tray table

First a message from Mars, with images of the Viking spaceship that no one could explain. Then a probe on a near-collision course with Earth and eerie predictions by Malcolm Raines that Voyager would return.

Now, apparently, confirmation that the space preacher was correct. Messages, images, and music from an American spacecraft launched three decades ago were brought back to Earth by a satellite that knew when to talk and when to be quiet. The modern world stampeded to Raines' door to discover how he knew what he knew and to seek his counsel.

Kerry was lost in thought and missed the first request for his fare.

"Ticket?" the Amtrak conductor repeated as she walked past rows of empty seats.

"Quantico," answered Kerry as he handed over the rail pass.

The conductor continued down the aisle and Kerry picked up the copy of the *Times*. "Message from Alien Craft Quotes Voyager." The headline read like a London tabloid. He skimmed down to the famous message from Voyager, repeated by the satellite on five separate frequencies using a mysterious tonal communication technique. A simple message launched thirty-five years ago but now known around the world.

> *"This is a present from a small, distant world, a token of our sounds, our science, our images, our music, our thoughts, and our feelings. We are attempting to survive our time so we may live into yours. U.S. President Jimmy Carter."*

Stafford, Virginia, rolled by as the Amtrak Express clattered up the rail toward Quantico and the FBI engineering laboratories. Kerry was glad his car was in the shop. It gave him time to ride and read, a rare treat in a lifestyle dominated by traffic, long hours, and travel around the nation. He looked out across the wilting hot green of mid-August and Virginia's dog days. The scene was remarkably peaceful compared to the chaos that had erupted in modern society . . . bombings, Iranians, and aliens. It couldn't get much more complicated than that. He read on with an insatiable desire to know more. More about something other than crime.

Voyager 1 was launched September 5, 1977, built to last five years and conduct close-up studies of Jupiter and Saturn. Along with Voyager 2, these spacecraft explored all of the outer planets of the solar system, forty-eight of their moons and rings, and many of their magnetic fields. Now eighteen billion kilometers away and twenty years past the edge of our solar system, signals from the spacecraft take over twelve hours to travel to Earth. Voyager 1 reached the heliopause in 1993, a demarcation widely regarded as the edge of the solar system, speeding away at a rate of five hundred and twenty million kilometers per year.

Kerry looked up again as the train pulled into Quantico, Virginia. The paper drew him back once more as the train coasted to a stop. He folded the paper over and read as he stood up, moving toward the door.

Under the direction of Dr. Carl Sagan, an international team compiled messages from President Carter and U.N. Secretary General Kurt Waldheim, along with music, images, and greet-ings in different languages recorded on a twelve-inch gold-plated copper disk mounted on the Voyager spacecraft as an outreach to communicate a story of our world to extraterrestrials. Modern digital recording capabilities did not exist in 1977, and instruc-tions were included with a needle to play the analog recordings on the remarkable phonograph. Each image, sound file, greeting, and printed message was replicated with perfect accuracy by the probe. NASA states that they have recently been in touch with Voyager 1 from a space communication station in Spain, and that the spacecraft is operating normally beyond the edge of the solar system, although it is virtually impossible to hear.

The conductor nodded to Kerry, and he stepped off the train. He skipped to the end of the article.

Reverend Malcolm Raines stated today that his prophecy of the probe's message was fulfilled.

Kerry winced. He stood at the edge of the platform as the train pulled away, still in wonder over the developments of the past twelve hours. Malcolm Raines' picture-perfect-politician pose jumped off the page below his quote.

"We must reach out to these new beings. God calls us, like Abraham, to sojourn to new lands. I echo that call, to reach out, to venture forth in this decade—yes—even within the coming year. Yet, not to the Moon, but to Mars."

22

"WHAT EXACTLY IS AN alien?" Malcolm asked, his eyes sweeping the coliseum's vast gallery of listeners. For an hour he'd pounded his revelations into his burgeoning flock—explaining the truth behind his prophecies—and now the crowd was just where he wanted them.

"Is an 'alien' someone from a foreign land or culture? Someone not like us?" He paused, letting the question sink in until heads nodded with understanding.

"I tell you, we were all aliens once!" he shouted. "Aliens in a new land . . . black sheep in our schools . . . marching to our own drum in family or job. I know what it's like to be an alien—I am one!" Approving laughter swept through the crowd, and Father Malcolm Raines laughed with them, his strong voice booming throughout the arena. He raised his hands, and the crowd hushed.

"'Alien' is a term we use to single out those who are different. I'm different—an alien because my skin is dark, but not quite dark enough. Light, but not quite light enough. I'm stuck in the middle, and no group will claim me. So I had to make my own opportunities. You know what they were—from Slidell, Louisiana, to Georgetown to Orlando to Oxford. No one handed me *anything*. That's the way it is for aliens. You start naked with what God gave you and pull yourself up from there.

"And—I'm an alien in my own country because I herald the word of God to an apathetic generation. There are fundamentalist believers—and you know who they are—who claim that there are no aliens. They'll tell you that God was too small to create an intelligent being other than a human, that He was too limited in a universe of a billion billion suns to place life on more than one small watery planet. They'll tell you all you need to know is in the Bible, and if it's not in the Bible, it just isn't. Am I right?" He opened up his arms, and the silence was replaced by a thunderous ovation.

"I am first a man of the cloth, not an astrophysicist or an engineer. My doctorate is in political science, not space science. Until this revelation from God, I had no strong interest in space. I have no ulterior motives. But there are people—and you know who they are—" he bellowed, sweeping his hand across the audience—"who would tell you that I am a false prophet. Well, answer me—did the space probe bring us a message or not? Which part of it did I get wrong?" Shouting, he lifted his hands high in the air as the crowd roared. Malcolm towered over the audience and the stage, a tall man with arms raised, sophistication and charisma wrapped into one package, exhorting a passionate crowd.

"Let me tell you a thing or two about prophecy, because that's just what God gave me. Prophecy means forth-telling, and that's what I do every day. This prophecy business didn't start with me. Remember that.

The message we all have heard came in a signal that NASA received—unexplained images of Mars and a long-dead spacecraft—sent to us by another space-faring race of people.

"Hear what the apostle Peter said: 'No prophecy comes about by the prophet's own interpretation.' The message from Mars or the probe wasn't my invention or a result of my imagination. You've all been witness to these times yourselves!

"I told you—not on my own, but through the wisdom of a higher being—that 'Voyager will return.' *Did it?*"

The crowd leaped to its feet, thundering applause while Malcolm raised his arms a second time in a show of victory. Applause and whistles roared for more than a minute while he strutted across the dais. After the crowd silenced, he moved close to the edge of the platform, his voice reverberating through the coliseum.

"This is the moment of truth—a historic juncture—a time for action. Will we retreat—or will we open our minds and venture forth?" He swept his hand from one side of the arena to the other.

As though on cue, most of the more than fifty thousand attendees sprang to their feet again, chanting as one immense voice: "Venture Forth!"

This rallying cry, initiated by Raines, was now being embraced by crowds across the United States, Europe, and Asia as the clarion call for a swift resolute response to the alien revelations. For many of the older generation, "Venture Forth!" had a sort of *Star Trek* ring to it, evoking a pioneering spirit of new vistas and new lands. It tugged at heartstrings, and the power of fifty thousand voices chanting in unison was hypnotic for all present, including Malcolm Raines.

With a broad smile, he raised both hands one last time, like a conductor escalating the crescendo. His deep bass voice boomed: "Venture Forth!"

Ten minutes and two encores later, Raines stepped off the stage. An aide escorted him outside the coliseum through a rear corridor, beyond the range of pressing fans and reporters.

"Someone sent a limousine, sir. Just for you." The aide held the door as Raines stepped into the stretch black Suburban.

"Nice touch. I'm honored. But who—?"

The aide pointed toward the driver's compartment and handed Raines a card, inscribed with calligraphy: "Please accept this as a token of my appreciation for your honesty."

Raines nodded, dismissed his attendant, and got in. He was alone. The black vehicle whisked away through downtown, and soon was on the freeway headed toward Raines' hotel.

An opaque window in front of him lowered enough for a hand to reach over the top. A woman's white gloved hand emerged, holding a large gold-embossed envelope. She didn't turn, but Raines could see long black hair braided under a delicate red scarf.

"For you. For your ministry," she said. "For the future."

Raines reached up, unsure what to expect, and took the envelope.

The window went up and a voice began to speak through the speakers that surrounded him. A man's voice, rich and cultured. "You were right. Voyager did return. I'm impressed."

Raines tried to peer through the opaque black glass ahead of him, leaning forward and placing a hand on the divider. It didn't move.

"Best that we keep it this way, for now. My identity isn't important, but my resources are."

"Very well," said Raines, and he sat back in the seat, putting his left arm up on the seat back and crossing his legs. "How can I be of help?"

"Speak your truth. Watch for opportunity. Nothing more."

Raines opened the flap of the envelope and lifted out one hundred thousand dollars in mint-fresh large bills.

"This is a generous gift, to be sure. But what are the strings?" Raines asked, placing the money back in the envelope and closing it. He put the package on the seat in front of him, just below the black glass window, then sat back, relaxed. "Certainly I'll need to understand your side of the bargain before I can accept such a magnanimous gesture."

"Of course," the voice said. "No strings. Call it an investment in truth, Father Raines. You are one of a kind. I invest in blunt, action-oriented businessmen. Now, I can at last invest in the clergy. Continue to be a reliable voice, and you will worry for nothing material. I can provide significant support—as long as you continue to share your vision and speak your truth."

Raines reached forward and retracted the envelope, placing it within his briefcase. He adjusted his glasses and his tie.

"A fair partnership," he said. "I accept."

| TUESDAY, AUGUST 16, 2011:
| COLORADO SPRINGS, COLORADO

". . . coverage of yesterday's attacks against terrorist strongholds outside Tehran, and bunker complexes near Qom, Iran."

The news commentator caught his attention, and Agent Kerry cranked up the volume of his motel room television.

"In a lightning strike by two Navy carrier battle groups and Air Force bombers, a volley of cruise missiles began the first phase of a military campaign in retaliation for terror attacks on the American homeland."

Kerry fell into a cheap chair in front of the set.

"Only hours ago, in the early morning hours here in Iran, more than seventy air- and sea-based cruise missiles hit their targets around the outskirts of the capital city. The missile attack decimated military facilities, weapon storage depots, and headquarter elements, all linked to Iranian terrorist cells deemed responsible for the devastation of March 21.

"The Iranian government issued a scathing denial of any involvement in terrorism, calling for holy war against the American aggressors. In a rare show of unity, the Arab League and OPEC have joined with Iran in calling for international sanctions against the U.S. in retaliation for a 'continuing series of bloody and unprovoked attacks.' Iran's ambassador to the United Nations insisted today that his country would soon possess a nuclear-tipped intercontinental missile capability and would not hesitate to use it against American interests. The United Nations Security Council, deadlocked for the past five weeks on the issue of U.S. retaliation for Iranian-funded terrorism, today issued a call for an end to hostilities. The U.S. ambassador walked out of U.N. deliberations pending further discussions with President—"

Kerry snapped off the volume and paced his Colorado Springs motel room, then he kicked the bedside in frustration. He moved to the window, staring west toward a predawn Pikes Peak. Purple, pink, and orange lit the bottoms of the high wispy clouds near the top of the mountain, silhouetted against the intense blue of the clear western sky. Ignoring the colorful view, he leaned his head against the cool glass, his temple throbbing against the pane.

"Why? It's too soon!"

But he knew the answer. An election year was coming. The administration beat the drums of war louder every day. "We have the proof, we have our targets, and we will crush those responsible." The vice president made the administration's position very clear. The FBI's stunning Al-Jihad evidence exposed a national network of deeply embedded, technologically advanced, Islamic terror cells spread across the nation. The CIA followed Al Salah connections to Syria and North Africa, with funding originating in Iran, all tightly linked through a complex digital network. A real terror network connected to Iranian nuclear bomb programs, test flights of their new missiles across Iraq, Jordan, and Israel, and embedded agents, identified by name, in a dozen western countries. Incontrovertible evidence. The network was real.

But were they to blame? Kerry had shared his suspicions with FBI leadership, his unnerving hunch that there was a dangerous hole in the mountain of damning Islamic terror-cell attestations. He dared not yet share his deepest fears, his domestic terrorism theory:

Americans attacked us and set up Iran to take the rap. The perfect cover.

He wondered if the FBI—or any agency—would ever crack this case. He looked back at the muted news images of last night's military destruction. Muslims were to blame. Whether for the March attacks, or because of their terror cells, or to punish them for nuclear and missile programs, Iran would have to pay. But Kerry couldn't shake a nagging conviction that his nation's thirst for Muslim blood had obscured a deeper truth. A truth that would point somewhere other than Iran.

Now their blood is on our *hands.*

"Cynicism thrives on the seamy side of honor, Agent Kerry," John said, his voice somewhat muted. "I've seen enough of the dark stuff in the military to know that you should never be surprised—and I'm not alone."

"You think that what I just shared about General Fredericks might actually be *true?*" Kerry asked, his voice ending on a high note.

"I do. And what you say to me stays with me, Kerry. I understand your dilemma, by the way. If I doubt what I'm seeing in this alien news, I'm at odds with three-fourths of humanity—the ones who watch news. Like you. If you suspect someone other than Muslims bombed America, you're up against a wall, too." John paused, gathering his thoughts. "So I feel your pain."

"I like that analogy," Kerry replied. "So, if you doubted that was an alien craft that you photographed, how would you proceed?"

"Didn't say I did, but to answer your question, I'd pursue it quietly. If I raised my voice against Raines or the UFO-ologists, or even against NASA or SETI for that matter, I'd be snubbed. So I'd keep my eyes open, keep my mouth shut, and follow my gut."

Kerry thought about that for a moment. "All right here's the deal. We work outside our own systems on this—partners—few if any at FBI would overtly support a theory like the one I'm carrying around in my head. Same for you."

John's delay in answering bothered Kerry. He wanted immediate confirmation that the astronaut was with him.

"I'm glad to help. But I'd rather keep my alien theories to myself, thanks. Let's nix any discussion of what I think about that. Okay?"

Kerry shrugged as he nodded. "Fair. So, what's the dark stuff?"

"Beg your pardon?" John asked.

"The dark stuff. You said you'd seen enough to suit you. What is it?" Kerry hit the button for speaker and picked up his cup, crossing the office to the window.

"You mean in the military? Like Fredericks?" John asked.

"The same."

"Oh, there's isolated pockets of the military services—like in any large organization—that aren't true-blue. A sordid underbelly that's concerned more about careers and success than integrity. It's well hidden, but you can find it if you pry."

"Give me an example," Kerry said.

"People who participate in activities that are flat-out wrong . . . like drunk driving, adultery, theft, fraud, kickbacks—violations of all sorts that are covered up to save careers. Selective enforcement of sexual misconduct, ethical breaches, intimidation, even rape. You name it. From what you've said, Fredericks was probably someone like that." John paused a moment. "His nickname is a dead giveaway, you know."

"Boomer?"

"In the naval aviation community, that was a term of endearment for a wildly popular guy who was a huge boozer and a party animal . . . somebody who knew how to scam the system—and did. I'm guessing that Fredericks fits the profile pretty well."

"He does," Kerry said as he turned back to the speaker phone. "So, what's your theory on this? I want to hear the outlandish unsupportable hypothesis that could ultimately save our nation." He smiled as he said it, fearing that he might one day have to share his deepest suspicions.

"I've given that question a lot of thought," John began. "This was a calculated move against the space surveillance system of the United States—and it worked. I'm convinced that when you—when we—find the answer, it will somehow connect back to space-based missile defense." John paused. "By the way, I'm looking down on Denver as we speak."

"Awesome," Kerry responded, looking out the window up at the morning sky.

"The question is, who'd want to blind us in space, maybe for just a little while?"

Kerry kept looking out the window, up at the bright blue, wondering where in that background the astronaut's voice was coming from.

"From a missile defense perspective, the Iranians are very likely culprits," John continued. "Or their neighbors to the north and east. But it's also possible you're chasing all the wrong leads."

"How's that?" Kerry asked, turning back to the phone.

"Maybe it *was* the aliens. What then?"

23

THE MASSIVE DELTA-V *Ares* rocket roared to life on the pad at Cape Canaveral, Florida. Huge plumes of blue flame and billowing clouds of white water vapor erupted from the base of America's largest and newest expendable launch vehicle as it struggled inches upward in the first second of the ignition process. Enclosed in the rocket's bulbous nose cone, America's next mission to Mars left Earth for an eleven-month journey to the elusive Red Planet.

Dr. Robert Kanewski crossed his fingers as he watched from Mission Control at Kennedy Space Center. This was a risky business, and failure was sometimes part of the equation. He watched his precious Mars Rover 3 sail off into the August sky, tucked away in the nose cone of Rex Edwards' belching liquid-fueled giant. Fingers still crossed, he watched the white trail of vapor disappear to the east as the launch vehicle made a flawless climb toward low Earth orbit. The control center erupted in cheers.

"Rover 3 is headed to Mars! This report from Cape Canaveral, Florida, where America has just launched the first of what may be a wave of new missions to explore the Red Planet and the mysterious possibility of alien life." CNN reports overpowered the background noise in the busy facility.

Robert glanced at the news feed on a monitor and then looked back at the faint white plume high in the sky. It was all a blur now. Ten years of design and construction, punctuated in this last year by the phenomenal news of possible alien life—on the planet that his spaceship would soon survey. His timing—NASA's timing—couldn't have been better.

"What's next, Doc?" an Air Force colonel asked as he put his hand on Robert's shoulder, the two of them watching the monster *Ares* rocket slip from sight.

"Next?" He turned and grinned. "Eleven scary months hoping that nothing goes wrong on the way to Mars. Probably a heart attack from all the attention we'll get when we take the first images of the Viking 1 site and the possible aliens." He laughed. "If they're still there, that is. We've got to wait nearly a year for the mission to get there."

"Get Kanewski to a terminal!" someone yelled. A voice rang out from near one of the television monitors. "Check out Fox!" Quickly, a controller piped the news audio into the control room speakers.

". . . reporting live from the White House newsroom, where the president plans to make a statement on the Mars Rover 3 mission, launched a few minutes ago in Florida."

Every eye that wasn't controlling the *Ares* was watching or listening to the news as the president strode to the podium in the White House briefing room.

"Ladies and gentlemen . . . members of the press . . . fellow citizens.

Thank you for this opportunity to address you on a momentous day. As some of you are aware, our next robotic mission to Mars, Rover 3, was launched only minutes ago toward a rendezvous with history. I want to personally thank and congratulate all the members of the NASA and contractor team that made this possible. But I want you all to know that a rover on Mars should not be our only response to the recent questions about the existence of intelligent life in the solar system. Therefore, I will use this occasion to propose a far greater mission—an exploration of historic import.

"It is time to commit our resources and national will to send men and women to Mars. Not just to resolve the questions of the images, the probe, and the mysterious transmissions—but because it is right for America to do this. It's time for humanity to venture forth.

"In little more than a year we will all go to the polls. These are critical weeks, times when many politicians will pick their words and their battles carefully in order to win election. Prevailing wisdom says that I, of all politicians, should play it safe and avoid divisive issues. After all, we are at war with terror on many fronts, and there are many issues we must resolve at home. Yet I've struggled with the events of the past five months, just as you have. As your president and as a citizen—not as your candidate—I've decided that this is a time for action, not risk avoidance."

The president took a breath and seemed to stand a little taller. "Fifty years ago, before many of you were born, John F. Kennedy made a historic and passionate call for us to land a man on the Moon within the decade. Yet in the nearly forty years since we last set foot on the Moon, humanity has not ventured beyond low Earth orbit. I say it's time to go. President Bush started a program for a mission to the Moon and Mars, but it died—for a variety of good reasons, and some bad ones. I am proposing that we leapfrog over the programmatic failures of the previous administration—and this administration—and head straight to Mars. Fast.

"I want a vote on a manned mission to Mars before the end of this fiscal year, a vote that will tell us all where every representative and senator stands on this issue as we go into the polls. I want a special session of Congress, convening during summer recess, to approve a special appropriation of fifty billion dollars. I want this mission, and I want accountability from every member of Congress."

He gripped the podium, seeming to square off. "Pundits, advisors, television ads—and some of your own senators and representatives—will oppose this proposal. They'll tell you it's political suicide to call Congress back to Washington in the summer before a presidential election year, that you can't appropriate funds out of cycle, that no sane representative would vote on such a measure so close to election time. Trust me. I've heard it all a hundred times this past month and, frankly, I'm tired of business as usual. For those who question our ability to accomplish this task, watch out. We can do it. And we will.

"I'm willing to gamble on American spirit, courage, and resourcefulness. This is the right time to forge ahead—even in the face of a hostile political machine." The president paused, folded his notes, and then bored into the camera with a steely gaze. "I say this to Congress and NASA. Fate has laid the opportunity of the millennium at your feet. We must not miss this chance to learn more about the universe into which we were born. Do not squander the future of mankind. Make this opportunity happen now!"

He jabbed a finger into the air.

"To Mars!"

Robert Kanewski stood near the back of Mission Control in Florida, watching the drama play out before him as technicians pointed *Ares*

toward low Earth orbit and the president pointed the nation to Mars. An image of Rex Edwards flashed on Fox News, his belching *Ares* on the climb in the background, and his finger-in-the-camera defiance of NASA to call his bluff. "To Mars. Launch in three hundred days," scrolled across the ticker below his massive bulging neck and red bow tie.

Less than a year from start to launch — if Rex Edwards has his way. And apparently, he did. Robert shook his head in wonder as he surveyed the watch floor and *Ares* on the climb to four hundred kilometers. He subconsciously ticked off the thousands of days and hundreds of people involved in the launch of his comparatively simple unmanned robotic craft. *Only three hundred days?*

His heart raced, suddenly seizing on the genius of Rex's proposal, the president's timely mandate, and the opportunity this very moment afforded *him*, Dr. Robert Kanewski, America's leading Mars explorer. *His* opportunity.

Perhaps — just perhaps — it could be done.

LOS ANGELES, CALIFORNIA

Foster Williams and Parker Hannifin bantered back and forth in their evening news analysis hour, neither taking a conservative or liberal view, but both going for the jugular of their partner in the newest rough-and-rumble television commentary.

"He's a fool," Parker Hannifin asserted. "The president can't expect Congress to quit their vacation, run home to Washington, vote a major appropriation out of cycle, and lay down like a mat at Manchester's feet. The president is smoking something illegal — and he's inhaling."

Foster flashed his pearly teeth and took a more restrained tack. "Wrong again. Ladies and gentlemen, my colleague forgets the power of the almighty vote. America is anxious. Anxious about terror, anxious about aliens, and desperate for leadership. There's a presidential election brewing, and for the first time since George W. Bush led us into a war on the backs of brawn and bravado, we are finally headed somewhere."

"Iraq?" Hannifin responded. "You use Iraq as an example of why Manchester's Mars proposal makes sense?"

Foster smiled. "Not Iraq. I'm talking about bold leadership. In-your-face risk-taking guts. Like Kennedy. He made no sense when he sent us to the Moon. Why go, for crying out loud? But we did it, and it transformed this nation. Manchester is challenging us in the same way that W and JFK did. And we'll be better for it."

"I take it back," Hannifin said with a smirk. "The president's not the one smoking weed. It's you. But let's not quibble. Let's bring an expert into this friendly mix. Tonight with us, the progenitor of this rousing discussion, the multibillionaire himself, Rex Edwards, owner and chief engineer of Delta-V Corporation. Good evening, Rex." He pointed to the large plasma screen to his left.

Edwards smiled, but did not immediately respond.

"Can you hear us, Rex?" Foster asked, thrown off by Edwards' silence.

"I can, yes, Foster. I was composing my opening line after Mr. Hannifin's eloquent tirade against our commanders in chief. My response was this: I am no longer a multibillionaire. My billions went into a secret research program—a very successful program by the way—to develop an alternative vehicle for manned interplanetary space flight. One I hope that I will be able to sell when the administration passes this funding appropriation, or when the space shuttle finally runs out of gas."

Hannifin coughed. "I'm honored you consider me eloquent, Mr. Edwards. Tell me, do you expect a sole-source contract for that fifty billion or so? That might help with your dwindling bank account."

Foster shook his head. "Parker. Really. No need to dig so low."

"My checkbook is fine, Parker," Edwards responded. "It might be worthwhile to point out that I have seen none of the nearly one hundred billion dollars funneled into the manned space program since the year 2000, yet I have the *only* manned spaceship that is ready to go to Mars. The prime contractor for the shuttle follow-on program can't say that. Neither can the vehicle contractor for our anemic moon lander program. Perhaps my commercial entrepreneurial spirit offends you?"

Foster picked up the line. "No federal monies, Rex, for your manned space work in all those years?"

"No. In fact, our *Ares* launch vehicle, which launched Rover 3 yesterday, and all of our other aerospace research developments have been *entirely* self-funded. I do not support public welfare programs, of any sort. I design and develop what we sell. If it won't sell without public largess, it's not worth making. I challenge the rest of the aerospace industry to adopt my model. It works."

Hannifin responded quickly. "He's got me there. I applaud you, Mr. Edwards. But my question about a sole-source contract still stands. What is your connection with the president?"

"Probably the same as yours. I've never met or talked to the man. What he knows of me, he has read about, or heard from others. My work stands on its own merits. My Ghost Works has a completed interplanetary vehicle that I can launch in less than a year. It will carry three humans to Mars, land two of them, and bring them all home safely. And I don't need fifty billion dollars to do the job. Just thirty. I suspect the larger number that the president threw out is part of his risk margin—to pay off the thirsty NASA beast while I do my part fixed price."

Edwards shifted in his chair, his face broadcast on a large screen between the two hosts. "If NASA would match my level of efficiency, you could give back nineteen billion or more of that money the president asked for. I certainly don't need it."

Foster jumped in. "Rex. Quickly. Give us a snapshot on how you got here. What's your secret?"

"For starters, simplicity. Pure simplicity." Rex Edwards began to gesticulate with his hands as he spoke. "Simplicity is the antithesis of NASA. Our space agency hires tens of thousands of people to do a job that should be relegated to a few hundred. They launch spaceships on mountains of paper. Spaceships that fail. All of my rockets are powered by safe, reliable, liquid-fueled engines. I build solid, no-frills hardware and fly it. No exorbitant money-wasting studies, just good solid engineering. I use proven technologies, and I finish my projects ahead of schedule and below cost.

"Second, I don't lose sleep over risk. NASA, on the other hand, has become insanely focused on risk avoidance. I think it's the epitome of irony that both times we lost an orbiter, our risk-averse NASA was ignoring the very warning signs that could have saved the crews and the vehicles. Solid rockets . . . frozen O-rings . . . and flying foam. Rather than avert it, we must *accept* risk—sometimes big risks—and quit the obscene focus on six-sigma reliability for manned systems. Here's an aerospace conundrum for you, Foster: When you put armies of people in charge of reliability and risk avoidance, you get the very demon that you set out to conquer. Complexity, the mother of risk. At Delta-V there are no armies of risk and reliability engineers. We design a solid solution and accept a measure of risk in everything that we do. In the end, simple things perform more reliably. A lesson, by the way, that the Russians have never forgotten."

Rex's gathering frown deepened with each word, and he clenched his right fist. "Finally, I focus on incentive. NASA has no profit motive and, as a result, it has squandered its inheritance. Tens of billions of dollars spent on dusty studies and no hardware, and tens of thousands of smart but largely unchallenged employees languishing in six major centers that squabble with each other for resources. My employees, on the other hand, work closely together, are challenged to the limits of their abilities and are generously rewarded—when they perform—with financial inducements far beyond their expectations."

Rex folded his hands smugly. "Simplicity, risk, and incentive. Those are the keys to my success."

24

"HELLO!"

Malcolm Raines tapped Dr. Felicia Bondurant lightly on the shoulder, surprising her from behind as she waited at the security checkpoint of the Old Executive Office Building next door to the White House.

The director of NASA's Jet Propulsion Laboratory was overcome with surprise. "Father Raines! Are you part of this parade today, too?" Around them, dozens of dignitaries filed in from around the world, converging on the pivotal decision meeting about the coming Mars manned mission, a meeting chaired by Vice President Lance Ryan and staffed by his entourage of national space experts.

"Yes, I guess I'm part of the circus, Felicia. The vice president invited me to contribute my concerns about the mission. Now that it's funded, that is. I presume you're here representing NASA?"

"Yes." She lowered her voice as they moved together through the checkpoint, handing over their briefcases. "What have you heard?"

"The appropriation paperwork will be on the president's desk this afternoon," he said. "It was a tough budget fight to the end, but we—he—got it through."

Felicia raised her eyebrows, and patted him lightly on the back as they stood in line. "Well done!"

"Another tidbit? The Russians will decline to join a manned mission. They think the alien messages are a hoax, and they don't want to get caught in the maelstrom when it breaks." He pointed her away from the stream of people as they cleared the metal detectors. "It's just as well anyway. They'd have been a distraction. Let's talk over here," he said, pointing to an alcove off the central hallway. "You know, the Russian decision to decline is the worst kept secret in town."

"Well, I hadn't heard it," Dr. Bondurant said, raising her voice as they moved away from the rest of the visitors. "Then, of course, I don't dine with the vice president." She winked at the charismatic new leader, despite being old enough to be his mother.

Raines leaned toward her and smiled. "Perhaps not, but we could arrange that," he said, returning the wink. He took off his signature round glasses and polished them with a smartly folded handkerchief from his suit pocket.

She locked eyes with him. "Would you?" she asked, her voice lilting. "Arrange it, I mean? I owe you a great deal, you know. Personally speaking." After he put away the cloth and his glasses, she took his right hand and held it.

Raines flashed a perfect smile. "I have a favor to ask, if I might," he said, his voice lowered as he bent over to speak close to her right ear. "I need your support—"

"Of course!"

"—for the selection of open-minded astronauts who are particularly well suited for the mission. Strong credentials, with views that are not hardened by personal spiritual convictions. Together, we can leverage each other in the crew selection process."

"I'll follow your vote, Malcolm," she said, her eyes locked with his, though she was a foot shorter. His sharp jaw and a hint of cologne caught her attention. She still held his hand.

Raines nodded, releasing her grasp and leading her away from the alcove toward the auditorium. "Felicia, you are of course aware of the Heisenberg Uncertainty Principle?" he asked as they continued down the hall, his arm under hers.

"Of course. Observation affects data, to be brief. But it's more complex than that."

"Exactly. Heisenberg's perspective, extended to general science, was that the very act of observing the world alters it. Our arrival on Mars will surely contaminate the landing site in some way, and our perspectives will influence our observations, even our decisions about how to deal with the aliens we encounter there. It will happen, no matter who we send. So it seems we ought to send those with the most open minds, and not those grounded in a worldview that denies the very existence of alien life."

"I agree. But I promise you, Malcolm—the Houston space mafia will push their agenda. Plan on it. Greg Church, the director at JCS, is a skilled political animal with incredible survival instincts." Felicia thrust the black hair back from her forehead and narrowed her eyes as she stopped at the door to the meeting room, pulling him aside to a corner of the hallway, out of the stream of dignitaries.

"You have my complete support." She extended her hand, and he took her grip.

"And you can count on me any time, Felicia." His hand swallowed hers in a firm shake.

Dr. Felicia Bondurant gave Malcolm Raines a heavily lipsticked, wrinkled smile. Walking into the ornate room on his arm, she wondered if she should try a new hairstyle or outfit when she returned to Los Angeles.

She had support in high places now, and she'd do anything to keep it.

FRIDAY, NOVEMBER 18, 2011: SPACE STATION ALPHA

"Kerry."

"Hello there. It's John. This a good time to call?"

"In fact, it is," Kerry said. "I'm at home, in Fredericksburg. Taking the day off for my son's birthday. What's up?"

"I am," John responded with a short laugh. "Get it? Space? You opened yourself up for that one."

"You never were one for good jokes, were you?" Kerry asked with a chuckle.

"Guess not. Did you get my last e-mail, the one about the specific periods of vulnerability for missile launches on 3/21?"

"I did," Kerry replied. "You put the high probability on the Pacific and East Asia. And the rest of the world was pretty much covered by other sensors. So where does that leave us, John? I mean, at this point, we've got negotiations proceeding with Iran on the subject of Al Salah, and you know I called off the tail of General Fredericks tail last month. My motivation's on the wane, to tell you the truth."

"I think I've found something else you should consider."

"All ears," Kerry said.

"Iran couldn't launch anything. The entire Middle East had duplicate radar coverage, and there's enough human intelligence operating behind the borders to back up the picket ships if they had failed. Ditto for India, Pakistan, Japan, China, Korea, and most of Russia. Draw a line from the middle of Africa all the way to Japan. Nothing could launch in that arc. With me so far?"

"Uh-huh. Go on."

"That limits any missile launch to far eastern Russia, the East Pacific, West Atlantic, or the Americas. When you look at who has launch capabilities in that area, there's only three candidates. The U.S., Russia—and France, in French Guiana. We know there were no hostile missile launches that flew to an impact, so whatever was done—if there *was* a launch—went to orbit, and it was put up by one of these countries. The next question is why."

"That settles it. The French did it," Kerry said, laughing.

"Good try, but no cigar. I consulted the launch declaration databases, and each of those countries had a launch planned in the two-day period when the U.S. was blind. The U.S. launch from Vandenberg, for missile defense testing, was cancelled. That makes sense. Local sources— people I know who watch launches—confirmed that nothing went up for several days. Rex Edwards launched a set of space tugs from his East Pacific complex on Baker Island, and they're precisely where he said he'd put them. Well . . . most of them are. One of them plucked a Navy satellite out of orbit, if you recall."

"Sort of. News conference about a month after the attack, right?"

"The same. The European Space Agency—the French—had an *Ariane V* launch planned, and it also went up as scheduled. Local sources in French Guiana told me that only one rocket was launched in that timeframe. Best we can tell, no one snuck anything extra into it. They declared the orbit, and I checked it out. They said they'd launch a communication satellite, and it's right where they said it would be. The

French are clean … this time."

"I wouldn't normally give the French a bye," Kerry said with a chuckle. "You say old man Rex Edwards was on that list, too?"

"Yes. He declared one launch. An *Ares*. Five space tugs."

"Interesting."

"So, that leaves three remaining options. One—the Russians made a mobile missile launch from the far eastern side of their country. Intelligence reports have speculated for some time about a small cosmo-drome on the Kamchatka peninsula, near Petropovlosk. Not a major site like Baikonur, Kapustin Yar, or Plesetsk, but nevertheless capable of a launch to orbit. The Russians have this launch business down to a fine art. You ever watch a Soyuz launch?"

"No," Kerry said. "Why?"

"It's simple. Nothing fancy," John replied. "They roll the rocket out on a rusty old train and it chugs down to the launch gantry. The Soyuz vehicle is hoisted up, people hug and kiss and drink vodka together, and then the cosmonauts walk up on the platform, strap in, and take off. Very elementary operation, and it works."

"Sounds like Rex on that television interview, doesn't it?"

"You got it. Option two. Somebody else can launch rockets, but we didn't know about it. Like a South American country, Marshall Islands, or the Brits down in the Falklands. Something out of the ordi-nary like that. But if it happened that way, unless it was really out in the boonies—and I mean, *way out*—someone would have said some-thing. You don't throw a rocket into orbit from land without someone noticing."

"Agreed. Too hard to pull off something like that. Third option?"

"Somebody launched at sea. The Sea Launch complex was in port in San Diego, so they're clear. But it's not beyond the realm of the possi-ble that another country could build one just like it and float it into the

Pacific or Atlantic. You could throw rockets up all day long from the middle of the ocean, and no one would ever know, as long as it was in the missile detection dead zone that I've described. There's also a fourth option, the scariest of all."

"I thought there were three."

"I can't count. Actually, it's a subset of option three."

"And that is?"

"A nuclear submarine sea launch. It doesn't take a huge modification to change a ballistic missile into an orbital payload platform."

"Uh-oh," Kerry said, his voice getting quiet.

"Uh-oh is right. The nuclear submarine launches its weapon into orbit . . . maybe multiple weapons into multiple orbits. Perhaps a nuke or a fleet of antisatellite weapons. Who knows?"

"Who can do this?" Kerry asked.

"The U.S., French, British, Russians, Chinese, and Indians."

"India?"

"Yes. Sagarika missile. Deployed last year."

"It's a dangerous world out there, John."

"Exactly. Scary part is — the vast numbers of submarines that we can't account for are in the hands of the old Soviets. Theoretically, many of those subs have been ground into razor blades, or sunk. But you just never know."

"Summarize for me, John. Where do we stand?"

"I'm still convinced that something happened in that forty-eight hour blind gap, Kerry. I don't think we should rest until we ferret out all the possibilities. But getting military intelligence help will take some suave on your end. No one wants to admit that there was vulnerability in the first place. Admitting that failure would set off a huge panic, or God forbid, copy cat attacks meant to blind us again."

"Check."

"So, you—we—are going to have to analyze these theories on our own. We have to pick one or two options. I recommend that we exclude all the options except sea-based weapons headed to orbit."

"Launched by whom?"

"Russia, or—"

"You broke up there, John. Russia or *what*?" Kerry said, the volume of his voice increasing.

"Us—the United States—domestic."

"You've gotta be kidding."

"Nope. Until all possibilities are excluded, each is as possible, although not as probable, as any other. It could have been an American boat, or an American interest, that did this. We can't exclude that possibility—at least not yet."

Kerry didn't respond. "You still there?" John asked. "Kerry?"

"I'm still here. You touched a raw nerve. Remember I asked you to postulate your hairy bodacious theory that you thought would save the nation if it could be proved true?" Kerry asked.

"Yeah. I just shared it."

"I've been working on a motive that I haven't shared with you yet, John—or anyone else in the Bureau. What spooks me is that you've arrived at a similar conclusion."

"So . . . let's hear your version."

"All right. This was not the action of a foreign power. It was perpetrated by someone inside our own system. This was an act of domestic terrorism carried out by someone with enormous insight into counter-terror intelligence. Someone who left the Iranians—valid terrorists in their own right—holding the bag. The perfect scam."

John let the microphone float as he watched the communication display in front of him. He gulped, trying to form his words.

"If we have independently arrived at a similar conclusion, then there can only be two possibilities," John said.

"Bad jokes and perfect logic?" Kerry asked. "Who are you—Spock?"

"Good try. I'm honored. Either we're incorrigible conspiracy theorists," John said, pausing to take a deep breath. "Or we're onto something."

"For America's sake," Kerry said, "I hope we're wrong."

25

DIRECTOR GLEN NOBLE OF the FBI pointed to the special agent at his side. "Mr. Vice President, this is Special Agent Kerry. I believe you've met."

"We have met. You had something important to show me before the National Security Council meets tonight?"

"Yes, sir." Director Noble said, cutting Kerry off before he could speak. "Our field time has paid off. We've been working hard on an alternate motive for the attacks, following a tip that there might be insider support for the attacks on Colorado Springs and Washington. We've mined quite a lot of intelligence, and indications are that the Islamic terrorists had help—from U.S. citizens."

That last bit of news ignited the vice president. "What did you say? Not Iran? Have you been watching the news, Noble? Three weeks ago we dropped fifty tons of high-precision ordnance on the outskirts of Tehran because we were sure that the conspirators were Muslim fanatics. And because that waste-of-oxygen, the United Nations, couldn't get a unanimous vote to go to the bathroom, much less deal with terrorism. Al Salah *admitted* responsibility, the Iranians *admitted* they funded al Salah, and we pulled dozens of certified human intelligence sources to substantiate those claims. Now you're telling me that we might have a line on someone else?" The veep released a bitter string of profanities as he paced his office.

Kerry stepped in to take some of the heat. "Sir, if I may. The new evidence we have now is preliminary. We all know that the cells we hit in Iran were legitimate terror organizations. Certified. However, the evidence is also very strong that the execution phase of the al Salah operation used, at least in part, American citizens." Kerry exhaled deeply, clenching his hands behind his back as he forced out the next words. "And it may be possible that domestic terrorists craftily pinned the entire thing on the Iranians. We can't afford to ignore that option."

The vice president stopped his pacing for a moment and looked Kerry directly in the eye, his jaw falling. Sweat was visible on the back of his neck and brow as he shook his head from side to side. "Al Salah, Kerry," said the vice president quietly as he resumed his pacing. "Keep repeating that to yourself, and you'll save yourself lots of sleepless nights. Al Salah."

"I understand, sir. Please let me finish my explanation and the connection will be clear. Beyond clear. After we processed the al Salah claims and evidence, the first new tips we had on this case were the sources of the stolen twin-engine aircraft. Early in the investigation, we pieced together an elaborate network of stolen rental aircraft. All the planes were lifted from small out-of-the-way local fields ranging from Moontown, Alabama to Skagway, Alaska. The terrorists were smooth operators, renting planes and learning the airfield ropes for months before the theft."

"We've already been over this." Vice President Ryan faced a copy of the Constitution on the wall while Noble kept his head down and Kerry talked.

"Yes, sir. We have. Based on that evidence we searched for some common threads beyond the obvious al Salah rental records. In a second round of forensics, after Thanksgiving, we used a special scanning electron microscope to lift parts of two prints off custom T-handles used to control the planes on the ground before launch. These guys were very nearly perfect in avoiding prints. But we found a needle in a field of haystacks, so to speak."

Kerry held out a pair of photographs, but the vice president didn't turn to look. "Red Henckey, real name Tobias, and this man, Cliff Farnsworth."

"Cut to the chase," the veep said, facing the wall. "Have you found them yet?" He wiped his wet face with a gold embossed paper napkin.

"No, sir. We're working on that."

"Spare me," the vice president hissed, turning to Kerry and snatching the photos. "You goons are always 'working on it.'" He flipped through the pictures.

"Each of these men has a record, sir. CIA ran a special filter on our data and linked them to this big fellow, Billy Carlisle, who played in some of the aircraft rentals." Kerry handed him a third photograph. "You wouldn't forget Carlisle if you ever met him and neither did those airfield operators. Finally, we had a lucky break in Colorado a week ago. A migrant family in Pueblo reported seeing him the night before the attack. Nailed him from a photo we showed them. He had a large truck, loaded with supplies, generators—you name it. We ran a likely range for that truck. Bingo."

Kerry produced a mounted Colorado map showing an abandoned airstrip and mine. "We found a small amount of dirt debris in one of the tires of the aircraft that hit NORTHCOM. That specimen matched the soil from this abandoned hangar complex and silver mine."

"Again, I ask you. Where are they now? Don't tell me you're still 'working on it,' Kerry. Not if you want to keep your job."

"He won't, sir. Will you, Kerry?" Director Noble interjected.

"Actually, sir, I can tell you whatever you want to hear. But if you want the truth, we have solid intelligence sources that are pointing us to Central America."

The vice president cursed again. "That's an awfully large place to hide, Special Agent."

"Sir," Director Noble interrupted, "I'm sure Kerry has another explanation. Right, Kerry?"

"Shut up, you suck-up. At least Kerry has the guts to take me on. Let him finish."

Kerry was deadpan, yet straining to hold his calm. "We don't have them, sir. There are no records of Henckey, Farnsworth, or Carlisle from that day forward. But we do have their scent, and it leads south. Sooner or later they'll make a mistake or drop another lead."

"You're an idiot, Kerry," the vice president exclaimed, facing the agent head on. "Gutsy—and innovative—but stupid. The Muslims beat you on this one when they got away with it the first time. Now you've invented a fantasy of domestic terror relationships to cover your own incompetence. Drop this line of investigation right now, get your butts in gear, and find me the rest of these jihadist fanatics who attacked us." He threw the three photos and map on the table, staring down both men.

Director Noble started to say something, but the vice president slammed the table with a flat hand, raising his voice again. "I am *done*, Noble. Good-bye."

SUNDAY, DECEMBER 11, 2011:
LOS ANGELES, CALIFORNIA

"We will lose contact for a time, and then we will hear from them again." Malcolm Raines' face filled the screen for a moment, and then the camera swung back to Foster Williams in the studio.

"There it is, folks. The next prediction from our exclusive guest, Father Malcolm Raines, a prophet for our times."

"In the face of overwhelming proof, Foster, even with a manned mission that eventually touches intelligent life on Mars, some people will refuse to believe. They are beyond my reach, lost in unbelief. I cannot help them. For the rest who embrace my message of hope, there is a future."

"Any last words as we close tonight, Father Raines? A summary of your vision?"

"Yes, thank you Foster. Two words. 'Believe'—and 'watch.' Look at the evidence for yourself and ask why you deny the proof before you. Believe. And then watch. I told you 'we will lose contact for a time, and then we will hear from them again.'"

PASADENA,
CALIFORNIA

"Where does he get this stuff?" Scott leaned over the back of his terminal, fishing for a cable while the Foster Williams show droned on in the background. "Gotcha!" Scott snagged another connector from behind the console and plugged it in. The new large-format video monitor on the wall sprang to life. "Merry Christmas, team! A new TV!" Scott bellowed. "Believe!" He sprang to his control station, hit three buttons, then sang out again. "And watch!"

As Scott spoke, a life-size image of Viking 1, imaged by the mysterious source on Mars, filled the center's new high-definition three-meter-wide screen. He swept his hand in front of the crowd of engineers. "Picture looks pretty healthy to me."

"I wouldn't count Raines out yet, son," Dr. Alex Watrick said.

Scott held his hands high and stretched out the kinks in his back. "Tell me you're not one of 'Raines' Ring.'"

"One of who?" Dr. Kanewski interjected, as he watched the large-format display.

"You know, Doc—you've heard of them."

"I haven't," Dr. Kanewski insisted, with a frown.

"Raines' Ring," intoned Scott, raising his voice comically. "A gathering of open-minded men and women of faith on planet Earth who aggressively embrace change and opportunity, linking their limitless minds and infinite God-energies in pursuit of the great challenges of the Universe." The entire operations crew erupted in applause.

"No kiddin', Doc," Scott said. "Mom, hotdogs, Chevrolet, and apple pie. With liberty and justice for all. It's their tagline. I couldn't make up something that corny."

The mission director shook his head again.

"No TV, huh?" Scott asked, with a smile.

Dr. Kanewski shrugged just as Alex Watrick let out a low whistle. "Well, I'll be."

Scott, Dr. Kanewski, and the rest of the Mars crew turned from the fun and looked at white-haired and rumpled Dr. Watrick, then followed his gaze toward the new screen. Prominently displayed across the monitor was an error message, overlying a frozen and half-formed image of Viking and the Martian horizon in the distance. "Signal Interrupted. Data File Incomplete."

Scott rushed back to his terminal, typed a flurry of commands, and then slammed his keyboard, vanquished. "Signal's gone, folks. Somebody—or something—just pulled the plug."

Dr. Watrick shook his head, laughing as he walked out of the operations center. "He's right again. Honestly, I'm going to ask Father Raines to pick the number for my next Powerball ticket."

26

"YEAR 28, DAY 115, 2042 Universal time."

A prominent digital clock ticked off an unusual time above the computer terminals in the Mars Mission Control Center. An uninitiated observer in the complex would think that Californians were on some obscure timetable. It was Mars time, day 115 of the twenty-eighth Martian year since the Viking 1 landing, the only time that mattered to this eclectic crew of earthbound explorers.

"Midnight soon, Alex. Your shift's just about up," the young female technician said, yawning.

"I guess it is. Hard to get used to setting my clock by Mars, no matter how many years I've been doing this."

She chuckled at the eccentric old Dr. Watrick, who clung to his long-time duty as an operations supervisor in the control center. "Spring on Mars," she said, "and December on Earth. Sun's just setting on

Viking, and it's pitch dark in LA."

Dr. Watrick nodded as he toyed with a computer file they would send tonight to the mysterious alien device that was transmitting Martian images and which responded to video commands just like Viking. His hair was askew, and his right cheek flinched several times a minute in a characteristic tic. He'd reviewed the command file a dozen times already, but had forgotten he'd done it, and checked his work again.

"Mars sets in another hour, Dr. Watrick. Do you want to upload the Viking command set now or have me hold it for tomorrow?"

The elder scientist shoved away a jumble of papers as he rearranged his keyboard. "What? Oh yes. Yes. Tonight. Definitely. We should do it now." He stared at the terminal for a long time after the computer registered that the message was on its way.

"We'll have a receipt acknowledgment in about twenty minutes, sir. It's a ten-minute one-way trip to Mars tonight."

"Yes, it is." The old space scientist seemed lost in a blank stare.

"What's up?" she asked, rubbing her eyes.

"Doing some math in my head. Simple, really." He paused, watching the ceiling as if it were a calculator. "This is the sixteenth of December, and the new year is fifteen days away."

"And?"

"If we launch a manned mission approximately eight months from now . . . let's see, that will be Martian day 342, or about midnight local time, thirty days before the Martian autumnal equinox. Late Martian summer . . ."

"How do you keep all that stuff in your head?" she asked, pushing back errant black bangs, her head cocked.

"Years of experience, I guess. But oh, gracious, no, that's not what's important. Follow me here. If we launch on August first and fly the planned trajectory—let's say two hundred twenty days—then our astronauts will be in Martian orbit around March 2013. Aries 563, if you live by a Martian calendar. One Martian week before the end of the dust season."

"Is that good?" she asked, suppressing a yawn.

"Yes. Wonderful. We use less fuel on the way out and miss the dust season entirely. Nice weather. Yes. We'll be able to fly home in about 250 days Earth time, given that we still have some fuel left. What timing!"

"Illuminate me, great one." she joked, blinking hard to stay awake.

"Don't you see?" he asked, his old eyes alive with excitement. "We launch in a blaze of glory in August as we're headed into the presidential elections. Assuming the launch is successful, it catapults Manchester and Ryan into their second term. All very convenient, don't you think?" Dr. Watrick pointed at her, his face alight.

"Yes, then 250 days after we leave Mars, and just a few days before Christmas, we bring our heroes home to safety. What a present. So fast, and it will all be over. Hmm. I wonder." Dr. Watrick stared back at the monitor, contemplative.

"Wonder what, Doc?" she asked.

Dr. Watrick burst out of his seat, a comical grin plastered across his sagging face. The glint of mischief sparkling in his tiny eyes behind bent dirty glasses emphasized his idiosyncratic genius. He waved over his shoulder as he left the operations center, shuffling and muttering to himself. His worn Birkenstock sandals slapped against his feet and the cold linoleum of the hallway.

"Yes, yes. What a campaign theme! And right on time, too. Manchester and Ryan. The Mars Team. My, my."

"Discovery, Houston. You're 'GO' at throttle-up."

Chills ran down John's spine, and the spines of many of the seasoned space enthusiasts, as those fateful words were uttered, reminiscent of tragedy twenty-five years before. At this point in 1986, the space shuttle Challenger had disintegrated over the Atlantic Ocean as pilot Mike Smith pushed the shuttle engines to maximum thrust. All eyes watched, and many observers prayed, as the mission to relieve the crew of Space Station Alpha powered through the most critical part of its liftoff maneuver.

"Roger, Houston. 'GO' at throttle-up."

John and Station Commander Al Rogers watched the ascent on the NASA channel, anxious as Discovery continued her thunderous climb on a bright clear December morning, only days before Christmas. They'd each experienced this ride three times, and now they were reliving the experience vicariously through the magic of live television.

"They'll be on board in time for dinner, Hawk," Al said, as the orbiter released the solid rocket boosters and continued its climb toward orbit.

"I've been thinking about that meal more than this mission," John said, his mouth watering in anticipation of the fresh Texas barbecue headed to the station, a tradition ever since Captain Danny Bursch and his record endurance crew started the meal express ten years ago.

Fifteen hours later, Discovery closed on Alpha, her charred nose and black-and-white colors a welcome sight for the crew that had waited months for a visit. The Progress module shipments from Russia had kept John and his friends well fed and able to maintain a core set of functioning equipment, but the crew was desperate for human contact.

Without regular resupply missions by people, seven months was a long time to be in close quarters with three other humans.

Discovery made her delicate forward roll as she closed on the station, a maneuver to evaluate possible tile damage on the bottom of the orbiter, and a regular practice since Colonel Eileen Collins first did it in 2005 after the return to flight. Every time he watched it, and this was his second time, John marveled at the giant spaceship gently tumbling toward them. He and Elena photographed every square centimeter of the belly and wings with the same telescope that had imaged the golden probe four months ago.

"Stand by to dock" echoed through the station two hours later as Discovery nudged into her berth with a gentle bump. At last, Alpha and Discovery were one. John's heart quickened as he grasped that his trip home was here at last.

The station crew hovered near the docking port while the orbiter crew opened their side of the airtight lock. John hadn't expected to be so glad to see new faces, or so ready to leave. His mind raced through the emotion and excitement of the past thirteen months, every part of him aching to be on the shuttle headed for home. The hatch opened, but his mind was on thoughts of Amy and the children, and a reunion on Earth.

The bear hug from Jake Cook shook John out of his momentary reverie. "Hey there, Hawk!"

John grabbed his old friend in a return hug that somersaulted them both away from the hatch. "You big ox. It's about time you came to see me. Who's got the takeout?"

Jake winked and reached into the back pocket of his cargo shorts. "Takeout's on its way, buddy. But here's something for you while you wait." He sent a small envelope spinning like a Frisbee toward John.

Scented and secured with a pink bow, the envelope was a package of pictures of the children from their activities during the past seven months, tucked inside a short love note from his bride. This was Amy's special tradition, one she'd begun during his first deployment in the Navy and kept up ever since. Whenever he was away for a long time she would always send a gift. She never forgot.

John's heart pounded as he opened the note at once, suddenly oblivious to the specially packaged pints of smoked pork, baked beans, sliced brisket, and spicy smoked sausage that floated past him.

In his mind's eye, as he stared at the pictures of his sons and daughter and smelled his wife's perfume, he was already headed home.

27

"DISCOVERY, YOU'RE LINED UP for HAC. Winds 180 at 12, crosswind component 4 knots."

"Copy. Standby HAC intercept."

The orbiter roared over Florida faster than the speed of sound, its twin sonic booms rumbling across Cocoa Beach and the Kennedy Space Center. In a few minutes, the thirteen-month adventure would conclude, long months punctuated with confusion, separation, terrorist attacks, messages from aliens, emergencies, equipment failures, and unsettling unknowns.

Discovery rolled out on final approach, vortices streaming off her wingtips like huge white corkscrews that spiraled to the ground in the humid Florida air. As the orbiter crossed the runway threshold, Bart McKinley gently pulled back on the controls and flared the flying brick to a flawless landing.

"Touchdown! Shuttle Discovery with 170 orbits spanning more than six million kilometers has returned from a historic mission to Space Station Alpha!" The NASA announcer heralded the returning crew, avoiding comment on the highlight of the station crew's accomplishment—imaging the passage of the alleged alien probe.

The orbiter stood tall above the runway as it rolled to a stop, support vehicles racing to its side. Down in the lower deck, unable to watch the landing or the cockpit operations, John squirmed under the new weight of a body that had been weightless for exactly 400 days. He hated to fly in "the cave," the windowless science payload area below the main deck. Yet he loathed the sudden burden of gravity even more. This was always the big test for long duration space flight—the return. Some resourceful Mir cosmonauts had been in space longer than John, but most of them had been carried out of their Soyuz return module. John was determined to walk off under his own power.

Michael Fincke's lifetime U.S. record of 381 days lay in ruins now that John Wells was on the ground. With a lifetime 432 days in space, John still had a long way to go to beat Sergei Krikalev's 803 days. However, being the U.S. leader gave him a strong sense of accomplishment as he groaned under the painful and burdensome load of his weighty flesh.

One of the tricks to a rapid transition back to gravity was to maintain excellent fitness in orbit. John calculated that he'd pedaled over 22,000 kilometers in orbit during the mission. Two hours a day on the cycle ergometer, averaging twenty-eight kilometers per hour on a simulated bicycle, but flying at 28,000 kilometers per hour in the spaceship. Eight hundred hours and 22,000 virtual kilometers on the pedals with no scenery, no wind, no sounds or smells, nothing to see but the boring white and grey aluminum walls of the station. A simulated cycling display, linked to the Internet, enabled John to occasionally race earthbound cyclists as they pedaled furiously through digital terrain on their own computer-enabled trainers. Walking off unassisted today would prove the value of riding for eight hundred hours at forty times the speed of sound.

An hour after landing, the communication link chimed. "Discovery, the vice president's ready to move into position. Confirm the Doc's completed his checks. Over."

"He's just about done probing us. Stand by," Bart McKinley replied from the pilot station.

John used the radio call as a catalyst for action. "I'm fine, Doc. Really!" John crossed his heart, ribbing NASA's flight surgeon, and anxious to get on the move. "You've poked everywhere. If I have a problem, I'll let you know." Despite his show of confidence, he knew it would be hard, perhaps impossible, to walk off unassisted. Yet he was determined to try.

The doctor shook his head, frustrated, John knew, with the hyper-egos of his senior astronaut patients. "All right, Hawk. You pass—for now. But don't try to be a hero. Please."

"Scout's honor," John said, saluting with two fingers. He struggled to push himself out of his seat, and several hands reached out to assist. Elena laughed aloud as she watched. "You are donkey, John."

"I think you mean stubborn as a mule, Elena," John said with a groan as he stood for the first time.

"That too," she offered as she tried to lift herself out of her seat.

The crew, led by Mission Commander Colonel Jack Montoya, began to descend the steps. Some exited more gingerly than others. This was the fifth space mission for Jack, and he nearly bounded down the stairs, like Captain Bob Crippen had three decades before him on the first shuttle mission—when Colonel Montoya was still in seventh grade. The shuttle fleet would soon be older than some of its astronauts.

The vice president, the NASA administrator, a dozen Secret Service agents, and a host of dignitaries stood at the bottom of the steps, waiting to congratulate the historic mission crew. John wanted to vomit as he stood at the top of the stairs, his head swimming while his vestibular system worked overtime, active for the first time in months. Gingerly, with hands clutching both rails, he took his first step, teetering as he stood tall in the cool bright Florida morning.

Salt air . . . warm sun . . . the odors of diesel fumes and marshes . . . images of saw grass . . . the ocean! Wind! A sugar-white coast rippled in the distance beyond undulating waves of green. His senses overloaded. The sterile world of Alpha had deprived him of sensory inputs he'd forgotten long ago. He was drunk with olfactory wine, and he stumbled as though he would pass out.

John felt like an elderly patient in a rehabilitative hospital as the NASA workers helped him down the steps. Barely able to hold himself erect, he was nevertheless determined to press on. The cycle ergometer had helped, but it hadn't completely prepared him for this. He ignored the cheers, the VIPs, and the bunting, as he tried to make each step count. A fall right now would be humiliating, or worse; his bones might be dangerously brittle after more than a year in space. He babied every step.

At the bottom of the stairs all thoughts of the difficulty evaporated as he met the dignitaries and began to ply their sweaty hands. They offered platitudes that he neither remembered nor cared to hear. Then he spied his family, impatient but maintaining their place behind a distant rope barricade and a bevy of federal agents.

John resented the VIPs and their Secret Service agents who kept Amy and the children bottled up. He completed the reception line as fast as his balance and strength would allow and then pushed out of the queue to walk, unsteadily, toward Amy and the kids. Two NASA technicians followed, one on each side to catch him if he stumbled. For John, all thoughts were gone of space flight, of aliens, of probes, and the loss of his friends at NORTHCOM. There was no space rescue or endurance record or heroism or space sunrise. His only focus was the most precious element of his life: his family.

Amy shook her head and grinned. It was just like John. Out of step and on his own.

His separation from the ranks of the other astronauts was all the inspiration that young Alice needed to make the break and get free. She darted out from under Amy's watch, dodging the G-men and the rope, and ran with abandon across the warm tarmac—a darling little girl in a bright blue dress and pink ribbons, perfect for the cameras. Amy tried to call her back, but it was fruitless.

Amy saw a Secret Service agent start to respond when Alice pushed free, but he let her go as he appeared to answer a call with his cuff mike. Amy yelled for Alice to turn around, and the boys pressed at the rope when their sister bolted. The agents complied and let them all go as the Secret Service suddenly hustled VIPs out of the area. CNN cameramen joined the dash with Amy and her children. The VIPs were soon forgotten. Amy, in a black skirt and blue sweater to match her daughter, chasing little blue Alice—with three blue-jeaned sons at her side—were racing pell-mell to join this historic reunion.

John turned to his handlers, near the end of his strength, with a silent nod for help. For the first time in more than a year, he stood in the sun sweating. Tiny rivers of salt ran down his face, his chest and back. It felt so good, wrapped in the humidity of the seacoast. With a steadying hand under each elbow, John stopped, watching his family and a dozen others run across the pavement. Shimmering heat waves rose in the distance beyond them, an eerie backdrop to a scene he would never forget. John's heart was bursting with love for the outdoors, the sights and sounds, and the bundles of billowing blue, black, and pink on the run toward him.

As Alice neared, he carefully knelt on the concrete in his baggy orange space suit, relieving the demands on his balance system, and opened his arms wide. Little Alice dove headlong into her father's weak grasp with a tearful smile, screaming with glee. "Popp-ee!"

Then Amy was with him, kneeling down and reaching over Alice to embrace John in a long tearful hug.

"It was so long—" she said, choking back what he knew was thirteen hard months of strain. She took his face in her hands, fingers running along the prominent lines of his cheeks and jaw. Children pressed in all around, and the handlers released him to the steadying vise of three boys, a wife, and daughter.

"You're skinny, John-boy," Amy remarked with a laugh after he stood and they embraced in a long kiss. Salty rivers cascaded over her grin into her mouth, her eyes sparkling in the bright sun of the Space Coast.

"You know how I hate to cook . . ." John said, with a broad smile. He kissed her a second time on her forehead, breathing in her familiar scent. Amy's hair fell past her shoulders as John ran his hand the length of it, letting the fine brown silk slide through his fingers as he held her gaze.

"I have a cottage on Galveston's west end," she began, tilting her head back as he stroked her hair slowly. "It's a small place on the beach." She raised her eyebrows with her pixie smile. "A private getaway while Dad and Mom spend time with the kids at our house."

John's smile bridged his ears, crow's feet lining his eyes as he listened to the voice of his bride and marveled at the gleam in her eye.

"I accept," he said. He took her hand in his and placed a steadying hand on her shoulder, as he stooped to kiss her once more. Amy pulled him close in a prolonged embrace.

He touched her lips as they parted. "I've been dreaming of this moment for four hundred days."

She smiled and added, "Me too."

Then he placed a steadying arm on Abe, his teenage son, and another on Amy's shoulder, as the humidity and the gravity began to overwhelm him. Arthur, Albert, and Alice tagged along, tugging at him, as John and his "A-team" began a slow walk toward the crew reception van.

It was time to rejoin humanity and learn how to live on a planet again.

SATURDAY, JANUARY 14, 2012: RICE UNIVERSITY, HOUSTON, TEXAS

Undulating like a nest of snakes, 90,000 ecstatic followers of Malcolm Raines swarmed Rice University's stadium on a crisp mid-January night. Despite the chill, the feverish crowd was a mass of sweating bodies, twisting, raising their hands, and yelling in response to Raines' inspiring exhortations. He raced from one side of the stage to the other, whipping up a frenzy that could be heard far across South Houston. This was no game, but the fervor would have rivaled a powerhouse football grudge match between Rice and Texas A&M.

"You shall not live by bread alone but by the word of God! I bring you that word. Does anyone doubt me?"

Ninety thousand believers bellowed a thunderous "NO!" He raised his hands high and leapt into the air.

"Have I prophesied tonight to confirm that I speak with authority? That I speak for Him?"

The upper and lower decks of the stadium thundered with an ear-splitting "YES!" that reverberated beyond Rice University's legendary tall hedges.

"Tonight I will again proclaim the word." He strode back to the center of the stage, placing his hands on either side of a large garish podium, and cleared his throat. Rushes of "Shoosh!" and cries of "Be quiet!" rippled across the crowd. The next words from Raines were guttural and eerie.

"Women and men of Earth, hear me speak." The voice was rich and deep, an amplified baritone so loud that many felt it rumble in their gut.

"Trust my servant! Believe my word! Do not doubt!"

Raines paused. "This is my word! Remember it—and remember him who proclaims it." He paused again, frozen and erect. He stared straight ahead, his round glasses like two gold-rimmed windows into the soul of some disembodied creature. No one in the crowd moved or spoke.

"You will see my children. Where once there was one, there soon will be two. Do not fear. We are many."

Malcolm Raines blinked once, then wilted in a sudden slump to the floor, like a tall dark body that had lost all its bones. Aides rushed to the platform and caught his head as he fell to the carpeted dais. A burly young man propped up his limp body. In an instant, the stadium went from an eerie silence to pandemonium, screams arising across the mob as people jostled and strained to see. The big TV screens put every person into Raines' ashy face, and soon they saw him begin to stir, as if shaking off a bad dream. Another aide rushed to the podium microphone.

"Please, be silent. Father Raines speaks!"

The tall strong Raines struggled to sit up but flopped back on the floor. He raised his hands and nodded in a silent "I'm okay" gesture to his followers. An aide held a microphone for him, his arms too weak to handle the light weight. "God has spoken!" Raines croaked, his voice raspy and gurgling. "Did we hear him?" The resounding roar, in bone-chilling unison, rattled windows four blocks away.

"YES!"

"Then carry this message! Tell everyone that God speaks. Proclaim the truth. We are called, my friends, to Venture Forth!"

The famous three syllables rose from Rice Stadium like repeated triple blasts from an Army howitzer in the deafening unison of "Venture Forth." Feet stomped and hands clapped. The voices were at last overcome by the *whump-whump* of a blazing fireworks display erupting from the dais. Raines and his entourage slipped away under a rain of sparks.

Offstage, Malcolm Raines recovered in an instant, showing no signs of the spell he had experienced moments ago. He removed his portable microphone and handed it to an aide, then took a comb from an assistant to reset his wave of greased black hair. An armed assistant passed him a note, took the mike and comb, and then disappeared around a corner without speaking to his boss. For a moment Raines was alone. Then, from the shadows, a voice spoke.

"There will be two?"

Raines jerked, eyes probing the darkness as he recognized the man's distinctive voice. He didn't move. "Yes—we will see them. Two. Very soon."

"Good. I am anxious to meet them one day."

"As am I, sir. Perhaps, too, someday, you and I will meet."

"Perhaps. But not soon. Continue to speak your truth." A rustle in the shadow indicated that the visitor was gone.

Raines peered into the dark corner and down a narrow corridor that led under the stadium to the football lockers. As the athletic Raines slipped around the corner, a sudden assault threw him backward against the wall. He was unable to make a sound. Blood-red fingernails dug viciously into his neck, and a slender hand gripped his throat like a vise, forcing him back into the concrete block. He could barely make out a young woman in a tight black jumpsuit, her waist-long braided black hair twisting with her smooth movements. He relaxed.

The woman grabbed his left arm and steadied him, her beauty belying remarkable strength. She released his throat, shaking her head in a silent warning for him not to run, and then beckoned him into the shadows. He followed her into the blackness, compliant and expectant, noting with intrigue the deep red lipstick on her perfect mouth.

28

"WHEN DO YOU HAVE to be back in Houston?" the slender white-haired woman asked as she served a dish of boiled new potatoes, smothered in sweet butter.

"In a week," John replied. "We're about ready to start our 'round the world tour. Doc says I'm good to go."

Becky Wells presided over the family dinner at the farmhouse like a mother hen tending her brood. The food never stopped flowing from her small stuffy kitchen, fueling a dining room that buzzed with Wells family talk. Her old apron slapped the door as she brought a fresh platter of homemade bread to the table. John's mother was always on the move, dressed in her traditional blue chambray shirt and white jeans.

"If you stay through Wednesday, you and the boys could help your dad finish the new stalls—that is, if you're up to it, son. I don't want you to overdo anything," she said, as though pretending to scold him.

She offered John part of a fresh loaf of honey-wheat.

Abe groaned, and John kicked him lightly under the table. "A few days on the farm will be good for us. And I'm well recovered. At least, I think so." He nudged Abe's leg again. "What I can't do, I know Abe'll be glad to finish. Right?" John smiled, but Abe just looked down at his plate.

"The kids want to see some snow, so we're going to drive over to Charlottesville and spend a day up on the Blue Ridge Parkway—if it's open," John said. "A day hike. I think I'm up to that."

"Day hike in the *winter*! I'm *not* up for it," Amy interjected. "We're going for him—not us. But don't sell him short, Mom. Has he told you what the doctor said?" she asked with a lilt in her voice. "If not, I've got to brag on him."

"Please don't—" John began.

"What am I missing here?" Mrs. Wells asked as she began passing the serving dishes around the table. "Tell me more."

"John has the spaceflight version of Lance Armstrong's body," Amy began. "Or else his bicycling really paid off. For the first time in history, apparently, we have in our midst a man who suffered no bone calcium loss or muscle atrophy from long duration space flight. The U.S. space endurance record—yet impossible as it seems, he's as fit today as he was when he left. His muscles are a little weaker, but no worse for wear." Amy beamed at John. "I got him back in one piece. Somewhat of a medical marvel, it would seem."

John blushed and shoveled some food onto his plate. "Nothing to make a fuss over. Let's bless it and eat."

Becky Wells led the family in their traditional rendition of the Girl Scout's "Johnny Appleseed" song, somewhat out of the ordinary for most families but right at home for Becky's brood. The kids sheepishly joined in, unsure of the words. Everyone else sang with gusto and off key. Once the food was blessed, fried okra, green beans, squash casse-role, potatoes, homemade garlic pickles, baked ham, brown gravy, homemade bread, honey, and pitchers of sweet iced tea were passed around the trestle table where John, and three generations before him, had grown up sharing meals. John's father ate quietly at the head of the table while the family chattered and cleaned their plates.

"Pass the honey, please." The elder Mr. Wells spoke his first words of the evening, still dressed in faded denim work clothes and his ever-present green John Deere cap. He broke the hot loaf for his usual dessert of hot bread and clover honey. His salt-and-pepper beard covered a gaunt and deeply wrinkled face, flecked with bits of hayseed from pitch-ing dried timothy and clover to his barn-sheltered cows. After more than sixty years of work on this farm, the suns of countless days had weathered him like a land version of Santiago in Hemingway's *The Old Man and the Sea*, the gray around his mouth casting the gruff look of a permanent frown. Even in his late seventies, he spent twelve hours a day taking care of the family homestead. He lived according to his motto, "Hard work is the essence of the good life."

Mr. Wells finished off the last bite of bread and honey as he shifted his weight in the old ladder-back chair. "So, John. What's all this talk about aliens?"

John paused, choosing his words carefully. "Jury's still out," he finally replied. "But the evidence is pretty convincing. Pictures of our Martian lander have been coming in every day for months. A spherical golden spacecraft, which I witnessed, raced here from Mars and trans-mitted an exact copy of Voyager's Golden Record using an unknown radio format. It's circumstantial, I'll grant you, but on the surface the evidence of intelligent alien life is very convincing."

John grabbed for another crisp garlic pickle, his tenth that night. His stomach would revolt before bedtime.

"Dad says he might go to Mars and meet the aliens, Gramps!" Alice said, squeezing into the conversation and capturing her grandfather's attention. John nearly fumbled the pickle jar.

Becky froze in place. "Is this true?"

John threw his hands up in mock surrender. "Now, just a minute! Nothing's planned. I just meant that it would be pretty neat if I *could* go." He gave his daughter a wink, the left side of his mouth pulled up in a grin, and Alice made a cute thumbs up sign. "They'd never pick me anyway—not if Raines has his way."

He closed the pickle jar and pushed the spicy temptation away.

Amy smiled and wagged her head. "I saw that, John Wells. Something's up."

John raised his hands in surrender a second time. "What? A dad can't smile at his little girl?" He winked at Alice again, and she hid under the table.

"Becky, your son has assured me that if he ever really were considering going to Mars, he'd show us the courtesy to at least ask first. Right, John?" Amy said, staring him down with her famous one-eyed squint.

"You betcha. And if I go, I'm taking Alice with me," he said as he reached under the table to pull the blonde bundle free of his shoes, and stop her attempt to tie his laces together during dinner. With Alice plopped back in her chair and the food moving again, the conversation resumed.

"Why not?" his father asked quietly during a lull in the din.

"Why not what?" John asked.

"Why wouldn't NASA pick you? And what's that have to do with this fellow—what'd you say his name was?"

"Raines, dear," Becky said, with a wink toward John. "He still doesn't read the paper, son. Too busy . . . as always." His mother got up from the table to begin clearing the dishes.

John smiled and nodded slightly, "Malcolm Raines is a preacher from Phoenix, Dad. He predicted that we'd hear from the Voyager spacecraft. When the probe transmitted the Voyager messages and images, lots of people assumed he had all the answers to their questions. Now he's a leading advocate for the manned mission to Mars. Some say he's also the catalyst for the president's Mars initiative. An impressive, effective, and politically savvy fellow. He's also the guy who whipped up a fuss two weeks ago predicting there are 'many'—by which he presumably meant many aliens." John looked away. "But I don't like him."

"Why not?" his mother asked as she picked up more plates from the table. "You said he's 'impressive.'"

John saw Amy look back at him from the sink a room away and shake her head, but John plowed on. "As a public speaker and a basketball player, he's the best. But that's not what I meant." John paused, watching Amy as she stared directly at him. He looked away, and back at his father. "I think Raines is a false prophet."

John turned to see Amy sigh, roll her eyes, and bend over the dishes.

Walter Wells's bushy eyebrows drew down. "I asked about the aliens, son, not about church."

"Like it or not, Dad, church is where this conversation is headed. And not just at our dinner table, but all over the world. We need to talk about this. Everyone does. Lots of people are scared, and this alien thing takes them to the raw edge of their faith. They don't know what to believe. Plastic preachers like Raines take advantage of that confusion."

The uncharacteristic silence was a sure sign that fireworks were coming. Mrs. Wells scurried into the kitchen. Amy called to the children who took the cue and disappeared. In an instant, John and his father were alone at the worn table.

The old man sighed and leaned back. "Why does everythin' we

ever talk about come back to religion?" His scowl was intimidating.

"You asked who Raines was. He's a national celebrity. It's not my fault you don't read the paper or watch the news."

"Might if I had the time. Not my fault I'm the only one left to run this farm either, is it?"

"We've been through this a hundred times, Dad. You had two sons. One left home and joined the Navy. The other got married and moved a mile down the road. Neither one of us is here to help you every day, yet you resent me . . . not him. It's old news, Dad. Thirty-five-year-old news."

"At least your brother stayed close to home. When I need him, he comes."

"Great! I'm happy for him. I love this farm, and I loved growing up here. But it's not the life I wanted." John toyed with his last piece of bread in frustration. "Do we have to plow this ground every time I visit?"

Both men sat in silence, their wives rustling in the kitchen behind them, on occasion peeking in through the crack in the swinging door.

"This farm's been in our family for four generations," his father said. "Someday—not long from now—I won't be able to work it anymore. Your brother's not gonna live here, and you're certainly not. So, where's that leave me—and your mom?"

"It leaves you both doing the good job you're doing now, not spending so much time worrying about whether I follow in your footsteps."

"Easy to say. Lots harder to do," the old man said, picking hay chaff from his beard. "So—what does this Raines fella have to do with Alice pipin' up about goin' to Mars? You're as qualified as anybody."

"I *am* as qualified—probably more than most. But Raines thinks people like me will try to sabotage any effort to learn about aliens because life on other planets supposedly conflicts with what's taught in the Bible."

The scowl on his father's face grew ever deeper. "Well, does it?"

"No. If you gave me ten minutes, I could show you the proof. But the fact of the matter is that NASA's very political, and politics usually drives the selection process. Raines is close to the vice president, and he's been trying to sway the crew selection his way. It doesn't matter anyway. I'm out of the running, for several reasons, not the least of which is that I just got back from a thirteen-month mission."

"Maybe if you'd stop wearin' your religion on your sleeve, you could get through life a little easier."

"Is that really what you think, that I wear my faith on my sleeve? That I parade it around?"

His father plucked a burr free from his chin and turned to face John. "Yes. Like tonight. You look for every chance to bring up the God stuff. I'm tired of it."

"At least we're talking, right?" John looked straight at his dad. "But I disagree with you about whether I push my beliefs on people."

"You tell them they're wrong if they don't think like you do," his father replied, his deep-set eyes boring into John.

"Sometimes it's better to tell the truth than to tell people what they want to hear. What do you tell Everett Kile if he's planning to cut hay just before the weather service says we'll get three days of rain? Do you tell him he's wrong or compliment him on his rugged individuality?"

"You tell him he's stupid, that's what. Anyway, Everett knows better than that. But it's still pushin'. Like tellin' folks that they'll go to hell if they don't get right with God—that's a bunch of bull."

"How can you be so sure?" John asked.

"What do you mean, 'how can I be so sure?' Show me the proof, son. I'm listenin'."

"Okay. Look at it this way." John used a pen from his pocket to draw a circle on the paper napkin that Amy had left behind. He pushed it over to his father. "Suppose this circle represents all the knowledge in the world. Fill in the part of the circle that represents the part that you already understand."

The gruff farmer growled under his breath. "Don't insult me, boy, just because I don't have a college degree. I know a lot of things about this life that you'll never learn." His father snapped his chair back from the table and stood up, eyes narrowed into little slits peering out from under bushy brows.

John's voice rose right along with his father's. "I'm not putting you down. I'm answering your question. Why can't we have a rousing conversation like two adults without you running off every time? Hear me out, will you?"

The elder Wells stood over the old trestle table his grandfather had built for his own wife, eyes flashing fire.

"I'm not talking about school learning, Dad. The point I want to make is that all of our individual knowledge surely doesn't even represent more than a dot in this circle when compared to all the knowledge in the world today." He imprinted a small blue dot in the center the napkin.

"So, if all I do understand is only a small dot in this circle, then isn't it possible that there's an awful lot I don't know? Isn't it possible that there may be some answers I don't have, that there might be a God, might be an alien, might even be a possibility that I haven't thought of?"

The old farmer stood over the napkin and stared at the circle, pushing his sweat-stained green cap back on his head, exposing gray tufts of hair where there had once been a hairline. Then he reached over and crumpled up the napkin, tossing it into his sticky dinner plate. "It's possible."

Walter Wells turned, walked out of the dining room onto the porch and headed out toward the barn. The old screen door slammed behind him as the spring snapped it shut.

John's mother looked up from the sink in the kitchen and then lowered her head, shaking it slowly from side to side. Amy put down the drying towel and went out to the dining room where John sat with his head in his hands. She placed both hands on his shoulders, waiting silently.

"I could use your advice," he finally volunteered. "I did it again."

Amy massaged his shoulders, then sat down beside him. "I hope you'll give me the benefit of some advance notice if NASA really did want to talk to you about that mission," Amy said as she caressed his neck, watching some of the tension drain from him. After a few moments of silence, she said, "Now, go after him. Don't let it end here. Keep reaching out. That might be all it takes. He's more stubborn than you are, that's for sure."

John looked up and managed a smile. "Okay. I'll go. Pray for him—for us," he said.

She squeezed his hand, nodding.

John pushed the porch door open; it creaked as the rusty spring stretched for the millionth time. A light dusting of snow fell off the cracked white paint as it slammed shut once more.

All around him were the works of his father's hands, his own hands, and those of his brother. The red barn still showed signs of the two coats of paint he had applied when he was twelve years old—weeks of hot work and ruined clothes. The old bull pen was proof that he'd sunk railroad ties in frozen December ground with the help of buckets of hot water, a dull posthole digger, and lots of muscle power. The garden was still surrounded by the old white picket fence he'd built as a young boy for summer spending money.

As he walked to the barn in the cold West Virginia night, he remembered his last trip home, the magical and frantic summer of 2010 before his mission to Alpha. Fireflies had danced above the distant clover fields by the thousands in a mating ritual that rivaled any fireworks display while a whippoorwill called down in the creek bottom behind the house. The evening fog, the sights, the sounds, the sweet smell of the drying clover hay, all had flooded John's senses with memories of thousands of nights as a child on this farm. They were also vivid memories of a passion to break away, to fly, to get up into the sky and touch the stars. He remembered so many nights of lying on his back in the fields, watching for satellites and meteors, dreaming of escape. He wondered if he'd ever contemplated the pain that his departure would create in his relationship with his stoic father. The successes he'd found as a pilot in the Navy, and in astronaut selection, seemed bittersweet tonight. They'd torn him from the family that he loved.

The elder Mr. Wells stood with his arms draped over the top rail of the bull pen near a graying oak cattle chute. He was motionless, hands clasped, staring off into the distance toward Middle Island Creek beyond the barn, shivering slightly in the cold wind.

John knew the stare. It was his "thinking" look.

Amy had called his dad stubborn. And Walter Wells, all one hundred kilos of him, sinew and very little fat on a gray and wrinkled body, was indeed that. He was a mule of a man at work and in person. John had inherited a good dose of that mule himself.

Father and son were silent for several minutes, until the elder Wells spoke. "Expect I'll probably cut the equivalent of twelve thousand square bales next year. Want to see my new round baler?" he asked.

John nodded.

Both men walked into the pole barn and made small talk under the light of a buzzing sodium lamp as they admired the tall red New Holland machinery. The hay in the big barn was stacked to the roof in huge round bales, and the air was pungent with the aroma of cured clover and timothy, mixing with the diesel scent of the tractors. They inhaled deeply in the cold night air.

"Somethin' over here I want to show you, son." His father pushed aside some old implements and dug into a corner near the silage silo, eventually pulling out an ancient garden cultivator with long weathered oak handles, an ancient iron wheel on the front, and rusty tines.

"You ought to put that out in front of the house, Dad. Some city lady would pay you good money for it." They both laughed. Once a woman from Parkersburg, lost in her travels in the country, had bought all six chairs at their dinner table for fifty dollars each. The family sat on apple crates for a month while his father made a new set of ladder-backs with rush seats, and his mother hoarded the money.

"Yeah. Somebody might buy it, but it's not for sale. This old girl has a story she needs to tell. Tonight's as good a time as any."

Walter Wells wasn't a storyteller. In fact, he wasn't much of a talker. Tonight John listened as his father began to weave the tale of a hot dry summer, parched earth in the garden, and his grandfather's attempt to cultivate baked West Virginia clay. The old man looked at the ground and away from John.

"Your Gramps was stubborn, I reckon. Every time I see this old cultivator, I think about him. Never been able to turn this loose," his father said, admiring the ancient sod buster. He pulled the rickety tool over against an oil-stained wall near the tractors, then leaned back against a giant tractor tire, slumping as though under a heavy weight.

"My dad wore his religion on his sleeve, too, John. I guess that's why sometimes you grate on me so much." The old farmer's voice cracked; he seemed to be forcing the story out.

"Dad was a hardline Church of Christ man, and he didn't mind tellin' you so. Every Sunday he packed the seven of us into the old wagon, and off we went to the church in Pursley. Three miles each way, rain or shine, in any weather. At first, I went 'cause I was s'posed to. But I was the oldest, like you, and I resented it—resented his stubborn attitude and a hard-core religion that ate up my only free day." His voice grew softer, his hands now jammed into his overalls.

"I started to identify church—and Sunday—with all the pain I felt as a kid. I wanted out of this farm in more ways than I could count. But Dad was determined that I'd take over the place. I tried to enlist when Korea broke out, but they sent me home classified 4-F. I looked for a job in town, applied for work in Wheeling, even thought about going to the steel factories in Pittsburgh. I tried to reason with Dad, but he wouldn't hear it. Years went by, raisin' cattle, mowin' hay, shovelin' snow and manure. Somehow, I was still here."

John winced.

His father pushed away from the tractor tire and again took the cultivator in his hands. "One summer, Dad hitched up the mule to go out and bust up some dirt. No real reason to. It was so dry that August that nothin' would grow, but Dad couldn't ever sit still. It was hot as blazes—no breeze. The mule was in no hurry to go, and it took him a while to hitch her. Finally Dad got her out into the garden, such as it was with no rain, and tried to break the dirt. The old cultivator just skittled along on top of that hard clay and never dug in. Finally, he jumped on the rear tines, but the mule couldn't pull it, with him on, and it spiked into hard earth. So he got off and whacked the mule with his belt . . ."

His father paused. John watched the old man's cracked, powerful hands caressing the ancient oak handles, touching the tines with his boot, as though reliving that moment of so many years ago.

"Mule wouldn't budge. He kicked the old thing, but she stood her ground. Then he went over to the side of the barn and grabbed a two-by-four. He brought that wood back and walked up to the mule's head, grabbed the bridle, and started yellin' at her. I watched 'em from the porch and almost laughed myself silly, Dad yellin' at that dumb old mule. I'll never forget what he said, though. Can hear it like he was standin' here now.

"'You dumb mule, you'll never win. Now pull that thing or else.' The mule stood still, and Dad took that pole and whacked her up side the head. At first it was funny, but he kept hittin' her—hard." Walter coughed and quickly turned away. Then, with eyes moist but free of tears, he turned back, kicking the dry dust of the barn floor while he massaged the handles of the old cultivator, oblivious, it seemed, to John's presence.

"After a while, it wasn't funny any more. I ran off the porch and asked him to stop beatin' her. He glared at me and sent me back to the house. I was scared. He kept sayin', 'You'll never win!' I can't forget that. I felt like he was beatin' me. I stumbled back to the house and watched from the step. He beat that mule for near on five minutes. Each blow took somethin' out of him—and her. Gradually, he got to where he couldn't hold up the wood, and the mule couldn't quite stand. They fell on the ground at the same time. I just sat there."

John's father choked on his words, his voice trailing off, hands massaging the handles, an occasional foot kicking at the red clay and hay chaff.

John hesitated, then put his hand on his dad's shoulder. He wasn't sure whether to hold him, or watch him.

His father turned, deep-set eyes swollen, pointing back to the cultivator handles. He coughed and pulled out a soiled bandana to blow his nose. "I . . . I sat there, on the porch, watchin' 'em both lay in the garden. I got worried . . . and went out there, mostly, I think, to check on the old mule. She was hurt and pantin'—but Dad didn't move. I called to him. Then I kneeled down and realized he wasn't breathin'. I shook him, but it didn't help." He let go of the cultivator and leaned back on the tall tractor tire, his cheeks flush with the pain his eyes wanted to shed.

"I yelled for Momma. She came a runnin', started screamin' when she got close and saw what'd happened. She fell on him cryin' and tryin' to revive him. I just stood there, stuck on his last words: 'You'll never win.'" He paused for a long minute, eyes focused on something far away.

John reached out to touch the weathered oak handles of the old implement. He remembered trying to push the cultivator through the garden when he was a boy and his dad watching from his tractor seat, frozen stiff like a statue. Now that he knew this story, many memories flooded back, dark family mysteries answered at last. "I'm so sorry, Dad."

"Don't be sorry, John." His father choked a half-laugh. "No, don't be sorry. No one's ever talked of it. We didn't want anyone to know your Gramps died 'cause he lost his temper and beat a mule senseless. We pulled him 'cross the garden and back to the porch, got the neighbors, and—well—you know the rest of the story. Far's anyone else in Sistersville or Middlebourne knows, he died of a heart attack and fell outta his rockin' chair."

The old man walked away from the tractor and out into the night beyond the barn. John followed, taking deep breaths of the icy night air, clover scent mixing with the heavy damp smell of the creek bottom.

"Somewhere between the garden and the barn," his father said, "leading away that half-dead mule, it hit me. He was right. I was never gonna win. My father was dead. As the oldest son I'd have to pull the family together, run this farm, and carry on. My dreams—they weren't big dreams, mind you—but my dreams all died that day with him. I resented him for killin' himself and stickin' me with the farm, for his pushin' church on me, for lots of things." He took several deep breaths as John stood by his side in the shine of the bright farm lamp.

"Then you come along, all full of vim and vigor, determined to get off the farm and conquer the universe. I was determined that you were gonna stay here with me and work this place. Wasn't 'til you were up on that space station that I realized why I wanted that so bad—why I wanted to make sure you stayed." He kicked a dry cow pie.

"Dang it, son. You just marched right out of here against my will, like I didn't have a rein on you or nothin'—to college, to the Navy, to astronaut. And here I was, still pushin' cow dung." He kicked another cow pie, much harder this time, and it shattered into dust on his muddy boot. "The day you left for college, I could still hear your Gramps tellin' me I'd never win."

He turned and faced his son, putting his hands on his John's shoulders. He drew in a deep snort. "When you left, I resented you, son. I resented your freedom, your success, and especially your escape. When you 'found God,' as you called it, and started tellin' me all about it, you scratched some deep scars. So—I resented your religion, too." He looked down at the ground. "I'm sorry for that."

John's heart cracked as his father bared his inner self, no longer the proud stoic. This sudden outpouring was a moment John had hungered for his entire life, yet it scared him. He wanted to hug his dad, but he hadn't done that since elementary school.

The elder Mr. Wells backed away, giving John some room as he continued.

"Your Momma was wrong, John. I do read the paper. Usually pull it out of the trash in the mornin', while she's asleep. Read it front to back, coffee grinds and all. I read all about your rescue of that Russian fella, and it got me to thinkin'. I burned about a hundred gallons of diesel in the tractor wonderin' 'bout you and how you handled that problem, and me watchin' my dad from the porch step. You took matters in your own hands when all hope was lost. You didn't give up, even when you had no chance of gettin' that Russian in alive. But I gave up. I didn't help Dad when he was tirin' out. I didn't leave and strike out on my own. I just stayed. I love this place now, mind you. But I didn't grab my opportunities like you did. For a long time, I've resented you for that." He looked John straight in the eyes. "I'm sorry."

John was speechless.

"I was—I *am*—like that mule. Determined to make up my own mind about who God is and not let Dad beat his ways into me with that two-by-four he called 'Sunday.' I'm just like your Gramps, too. I won't move, and I won't quit. I'm so stubborn that I keep beatin' a dead horse." He put his hand on John's shoulder. "I was wrong, son. Wrong to try to hold you back . . . wrong to be so mad about you leavin'. I don't want to be that mule—or your Gramps—any more."

The old man, his craggy face wracked by emotion, with an uncharacteristic smile breaking under the unkempt, graying beard, stood all alone. For a long moment neither man moved. Then John, who wanted the hug he'd not felt since he was a little boy, stepped forward and embraced his father. The moment broke them both. Two generations of strong Wells men hugged each other tight, both filled with joy and regret in the frosty January night air.

29

THE YOUNG ROBED PRIEST surveyed the flock of his small Episcopal parish in historic Fredericksburg, Virginia, on a cold winter Sunday morning. The crush and rush of the holiday season was over, and his mostly-white-haired congregation was dwindling again in the doldrums of a post-Christmas spiritual morass. How he'd love to be rid of the hype and keep the season sacred. At least his people wouldn't be so tired. He wanted to scream "Wake up!"

He shook his head as he took his usual place at the lectern, moving his sermon notes about. He took a deep breath, then another, and looked up at the congregation at last, determined to press forward with renewed vigor. Determined to end their blind embrace of falsehood.

"We're being lied to." He kept his eyes focused on the sleeping people in the pews.

A few heads popped up and even more as the silence endured.

"*You* are being lied to," he said, pointing a finger toward various members of his flock, then pausing again, as he waited for a sea of eyes to meet his. "We are—you are—being fed a false gospel that is magnified and manipulated by the media. It needs to stop."

He felt his heart pounding but was renewed by a surge of courage as he brought this important word to a tiny sliver of the kingdom. He would not fail in delivering the message he felt called to preach.

"Hear the words of the apostle Paul in his second letter to his friend Timothy: *'I give you this charge: Preach the Word; be prepared in season and out of season; correct, rebuke and encourage—with great patience and careful instruction. For the time will come when men will not put up with sound doctrine. Instead, to suit their own desires, they will gather around them a great number of teachers to say what their itching ears want to hear.'*

"Two weeks ago, the charismatic so-called preacher, Malcolm Raines, held a massive rally in Houston, Texas. He had some disparaging things to say about those of us who claim Jesus Christ as King. He lifted up his prophecies as God-given messages and twisted the meaning of Scripture. I don't normally tackle current events from this pulpit, but I feel as called to preach the Word in and out of season as he does to manipulate it to his own gain. You are being lied to, and used, by Malcolm Raines."

The parish, what there was of them, fidgeted in their seats, uncomfortable, he was sure, with this departure from the usual book report or dry-bones apologetic. He turned up the heat and drove on.

"I don't know whether there are aliens or not. It doesn't matter to me, and it doesn't affect my faith. I believe what I read in Scripture. In Genesis. *'Thus the heavens and the earth were completed in all their vast array.'* There's plenty of room in that statement for other life forms, if need be. But when Raines stands up and tells the world that he proclaims the word of God, and then lifts himself up as an oracle and an object of praise and worship, he has gone too far. You need to be discerning and pay attention to what's happening around you."

He swept his arms across the congregation, some heads nodding approval. "Malcolm Raines is a *false prophet*. He said that Christians would proclaim him so, and he was right about that one thing. He calls on our government to apply a litmus test to those who can participate in the space program, in this new mission to Mars. A litmus test of faith. Again, be discerning. We are in the midst of a spiritual battle, and we must be heard."

The young priest tapped his head. "God gave us inquiring minds, and we need to seek wisdom to connect what we observe with the truths that He teaches. Science is a God-given tool to help us discover truth." He paused as he drew in a deep breath, and leaned forward into the lectern, toward his audience.

"We are commanded to never be lukewarm. We need powerful, outspoken faith in Christ as part of this national quest for answers about alien life. Consider this before you pass judgment on the role of faith in our space program: Perhaps these aliens, if they do exist, are reaching out to *us* for the answers."

MONDAY, JANUARY 30, 2012: WASHINGTON, DC

"L'Enfant Plaza Station!" cried the conductor on the Virginia Railway Express.

Marv Booker shook himself from his thoughts and peered out the window of the train as it crossed the new Potomac River Bridge. He longed for the quiet five-minute drive to work from his Clear Lake City neighborhood, a short half-mile across the highway from the space center near Houston. He shifted his tall cowboy frame in the painful molded plastic train seat, his broad leather belt pressing sharply into his back. Today, in the midst of the gray winter cold, Texas seemed so very far away.

Marv had spent all of his adult life in the space business, and most of that near Houston, Texas. Born on the Gulf Coast in Galveston, raised in nearby Texas City, a loyal Texas Aggie with thirty years of service to NASA in flight operations at the Johnson Space Center, Marv was now rewarded with the famous NASA golden handshake—what he viewed as an ignominious promotion to a headquarters job in Washington, DC. As NASA's associate administrator, Marv was in charge of all manned space flight. That was the good news. The bad news was that his job made him the focal point of the most heated crew selection process and media frenzy of his career. And instead of being in good old Texas, he was in Washington, a crazed metropolis where people ogled his oyster button shirts, pointed boots, and broad belt buckle, sometimes whispering that he must be a retired rodeo performer.

Marv stopped at a small coffee shop before he reached NASA Headquarters. Outside, a homeless woman tipped an empty soft drink cup in his direction. Marv waved at her, went on in, and bought a small mocha. He sat in the back corner, where he cradled the hot cup between his hands, deep in thought.

Marv was a lifelong Episcopalian, raised from the cradle in St. Michael's Episcopal Church in La Marque, Texas. He'd been baptized and married in that church, and was an active member of the congregation for the thirty-plus years since his marriage. He'd seen many controversies come and go in the Episcopal Church, and he'd weathered some thorny ones that never seemed to die.

Yet, until yesterday's sermon at his new parish in Fredericksburg, he'd never come face-to-face with his personal beliefs. Now he wondered where he really stood in this faith of his, and whether it was a faith he was willing to risk persecution for. He craved the conviction that his priest had shown in the past twenty-four hours. Was he willing to take on the NASA system, perhaps even the White House? Was he willing to insist on the best man for the job, even if it meant taking a stand against the Rocket Reverend and his politically correctness test for astronauts?

The coffee warmed his hands as he considered his options to make a difference. He could weigh in heavily in his role as Associate Administrator for Manned Space Flight. He was at the pinnacle of his career with little to lose, headed toward retirement. With the biggest exploration mission of his life ahead of him, he wanted with all his heart to stay on, even if it was in Washington. Yet Sunday's words haunted him.

He dialed a number on his cell phone. Jack Schmidt would be in his office at the Johnson Space Center, early as usual. Jack was his closest friend and the new director of flight operations, promoted into Marv's old job. The phone rang three times before Jack picked it up.

"Hey, Marv. What's on your mind?"

"How'd you know it was me?"

"Caller ID, pal. It's been around a long time. I got me a real phone when you left. Yours must have been twenty years old."

"Twenty-five, actually," Marv replied. "At least it had touch tone."

"So, what's up?"

"Selection issues. There's a new twist I heard yesterday that has me ready to finally commit on a crew roster." Marv jostled the hot cup as he searched for the right words.

"Wow, this is a first!" Jack said. "You've never been one to jump on a decision before its time, Marv." Both men laughed because Jack was right; Marv was a consummate politician in the NASA job, and that had proven to be a valuable survival skill over time.

"It's about Hawk," Marv said, hoping for Jack's support.

"Yeah. Figured as much. You know, we haven't even talked to him about it yet. Suspect he'd jump at the chance, though, if I know him. But he's way out on the Bible-thumper limb, Marv."

"So what? We need a Mr. Fixit on this mission, Jack. With old man Edwards' cheap rocket, we might need a downright miracle worker. Look at the roster. Every astronaut wants this mission, most have the experience, and many have the science credentials. Some even have political backing. But no one in the astronaut corps has this guy's combination of flight experience, time on orbit, and mechanical savvy. And I'll bet none of them have the tolerance he does to zero-G. D'you see those results from his post-flight medical report? Incredible."

"Yeah. He's got all that going for him, and more."

"Religious or not, if we have to patch this thing together halfway back from Mars, he's the one I'd want in the flight engineer's seat." Marv hesitated a moment. "And I'm willing to take on the system to get him on the crew."

"You are? I've been around this selection pole a hundred times, Marv. Few people I know make the grade, and Hawk's probably one of the best. But you know what I'm up against. Director Church already has his own ideas about this roster, and he'll be impossible to stop. Then, of course, there's this Raines guy. Very powerful. And close to the veep."

"Don't cross the director, Jack. Or the vice president. You still have a career down there, at least until they ship you up to DC like they did me."

"No thanks."

"My point exactly."

"Are you gonna crucify yourself to win this one, Marv?"

He thought about that comment, and yesterday's sermon, for a moment before he answered. "Interesting choice of words. Yeah, I guess that's what I've decided to do. Put it all on the line, so to speak. Sometimes you have to take a stand, and—I just can't let this one slide."

"It's your life, Marv. But I agree with you, off the record of course. I wish John and the rest of his Bible-thumpin' crowd here in the astronaut office could keep their Jesus-talk to themselves, but there's no doubt he's the right guy for this mission. So, what do you want me to do?"

"Tell me what Church is up to. If the director starts a big push, I need to know. My position at headquarters will be that Wells is the best mission specialist we have, and the only one with the engineering and fix-it skills to make this mission a success. He holds the U.S. space endurance record and he's the only person to ever conduct a rescue in EVA."

"Not good enough."

"And his bones won't break. Come on, Jack. I know all that won't beat the vice president, Malcolm Raines, and Director Church. But wouldn't it at least be good enough for fourth place?"

"You mean, get him on backup, and if someone falls through, he flies?"

"Now you're talkin'. It's the same approach we've used a dozen times. Sometimes we get our best crews that way."

"It's our only option at this point. Hawk as the alternate. Will you push it hard in DC, so I can deflect some heat down here?"

"I will. I appreciate this, Jack. I really do."

"Don't thank me, Marv. You're the one who's putting it all on the line. Just promise me you'll watch my back."

FRIDAY, FEBRUARY 3, 2012: APPALACHIAN TRAIL, NEAR SWEET RUN GAP, VIRGINIA

Sweet gums, red oaks, poplars, and maples stood stark naked against a gray sky, tall sentinels along the Appalachian Trail where it ran adjacent to Virginia's Blue Ridge Parkway. John, Amy, and their children snaked through the cold woods and a dusting of snow as they wound their way toward a lunch stop a kilometer farther north. The only sounds were the rustle of feet on fallen leaves, the scamper of a rare squirrel, and Alice's frequent "Shhh! I see one" when yet another deer crossed their path. Clouds blew across the face of the ridge immersing the family in an icy, wet tumbling fog.

"I'm freezing, John," Amy said with a shiver while they walked, pulling her coat tighter. "But I have to admit, this is incredible. Hiking never was my idea of a good time, but you might change my mind. Are you sure the boys are okay?"

"They'll be fine," John replied, watching Alice a few meters ahead in the freezing mist. "You can't get lost on this trail as long as you don't go down hill. The parkway is only thirty meters to our left."

Alice stopped with her finger to her lips, bending slightly at the knees. Amy and John crept up behind her, following her point to a large dark shape in swirling clouds ahead of them.

"Look at the rack on that one!" John whispered as he knelt beside his spellbound daughter, the three of them entranced by a massive twelve-point buck that had materialized out of the mist. Alice grabbed her daddy's hand, her heart pounding in his grip. The boiling mountain fog whispered gently as it blew across them, the only sound in the hush of this winter mountaintop forest.

Still as a statue, the regal buck regarded the family impassively, exhaling a cloud of vapor about his face in the cold air. Suddenly, the animal turned its head in the direction of the trail to the north, sniffing swirling currents and ignoring John, Amy, and Alice.

As quickly as the buck had appeared, it bolted from view, to escape whatever threatened it in the fog beyond. Crashing through the once-silent woods, the majestic animal disappeared down the mountain. The three Wellses crouched by the trail in awe, watching the creature bounding downhill through the bare gray woods.

At that moment, seemingly out of nowhere, a hiker emerged from the mist. "Hullo there!" the young man hailed them, pulling up short as he suddenly made out the shape of three people crouched in the snowy trail.

John held Alice's hand as they all stood up. "Hello yourself. Did you see the buck?"

"Yeah! He was a monster, wasn't he?"

"He was. Where you headed?" John asked, reaching to help Amy up with one hand.

"I'm, like, a ridge runner for the Potomac Appalachian Trail Club. You a day hiker? Not many folks crazy enough to come up here this time of year."

"Crazy? How'd you guess?" Amy joked, her ice-covered fanny pack slung over her shoulder for the moment. John saw her shiver now that they'd stopped moving.

The young man took off his light pack and leaned it against a wet rock outcropping as he spoke. "You must be John Wells."

John's jaw dropped, and he pulled Amy and Alice closer. Both of his girls were shaking now.

"How'd you know? I mean—yes—I am. And you are—?" John extended his free hand, a puzzled expression on his face.

"Mack Bakken, and it's an honor, Mr. and Mrs. Wells. It didn't take too long to find you." He laughed. "You're the only people—I mean the *only* ones—on the trail today."

Amy poked John in the side and pulled her wrap closer, then snugged Alice's hood tight. Her gaze bored in on the stranger. "You were looking for us? Did you see three teenage boys up ahead?"

"Yes, ma'am. And they're fine, taking a break up at the next bend. Beaned me with a snowball. Scared the wits out of me at first. But no harm done. Anyway, folks in Houston knew you were somewhere up here. That's why they sent me."

"Has there been an accident?" Amy asked, grabbing John's arm.

"No, ma'am. Everything's fine, you know. There's some news, though, that NASA wanted to get to you. It's awesome."

John grinned at the throwback speech of this college-age boy. "Go on, Mack. You've got our attention."

"Great! You know, the radio communication with the alien ship, or whatever it is on Mars, has been off for a while? Yesterday that Raines guy came on CNN and all and said that God had given him an awesome vision of the sun setting on the human race if we don't embrace change and open our minds—or something like that. Anyway, you know, he's pretty strange."

Mack's parody of Raines' voice brought laughs from everyone including Alice. "Sure enough, that radio with the alien on Mars, or whatever, is fixed and working now. What's really freaky, you know, is the first image from Mars was a sunset, just like he said in his vision. Weird, huh?"

"That's an understatement," Amy replied, stroking Alice's misty-wet coat while she stood gaping at the news and the messenger. She shoved her hands in the pockets of her parka and stamped her feet.

John stared in the direction the buck had fled. "How could he know the Mars link would come back up?" he asked, of no one in particular.

"Old Raines' got people pretty freaked out and all. NASA called the Appalachian Trail folks in Harper's Ferry, and they called us at Big Meadows. Sent me after you. Anyway, that's not all they wanted me to tell you."

"There's more?" Amy said, wrinkling her wet brow.

John tried hard to suppress a smile. He knew his wife wasn't amused by the boy or his news. And everyone, including John, was cold.

Mack looked at Amy, down at Alice, and then back to John, savoring the message as though he'd considered how to deliver it for twenty kilometers and three hours of freezing trail. The whisper of the blowing freezing mist was barely audible in the silence of the boy's pause.

"The second message is really sweet." He took his time, soaking up the moment. "NASA wants to talk to the senior astronauts right away — to decide who's going to Mars."

"You just got back! How can they?" she cried. "I don't know if I can do this, John — be the wife of a Martian astronaut." Amy bowed her head, her shoulders slumped from the sudden stress of the runner's news. Her heart raced again, and she knew exactly why this time. She ignored the pounding. "I know that's not what you want to hear — but it's the *truth*." She looked up at him and touched John's cold face with a trembling hand. "Please, please John. Promise me that you won't do this."

John cradled her in his arms as they sat by the trailside in silence, their four children looking on and the ridge runner long gone in the direction of Big Meadows.

Abe, Arthur, Albert, and Alice, the Wells "A Team," ages thirteen, eleven, eight, and six, were all together now, silent. Their daypacks still on their backs, the four children stood stamping their feet and watching their parents, huddled tightly together by the side of the Appalachian Trail, pondering the possibility that, of six billion people on planet Earth, John might be one of those chosen to fly to Mars.

"What's everybody so upset about? This is great!" Arthur exclaimed, breaking the silence. "But we gotta get going or I'm gonna freeze!"

Amy nodded silently toward her son. John's arms were wrapped around her while she leaned into him from her seat on the ground where she'd collapsed in tears and shivers minutes earlier. She began to speak in a quiet voice, fighting the cold as she measured her words carefully, and reached out to Alice to pull her close.

"Sit down for just a minute, boys," she said. "I know you're cold. We all are. But I have something to say."

Abe took off his pack, and his brothers followed his lead, the three of them in a campfire-like semicircle around their parents and Alice, jackets drawn tightly about them.

"John, I've always tried to be the loyal, supportive Navy wife. I've worked hard to put a happy face on whatever test life dealt us—including this day—and I want you to know, I won't stop doing that. I will always be there for you, and somehow," she said, wiping the frozen drizzle from her face, "with God's help, I'll smile my way through this next trial if I have to. But—" she began, stopping to take a deep breath, her voice quaking. "—you need to hear something I've kept bottled up for a long time." She took two long breaths, no one speaking.

"I've followed you everywhere, John Wells. Through half a dozen household moves in twenty-five years, a war, three years of separation on Navy deployments, nearly fourteen years of astronaut training and space flight, three awful shuttle launches on rickety old spaceships, and thirteen months with you stuck in orbit while someone attacked our country and some alien thing landed on Mars—never knowing if or when you'd come home. I've been there for you through four hard pregnancies—" Amy looked up at her wet shivering boys, smiling as she swept her head in an arc, regarding three healthy well-adjusted young men.

"—four at-risk pregnancies in my thirties when I was sick as a dog or stretched out like a drum—four kids I've pretty much raised by myself. Until Houston, there never was a real home we could call our own, just base housing or tiny rentals with roaches and ants and leaky pipes and nasty landlords. We moved to Houston, just for you, John. A sterile stucco wasteland of concrete, heat, and traffic while you worry us with your trips to space." She turned to face him, eyes puffy but dry. "Although right now I wish we had some of that heat," she said, with a tiny smile.

Alice nodded.

"I know this is your greatest dream, honey. We'll find a way to support you in this, and enjoy it—somehow—but I'm asking you, now, before we go home, before we're under the lights of the reporters and surrounded by our neighbors and other astronauts—while it's just us, a *family*—please don't do this! Let's be a family, for good. Let's watch the kids grow up and then slip into old age in a quaint little home in Brunswick while we bounce grandchildren on our knees. We've climbed the mountain, John. Now let's take a rest. Lord knows, we both deserve it."

Amy stopped, taking another deep shaking breath. She looked down at Alice's head in her lap, her daughter a bundle of blue L.L. Bean material. Amy poked some frozen blonde strands under her hood in silence as they all sat together, cradled in the gentle whisper of the swirling mountain mist.

John watched Amy's trembling hand caress their daughter, his own hands on Amy's shoulders as she leaned back against him. The boys waited in silence, knees pulled up to their chins, arms wrapped around for warmth.

"It's cold, and we need to get moving," John said after a long delay. "But you're right. We *have* climbed the mountain, and largely thanks to you. I recognize that, and you know how much I appreciate it. We've discussed this before."

"Yes," Amy said, still facing Alice.

"You have my promise, Amy." He pulled on her shoulder, encouraging her to look up at him.

"Your *promise?*" she said, her voice cracking.

"I've got to admit . . . I've seen this news coming, and I've worn my knees out in prayer over it. But I kept it to myself. You know how much a mission like this would mean to me—but I also want that life you dream about, the little home in Maine, the grandchildren—more time at home and less stress. Yes, I did just get home, from a difficult and long mission. But somehow—that little Voice—keeps saying that there's something important that I have left to do."

"I was afraid you'd say something like that," she said, lowering her head.

"No. Look at me," he said, pulling her wet chin up gently with his hand. "My promise to you is this. I will *not* go—unless we have both, and I mean both, of our own free will and prayer, come to the decision that this is where we are led to go. I'll tell NASA that I cannot . . . *will not* . . . commit without your blessing. That's my promise—to you all."

He looked up at the boys. Alice raised her head from Amy's lap to meet his eyes, her shaking gone for the moment. Amy turned around on her knees to face him, a smile gathering on her puffed and flushed face.

John took her free hand in his, his warmth in stark contrast to her frigid wet fingers.

"We're in this together, Amy—or not at all."

30

"WHITE PAPER?" JOHN ASKED. "You guys do those, too, eh?"

"Hate 'em," Special Agent Kerry responded. "But it's part of the routine. Sometimes the only way you can get someone's attention is to put it in writing."

"What'd you tell them?" John asked, his voice garbled over the cellular connection.

Kerry dodged a car that darted in front of him. A "Hang Up and Drive" bumper sticker was plastered askew on the rear bumper. *Who's the bad driver?* Kerry wondered. "Since I'm on a cell phone," Kerry said, releasing the steering wheel to wave a hand in anger at the errant driver, "let's just say I shared my alternate hypothesis. The one that got me thrown out of the big guy's office the last time. Felt I had to give it one more try. Director Noble supports me on this."

"I can relate. Never give up. Anything I can do to help from Houston?" John asked.

"No. Got what I need for now, but keep your ears open. What's up with you and the Mars thing, by the way?" Kerry made the turn onto Fourteenth Street and crossed the Mall. Beyond Independence Avenue, the street was a sea of red lights. *Gonna be here a while.*

"Good question. Amy's out of town for a few days visiting her folks while we're working through that decision. I told NASA I wouldn't be available for the mission slot unless Amy and I agree on it." John paused. "We're doing a lot of praying over it, that's for sure."

"Praying about it? Never figured you for that kind of guy," Kerry said with a brief chuckle as he inched along in traffic.

"And what kind of guy would that be, Special Agent Kerry?"

"Didn't mean anything by that, John. Just wondered why you wouldn't jump on the Mars opportunity—with both feet."

"No offense taken. But it's important for me to do right by Amy. And I pray for wisdom about where God wants me—what He wants me to do. How about you?"

"Me?" asked Kerry.

"You ever pray about tough problems? Like for insight on this case?"

"Never considered it," Kerry said, hitting the steering wheel as the light cycled through red again and no cars moved. Gridlock at Fourteenth and Constitution.

"Let's talk about it sometime. Gotta run now though. The pizza guy's here, and the kids are hanging on my heels." Kerry could hear the doorbell in the background and children yelling for dad to bring money.

"Good luck with that white paper, by the way. Maybe the prez will give you the green light you've been waiting for. I'll pray about it, okay?"

"Yeah. Do that. Sure can't hurt," Kerry said, staring at the snarled mass of cars ahead, but lost in thought. "I'll call if something breaks."

John stood in south Houston's Hobby airport, waiting for Amy to exit the concourse. After four days with her parents, she was coming home. Four fun and busy days of holding down the fort and bonding with his children while Amy enjoyed a much-deserved vacation. And four nights, once he had some private time, of earnest prayers seeking God's insight—answers about what path to take with NASA, and Mars. The toughest decision—what he felt was an immediate answer to his deepest angst—was the peace to be able to walk away from the Mars quest if God closed the door through Amy's decision. She had to come first.

"Mommy!" Alice screamed as Amy emerged from the tunnel past bored security guards.

"Aliki!" Amy exclaimed, using her Greek nickname for their precious daughter. Amy knelt in the flow of the crowd and took the tiny blonde bundle in her arms, nearly bowled over by the embrace. She pulled out a new cross-stitch kit from her purse and handed it to Alice as she regained her balance. "Look what Grandmommy sent!"

Alice held the gift close and squeezed Amy's neck, as Albert and Arthur piled on.

John watched the reunion, remembering his own return only months ago and how precious that moment was for him. After only four days with the kids, he wondered how Amy had survived for thirteen months alone. He tried to shake off thoughts of that mission—and anxiety about the Mars opportunity—as he pasted on a smile.

John saw an opening in the pile of children and took Amy in his arms, above the din and clutches of three others. They kissed, and he held her close for a long time.

At last, Amy pulled away, rearranging tousled hair. She seemed to

John to be glowing in the adoration of her family. *She's always smiling, even now,* he thought.

Amy amazed him. He wished he had her remarkable ability to persevere with a clarity of family purpose and optimism that he never seemed to be able to match. The public adored the astronaut. No one knew, as he did, how much more they should adore his incredible wife.

"I hope you guys missed me!"

"We did!" Albert exclaimed. "Dad didn't do the dishes until we left for the airport. And we had pizza and ice cream every night!"

Amy cast a baleful eye at John. "At least you fed them," she said with a grin, then turned back to the kids. "Did you all have a good time?"

Arthur piped up. "Yeah. You might be amazed, Mom. We cleaned our rooms, put the lid down on the toilet, and said our prayers every night. All that stuff."

"Really?" she asked, wrinkling an eyebrow as she stared down her second son. "Well, I did some praying, too," Amy said, stopping in the middle of the ticket area as they were headed out to the car. "Lots of praying, in fact." She pulled on John's arm to turn him toward her. "Know what I read?" She took his hand and squeezed it, bouncing on her toes.

"No. But I'd like to." He looked for a long time at her face, always amazed that they knew each other so well, yet had so much more to learn. This was one of those moments when he was thankful God had saved her just for him.

"I read the Book of Ruth. Who remembers Ruth?" she asked, looking down at the kids.

"Uh, Mom, maybe later, okay?" Arthur said. "We can talk in the car."

"All right, but let me tell your dad something important before we leave." She kept a hand on Albert's shirt collar, an arm around Alice, and an eye on Arthur as she faced her husband. "Here goes. You ready?" she asked.

John nodded, afraid to hope where this might be headed.

Amy took a deep breath and straightened up for her recitation. "'Don't urge me to leave you or to turn back from you. Where you go I will go, and where you stay I will stay. Your people will be my people and your God my God. Where you die I will die, and there I will be buried. May the Lord deal with me, be it ever so severely, if anything but death separates you and me.'"

John set her travel case down.

Amy let go of the children and put her hand up to the side of his face. She stroked his cheek slowly and her voice quavered when she spoke again. "Do you still want to go to Mars, John?" Tears welled up in her eyes, and the children stood by, transfixed.

John swallowed hard, trying to find his voice. "I want to go," he croaked. "God leads me to go. But I can't break your heart, honey. Honestly, I'm a basket case right now."

"I know. I could see that before I left." She reached up and placed her other hand on his right cheek, cradling him as she looked up. "John-boy, I guess you're just going to have to go." The tears flowed freely now, running down her cheek, across her makeup, and into her smile.

"I love you so much. I want to be your Ruth. If your family includes little green Martians, then I need to make them my people, too. Go, John, with my blessing. God seems to have answered my prayer with a clear peace that this is the right thing to do." She squeezed his face playfully, pulling on his cheeks. "Just promise me that you'll use every bone in your zero-G Space MacGyver body to get back home to us in one piece, okay?"

John's heart raced as he strode across the quadrangle from the medical facility to the astronaut office building. Anxiety swept over him, bringing to mind a hundred outcomes he sought to control, but could not.

The office was a beehive of activity, with a space station mission in progress, shuttle crews preparing for the last launches of aging orbiters, and the planning in work for a historic manned mission to Mars. Athletic men and women hurried through the halls in their trademark polo shirts, mission patches, and Dockers. The attire was casual, but the frenetic pace was 100 percent professional.

John stepped into a restroom to collect his thoughts and let his sweaty forehead cool, shaken by a feeling of *déjà vu*. Fourteen years ago he'd crossed this same quadrangle during his astronaut candidate interviews, and today he could see his life's dream perched on a precipice again. Any wrong move could sink him—a poor perception, a bad answer to a question, perhaps rubbing someone the wrong way, particularly the "Bubbas" who were closest to the center director and his backroom politics. He prayed silently for peace, but it eluded him.

He walked out of the restroom and approached Jack Schmidt's office with its imposing label, "Director of Flight Operations." He'd told Jack a month ago, and had repeated three times since, that he could not accept a Mars mission assignment without Amy's agreement. Most of the astronauts told him he was nuts. *You never let family get in the way of a choice mission slot.* It was difficult for many of them to understand, but Amy meant more to him than all of his astronaut dreams. He'd walk away from it all for her, as much as that might hurt.

Now, with his family's decision—Amy's decision—to support his Mars dreams, John couldn't waste any time. He only hoped it wasn't too late. "Got a minute?" he asked as he knocked and leaned into the doorway to greet Jack.

"Actually, I don't. But we need to talk. Come on in," Jack said, pushing back from his desk. "What's on your mind?"

John tried to sound calm. "I've come to a decision, and I wanted to see you right away." He began to feel more relaxed as he talked. "Amy came home Saturday from Pensacola. We had a long talk. The long and the short of it is—she supports the Mars mission."

"Oh, yeah. That."

"Let me finish, okay? You might think I'm tied to my wife's apron strings, but she put up with an awful lot for me to get here. The last mission, thirteen months on orbit, was hard on her. Amy's stood by me when times were tough. And—"

Jack interrupted him. "Hawk, that's all nice, but—"

"What?"

"You've got a lot of nerve, pal, rushing up here at the last minute. Lots of people have pressured me for a place on the Mars mission crew. You have no idea how much pressure, all the way up to the president. We went out of our way to push you for this mission—even after you had your shot on the station—and you told us you weren't sure you could go. I respect that. But you can't expect us to hold a prime mission slot open for you while you wait to make up your mind. For crying out loud—" Jack turned away to face the window.

John's heart began to race. "Jack, I was willing to walk away from this mission if I needed to for Amy's sake, and I still am. No regrets." He swallowed hard as he fought back the anxiety demon that plagued him. "But I'm here now to let you know that Amy and I agree it's the right thing to do. *I want that slot*, and I'm the best candidate for the job. Nobody in the U.S. knows long-endurance space flight the way I do."

Jack paced back behind the desk. "Talk about long endurance . . .

it's a shame you and Amy waited so long to come to this decision." He picked up a red file folder from his desk. "This is the approved final crew list from Headquarters." He reached across the desk to hand the folder to John. "It was endorsed by President Manchester this morning. You're too late, Hawk. It's done."

John went cold. "The final selection? Already?" He turned to face out the window, reliving the horrific moment of his first rejection notice from NASA in 1996, but magnified a million-fold. *Too late.*

"They were waiting on Malcolm Raines and the vice president to finalize this, if you can believe it. That preacher needs to keep his nose out of NASA business. But it's a good crew. Got the list from Marv Booker just half an hour ago." He paused. "You're welcome to read it if you want." He flipped the folder onto the desk. "Your choice."

John turned back from the window. "You kidding? Of course I want to read it." He stared at the red folder, labeled PERSONNEL CONFIDENTIAL. He couldn't bring himself to open it. He'd been willing to walk away from the Mars mission for Amy, and he was comfortable with that decision at an intellectual level. But his heart shredded as he stood there, the final selection list in hand. The portal to Mars had closed.

John opened the folder as if it might bite him. He scanned the names, pausing on the top two. "Sean O'Brien, Mission Commander. Shane Martin, Primary Flight Engineer." His heart skipped a beat, then another. At the bottom of the list, highlighted in yellow, it read "John Wells, Alternate Flight Engineer."

As soon as Jack let out the first bellow of laughter, Marv Booker stepped out from behind the office door, where he'd been hiding and listening. He, too, erupted in laughter. He grabbed John's shoulder and spun him around.

John felt ready to cry, then scream, then laugh. He grabbed for the hand of his old flight director, Marv Booker, squeezing hard, tears brimming. John could feel his mouth stretching so wide that it almost hurt.

Marv squeezed John's hand for a long time. He stuttered through the choked laughs, speaking up to overcome Jack's loud hilarity. "Congratulations, Hawk. You've earned this. You put us through the ringer, but we knew, somehow, it would all work out." Marv patted John on the shoulder. "I know it's an alternate assignment but—"

"—at least I'm on the list! This is huge!" John bellowed. "But I don't get it. I didn't make up my mind—I mean *we* didn't make up our minds—until Saturday. And you didn't know until *now*."

"Oh yeah. Well, there's this little secret, Hawk—" Jack got out a few words, but couldn't finish because he laughed so hard.

"What Jack's trying to tell you, but can't, is that Amy called me last Wednesday. She wanted me to know that she was going to say 'yes' when she came home and didn't want to keep you out of competition for the slot. She insisted that she tell you in person." Marv shook his head. "When you think about it, Jack and I must have been nuts to hold your name in reserve until the end." He took the file from John's hand. "But Amy saved the day."

"She called you? In Washington? Last week?" John shook his head, unable to absorb all the news and surprises. "And the director supported me too?"

"Yes—on all counts," Jack said, choking down belly laughs. "Dr. Bondurant at JPL, and that Raines fellow, tried to pull rank, using the vice president's office for support. But Greg Church took it personal and fought them all the way. He fired every silver bullet in his arsenal to get you in. I'm not kidding . . . Raines and the veep held this thing up till the end. Good thing for you!" Jack's smile took a devious twist with the last words. "After he won, Director Church nailed Felicia Bondurant's coffin shut. Shared some insider 'dirt' on her just to twist the knife. I suspect you aren't on her Christmas list anymore."

"Bondurant won one, too, though," Marv continued. "She's hated Church for years. And it wasn't a silent war this time. She pushed hard for Michelle Caskey and—"

John cut him off. "Michelle? She made it?"

Jack started the deep belly laughs a third time. "Come on, Hawk! She was just above your name—right below Shane's on the list!"

Marv nodded. "She's in, John. Primary slot, Chief Scientist. Should have heard her when we told her this morning. Man, can she scream!"

Jack cut in. He was still wiping tears, but his voice was serious again. "Hawk, if the list had come out, and the situation was different—I mean, if you and Amy . . . well . . . you know—"

"You mean if she hadn't said 'yes,' would I have turned down the assignment—alternate or otherwise?" John took the file back from Marv, scanning the names. He didn't answer for a long moment, then turned and nodded his head. "Yes."

Jack and Marv looked at him, their respect apparent.

"I know it's hard to believe. Maybe you think it's easy for me to say this now that I know I'm on the list, but I mean it. As much as I want to go, I was ready to walk in here today and turn it all down—for Amy. That was the hardest decision of my life."

John looked into the distance through the window again, as he imagined the alternative and how he would have felt. He shook his head again and turned back to Marv. "*Amy* called you? Incredible!"

Marv smiled. "There's someone else you should thank."

"I haven't thanked *you*, yet!"

Marv smiled. "Your reaction is thanks enough," he said, as Jack nodded silently.

"Is Greg Church around that door, too?" John asked as he pointed to Marv's hiding spot, his smile so wide he had cramps in his cheeks.

"Not exactly. Just a special guest we asked to tag along."

From behind the connecting door to Jack's administrative office, which had been ajar throughout the entire conversation, a beaming Amy stepped out to embrace John. If John was already in shock from the news of his selection, her appearance sent him over the edge. He didn't move. Amy threw her arms around his neck, shaking him a little to bring him out of the stupor. After a prolonged hug, she pushed away, hands resting on his chest.

"Rough day, huh?" she asked, her green eyes sparkling. "Thank you, by the way."

"Thank you?" he asked, through a huge smile. "For what?" He held her face in his hands, cradling her softly.

"For this precious gift you've given me!"

Jack and Marv slipped out, unseen, on opposite sides of the room.

John was puzzled. "You're the one who pulled the big surprise!"

She ran her fingers along his forehead and slowly caressed his cheek. Her new tears ran down onto his fingers and across the back of his hand. She couldn't speak for a long time, but her teary green eyes spoke volumes.

"With it all on the line, you stood up for me, John, even when it broke your heart and dashed your deepest dreams. You risked everything you've ever fought for. Just for me. Just like you promised." Amy pulled him close and buried her head in his chest. "No wife or friend could ever ask for more."

31

THE VETERAN'S MEMORIAL COLISEUM in Phoenix went dark except for two spotlights that bored in on Malcolm Raines as his weekly service, a Wednesday evening event, came to a climactic end. Father Raines slowed, then fell to his knees, his face pointed up into the eerie spots that tracked his every move from the upper galleries of the tall arena.

"He speaks!" Raines said, jerking his head and turning his left ear toward the brightness. He raised both hands into the twin beams, silent for the first time that night.

Malcolm Raines looked up into a sea of faces as he seemed to wait for an answer to some unspoken prayer. He was surrounded by thousands of faithful, who, with him, had outgrown every building the congregation had occupied. Their first rented church, a small Catholic property in a Latino neighborhood, had given way to a larger second home, then a much larger third, and now, his huge rented theater-cum-chapel downtown was history as well. Only the 13,000 seats of the Veteran's Memorial Coliseum would hold his flock. Wednesday nights, sandwiched between weekend special events and Thursday hockey games, were his. The cool air from the ice below the temporary stage sent ice fog rolling across the floor. Malcolm dropped his head.

"You will see us soon," said the voice through the oracle of Father Raines. "We have come together that you may see us through our own eyes. Believe." Raines' head bowed even further in the ensuing silence, then he looked up into the spots and raised his hands once more. He opened his eyes, the sheen on his sweating face reflecting the spotlights as his picture was displayed on the giant screens to either side of the stage. He leapt to his feet.

"They are coming!" he said at the top of his voice. He raised his hands higher. "They are coming, and we will see them. Soon!"

"You getting this, Director Noble?" Kerry asked, covering the micro-phone of his cellular phone to screen out the wild adulation in the background. He could barely hear his boss as he tried to take a call from an upper gallery seat of the Coliseum.

"Live on CNN. This guy's got connections or something."

"Something," replied Kerry. "Something wrong in his head, if you ask me. We ought to ask him to join the Bureau and ferret out all the motives we can't seem to figure out."

"Don't need him now. I've got you. The reason I called," Director Noble said, sounding as though he were shouting, "is that you got your wish." He paused. "You hearing me, Kerry? Get out of that blasted background noise."

Special Agent Kerry clambered across seats trying to get to the aisle and escape the din. He jumped over the last pair of legs and ran up the stairs into an access tunnel. "Hang with me, sir. I'm almost out," he said.

"Now?" Noble asked.

"Go on," Kerry said, safe in the silent perimeter near a popcorn stand. "What was that about my wish?"

"The president called me ten minutes ago. Hard to believe but it's true. He wanted me to know that he was personally authorizing an independent review of the al Salah case. I suspect that he won't be announcing that in the papers, and I don't want you blabbing it either."

"Agreed."

"It seems that the classified white paper you sent to the Oval Office last month had quite an effect on him. Bet I get a call from the veep complaining that we went around him."

"You will. But his job as a gatekeeper is over. We can move out now."

"So do it. No more goofing around worshiping the Rocket Reverend, got it?" Noble said with a growl, then a chuckle.

"No problem there. Thought I'd do some field research—"

"That's what they call golf," Director Noble interrupted. "Field research. Whatever you're doing, get back on the clock and find out more about your domestic theory. You have the president—and me—on your side now. So don't screw it up."

THURSDAY, MARCH 29, 2012: PASADENA, CALIFORNIA

Dr. Robert Kanewski stared out the window of his Pasadena office at NASA's Jet Propulsion Laboratory early in the morning, coffee in hand, and wondered where the roller-coaster ride he was on would take him today. He didn't have to wait long. The phone rang.

"Kanewski," he growled, resenting the interruption.

"Scott here. Mars will rise soon. Figured you'd want to know."

"Be right down. Any guests?"

Scott chuckled. "About fifty. It's pretty tight down here."

"Be there in a minute. Thanks."

Robert turned back to the window and the view of Pasadena. The last two months had been frenetic. Malcolm Raines' January prophecy that "we are many," whatever that meant, had the world stirred up. But last week's prediction that "we have come together that you may see us through our own eyes" was so eerie that the once-boring Viking 1 image in Mars Mission Control was now the hottest spot in town. NASA was besieged with visitors, most of them one taco short of a full Mexican dinner. Or so he thought.

Somewhere beyond his gaze the crazies queued up in the early morning cool, ready for another day of rabblerousing and demonstrations in front of an army of television crews. This was the news of the millennium for the modern world. As thrilled as he was to be at the center of this history-making opportunity, Robert sometimes wished for the quiet laboratory atmosphere he'd loved in his many years at NASA. Life had become a circus. He headed to the door, resigned to this distasteful mix of mindless media and historic science.

As he entered the Mars Mission Control Center, VIPs and media piled on him, seeking some proof of the Rocket Reverend's latest prognostication. Over several voices that pressed for his attention, Robert could hear Scott trying to communicate with the other payload operators and prepare for the day's first imagery downloads. The frustration in Scott's voice was apparent.

Robert had once wondered how a mother could, with utter clarity, pick out her child's voice in a pack of screaming children. In recent days, he'd developed the same skill, sorting out the voices of his dependable Mars team in the midst of the insane clamor of visitors.

"What do we have, Scott?" he asked when he'd finally escaped the madding throng.

"The image of Viking 1 isn't up yet. Don't know why."

"Pull up the files from yesterday's shot. They all look the same, anyway. Show 'em something." Scott nodded, huffing in frustration as he turned back to the computer. Robert thought about reprimanding him for his attitude—then thought twice. No one who worked for Robert could see the sense in this any more, not after months of watching the sun rise and set over Viking 1. Even he had come to doubt the reality of the signal that SETI insisted came from Mars. After the initial hullabaloo, interest in the Viking 1 images had evaporated in the past two months—until Malcolm Raines had opened his mouth. Would that a space scientist had such pull, Robert mused.

He turned to the multitude, his hands raised. "May I have your attention? We expect to see Mars rise in about two minutes. The first signals from Mars will be on display very soon. We're privileged to have you join us." In truth, he wished they'd all leave.

Scott flashed the last picture of the previous day on the big screen. The visitors all commented on the amazing clarity and the remarkable message of the picture. But it was an image that nearly everyone on Earth had seen a hundred times in the past six months. And it was yesterday's image. But no one could tell the difference as the crowd pondered the deep scientific and spiritual significance of what Robert knew was old data.

While they ogled the old image, Scott shifted his attention to the missing transmission, today's signal from Mars. He'd monitored this signal hundreds of times before, and it had always behaved just like a Viking system should. Yet, with all that experience behind him, somehow this morning he couldn't synchronize the data feed; the link quality was corrupted. Scott ignored the hubbub behind him, diving into new file screens on his terminal to determine the problem. The signal was there—he could see it on the signal analyzer—yet it was lower in strength than he'd ever observed. Some sort of noise degraded the transmission, and the imagery data of Viking 1 were sure to be affected.

"All right, what is it?" Dr. Kanewski whispered over his shoulder after five minutes of Scott's desperate searching through manuals and consulting multiple monitor screens. "Mars rose five minutes ago. No new Vikings; I know it's not sunset there—although none of these kooks seem to notice. Give me some answers."

Scott put the manual down and faced his mentor. "The alien signal is bad today. It's like the transmitter just lost half its power or got clobbered by noise. The link is down three decibels."

"Cut in half and no reasons why?" Dr. Kanewski asked.

"None. That is, none that made any sense until—" He winked.

"You haven't told me everything, have you, Scott?"

"Nope."

Robert knew Scott was going to make him pry this secret out. "I guess we'll just have to ask our visitors to go home, eh?"

"Be a shame to, considering—" Scott said, eyebrows raised.

"Considering what?"

"Oh, the news we could break today. Be a real shame." Scott went back to the terminal as he spoke, frantically typing commands, evaluating displays of signal level, and consulting his image processing system. "Yep, it—would—be—yes!—it would be a terrible shame." He hit the "Enter" button with a sharp tap of finality, and two images began to form on his monitor.

"I think you're about to tell me something that I won't forget, Scott. Am I right?"

"Maybe. If you're wearing socks, prepare to have them blown off. For good." The engineer leaned back in his swivel chair and grabbed both armrests. "Take another heart pill, Doc 'cause here . . . we . . . go!" Scott hit the final button and moved away from his terminal as though it might bite.

Dr. Kanewski and some stragglers behind him turned to view the now half-formed images on Scott's small monitor screen. A hush suddenly rippled through the room. Scott directed the video feed from his terminal to the big screen in front of them. There, in graphic color and exquisite detail, was a spectacular image of a sinister looking creature—or craft—against a stunning backdrop of Martian rocks and soil. An image taken at *ground* level.

Months of views of Viking 1 were forgotten as they saw, for the first time, someone—or something else—on Mars. Spidery jointed silver legs sank into the ruddy Martian dust beneath a large gleaming silver elliptical pod-shaped structure. Each leg, jointed in four places, tapered toward the ground, where sharp points pierced the soil. A strange ellipsoidal protrusion, perhaps an antenna or a head, rose out of the top front of the pod, pointing up to a salmon sky.

The silence shattered as everyone tried to talk at once. Scott turned to see a female reporter collapse in her seat, pale and sweating. It took his boss more than a minute to calm the frantic guests. Another reporter dashed for the door, and Dr. Kanewski motioned to stop her before she left.

"Please, ladies and gentlemen," Dr. Kanewski nearly shouted. "Before we rush to judgment . . . let's give Scott a minute to tell us what happened. Let's not tell the world yet about pictures we can't explain."

"We couldn't explain the first ones. That didn't stop you,"

complained the reporter at the door. She shook off the grasp of a lab technician who stood her ground at the entrance and guarded the exit. The rest of the room hushed.

"Thank you. Now, Scott. What is this? And where's the latest image of Viking 1?"

Scott shrugged. "Can't help you on the second question. As to the first—the original signal was down . . . way down in the noise, Doc. Half strength. I couldn't figure out why and ran some diagnostics to pull up the signal-to-noise ratio. When I did, I realized that there were actually *two* signals out there, both on the same frequency, which explains the signal reduction. This image," he said as he pointed back to the ominous silver spider-shaped thing on the large screen, "is from Mars. Same transmitter that used to be sending Viking 1. Perfect waveform match. No doubt about it."

Again, everyone began to talk at once, but Scott cut them off. "If I were a betting man, I'd guess that we have *two* landers on the surface and this image is taken of a second alien. If we could get an image from the fella we're looking at and compare the background images of the Martian landscape, that would about prove it."

"But we can't do that, right?" asked a reporter.

Scott glanced over his shoulder at Dr. Kanewski, who shook his head "no" in response to the question, and started to explain. Scott cut him off as he pointed at his monitor again.

"Uh, Doc? We . . . might just . . . have that proof."

The audience saw what Dr. Kanewski could not until he turned around. Scott commanded a split image on the large-format screen at the front of the operations room, feeding signals from the two competing transmitters on Mars. There, in frightening doubles, was the real reason for coming to JPL today.

A second spider. Menacing, silver, and towering over large dark-gray rocks in the soil below it, stood the twin of the first image. More frightening, though, was the image thumbnail that Scott cropped and expanded, exploding the upper right of the second scene into a new computer scene window: a familiar dirty white gangly lander with a United States flag stood in the distance about a hundred meters beyond the second alien. Viking 1. The antsy female reporter rushed out the exit, unchallenged. No one could hold this news back. Not now.

In the back of the room, from an unseen VIP, Scott heard an eerie baritone rendition of Malcolm Raines' oracle of ten weeks ago. Slow and deliberate, he parodied the rich disembodied voice heard by tens of thousands in Rice Stadium in January. A chill ran down Scott's spine, even though he'd heard the prophecy replayed dozens of times.

"You will see my children. Where once there was one, there soon will be two. Do not fear. We are many."

32

| LA MARQUE,
| TEXAS

RONNIE WILLIAMS DIALED THROUGH the spectrum on his old ham radio set while he waited for Mars to rise. The Allied home-built kit was forty-five years old, and in the modern digital world of amateur radio, his receiver was legendary. Since those magic days in the 1960s when he'd built it as a teenage boy, the ham radio had dialed through the international radio spectrum, including many nights of covert listening from the South Texas bedroom of his childhood home.

While he waited the last few minutes for today's Martian images to arrive, he caressed the smooth black knobs of his pet radio, picking out snatches of short-wave broadcasts from Honduras, then Cameroon, and finally South Africa. He never tired of bringing words from halfway around the world into his home with the quick twist of a hand. Modern digital radios denied most ham enthusiasts that tactile joy.

Ronnie wasn't just any ham enthusiast. He raised amateur radio to a new level with thirty antennas and twice as many advanced transceivers that could dial through the entire electromagnetic spectrum, from the lowest shortwave frequencies of yesteryear's Morse code, to ultramodern Ka-band satellite communications with gigabit-per-second transmission speeds and home-built tracking mechanisms to follow passing spacecraft or distant planets. No one he'd ever met or read about had ever invested the time and expense to attempt to build such an assortment of high-tech gear that could listen to any NASA payload, shuttle orbiter, or space station transmission. Living only twenty miles south of the NASA Johnson Space Center, this was Ronnie's life. A regular shift job at a chemical plant in Texas City paid the bills, but radio was his passion, headquartered in the "Radio Central" of his modest childhood home on Shady Lane in La Marque.

The little 1950s chemical plant town he and Martha called home had been overcome long ago by the sprawl along Interstate 45. Much of the area beyond his neighborhood was now one giant strip mall. Ronnie was one of only a few natives who hadn't moved to the historic houses in Galveston or the mind-numbing stucco subdivisions of Baytown and Clear Lake City. Martha begged him to move, with gentle pleas every payday. But Ronnie would look out at the antenna field covering half of the horse pasture behind their house and shake his head. A move would mean leaving more than his childhood home and his land. It would mean leaving his passion.

Mars began to rise.

A silent warning message flashed in the corner of his computer monitor. He missed it, engrossed as he was in the old Allied kit radio and the speech of a dignified South-African commentator. When he looked up at last, the daily alien signal from Mars was obliterated by noise.

Ronnie pushed back from his computer and squinted at the monitor, scratching his chin. In the background, singsong African voices warbled as another high-power shortwave emitter on the Dark Continent "stepped" on the Radio South Africa transmission he'd been listening to so intently. While he stared, surprised, at his high-tech gear and a computer screen devoid of the usual daily image of Viking 1, the old Allied speakers crackled again. Competing signals drifted in and out of tune, alternating between the lilt of native Ethiopians and the sharp accent of a South African. Ronnie spun around to face the antique kit radio and slapped his forehead. He'd missed the clue, and it took his old friend to bring him back to first principles.

In a flash, the radio genius configured a new program to port the incoming transmission to a digital signal analyzer. With deft strokes of his computer tool, he tore the corrupted transmission apart on a sophisticated waveform display. Overlaid on the distant alien signal he found another transmission, at the same frequency and modulation, but so slightly offset that the additional signal had a power-divider effect and pushed the original alien transmission into the galactic noise.

In less than a minute, Ronnie had separated the two transmissions, very similar but different. When the data popped on the screen as a pair of horrifying Martian images, he let out a yell.

Martha came on the run from the kitchen. "Ron? What's wrong?"

By the time she'd reached him, Ronnie was leaning into the screen, mesmerized by the dual pictures from Mars. Martha stopped short as she rounded the doorway, engrossed by the terrifying scene. Panting from her quick run across the house, she plopped weakly into a chair.

"Good heavens, Ron. What *is* that?"

Ronnie turned in his swivel chair and put an arm around his shaking wife. "I think it's what it looks like, honey. This, apparently, is what has been transmitting all the pictures of Viking—a very large spider. Or a craft that looks like one." He paused, panting from the excitement. "I don't think they came from Earth."

The figure was ominous, a giant egg sac suspended over long bony silver legs that ended in tips like eight silver spears. Martha shivered under Ronnie's pale white arm.

"I was afraid you'd say something like that. Please, Ron, let's move. Tomorrow. We'll get normal lives and join a country club." She squeezed his arm hard, pressing her point home. "This scares me. It might be fun for you, but for me it's awful. None of this—or you—is normal."

He rubbed his unshaved chin in quiet contemplation, and then spoke. "I know." Holding hands, they stared at the fearsome picture on the screen for over a minute.

"Data file transfer complete" popped up in a dialogue box on his monitor with a *ding*, reminding him that an automated function had been completed. Ronnie threw off Martha's hand and spun around in his chair.

"What now?" Martha asked.

"I forgot my Web program! It's been set up for the last six months to automatically transfer Viking 1 image files to my Web page. Oh, brother—"

"If you're trying to publish what's on Mars, isn't this what you want?" She toyed with her apron nervously.

"I don't want to peddle someone's hoax. We don't know what those things are—or where they came from."

"I can't believe we're having this conversation, Ronnie. How do you know that the Viking pictures you and the rest of the world have fawned over for the past months are real? They could be a hoax, too. It's crazy the way billions of people have watched the same Viking sit there like a statue. I'd rather watch grass grow. But then, Viking was better than this—"

Ronnie didn't respond.

"Please, Ronnie, pay attention! I want to move, and you're worried about whether you have real pictures of aliens!" She jumped out of her chair and paced around the room. "We'll never get a nice home in Clear Lake City," she said, plopping down a minute later with a resigned sigh. She softened, leaning toward him, as she placed a hand on his shoulder. "It's probably too late for you to pull those pictures off the Web, dear. You know people watch your site like a hawk."

Ronnie checked his server. The Web hits were rolling in by the dozens. "It's public, all right. No sense worrying over this now. But don't answer the door if anyone comes knocking."

"Are you sure there really are *two* aliens, Ron? Spiders—or whatever they are."

"I'm not sure of anything, Martha. But look here—" he said, pointing at the snapshot on the screen. "You can see Viking 1 in the background behind this guy. I'd bet they're parked in a line, each about a hundred meters apart. Just a guess, though. They're 150 million kilometers away."

Martha stood up and began to pace around the room a second time. After a few laps she stopped in the doorway to watch Ronnie work with his equipment. When she spoke, her voice squeaked, trembling as she formed his name. "Ron?"

"Yes, hon." He didn't look up from his keyboard.

"Do you remember what Malcolm Raines said when he was in Houston?"

Ronnie looked up. Something was very wrong with Martha. She held onto the doorframe with both hands, ashen faced. He jumped up to steady her.

"Martha! What is it?"

"Raines," she whispered.

"What'd he say? I usually ignore him."

She pointed a shaky finger at the screen and recited the now famous lines in a trembling voice. "You will see my children. Where once there was one, there soon will be two. Do not fear. We are many."

Ronnie looked back at the screen, then at his terrified wife. "You're joking—"

"This is no joke, Ron." She took a deep breath, reaching for him and grabbing his arm. "Raines was right."

| MONDAY, APRIL 2, 2012:
| CLEAR LAKE CITY, TEXAS

Arthur groaned as his father snapped off the television.

"Homework. Now." John commanded. "Vocabulary test tomorrow."

"Whatever . . ." Arthur complained as he skulked away, watching over his shoulder as he headed to his room.

"I'm glad you turned it off. I couldn't take any more." Amy dried her hands on a towel as she left the kitchen and followed John into the den.

"What was it you couldn't handle? Cartoon Network, Discovery Channel, or CNN?"

"Media saturation. Mars. Aliens. Giant spiders. Constant repeats of the same material, like watching the Twin Towers fall in on themselves over and over after 9/11."

"I know," he said.

"Know what?"

John recognized her tone. She was fishing. "I know how this wears on you. That's what."

"Nothing more?"

"No."

They sat together in silence, listening for the telltale sound of video games when their three sons were supposed to be doing homework.

"The world's upside-down, John. Alien spiders, from who knows where, have landed on Mars. They're sending us pictures, and no one knows why. They've flown giant golden golf balls by Earth transmitting thirty-five-year-old messages. A crazy man in Arizona can talk to them—or to something like them—and millions of people are turning to the sky for answers. My husband is training to fly off to another planet to take a look at a big silver insect with no guarantee he'll ever come back. People are losing their marbles everywhere over this news." She slumped on the couch, pushing her long hair into some semblance of order. "Every time the kids turn on the TV, it gets shoveled up in our faces again—and again. It drains me."

"Then turn it off," John said, his eyes following hers.

Amy shrugged. "I worked so hard today, cleaning, organizing . . . anything I could do to stay away from that stupid television. I'd be busy and forget about the aliens for a blissful moment. In total control of my world. Then I'd go back to the TV, and the anxiety would return. I tried to get the images out of my mind, of you a bizillion kilometers out there, maybe eaten by them, or zapped by some horrible death ray—"

He half laughed, then hiccuped, as she gestured with her hands, pretending to shoot a ray gun in his direction. Her eyes grew serious.

"I watched all those sad people searching for answers in this crazy time, and I realized that I *had* all the answers—that God had the answers I needed. But it struck me—as tough as these times are for everyone else, I was going to experience this alien nightmare worse than they could ever imagine. My husband might leave and go touch those horrible things. Part of me felt persecuted, but—despite my fear—I'll admit," she said with a smile, "part of me felt special." She smiled at him, her head canted a little to the side.

John sat still, staring off beyond her, in thought.

"John, does this scare you?" she asked quietly.

His gaze snapped back to her at once. "No. Is that okay?"

"It is," she said, somewhat reserved. "We've talked about this before, haven't we?" she asked.

"Yeah, but I don't mind." He got off the recliner to sit with her on the couch. "There's a line from yesterday's Sunday school lesson that applies right now."

"Uh-huh?"

"'Keep walking in God's will and trust Him with all the details. You'll be amazed at the outcome.' Pretty good advice."

"It is," she said, head down as she folded and refolded the damp kitchen towel in her lap, "when you have the gumption to stick with it. That's my problem."

"Amy?" he said, pulling her attention away from the towel and her unspoken worries.

"Yes?"

"You and the children are never outside God's grace, as long as I'm gone, or as far as I go. And neither am I. No matter what happens—no matter *what*—God will sustain us all with a mighty provision for just what we need, precisely when we need it."

She squeezed his hands in hers, smiling broadly, and her breath light on his cheek as she sighed.

"I know."

TUESDAY, MAY 1, 2012: NASA JOHNSON SPACE CENTER

John set the phone back in its cradle, heartsick, his skin suddenly cold. He looked up at the wall, at the poster of a silver spider with a NASA logo plastered to its side, Mars in the background, and a digitally enhanced picture of him with his bicycle standing next to the alien creature. It wasn't funny any more. Acid rolled in his gut.

The words from Jake Schmidt replayed themselves in his mind as his eyes wandered sightlessly from the gag poster. Shane Martin, the Mars mission flight engineer—his close friend—was dead. Someone, John noticed, pulled his office door closed for privacy. Shane Martin was a friend of everyone who worked here. One man's loss was about to be another man's fortune, but no one would have wanted it this way.

John was thankful for the momentary solitude. From his window he watched people gather on the quad below, sharing the painful news of a lost astronaut, some pointing up toward his office. He knew the routine. Rumors and speculation would rip through the Center. One astronaut lost from the lineup would open the way for the backup to fly. This would be perhaps the most famous backup since Ken Mattingly was grounded for Apollo 13 seventy-two hours before its launch to the Moon. John wanted with all his heart to go to Mars—but not because of this.

He grabbed his keys and headed out the door, to escape the questions, the congratulations, and the attention. Just down the hall, a friend waved him toward the back stairs. John nodded in his direction, and then departed out a back service corridor, avoiding news crews already on the hunt for him.

"Got your keys?" Keith asked as he met John in the back lot on a mutual mission to avoid the press.

"Truck's out front," John said. "Gold Silverado with a silver truck box."

"Roger that." He pitched a set of keys John's way. "My maroon Suburban's over there. Meet me at the Ramada, and we'll swap."

Five minutes later, at the Ramada Inn beyond the main gate, Keith voiced the words John knew were about to come. "I heard Shane hit a cellular tower," he said, shaking his head.

John nodded, closing his eyes for a moment. "Probably cloud surfing on the northern departure out of Moffett Field. He had a bad habit of doing that."

"I hope we're wrong," Keith said. "Did you get . . . the call?"

John shrugged and nodded again. Part of him wanted to jump up and down, to embrace his buddy, to yell and tell the world. But this was not the time.

Keith offered a strong handshake. "I wouldn't have wanted it this way, but congratulations, Hawk. Now go tell Amy. Go on—git." He pushed John toward the old pickup and they separated.

Amy was already at the bay window looking for John. The subdivision was tight. Houses weren't more than two lawnmower widths apart, and neighbors were close-knit. The word of Shane's death had already begun to spread, and a few neighbors were in each other's yards, undoubtedly talking it over. Amy knew that John would deliver this news in person, and she stood by the window, waiting.

As his old pickup rolled into the drive, she watched him, sheers pulled aside. He seemed to struggle out of the truck and into the house, laboring under a heavy load. She knew God had control of this moment, as He did the entire mission. She prayed silently for Shane's family, his wife Karen, and for her own husband.

Amy met him in the kitchen with open arms and a long hug. "It's true, isn't it?" she asked after more than a minute together in silence.

John's nod was all the answer she needed. Neither of them spoke as they held each other. Over his shoulder, she saw a neighbor intercept a newsman and keep him at bay. Amy pulled John over to the window, and they watched the gathering crowd through the blinds, marveling at their loyal friends who'd formed a human wall to hold back the press.

She turned to face him, dreading the next words, yet in some way hoping for the news she was sure he would share. Their entire lives together had pivoted, in many ways, on this next moment. "Well?"

"Well what, honey?"

"Don't pull that one on me, John. This is a tough time. Shane was my friend too, remember?"

"I do. I'm sorry." He pushed her bangs gently back over her ears and wiped away a tear from her cheek. "There. Need to get this just right for the cameras before we go outside."

"And why is that, John?" she said, managing a small smile, her heart leaping for her husband, yet crushed for Shane and his wife Karen. She willed away—for a moment—the despair that began to gnaw at her gut.

"Because," he said, "If my people are to be your people, like Ruth said in the Bible, then you'd better prepare to meet your new family. I'm going to Mars."

33

"HOW MUCH LONGER?" KERRY asked, repeatedly flipping his cell phone open, then closed, with a staccato *clop clop*. "Time's a wasting."

"A few more minutes," the intelligence analyst said, rolling her brown eyes when he looked her way.

He paced back and forth across her windowless office. "Anything yet?" he asked, less than a minute later.

"Almost. The last file is indexing now." The contractor continued tying together the latest prints, news reports, and bank records with a special software tool, as she sought to find a common thread through her rapid selection of multiple commands on a high-end computer prominently labeled with red "Classified Information" stickers.

Kerry watched her navigate the wide plasma screen with deft keystrokes and mouse clicks, pulsing a magic world of intelligence information that he could only dream about. He thought back to the meeting three months ago that finally gave him the green light to turn over the improbable rock. Kerry punched his thigh with a fist as he dwelt on the lost time, the squandered opportunities since he'd first proposed this line of independent investigation. The president himself had asked for Kerry's insights, for a new beginning. "Go find them." And he would.

Meanwhile America was going nuts, waiting for even more aliens to pop up on Mars as they stewed over the wickedness of radical Islam. Between the international hysteria over life on other planets, and a nuclear-capable saber-rattling Iran, he might have only days, or hours, before the world turned itself completely upside down. Except—he was about to turn America on its head again. He had proof now, absolute proof and a trail, that would link domestic terrorists to 3/21. His bodacious theory—the theory of domestic terrorists and cover-up that was too frightening to consider—was somehow turning out to be true.

Call John, he reminded himself. *He'll want to know.* He pulled out his pocket watch and checked the time, again. Maybe John was right; maybe the aliens bombed America. Or better yet, maybe the Iranians really did arrange for it and they deserved to die. That would make all this work so much cleaner. Let them burn.

"Bingo!" The analyst's cry snapped him out of his racist daydream. She pushed her straightened hair back into position and looked up at him.

Kerry rushed to her side. "Speak to me," he said, leaning over her shoulder toward the monitor. Her perfume distracted him.

She began to point at selections on her screen as she spoke. "I compared the warrants and arrest records for Henckey, Carlisle, and Farnsworth—the guys you sent me the prints for—along with records on the prints from the Nevada site and a global text search of all the world's news reports. Hundreds of terabytes of data, mind you. When I expanded the semantic indexing to include physical descriptions, bank records, domestic and international news reports, I got this—" She proudly handed him a digitized article from a Central American paper.

"It's in Spanish . . ." Kerry objected.

"No problem," she said with a grin. "Yo hablo Español. An international news clipping service pulled this report from Tegucigalpa, Honduras. It's about a shooting in Bluefields, Nicaragua. The Hondurans have been trying to shut down illegal trade activity coming from Bluefields. According to the clipping, a very large white man, speaking English, got in a shooting match with some rowdy stevedores in a Bluefields bar. The Nicaraguans died—all four of them." She scanned further down the page. "That was about the same time that space preacher made the big prediction in Houston—five months ago."

She looked up at him, setting the article aside for a moment. "What do you think about all this—I mean, are those space spiders for real?"

"Real as these goons are. I can't see 'em—Carlisle and Farnsworth—but there's plenty of evidence that they exist. Now, what else does it say?" He gave the analyst a gentle nudge on the shoulder.

She skimmed to the bottom of the article. "A local gringo saw the big guy, Carlisle, pull a gun. He leveled the sailors, point blank. I've been to Bluefields. It's a rough spot."

"What were *you* doing there?" he asked.

She blushed slightly, turning her head. "I was cruising the Caribbean with a Jamaican boyfriend when our radar broke. Tried to fix it but we couldn't afford the bribes for the Nicaraguan port officials. It's a crazy place. I blended in down there pretty good, so I was safe," she said, pointing at her own mocha skin. "We left one night under the cover of darkness and a loaded rifle, but I jumped ship two days later in the Corn Islands." She looked away from Kerry. "It didn't—he didn't—work out."

"Umm-hmm. Sounds like a rough place—Bluefields, I mean. Anything else?"

She pushed frizzy black bangs out of her eyes and sat up a little straighter. "Only one other hit. Carlisle. He shows up in lots of material related to coal mining."

"That may be worth its weight in gold, Shawnda. Good work."

"Will you be back soon?" she asked as she stood up, adjusting her top.

"Think so. I'm headed downtown now. Get that stuff to my office—pronto. I've got to get some of the bureau's feet on the ground in Honduras and Nicaragua. The clock's ticking and we're about to run out of time before more missiles fly in Iran."

He stuffed her analysis in his classified pouch and locked it, preparing to head out the door. "Keep up those semantic index queries. Search the world and help me widen the net." He pointed at her as he entered the doorway. "I'm depending on you," Kerry said as he left without offering a thank you or a good-bye.

"Stay in touch, Terrance," she said, calling after him as he ran down the hall.

Her smile was perfect, her voice lilting. As he rushed past the guards, he realized she'd just called him by his first name. No one ever did that. He made a mental note to come back soon, learn more about her, and check her ring finger.

SATURDAY, JUNE 30, 2012: BLUEFIELDS, NICARAGUA

Ten days later, Special Agent Kerry and his team were ready for business. The pristine Beech Baron 58 used by Billy Carlisle had flown from Bluefields, Nicaragua, three times in the past week. The big guy was always at the controls, and his prints, lifted from the controls on their initial visit to his plane, were a perfect match. The first terrorist was within their grasp. Long-range video and audio surveillance teams were in place at every one of Carlisle's typical destinations, ready to tail him and record his every move.

Late on their second night in Bluefields, Kerry's team returned to Carlisle's expansive tin hangar at a grass strip outside the seamy port town. Hispanic agents plied Carlisle and his minions with beers at a bodega near the port while their federal agent partners watched the airstrip. The plane, unguarded, was an easy target for a covert installation of a micro-miniature satellite-based tracking beacon and a digital tap on the radios. Disguised antennas completed the kit, and the team was out of the plane in less than two hours. The Baron was ready; they could follow it, remotely via satellite, anywhere in the world.

Billy Carlisle flew the next day. True to form, his first leg was to the Honduran capital, Tegucigalpa, and the satellite tracker worked flawlessly. Once on the ground, agents shadowed him in dilapidated cars, never more than a hundred meters behind their target. Carlisle took his FBI tail on a round-robin tour of the major Honduran banks, traveling in a series of cabs from one to the next, then back to the airport, and on to La Ceiba, a lively resort city to the north on the Caribbean.

Three bank drops, each one moving thousands of dollars in cash and securities, and every drop intercepted at the bank by U.S. and Honduran officials after Carlisle left. Every bill was checked, fingerprints were taken, and drop bags were analyzed. As he had done on each run in the past weeks, Carlisle's third leg took him to Roatan Island. If he didn't know better, Kerry thought, following the action remotely through satellite phone contact with his agents, this could be a Federal Reserve pilot in the United States on a weekly banknote run.

Following Carlisle across Roatan from the tiny west-coast landing strip, the FBI trailed him to a private Caribbean resort, a nest of fancy bungalows perched over azure waters, supported by a staff of dozens of white-jacketed waiters, a full dive shop, and a modern marina. Numerous luxury cruisers were tied up pierside, along with one sleek red Cigarette ocean racer. Carlisle disappeared into a bar for three hours, then a restaurant, half an hour in a bungalow, and back to the bar. Without a recording device on him, they could only guess as to his intentions. There were no major banks on this island, but he was running in the company of the ultra-rich.

Carlisle's visit was short, but it produced vital intelligence. At the end of his visit, an athletic man, dressed in expensive beach apparel, met Carlisle at the door of a large bungalow built over the shallow inlet and invited him in. Soon after they met, his host escorted Carlisle out, with a new package in hand. Using a long-range listening device and high-resolution optics, the pursuing agents got photographs and audio of the brief parting exchange.

As the big man stepped off the porch, he waved back to the well-dressed suspect in the door, sharing a hushed but clearly distinguishable parting: "See you, Nick."

THURSDAY, JULY 5, 2012: ROATAN, HONDURAS

Nick slept soundly, snoring lightly in the dark early morning hours. Below his bungalow, the faintest rustling of the water failed to stir him or any other guests at the Bender Reef resort complex. A dark body emerged below his elevated bungalow, silently rising from the water and scaling a wet piling to reach the underside of the thatched structure.

Moving quickly, clad in black that dissolved into the night, the figure clamped a tiny package around the coaxial cable feeding the room above, a miniature green light flashing once it was in place. The figure pushed the clamp and wire up into the sub floor, covering it with a tiny "Bender Reef Info-Tech Services" sticker, and descended the slimy pole.

In the water within sixty seconds, and under the surface without a ripple, the figure was gone. The night remained undisturbed and Nick snored until daybreak.

Nick reclined in the deep rattan chair, feet up on a padded stool, as he opened the laptop computer and began his day's work shortly before sunrise. Above him, a fan poured cold air as he lay in an open-collared shirt and Bermuda shorts, a tall iced juice drink on the table to his left. Opening an Internet browser, he was quickly about his business, connected to a computer on the Baikonur Cosmodrome, east of the Aral Sea in distant Kazakhstan. *Time for a message to an old friend,* he thought. *A message about family and the future.*

Below his bungalow, a dim green light flashed under the sub floor, hidden by an opaque plastic sticker. Above, Nick worked tirelessly into the noon hour, then closed the computer and went to the bar for lunch.

The green light went out.

THURSDAY, JULY 5, 2012: COLORADO SPRINGS, COLORADO

General Fredericks was never far from his computer or his wireless e-mail device during his last days as a military officer. His fascination with electronic mail had become an insane compulsion, he'd heard someone whisper behind his back among themselves. He had the volume dialed up on his computer to alert him as each message chimed in. The latest *ding* pulled him away, for the fifth time, from an early morning retirement ceremony conference with his chief of staff and military aide. He rushed to his desk again.

"Subject: YOUR CHILD SUPPORT PAYMENT IS DUE." The capital letters shouted at him.

The general looked up, ashen, and dismissed the frustrated staff. He knew this was the third meeting about his impending retirement that he'd canceled. The ceremony was only weeks away, at the end of the month. A staffer had recently recommended that the general extend privileges to his e-mail account so that she could handle that burden for him. He refused, insisting on complete privacy. "Eyes only, limited distribution," he told her.

The general cancelled the e-mail without reading it, but it popped right back. As it did, every time. He knew the drill; he'd dealt with a dozen of these strange messages, but none since he'd disposed of the previous laptop months before. *Why? After months of peace, now just days before my retirement, the menace is finally back.* He knew he had to read this mail to delete it. There was no other choice. His career, his reputation, and his pension, all hung in the balance.

He opened the message.

Did your late daughter know about your secret children? What were there—four? You'll get to meet them all soon. They're coming to say 'good-bye.' I'm sorry that I will miss your ceremony. It should be quite memorable. Enjoy your retirement.

General Fredericks's eyes widened and his face flushed as he reread the forty words. Then he swore out loud and lunged for the mouse to delete the e-mail, pounding the desk with his left fist. Instantly, a stabbing pain shot through his left eye socket, down his left cheek, racing toward his neck. His left jaw felt like someone was trying to pry it off with a crowbar. He gasped for breath, struggling against what seemed to be an elephant sitting on his chest. The message seemed to fade in and out of his vision, yet he was determined to somehow reach the mouse, to delete the dreaded file.

Searing hot pain, then numbness, shot through his left arm and down to his fingers, rendering his hand and arm flaccid. The staggering pain in his jaw doubled him over, his face crashing into the keyboard as he lunged for the mouse, vision blurred, in desperation to complete his only mission. Delete the e-mail and breathe!

The general's right hand flailed in a final frantic attempt to reach the mouse that he could no longer see. He missed, flipping a glass pitcher of ice water from the right side of his huge desk onto the carpeted floor, where it splintered in a muffled crash. One more time, some demonic force attempted to rip his jaw free as another surely drove a massive hot poker through his left shoulder and out his back.

General "Boomer" Fredericks's left side was immobile and riddled with searing pain and his chest was bound tight by some unseen force. His right arm was splayed out across his desk, and his face planted in his keyboard, drool oozing on the keys, when his executive assistant opened the door to inquire if her boss needed any help.

The e-mail was gone.

BLUEFIELDS, NICARAGUA

Kerry downloaded his e-mail through a satellite phone while he reviewed a map of the surveillance plan for the Bender Reef Resort on Roatan Island. He dropped the map when he opened the mail at the top of his queue, the subject highlighted by a red blinking flag.

Fredericks's pen-pal is back. Message attached. General is in cardiac ICU, Colorado Springs. Critical condition. Covert surveillance set up at the hospital, office, and condo. What do you know about these "secret" children and the motive for the e-mail?

Kerry hit the speed dial on the satellite phone and connected with his agents in Colorado. Minutes later he placed a call to a red phone in Langley.

"Shawnda? This is Terrance . . . Yes, I'm fine. No time for chit-chat. I'm sending you a text file. Run everything you have on the Commander, U.S. Northern Command—NORTHCOM—General Fredericks. Nickname 'Boomer.' Work that magic worldwide database and relationship tool you showed me the last time. I need any connection between him, this operation—and everyone we have the goods on. Also run a search of Fredericks against the images of the well-dressed guy in the bungalow—Nick. We know for sure now that he's the one who sent e-mail to the general, and a linkage to Fredericks might tell us who Mr. Fancy Pants really is." He paused, taking a breath as he mentally ran through all the connections that were falling into place. "Did you get all that?"

He listened, and nodded. "I owe you on this one. And Shawnda? Tell no one."

34

A MILE SOUTH OF the deserted resort, on a low ridge near the center of Roatan Island, an old panel van sat covered in mud and rust.

"I've got him," the first agent said, flicking a cigarette out the window. "Look at this. He's uploading the latest file to that server in Russia."

"Internet tap's working like a charm. And it's in Kazakhstan, you dummy," the second agent said as they watched the activity from Nick's computer in real time.

"Whatever. His routine hasn't changed since we planted it."

The radio beside them chirped.

"The plane's en route with a passenger. Tall fellow, cowboy. Probably Fister."

"Copy," the first agent said, setting a newly lit cigarette aside as he spoke into the mike. "We're ready. Ulrich is still on the Net."

"Everything's in place here," the radio barked again. "We'll get photos and audio at the bungalow. You watch the computer. We'll call if we need you. Bail out if he spooks."

An hour later, Tex Fister powered a Land Rover up a dirt road toward Bender Reef Resort. He barely noticed the old van at the top of the ridge, quickly dismissing it as just another abandoned car among many in the poor country. He continued down the ridge to his rendezvous with Nick.

"Uneventful, Nick. No tails," Tex said ten minutes later as porters carried two large boxes from the Land Rover to his boss's bungalow.

"Where's Billy?" Nick asked, opening the new shipment of computer equipment in his back room.

"Putterin' with the plane," Tex said, wiping off the sweat. "Man, you sure do keep it cold in here."

"I like it that way. But plane trouble, I don't like. What's wrong with it?" Nick put down the box cutter, facing directly at Tex.

"Planes break. He fixes 'em. That's the reason we hired him. Why ya' so jumpy, Nick? We've been here two years and no one's so much as poked around."

"Exactly. It's starting to seem just a little too nice."

"Well, I don't know about you, but I don't call a roach-infested bodega in Costa Rica with a window air conditioning unit 'nice.' I'm alive. I have all the money I need. I'm healthy. So, it's not so bad—but it ain't 'nice.'" Tex waved at Nick's thermostat. "You're welcome to move me into these digs any day, and I'll shut up."

"You talk too much," Nick said, hunched over the boxes from Dell. "Besides, you can afford better. You just choose not to."

"That's true."

Nick scowled as he pulled back a drape to look out the window toward the beach and the pier with its hyper-expensive luxury craft. "I expected to see some kind of indication by now that they were looking for us. Something to give us a clue what to avoid . . . where to go."

"Any ideas?" Tex asked, pulling a cerveza from the cooler in Nick's amply stocked kitchen.

"Yeah. I want you to go to Belize City. Red Henckey's over there. Send him to Isla de San Andres—Colombia—with wads of money. Head him off to one of those private gambling resorts, and tell him to have a good time. But follow to see who watches. He doesn't know where the rest of us are, right?"

"No, but—"

"Send him," Nick interrupted. "Load him up with cash and follow. You know the drill. Look for anything out of place. The Feds will stand out like blood on a T-shirt down there."

Tex was quiet, staring out the window over Nick's shoulder.

Nick spun around. "What?"

"Just thought of something," Tex said.

"Spit it out, Tex. I need to know everything."

"Something out of place. On the way in, an old dive-shop van I've never seen before. A clunker. On the ridge, 'bout a mile south of here."

"What's so special about that?"

"Parked on the side of the road. Nobody there. And no one trying to steal it."

"That's unusual?" Nick asked, picking up a wine cooler and taking a long swig.

"Not the stealin' part. It was labeled in Spanish. Why would someone label a dive-shop van in Spanish? All the shops on this island cater to Americans."

Nick said nothing but reached under the desk below his laptop and withdrew a loaded submachine gun. He drew a pistol from under his belt and handed it to Tex. He held a hand to his lips to indicate Tex should be quiet as Nick slipped out the back door of the bungalow. Tex watched him out the window as he headed down a plank walkway toward the palms, beyond the beach and the bungalows. A few minutes later, Tex went out the front door, tipped the porter, hopped into the Land Rover, and retraced his tracks up the low ridge.

Nick walked quickly to the edge of the resort, and then sprinted uphill through the palms to the spot that Tex had recalled, arriving only minutes after his partner. Tex was waiting at the roadside, a cigarette in hand, staring down the hill in the direction of town.

Nick panted as he leaned on the Land Rover's fender, the submachine gun at his side.

"Were . . . they . . . here?" he asked, catching his breath.

"Must have just missed 'em. Could still smell the exhaust from that old van. Went toward town. And they left this." He proffered a half-smoked cigarette. "There's about two dozen more over here. Winstons. This one was still lit."

Sweat pouring off his forehead and soaking his chest in the damp tropical air, Nick took the half-cigarette and examined it. "Anyone . . . in the van earlier?" he asked, bending to examine the pile of butts more carefully.

"No one. I would've noticed. I thought it was abandoned."

Nick looked down the road. "They're onto us, Tex."

"You sure?"

"I'm sure," Nick snapped. He turned on Tex with the gun raised and the safety off.

"Whoa, man!" Tex protested, backing up, hands in the air.

"See this?" Nick said, lowering the gun and thrusting the Winston butt in Tex's face. "Can't buy 'em on the island, or in La Ceiba. I know. I used to smoke 'em. The guys in that van were Americans. When we find out where they got that rat trap, we'll find Feds."

"What now?" Tex asked, wiping his face.

"Get back to the plane. Clear out of your place in Limon. Tonight. Take the fast boat to the camp at Miskito Keys and set up shop when you get there. I'll meet you with my boat in two days. Send Red from Belize to San Andres for a diversion. But warn him to keep his eyes open—and his radio on. Take the satellite phones for backup, but don't use them unless you have to. Assume we're being bugged and tracked. Ditto for the plane."

Tex wiped stinging salt from his eyes.

"Those guys might have been some local gringos, Tex, but not likely. Best guess is, the Feds are surveilling us, building a case. So we take advantage of that. They won't move too fast. There's too much at stake. Go on. You know what to do."

"Got it. See you at Miskito Keys."

MONDAY, JULY 16, 2012:
PASADENA, CALIFORNIA

"It never occurred to us to encrypt data transmissions from Rover, Felicia." Dr. Robert Kanewski said. "Why would we have complicated the vehicle design like that in the rush to launch the mission? Let's accept what we can't change and focus on the mission." He set a hardback book on the corner of her desk, keeping a safe distance from the temperamental woman. "You ought to read this."

She raised an eyebrow, Spock-like, under her jet-black dyed hair. "What are you trying to pull, Robert?"

"It's titled *Don't Sweat the Small Stuff*. Very apropos," he answered, backing away.

"Don't you dare insult me, Robert Kanewski. I can crush you like a cockroach. It's *not* small stuff. You fix this problem, or I will."

"Ronnie Williams is doing us a favor, Felicia. Thanks to his posting of the alien images — or whatever they are — the interest in our programs is at an all-time high. He's shown the world that they can touch us, that we're accessible — even if we're not. And this way, the data gets out without you having to take the fall."

"No! I won't take any falls around here!" she shouted. "But *you* might. Maybe you can't cover the transmissions from that spider thing, but you *will* find a way to protect your Rover's data before she lands — or else!"

An ashtray smashed into the wall. It wasn't the first time she'd thrown it in her ten years at the center, and it didn't faze Robert as he dodged it with a deft feint to the left. "You really ought to take pitching lessons, Felicia. You've got a lousy arm." He turned and walked out, slamming her door.

"Don't you dare walk out on me!" she yelled, her screeching voice blissfully muffled as he headed down the hall.

"Want a challenge, Miracle Man?" Robert asked as he walked into Mars Mission Control and placed a hand on Scott's shoulder.

The young man turned around, flashing a thumbs up. "Always. The harder the better. Gotta keep my edge."

"Find a way to protect the Rover 3 data stream. Take Ronnie Williams offline for the landing and the first forty-eight hours or so afterward. I want to see what's happening when Rover opens her eyes, and not have to worry about who else can see it too. Don't shut him down forever—just long enough to give us some control of the panic when Rover lands. And give me an excuse to provide us plausible deniability when he finally figures it out."

"Already on it, Dr. K." Scott said, as he turned in his seat and opened a programming application on his computer.

"You know," Robert said, pacing the floor of the operation center. "I kind of admire the guy, enterprising ham radio buff that he is." He took a quarter from his pocket and studied the Georgia emblem, then flipped the coin high in the air. "Can't imagine how he managed to put that space radio rig together. But good as he is, we need to get the wicked witch off her broom—and out of our hair—just for a few days."

35

VICE PRESIDENT LANCE RYAN took the phone call along with his boss in the Oval Office. The chief of staff and press secretary joined them. FBI Director Noble was insistent that he speak to President Manchester immediately. On speakerphone.

"What is it, Noble?" the vice president barked. "We're busy. Did you find them or not?"

"Yes sir, twenty so far. All U.S. citizens. And they're all on the move."

"Are you sure about this? You already set us up once . . . "

"Sir, I can't tell you for certain who funded them, or why, but I can tell you that these are, without question, the people who carried out the attacks—and they are definitely *not* Arabs or Iranians. If this was a Muslim plot, then the Islamists paid Americans to pull it off." Noble paused. "I have a recommendation, sir."

"I don't know if I want to hear it," growled the vice president.

"Let him have his say." the president said, his arms folded as he spoke up for the first time.

"Thank you, sir," Noble said. "I recommend that we put a lid on Operation Yellow Arrow. Parts of the Iranian connection don't add up, at least not from my perspective. We need more time to snag these perps in Honduras. I wouldn't expend political capital on another wartime action in Iran — at least not yet."

The vice president slammed his fist into the wall of the Oval Office. The chief of staff started to speak up, but President Manchester waved him off, with a deadly look toward Ryan.

"We'll wait," the president said. "But understand this, Director Noble. No matter who did the work on 3/21, we also know that al Salah is real. And dangerous. We won't be able to wait long."

MARTIAN CALENDAR DAY 326, MONTH OF SCORPIUS, YEAR 28: MARS

As the Rover screamed into Mars's thin carbon dioxide atmosphere on a rendezvous with destiny, the mushroom-shaped aero shield below it glowed a deep orange-red as it absorbed the energy of Rover 3's blistering approach speed. Eleven months distant from Earth, it was only minutes away from Mars.

As it slowed, Rover 3 deployed a series of chutes that blossomed above the spacecraft like three monster zinnias, with the robot unit and its aero brake dangling far below. The aero shield eventually tumbled away, falling ten thousand meters onto the rocky plain below where it shattered into hundreds of fragments of Earth litter.

The Chryse Planitia region lay on the near horizon as the trajectory of the bobbing spacecraft and its parachutes carried it northeast across the western hemisphere of Mars. The rugged western Ophir Planum region, with its thousand-kilometer-long canyons that would dwarf Earth's Grand Canyon, lay behind the descending spacecraft, her Vectran air bags inflating to cushion the impending impact.

Chryse Planitia, home to Viking and the alien visitors, was now in full view below. Basin-shaped low elevations lay to the north of cratered highlands. Giant outflow channels, the Martian rivers — long since evaporated, and known as Maja and Kasei Valles — had once drained these higher elevations and emptied into the Chryse Planitia.

Viking 1 had come here thirty-five years ago in search of water and life, to an area where channels converged and flat sediment areas made for fewer hazards to a lander. There could no longer be any doubt that this had once been a watery planet. Teardrop-shaped islands dotted the landscape to the south, where water had once flowed around the craters Bok, Lod, Dromore, and Gold, forming elongated tails of debris and sediment. Except for the craters and the ruddy red landscape, this could easily be Earth.

Monstrous Vectran fiber bags deflated as the craft slammed into the rock-strewn surface, like an interplanetary fall into a super-sized pole-vault airbag. The chutes separated at impact and floated downwind, away from the Rover, eliminating the possibility of fatal tangles.

Rover opened her eyes. Most residents of Earth might say that the surface of Mars looked like the Nevada high desert. Small and medium-sized rocks, up to half a meter in length, were scattered everywhere in the flat red dust. Rover's navigation systems also awoke automatically and began to triangulate her position based on the detailed surface mapping a decade earlier by the Europeans. She concluded that her position was northeast of Lexington crater and six kilometers southwest of Viking 1 with its alien visitors. After two hundred million kilometers of space travel, Rover was only six thousand meters shy of her destination.

With her telescopic mast, Rover pointed long-range digital eyes toward the northeast and located her quarry. There, on a small ridge of what was once dubbed the Yorktown region of Chryse Planitia, on a branch of the Xantha Dorsa ridge system, Viking 1 waited. Thirty-five years before, the gangly white probe had landed on America's Bicentennial, surrounded by a complex of craters named for the original thirteen American colonies. Viking 1 was distant, but her image in the morning light was clear. To the northeast along the low ridge sat Rover's ultimate prey. Reflecting brilliantly in the sunrise, two alien spider-like craft squatted motionless southwest of Viking, just as their own imagery had shown and Dr. Kanewski's team of professionals had predicted.

In a moment, Rover confirmed months of alien transmissions: the scenes matched. The visitors were, in fact, real.

What Dr. Kanewski could not have predicted was the true color scheme of Mars. Not the reddish brick color of so many older Viking 1 images, but more of a ruddy red-brown, darkening in the areas away from the sun, and more reddish toward the sun. Dull gray basaltic rocks were scattered across the plain and surrounded by thin broad patches of white frost and wisps of windblown red soil. Rover watched the frost sublimate away as the rising Sun warmed the soil, a real-time event that no one on Earth could appreciate through still imagery.

The Sun rose on an especially dusty day. A bright bluish-white ring, seen first in 2004 by the Spirit and Opportunity rovers, surrounded the solar disc. Away from the Sun, Rover gazed on a light amber sky, almost butterscotch yellow. It transitioned to a yellow-orange glow in the sky away from the sunrise. On Mars, the colors of the sky depended on the time of day, the sun angle, the persistence of dust, and the direction of gaze. Rover took it all in, as she scanned the horizon and the sky above.

The first commands from Dr. Kanewski's team reached Rover nine minutes after landing, and she was ready to move. There would be no days of preparation to roll off and explore. Only minutes. Rising up like a gangly colt on articulating legs and eight serrated wheels, Rover leapt to life and began a journey across the rocky soil to meet the alien visitors, face to face.

"Ladies and gentlemen, Rover has arrived on Mars!" Dr. Kanewski announced as he addressed a packed control room, while keeping an eye on his boss. Dr. Bondurant stood near the front of the crowd, frequently looking back over her shoulder, as if she expected someone to arrive.

"We have confirmation of a first signal, indicating that the package has landed safely. We'll know more shortly, after her autonomous navigation and communication systems update her position and transmit a first report on status and location." He pointed to a digital map, identifying the Viking 1 area and its geography, and the intended landing location of the new probe.

"The Rover's large cushioning bags will have deflated by now, relaxing her to the surface without a series of dangerous bounces. Soon, when her first imagery arrives, we will see her rise above the deflated Vectran material and drive away." He recounted the type of terrain, the erection of the antenna and camera mast, and the schedule for scientific experiments.

"It is late evening here, and at Mars, the planet is rotating out of view. We have planned this to allow us maximum time to observe the approach to the landing site. Rover will let us know she is fine, then get close to the alien landers and shut down. In about twelve hours, we will be ready to watch history unfold."

Scott interrupted, with the confirmation they'd been waiting for: "I've got a strong signal! The first Rover imagery is queuing now! We're there!"

| MARS

Rover was up on her spindly jointed legs, looking like an eight-legged version of a two meter-tall British pram with a satellite dish. Jointed linkages allowed the wheeled appendages to adapt to varied terrain, a drive system that had overcome every obstacle that NASA could dish up in Nevada. Her grand Martian test lay before her. Within minutes of landing, her wheels were churning as she rolled over the limp puncture-resistant material that lay on the ground surrounding the heat-resistant shroud. Downwind the huge chutes were strewn on rocky ground, the white material blending in with the early morning's frost.

At a moderate one-half kilometer per hour, Rover began the slow and deliberate trek toward the alien landers and Viking 1. With a camera ready on her erect mast, Rover used an autonomous navigation capability developed for Army robots in the battlefield. During her progress toward the Viking 1 landing site, Rover used preprogrammed terrain data augmented by twelve visual sensors that enabled the craft to detect size, predict depth with some certainty, and navigate based on an integration of imagery and onboard sensor data. A stream of information from onboard science missions that sampled the soil compaction, temperature, atmosphere content, and dust density, burst from Rover's high-gain antenna and headed back to Earth.

As Mars's western hemisphere slowly turned away from Earth and cut off direct communication, Rover continued on her own. During the next ten hours she would cross the plain to reach the alien site, then wait at a safe distance for the coming morning. And wait for new radio contact with

Earth.

By the time the Sun began to set, with its characteristic blue aureole in the dusty Martian sky, Rover had reached the Viking 1 site. She slowed her trek and stopped five hundred meters from the closest silver alien spider. Using an automated target recognition algorithm, Rover watched for any alien movement. She could react, without Earth input, to any possible activity. With a nine-minute time communication delay each way, her connection to Dr. Kanewski's team was tenuous. It was up to Rover to defend herself, or run, if necessary.

Rover settled down on jointed legs, resting in her cradle of eight wheels. A red beacon on top of her highest appendage pierced the night every second so that controllers might later watch her approach through the remote eyes of the visitors. If the aliens sent images of Viking, they might also send those of an approaching Rover. As darkness consumed the scene, Rover began to shut down all but her essential systems. The beacon pulsed bright red, awaiting the coming dawn.

On cue, as though they'd waited for Rover to sleep, both aliens stood up on powerful silver legs and began moving nimbly in single file to the southwest . . . giant mechanical tarantulas creeping toward the unsuspecting craft. As predicted, they recorded and transmitted images of what they saw, a Rover settled to the ground, with a bright beacon strobing the night above her. But hidden from Earth by the rotation of Mars, there was no communication connection to allow NASA, or Ronnie Williams, to watch them approach the newly arrived Rover 3.

Under a starlit Martian night sky, the two silver spiders closed on Rover to within a few meters, and then settled behind the Earthcraft on the opposite side from her northeast route of travel. They lowered themselves back into their characteristic pose, legs bent, as if to spring, bulbous bodies dangling just above the surface.

They waited.

36

MARTHA WILLIAMS STEPPED INTO Radio Central late at night, dressed for bed.

"When are you going to relax, Ron? You've been working on that computer all day."

Ronnie leaned back in his antique oak swivel chair and rubbed his eyes. "I can see the signal, Martha. I can record it, demodulate it, and get it into a data stream. But for some reason, after watching Rover fly all the way to Mars, I can't for the life of me decode the data. If I didn't know better, I'd say NASA has encrypted this thing. But I didn't think that was possible."

Martha began to rub his shoulders, and his head sank under the relaxation of her hands. "Don't beat yourself up about it. Remember, this is a hobby, not a job. Okay?"

"I know. It's such . . . a challenge . . . such an opportunity. I wanted to watch this landing live. NASA announced that it landed but they're not putting any images on their web page. Hundreds of thousands of people—and the news services—were depending on me. All I can tell them is that 'technical difficulties' interrupted my Martian pictures."

"Like I said, Ronnie, it's okay."

Ronnie tapped on the soft plasma monitor, his finger on a dialogue box depicting unintelligible data from the noncompliant Rover. "What's your secret, girl? What are you hiding up there and why don't you want us to know about it?"

WEDNESDAY, JULY 18, 2012: PASADENA, CALIFORNIA

Dr. Kanewski and the Mars Rover team, along with hundreds of reporters, news affiliates, VIPs, and NASA employees, were on hand the next day at Jet Propulsion Laboratory in Pasadena several hours before Mars began to rise. Outside, the streets were jammed with late arrivals who had no hope of a place to park.

Robert surveyed the gathering chaos from his office window. "What a circus, Gloria."

"It is," she said, scurrying about his office, picking up last night's used coffee cups and arranging his piles of technical papers scattered about the floor. "I'm glad I came in early."

"Me, too—no, leave *that* pile alone! Did we get the final list of VIPs?"

"Yes. And you-know-who is here!" she said, adding a "Whoopee!" as she twirled about the room tidying up the last of the piles of manila folders.

"Tell me it's not true."

"Sorry, Dr. K. The big guy himself, the grand poobah of alien muckety muck, the Right Rocket Reverend and most holy emperor of space ritual, our priest of the heavens and celestial beings, Father Malcolm."

"Hey. That's pretty good. Did you make that up?"

"I heard it on this morning's Bubba Dog show. Couldn't resist," she said as she strolled out of his office.

"So he's not here, then? You were joking?"

"Oh, he'll be here!" she said, wagging a finger at him from the doorway. "You've got a message from Dr. B on your e-mail—if you ever read it," she chided. "The boss lady wants to make sure you'll be there with her to greet him . . . in person."

"I can't wait," he said. "Send her a note that I'll be there."

"Already did," Gloria said with a grin. Her smile suddenly disappeared as she glanced back at her office a few meters away. "Uh, Dr. K, I think you ought to come see this . . ."

Robert got up and crossed the room. Gloria pointed into an adjoining guest area, where a television met the insatiable needs of news junkies like her. Right now, the screen displayed a "LIVE from JPL" news ticker and the face of Malcolm Raines.

Robert came into Gloria's office, sick at his stomach from the stress and from a nagging conviction that his day would be spent reacting to yet another Raines vision—not the real science he'd worked so hard to accomplish.

"Father Raines, please, a moment if you could." The CNN reporter had pulled Raines into the NASA press booth for a live news feed. Dr. Kanewski shook his head and groaned.

"Thank you, Cynthia. I'm glad to be here for this historic occasion. Truly historic. But God's spirit troubles me today. I've heard the same message many times in the past hours. I sense dread and doom . . . aggravation . . . possible aggression." There was an icy chill to his prophetic words.

"This is the message I hear repeated," he continued. "'You have awakened my people.'" He lowered his head for a moment of silence, observed across the planet on the nonstop news channel by a billion listeners.

"I do not have an interpretation for you, Cynthia, but I suspect we will see with our own eyes when this message is revealed to us today."

Gloria turned toward Robert, pale. She didn't talk, unusual for his melodramatic assistant. "Don't tell me he's getting to you, too, Gloria?"

"You have to admit—every time he gets on TV and says this stuff, it happens."

"Yeah. I wonder . . ." Robert murmured, rubbing his chin.

"How could he know? I mean, think about it, sir. He predicts what the aliens will do, and he nails it every time."

"I don't have all the answers," Robert said. "But every action in this universe has a cause and effect. There's a reason for everything, even if we don't understand it. This much I do know: We have a mission to run today, and I'm not letting that space priest upstage the biggest day of my career. So let's go greet some aliens!"

Gloria broke into a smile, spun again in her pleated skirt, and rushed down the hall toward the control center. "Don't be late!" she called over her shoulder. "I'll make sure you have a seat right next to the good Reverend."

"You do that, Gloria." He turned back to the post-Raines analysis on CNN, his head cocked to one side. "How *does* he do that?"

LA MARQUE, TEXAS

Mars would rise in two hours. There had to be a trick, a weak point, some hint as to how to pull these images out of the ether. The challenge of cracking Rover's code consumed Ronnie.

Martha brought a fresh cup of coffee and sat down next to him. She'd just risen; he'd been up all night. "You know, it's a good thing you weren't on shift today. Calling in sick just wouldn't be right."

Ronnie didn't look at her. After an all-nighter working this encryption problem he was in no mood for a nagging about workplace ethics. He thanked her for the coffee and stared at the screen. His fatigue was about to overcome his caffeine addiction.

"You told me once," she said slowly, her hand on his shoulder, "'when life hands you lemons, make lemonade.' Remember that?" She began to rub his neck.

"I do." He closed his eyes and took a break, aware that his wife was trying to get through his thick stubborn shell. And that he needed to let her in.

"When you told me that, you also said 'when all else fails, go back to first principles.' Remember?"

"Uh-huh."

"So, Ron, if this is one of those sticky points—and you always manage to get past them—go back to first principles. What do you know, and how can you make it past the parts you don't?" She squeezed his neck playfully. "C'mon, let's do it."

"You're serious?" he asked, staring into her familiar face.

She nodded as she squeezed his hand, and they walked through his problem, piece by piece, for the next half hour.

"What time is it, Martha?" he asked later as he worked feverishly at the terminal.

"Nearly eight. Why?"

"That means we've got about ninety minutes. Turn on the TV and we'll listen to the freak show at NASA while we try to solve this."

Martha clicked on the news just as Malcolm Raines came

on-screen. "You might want to come see this," she said.

As Ronnie strode into the den, there was the smooth man himself, and the shocking next prophecy: "You have awakened my people!"

Martha was clearly troubled.

Ronnie shook his head. "I don't know. This is all so crazy. And we only have a little time—wait a minute! Time! That's it! We know the time!" He turned so fast that he spilled hot coffee on himself and dropped his cup on the linoleum floor. "Ouch! Oh, Martha, I'm sorry—but I gotta go! I think I've figured it out!"

Ronnie raced back to Radio Central and his data files, talking himself through the process. "Let's see . . . the time code falls every five seconds in the main data stream . . . we should see some repetition on five second intervals . . . yes, there it is. If they hardwired this baby, I'm sunk. But if they ran a little scratch pad encipher to throw me off . . . then I can beat this." Ronnie coded up a program to filter the data and search for the time code. He tapped away on his keyboard, fingers flying in a race against time and the radio challenge of his life.

Slowly he toiled away, CNN droning in the background about the latest Raines pronouncement, his wife glued to the broadcast.

"Twenty more minutes, Ron," she called from the den, an hour later. "I know you're going to make it. You always do."

"Thanks," he said as he worked.

A few minutes later, Martha came into Radio Central, her hand to her ear. "Did you say something—I couldn't quite hear."

He suddenly punched the air with a yell: "Eureka!"

Martha, too, screamed for joy as random pixels transformed before their eyes into yesterday's saved, but previously encrypted, Rover images from the landing.

Ronnie had done it. He'd beaten NASA again.

"But how?" she asked, her plump face jiggling as she bounced on her toes in glee.

"You were right, gorgeous!" he said, jumping up and taking her in his arms. "Go back to first principles. Make lemonade. That's just what we did!"

She smiled and kissed him, and they danced together around the stuffy radio room. In their tiny wooden home on an obscure horse pasture in La Marque, Texas, two simple people had broken Scott's elaborate time-based scratch-pad encipher. Now the whole world could watch history unfold on Mars.

✳

JET PROPULSION LABORATORY, PASADENA, CALIFORNIA

"Mars is rising, Doc. This is it," Scott said from his terminal in the Mars Mission Control Center.

"All right, team," Dr. Kanewski said quietly. "You do the magic and I'll do the politics. You know your parts. Everybody ready?"

Seven experienced controllers smiled in unison, with thumbs up, and turned to their monitors. Robert beamed, proud of his select brood and honored to be in this moment. He turned to the assembled crowd of VIPs and press, seated in the conference area behind the control team, raising his voice.

"As you can see, we built this control facility for spacecraft operations, not media presentations," he said, sweeping his hand around the small, high-tech room. "Mars is about to rotate into view, and we're monitoring the strength of the incoming signal. The landing site was visible about seven minutes ago, which means that the signal, on its way to Earth, is about two minutes away. We'll soon have our first images of the landing craft close up, with a set of Earth's eyes on the planet at last."

"Dr. Kanewski," a visitor asked, "did the Rover approach the landing site last night?

"Yes. As you know, Rover sent her first images of the landing area, and the distant alien craft, during a short transmission window yesterday. She traversed most of the six kilometers to Viking in the past twelve hours. We scheduled those pictures to spool for low-priority transmission later today. What we see first will be the highest priority data that the Rover has determined we need to see—probably the last few meters of her approach to Viking 1 and the visitors."

"Give us a for-example, please, Doctor," Malcolm Raines, seated to the left of Dr. Bondurant, asked in his smooth monotone. "An example of the priority scheme and how it might take effect."

Dr. Bondurant flashed a wicked scowl at Robert. He decided to let Felicia have her day in the sun, and began to answer the space prophet. "If the Rover experienced a malfunction, or if she detected alien movement, such an event would constitute a high-priority transmission. If absolutely nothing's awry, and she's not moving yet, she'll send us streaming images of yesterday's approach to the Viking 1 site. And if she's on the move, we'll see that."

"Thank you, Doctor. And, if your Rover was attacked?" Raines asked, sitting ramrod straight in his seat, gesturing with his hands.

The audience gasped.

"I beg your pardon?" Robert asked, arms crossed and frowning.

"The Rover, if it were attacked. Would that constitute a high-priority message?

Dr. Kanewski shook his head and exhaled loudly, looking up at the ceiling, fists clenching below his crossed arms. He was about to blurt out an answer, but Scott cut in.

"If I could, Dr. K., let me take that one," Scott said as he stood up and saluted his mentor with two fingers, bringing a sudden smile to both their faces.

Scout's honor. Scott was coming to his rescue.

"Yes—go ahead, Scott. Please." Robert forced himself to turn and consult a monitor while he cooled off.

"Dr. Raines, if Rover 3 was, as you say, 'attacked,' this would be interpreted in one of two ways. First, that a mission system had failed to function. Let's say, the alien zapped the Rover's wheels with a death ray. That would about do it."

Raines started to protest, and Dr. Bondurant started out of her seat, but the chuckles in the crowd forced them both down.

"Second, if the aliens were to move and physically attack . . . yes, the Rover would notice their movement. If they approach her, she will move away. Images of an approaching alien would go to the top of the transmission queue. We wouldn't get to watch Rover turn and run in real time, but we'd get to watch it about nine minutes later. Of course, we'd be powerless to do much but watch. And, if we're lucky, we might be able to monitor the attack through the eyes of the aliens, much as we have been able to view the local scenery for months now."

The puzzled looks of the audience suggested that they still didn't understand. "Explain the path time, Scott," Robert said, his back to the audience.

"Gotcha. We're almost 160 million kilometers from Mars this morning. It takes a little while—8.96 minutes give or take—for the Rover transmissions to reach Earth. When you're being chased, nine minutes is an eternity. Nine minutes to get here, then time for us to fig-ure out what to do, then nine minutes to send the message back . . . at least twenty minutes round trip on a good day. There's no way we can drive that robot from here if it's being attacked." Many in the audience nodded. "Did that answer your question, sir?"

"Yes, it does," Raines said, looking around the room. "If you heard my prophecy this morning, I'm sure you'll understand the concern behind my question."

Robert turned and motioned with his eyes to "stop now." Scott shrugged and returned to his station.

"And on that note," Robert said as he nudged Scott back into his seat, "we have a signal! Our first data file will be displayed in just a moment!" He turned, leaning over the shoulder of his suddenly silent protégé—and coughed.

He grabbed the back of Scott's chair to steady himself as his eyes locked on the control terminal. Scott looked up, his mouth forming the silent words, *what now?*

There was only one option. "Put it on screen, Scott," he whispered. "Like it or not, here we go."

The image from Scott's terminal was redirected to the large plasma display at the front of the room. Across the top, in the command sequence dialogue box, were the words in red, "Priority: Activity detected."

Below the message, the image of an alien craft filled the lens, almost out of focus so close to the camera. It was a blurred likeness of a silver spider, probably less than a meter from the Rover. An upraised jointed leg and its blurry tip was pointed like a silver bony finger toward the camera. On another monitor, just as Scott had predicted, was a similar blurred image of Rover, seen through the alien's eyes, only a meter away.

"It's coming toward us!" Scott exclaimed. "And we're backing up!"

"Then back it up faster!" Dr. Bondurant yelled from her seat on the front row.

Robert turned from the control floor to face the gallery of visitors in seats rising up behind him, his heart racing. "Felicia," he hissed. "You can't control it. Time delay . . . remember?"

The drama shifted again to the big screen. They could all see in the images, transmitted every ten seconds, the foreground disappearing into the background as the Rover retreated, with her camera locked on the aliens. The alien craft—both of them—followed the Rover in their menacing eight-legged spider walk, their own cameras, transmitting live to Earth, locked on Rover. It was a real-life *War of the Worlds.*

Scott's hands flew across the keyboard, commanding emergency options for the Rover to consider nine minutes from now, and twenty minutes after the time of the actions they observed.

Robert ignored the audience beyond the gallery rail. He huddled over Scott's shoulder. "Where are you sending her? What's the plan?"

"I'm pointing her to the Viking 1 site. We can retreat, but apparently not as fast as those guys can move. We can swing in a large arc, east of the crater, and put Viking 1 behind us. That leaves only one avenue of approach—unless you have another plan. Eventually, we're going to have to deal with them—somehow."

Robert shook his head in disbelief. "Send it. But for all we know, they just want to shake hands." Here he was, at the pinnacle of his career, fighting a rearguard action against giant alien spiders on Mars with a time-late autonomous Rover under the watchful eye of the world's leading spiritualist. It couldn't be worse.

His cell phone began to vibrate and he heard other phones warbling in the audience behind him. "What now?" he groaned.

"The Web?" someone asked, speaking loudly to overcome the rising din in the room.

Robert recognized the voice of Cynthia, the female CNN reporter who covered Raines live outside the Center. She was talking rapid-fire into her cell phone; then she pushed across people in her row to reach the aisle. "Out of my way!" she yelled in her desperation to get to the prophet on the front row for a comment. She wasn't the only one; Raines was immediately mobbed by those around him. More loud conversations, more cell phones, and then two reporters, unable to get to Raines, stormed out the back of the room.

Robert turned from the madness and again huddled over Scott, whispering. "I've got a bad feeling about this. Check on Ronnie Williams's site. Keep it on your terminal only."

In a flash, Scott pulled up the bookmarked site, and there was the Rover data feed—clear images of what many would assume to be attacking aliens, and a warning message, all in living color and live downlink to anyone on Earth with a Web connection.

"I thought—" Robert began, his mouth falling open.

Scott shook his head. "I fixed it, Doc. Really! He'd have to be a genius to have broken the seed and the cipher that fast."

"Well, he *did*—" Robert was cut off by a shrill scream behind him. He knew that voice.

"NO!"

Dr. Bondurant, suddenly aware of what was happening, flew out of her seat, both hands on the gallery rail and screaming at Robert in full shrewish fury, audience forgotten and Raines left behind. "Robert, tell me that what I just heard is not true! This *cannot* be happening!"

Robert watched as Malcolm Raines, on a live audio feed with Cynthia and CNN, turned toward Dr. Bondurant and pulled her away, gesturing to the cameraman to hold the interview for a moment. Raines escorted Felicia toward the rear door as she ranted about firing both Scott and Robert.

As they disappeared, Robert could hear Raines raise his voice in a desperate attempt to answer reporters' questions while he pulled Felicia out of the fray. Robert shook his head in wonder at the sight, news crews fawning over the space preacher while history unfolded on Mars.

"Raines Was Right!" read the CNN ticker below the image of the prophet leading the director of JPL from the control room, an image of

Rover and pursuing spiders on the big screen in the background, and Dr. Robert Kanewski dimly visible, standing alone at the gallery rail.

The transformation was instantaneous. The room was suddenly clear of everyone but payload controllers and scientists. In the eerie silence of the aftershock, they all looked at each other, then back to the big screen. There they could see the Rover making valiant attempts to retreat, as both aliens pursued it like hungry mammoth spiders stalking a fresh robot meal. On Scott's Internet browser, the same images played out, just as they were seeing them in Pasadena.

The science in Robert's control room had been forgotten by media and visitor alike, and he didn't mind at all. *Thank you, Mr. Williams!* Robert thought, watching the eerie pursuit simultaneously through the eyes of Rover and two aliens.

"She doesn't have that last command yet," Scott explained. "If she takes off too fast, she'll hit a big rock and we'll lose the whole shebang."

"No, she won't. She'll back up with care. We didn't program in hysteria, remember?"

Scott waved at the empty gallery behind them. "Who's hysterical?"

37

THE HORROR OF THE past two hours had seared itself into their memories. Martha was cradled in Ronnie's arms as they sat, transfixed, in front of the monitors, watching an epic pursuit from two perspectives—alien and earthling.

Across the top of Rover's data screen, the command warning continued to flash red. "Priority: Activity Detected." And below, every ten seconds, a new image appeared of two hideous alien craft at very close range. Like a stop-action movie, they could see the aliens lift their long silver legs, advancing in pursuit of the Rover. And in the eyes of the aliens, Rover was backing away, with Viking growing closer in the background of every new picture. Two hours and more than seven hundred images later, they watched a stop-action movie of *Rover Runs Away*, transmitted from across the solar system.

An hour and a half after the first gripping scenes had arrived at Earth,

Rover had closed to within meters of the original Viking lander. For half an hour the autonomous robot stood within what seemed to be arm's reach of the first Martian explorer, and for a brief respite, the spiders stood safely at a distance. In the past three minutes, though, the aliens continued to advance, drawing within a meter of the Rover, on either side.

In Rover's image, Ronnie noticed two appendages descend from one of the silver craft, short mechanical grapples that reminded him of the claws on a lobster. They were blurry as they came in close to Rover's camera, but unmistakable. These were not legs, and they reached up on flexible hose-like appendages, apparently snapping for Rover's elevated eyes, her camera on an elevated mast two meters above the surface of the planet.

Martha began crying softly as she sank her head onto Ronnie's shoulder. He felt oddly responsible for the panic that was no doubt sweeping Earth, as people watched these same scenes through his website. He felt as if he'd opened a Martian version of Pandora's Box. America was on Mars—the aliens were real—the prophet was right again—and Rover was under attack. Ronnie leaned back in his swivel chair, his head tilted against Martha's, both their hearts racing, as he whispered quietly into the fragrant curls of her thick gray hair. "Good heavens, Martha. *What next?*"

BAYTOWN, TEXAS

Michelle's heart raced as Keith held her in his arms. The two were on the couch in their new home, unaware how tightly they gripped each other. Their attention was devoted entirely to Ronnie Williams's riveting images, graphic pictures that had been spooling to the Web, and then to the television networks for the past two hours. Ronnie's interplanetary snapshots poured into their living room.

This scene was personal for Michelle. She was going to this forsaken place, this robot battleground, hundreds of millions of kilometers away. And far from Keith. She would leave for Mars in two weeks; in only four days, she would be in pre-flight quarantine. She had less than ninety-six hours left, precious little time remaining with her new husband, and now this . . . the battleground of her future. They watched intently.

Keith reached for the remote control, switching off the drama, and bringing an immediate protest from Michelle.

"Keith—"

He shushed her with a finger on her lips. "I don't know what to make of the events today on Mars. But I do know this: I love you more than my own life." He pointed at the blank screen and its imagined drama beyond their sight. "I understand that you need to know—personally and professionally—what's happening out there. Trust me, Michelle, there will be plenty of analysis and reports to tell us what we miss in the next few minutes. But don't let what's happening on Mars steal you from me for the rest of this day—and the few days we have left."

He paused, breathing deeply, she thought, to regain his calm. But the sweat stains on his thin polo shirt gave him away. She smiled, at ease with this man who worked so hard to open himself up to her.

He moved off the couch and knelt at her side, her right hand in his. He pulled a small box from his front pocket and placed a ruby in a gold setting on her right hand, his pulse throbbing in her grasp. "A Mars ring, for you. Something to remember me by when you're way out there doing something historic, and I'm back here shuttling old fat men to meetings in Washington."

Michelle chuckled, her hazel eyes wet with emotion. She rubbed them dry with her left hand and pushed back the auburn bangs that hung limp over her cheek.

"It will be over and done with before you know it, Mr. Caskey. Thank you for this. I'll see you every day in this wonderful stone. I'm so glad to be your missus." She giggled for the first time in what seemed like years, put her arms around him, drew him into a kiss, and then released him. "You have *no* idea how glad," she said as she locked the memory of this special moment deep within her heart.

Alice whimpered as she laid her head in John's lap; Amy sat at his side. The three of them watched in horror as Ronnie Williams's images filled their television screen. Now midday on Wednesday, John's family waited with Rover, NASA, and the rest of the world. His youngest son watched from the couch; two other boys split their attention between Mars and a portable video game. The family had planned an outdoor hamburger barbecue today, one of their last together before John left for five hundred days. But no one wanted to leave the room, captivated as they were with the focus of John's upcoming journey. The uncooked patties waited on the kitchen counter.

At one level, John wanted to turn the television off, to protect his family from this horror. But he knew that this news, this conflict millions of kilometers away, would blanket the planet. Of all people, his wife and children deserved to know.

Amy held the remote in a quivering hand, stroking Alice's blonde curls with the other while Alice gripped her dad's leg. John's little girl and her mother shivered in his grasp as they watched with him.

Suddenly, the two sinister craft began to move. The chase and standoff of the past two hours was ending. The aliens moved abreast of Rover, each extending a pair of metallic grapples as if to tear or snip off part of the earth robot. One claw, seen through an alien's camera, grasped at a front wheel, slightly rocking the robot. A second grapple, from the other alien, took hold of another front wheel on the opposite side and together the two lifted the front of the earth visitor a few centimeters off the ground, then lowered it and released their grip. Rover's camera pitched up, imaging the Martian sky for a brief moment—pitching the stomachs of earth's observers with it.

Rover had nowhere to go, forced as it was into a cul-de-sac and into the clutches of hostile pursuers. Rover didn't—or couldn't—fight back. It was an exploration vehicle, after all, not a battle-bot. But this position, cornered with a dead Viking at its back, wasn't the dignified or courageous way to die that John would have chosen. He filed the moment away in his memory—should he ever be faced with the same dilemma—and the same silver foe.

John, Amy, and Alice watched through Rover's eyes as the spiders' pincer-like arms released the wheels and curled up in curious loops, drawing underneath and inside each of the alien bodies. The pairs of claws disappeared inside the separate bellies of the craft and emerged, each with a package in their grasp.

Chills ran down John's spine as he held Amy tighter. The aliens surely would pull out a weapon now, or perhaps some smaller ravenous version of themselves, to dispatch poor Rover. All that the residents of Earth could do was watch.

The next pictures relayed by Ronnie Williams to the Internet, and to the world, changed lives around the planet. Even Raines had failed to prophesy the remarkable event. Each craft—or, perhaps, alien creature, since no one knew for sure which it was—brought out of its belly a small golden orb, held gently in the clutches of those chilling pincers. The orbs glowed a brilliant copper, then brassy yellow, then gold. They must have pulsated because their brilliance changed with each frame of the still action from Mars. Together, the two craft lowered the orbs from within their bellies, and the pincer arms stretched out in front of the aliens toward the Rover, gently balancing their perfect spheres.

The once-hostile aliens were passive now, as if each waited to present an interplanetary offering—two golden spheres—to the gangly earth machine. Or perhaps the spheres were weapons that would dispatch Rover in the next image frame. There was no way to know, here or on Mars. Rover's inelegant head pivoted on a tall mast, and her wheels ground down to their axles in the Martian dust. Like a Dr. Seuss standoff, Earth lander and alien stood together on the plain, contemplating the gifts, each waiting for the other to react.

Then, in an unprogrammed autonomous move that surprised even Rover's designers, she reached out her single articulated grappling fixture to touch one of the golden orbs. As Rover and alien connected on Mars, the spheres flashed a brilliant blue, their brightness overpowering Rover's digital camera. The aliens set their offerings in the dust in front of her, squatted in a strange intergalactic curtsy, and backed away ten meters, where they settled down, bellies on the ground.

The Voice spoke.

John recognized it at once as his family and the news somehow faded instantly into the background. Everything was silent around him.

All of his experiences seemed to converge on this moment. In his mission to Mars he could now see the fulfillment of that promise given him so many years ago—the promise that he would make a difference.

For the third time in his life, God spoke to John's heart with a vibrant clarity and an unmistakable presence.

I have called you for such a time as this.

38

"**EVERYTHING'S READY. WE SHOULD** have a 'go' from Washington in less than an hour," Kerry said over the internal communications circuit. Five close-shaven heads nodded in response, tight-lipped warfighters in the battle management center of the Air Force AC-130U *Spooky* gunship.

Arrayed around the remote Miskito Keys off the Caribbean coast of Nicaragua were hundreds of U.S. Special Operations Forces, or SOF, ready to pounce on the most notorious terrorists of the decade. On board the *Spooky*, tonight's lethal airborne command post, Special Agent Kerry was the only federal man in a crew of ten men and women that orbited thirty kilometers west of the remote archipelago. FBI agents and Special Forces teams were dispersed around Central America, with support from Honduran, Nicaraguan, and Colombian military units. Hundreds of U.S. personnel had infiltrated virtually every Central American country and the northern reaches of South America, once Nick's complex computer code was broken that located him and his men.

"Mike Niner X-ray, this is Papa Gulf, over."

"Go ahead, Papa Gulf," Kerry replied into his headset microphone.

"Belize reports two more down. Prints are confirmed. Picked 'em up headed out of Tuneffe Island on a 'go-fast'."

"Copy Papa Gulf," Kerry said. "Your aircraft is on the ground waiting in Belmopan City. Extradite and get them to Miami. Local military will meet you plane-side and smooth the paperwork."

"Papa Gulf copies. Out."

"Kerry?" A muscular Hispanic man in a tan flight suit seated next to him tapped the special agent on his shoulder.

"What you got, Tech Sergeant?" Kerry asked, pulling back one earphone to be able to hear him.

"Go up Comm 1, sir," the sensor operator said, his voice raised over the whine of the turboprops.

Kerry nodded, replaced his earphones and switched to the private intercom channel. The warrior to his left began to talk, while facing his equipment and managing the gunship's long-range imaging system.

"We've got a call from Isla de San Andres, sir. Henckey and two others are in custody now. Colombian military's assisting." He pointed at the Tactical Situation Map, or TSM, in front of him, indicating a small island to the southeast, labeled "Colombia."

The sensor operator continued as he hit a sequence of buttons on his green-glowing plasma panel. "Navigator got the report over satellite phone five minutes ago. Henckey's buddies matched the profile you gave us." He paused, looking at Kerry as though sizing up the agent before him. "So, how'd you nail 'em? You've been chasin' these guys for a while." He turned back to his monitor.

"Steganography."

"Digital watermarking?"

Kerry nodded, following the battle command updates on his own tactical map as he talked. "We're pretty sure the leader's a U.S. citizen—Elias Ulrich. Goes by 'Nick.' He's a smart cookie. Built up a covered Web-based communication network all over Central America, with at least sixteen other covert networks spread across the globe, using the most complex code and steganography we've seen yet . . . spread across the Internet from South America to China. Tens of thousands of keys across millions of Web pages. We got lucky on a single fingerprint that one of his people left behind. From that print, CIA led us to some foreign intel, and from there to his computer in Roatan. After that, the floodgates opened."

The tech sergeant turned toward Kerry, removing his headset, and indicating for Kerry to do the same. He pointed to the back of the plane and motioned with a tilt of his head that Kerry should follow him.

"I know him." Tech Sergeant Leon said a moment later when they were both alone near the rear of the aircraft. He was stone-faced, arms crossed.

"You what?"

"Ulrich. I know him," he repeated. "Served under him a long time ago. He'd just come out of Special Forces and transitioned to space operations. I was junior enlisted, at Vandenberg Air Force Base." Leon paused. "Ulrich mentored me . . . he encouraged me to do this." He waved his hand about the radio and weapon-laden aircraft. "So, I did. And no regrets. I'm the sensor operator on this beast . . . one of the few enlisted in the Air Force with this much firepower at his disposal."

Kerry stared in disbelief at the copper-skinned man standing over him. "You served with Ulrich? Did you know he was our prime suspect before now?"

"No, sir. Not until I heard the navigator's call from Homestead Air Force Base a few minutes ago. That's why I wanted talk to you. In private." He motioned with another tilt of his head back toward the battle-management center. "Away from them. I don't want to be tied to him—to Ulrich. But you need to know, he's unpredictable. He's much smarter than you might think."

Kerry shook his head. "That much I'd surmised. But help me here, Tech Sergeant. This guy doesn't compute. Until a drinking incident in Colorado, he was a senior master sergeant in the Air Force with a stellar career. Nothing that would indicate domestic terrorism or that he's a homicidal maniac. Why'd he flip his wig and do this?"

"Don't know, Kerry, but whatever the records say, Ulrich was the best. I know the official story about Colonel Fredericks and the trip to Cripple Creek, if that's what you're referring to. Trust me—that conviction was a sham."

"Seems you're the only one who believes that, Tech Sergeant. The evidence is damning."

"Don't believe everything you read, Agent Kerry. Ulrich was set up. And don't underestimate him. He's the most meticulous planner and detail-oriented guy I've known. If it's Ulrich you're up against, plan for the worst." Tech Sergeant Leon turned toward his tactical station, but hesitated. "And don't cross General Fredericks. He'll crucify you." He pointed a finger at Kerry. "Let's keep our little talk between us. Okay?"

Kerry nodded. Tech Sergeant Leon started to leave, then turned and rested his hand on the plane's Howitzer-like 102-mm cannon.

"Oh, yeah. One more thing. I don't know if it shows in your intel, but Ulrich had an odd side. A really weird fascination with clowns."

Kerry wrinkled his eyebrows. "That doesn't show up in any of his background. You sure we're talking about the same guy?"

"Sounds crazy, I know. He had a huge collection . . . all kinds.

Mostly Russian clown dolls and framed pictures of Russian circus performers. I accidentally stumbled onto his collection once when I picked him up for work. He was real mad—didn't want me nosing around. But I asked him about them, since he was mentoring me and all. What he said might be important."

Leon paused, eyes locked with Kerry under the glare of the red overhead lights. He steadied himself as the plane banked to the left. "He had this favorite saying . . . that clowns were the perfect proof of what he called 'Ulrich's Law: Everything is not what it first appears.'"

Tech Sergeant Leon gripped Kerry's shoulder with a hard muscular hand, as if to get his attention. "I'd presume the worst. Ulrich is smart, and he always—I mean always—has a way out."

CIA agents and Army Special Forces loaded into three armed MH-60 *Pave Hawk* helicopters on the moonlit beach of a tiny Nicaraguan island that had been transformed into a U.S. military base camp. Beneath a swaying canopy of coconut trees, three portable shelters housed a thriving operations center that coordinated over two hundred Special Forces poised to capture four men on the Miskito Keys to the north.

Fifty islands of keys and inlets, most measured in square meters, were arrayed in Nicaragua's protected Miskito Keys National Park east of the barren Central American coast. Ninety kilometers northeast of Puerto Cabezas, the islands were the occasional destination of eco-tourists in search of green sea turtles, azure waters, and thriving lobsters that swarmed the walls of the bountiful tropical reefs.

Tonight, one weathered lobsterman hut in these islands was the focus of America's largest manhunt since the invasion of Iraq. Two Cigarette boats, sleek craft that could cut the run from Puerto Cabezas down from three hours to one, sat anchored off the beach near the hut.

A single lamp blazed in the hut's single window, a beacon clearly visible thirty kilometers away with the long-range eyes of the aircraft's low-light level TV and infrared suite, both under the control of Tech Sergeant Leon. Men were moving inside.

"They're still in there. Three, maybe four of 'em," Leon said.

Kerry nodded. "Four." He watched images of his prey from his tactical station, glad that the same pictures were winging their way to the operations center on the island in the Pearl Keys. He waited only on word from Washington before striking.

"It's Carlisle, Farnsworth, Ulrich, and the Cowboy. They were all seen boarding the boats in Bluefields. Those four, plus the sixteen we've nailed so far. Pretty sure this is the leadership," Kerry stated. Sweat formed on his forehead despite the intense chill of the conditioned air in the plane. "Looks like one of 'em's coming outside. Zoom in tighter on the door, Leon."

The compact electro-optic system, able to clearly see a man at thirty kilometers, trained its sensitive eyes on the hut. "Carlisle," Kerry said over intercom. The hulking frame of the man was a familiar sight to him by now.

"Train your magnification on the window." Kerry's heart pounded as he watched the minutes tick by without attack approval from Washington and the State Department.

"There's still three in there, sir."

"But what's Carlisle doing? He's headed to the boat!" Kerry yelled as he watched Carlisle, then three more men suddenly dash out of the hut, running toward the shallow surf. "They're leaving!" Kerry cursed in frustration at the slow response from the bureaucrats. The White House demanded the final say on this operation, for whatever reason. He swore again.

"Mike Niner X-Ray, this is Charlie Tango, over." *Finally*, Kerry thought. *The White House is responding.*

Kerry answered the call. "This is Mike Niner X-Ray. Go ahead."

"You are cleared for pickup. Nicaraguan authorities are on standby in Managua. Proceed."

The interior of the crowded gunship exploded into action. Men at every station readied their sensors and weapons should the aircraft be called into action. The fire control officer and mission commander relayed calls to their charges in the armed light attack boats waiting below them. From a five-kilometer perimeter around the spit of land, converging from six directions, Navy SEALs in sleek black boats raced toward the tiny island and its departing tenants. Three black *Pave Hawk* helicopters lifted off the sands of the island in the Pearl Keys, skimming across the water at two hundred knots in a desperate rush to stop the escape. The approval from Washington had come, but just minutes too late.

The long-range airborne optics and infrared suite captured every movement of the men, all four wading rapidly toward their boats. Kerry slammed his fist into the armrest of his tactical station as he watched. *Someone tipped them. But who?*

Over calm waters and through the air, U.S. Special Forces sped toward their target. Less than a minute after the fateful call from Washington, both of the terrorists' v-hulled ocean racers were on the run, headed away from their shallow anchorage and east into open sea. The SEALs were less than two kilometers away when the fleeing speedboats slowed, pulled alongside each other, stopped briefly, and then roared away in opposite directions, north and south, at top speed.

"Leon! Give me tracks on both craft," the fire control officer yelled. "Charlie One, vector to north target, Charlie Two vector to south target. Charlie Flight Leader, take the island." the lieutenant colonel said as he barked orders to the nine converging boats and helicopters. "All units, weapons free! Read back, over."

Kerry shook his head slowly. This was about to become a shooting war.

"Red boat team copies. Weapons free."

"Flight leader copies all. Weapons free."

"Weapons free," replied the pilot of the gunship. "We're moving in to four kilometers. Stand by to descend." Kerry grabbed the arm rest of his seat as the plane took a steep diving turn to the left.

Within minutes, the *Pave Hawks* swooped down alongside the long race boats, firing 50-caliber bursts across the bows of the two craft that raced north and south in open water. Blistering gunfire boiled the waves in front of the boats, an unmistakable warning even in the dark, as microscopic marine life glowed green when the large-caliber slugs shredded the night sea. One gun pass, then another, firing in front of each boat, yet neither altered course or speed.

"I've got a fire control solution now on both targets," Leon said calmly. "Good tracks. Ready to engage on your command."

"Lost 'em," another voice said.

"Lost what?" the fire control officer demanded.

"Optics can't see the boat drivers, sir. Having a hard time tracking 'em cause they're jumpin' around so bad on that water."

The seas became choppy, beating the boats as they smashed up and down through whitecaps farther from land. The high-pitched whine of the huge racing motors could be heard by the SEALs over the roar of their own engines. Like watching an insane boat race on rough lake waters with the roar, whine, and roar cycle of immersed, airborne, and then immersed engines, the two fleeing go-fast boats played out identical dramas north and south of the Miskito Keys.

Back at the island, the flight leader swooped in on the lobsterman hut, a single gas lamp burning in the window. As the helicopter slowed its approach, two fiery missiles arced out of the top of the building toward the aircraft. Only seconds after the pilot screamed a warning and pitched headlong toward the water in an evasive maneuver, each of two Stinger missiles found its mark in the engines of the helicopter. Moments later the aircraft and the charred remains of ten men rained in a hail of fire on the tiny beach.

"The hut was manned!" shouted the gunship pilot. "Countermeasures, now!"

"Deploy flares!" The fire control officer to Kerry's left commanded the flare dispensers as the gunship banked in a hard turn, eight kilometers west of the island. Pods under the wings spewed a hail of burning phosphorus behind them in a glowing arc of flame that would sucker off any incoming missiles headed for the plane. Kerry grunted against the G-force of the tight turn as the pilot put a wall of flares between them and the missile-armed hut.

The flares were barely deployed before additional Stinger missiles arced from each of the Cigarette boats into the humid night air toward the remaining choppers. The northbound boat fired first, and the pursuing *Pave Hawk* aircrew had only moments to respond, the pilot banking hard into the coming missile so as to minimize the infrared signature of his engines. The defense was too late, and the helicopter careened wildly out of control as the missile flew through and sheared the blades of the chopper. The sudden loss of rotor symmetry homogenized the helicopter as fifty G's of alternating, wild oscillations snapped bodies into pieces and sent black rubble hailing down into the wake of the escaping speedboat.

The *Pave Hawk* to the south had more time, banking hard into the Cigarette boat as an errant Sidewinder sailed within a meter of the pilot's windscreen and disappeared behind him. He dove for the water, his copilot arming guns and rockets in swift moves, the aircraft ripping along in the dark at a dizzying speed only meters above the water. The pilot banked left, two kilometers behind the southbound boat, keeping the exhaust of his engines pointed away from more missile attacks, as he captured the boat in his target acquisition window and rained death on the enemy. Hellfire missiles sliced off the weapon rail headed to the laser designator on the engine cowling of the race boat. As the pilot continued to swing left, 50-caliber gunfire shredded the rear of what little was left of the racing vessel. Five minutes after the first gunfire, one of the terrorist's boats were destroyed, along with two Special Forces helicopters and twenty crewmen.

"Charlie Two, intercept northbound target."

"Interrogative status, Charlie One?"

"Flight Leader and Charlie One are down. Your intercept vector zero one zero degrees, target hostile."

"Copy that." Adrenaline surged as the angry flight crew bore down on the escaping northbound boat and sliced through it with three more Hellfire rockets, and then shredded the remaining hull with a blaze of guns on a second pass. SEALs in their own fast boats watched as their airborne brethren finished the swift attack. On the beach at Miskito Key, the lamp burned brightly until Gatling cannon fire from the gun ship shredded the hut and pummeled the tiny island. Half an hour after the operation began, the attack was over.

Kerry's head sank into his hands, weary of the chase, in pain for these brave men he had prepared, then lost, and frustrated that his quarry was now sunk, along with all of the motive and tactical intelligence he had fought so desperately, and for so long, to obtain. In the darkness of his covering hands and the dimly lit plane, Kerry wept unnoticed.

✳

An hour later, orbiting above the Miskito Keys in the gunship, Kerry shook his head in disbelief. "No one? Not even parts of bodies? Blood? Anything?"

Tech Sergeant Leon shook his head, a mixture of anger and sadness covered by his blunt professional demeanor, the product, Kerry was sure, of many missions and lost comrades. Leon pointed to the tactical situation map and a saved infrared image. "No, sir. Nothing at all on infrared, and nothing the SEALs can find at sea in the dark."

Kerry stared at the man as the plane banked hard to the right, headed toward Managua and a debrief of the disastrous evening. No one wanted to go home empty handed. Bodies of the terrorists—body parts—would have been better than nothing at all. Tech Sergeant Leon was too much the professional to say what was on his mind. Kerry wanted to hear it, yet dreaded the man's words.

He dismissed Leon and turned back to the battle-management console, replaying the stored footage of four men running to the Cigarette boats anchored at the islet. *How had they known to leave?*

He hung his head, recalling Leon's words to him earlier that night: *Everything is not what it first appears.*

39

"I THOUGHT YOU'D LOOK older. Must be all that bicycling," Kerry said with a grin. He held his hand out, taking John's with a strong grip as they met at the front door of the Wells's home in Clear Lake City in the late afternoon of a hot July weekend.

"Come in!" John crushed the agent's hand in a playful contest of grips. "Good to meet you face to face, Special Agent Kerry, after all this time. And it's not the bicycle," he said as he pointed Kerry to the left and into the living room. "Einstein predicted that the faster you move, the slower you age. So space flight must be the fountain of youth. What d'you think?"

"Better you than me. I couldn't lock myself up for two years in a tin can." Kerry grinned, shaking his head. "But congratulations on the Mars assignment. You go into quarantine tomorrow?"

John nodded. "Spaceflight does have its drawbacks." He pointed to the couch, indicating a place for Kerry to get comfortable. "What brings you to Houston?" he asked, offering Kerry a tall glass of fresh-brewed sweet tea with lemon.

"Business. And chasing down leads," Kerry said, leaning back into the sofa and sampling the cold drink. "I need your help. Again."

"Where do you stand now? You caught what . . . eighteen?"

"Sixteen. Three days ago," Kerry replied.

"I understand you ran the dragnet in Central America. Got an intel brief on it yesterday. Your hunch proved correct."

"It was your hunch that confirmed it. And the guys we got are a wealth of information. Spilling their guts to plead their way out of lethal injection. Lots of expertise in that group." Kerry looked away from John toward the bay window. "At least, those that we caught."

"Yeah. What about the top dog? What was his name?"

"They called him 'Nick.' Real name's Elias Ulrich. Their descriptions match Ulrich to a tee. But it's a funny thing . . ."

"What?" John asked in the lull.

"None of them knew his *real* name." Kerry looked back at John, shaking his head. "They were clueless when we laid his background in front of them. The man must have been a master of deception. His own men, working by his side for nearly two years as they planned and executed that attack, had *no* idea where he came from or how he learned so much. He paid 'em well. They never asked." Kerry got up from the couch and walked to the window, staring out as he leaned against the jamb.

"Tell me about him," John asked, watching the agent from across the room.

Kerry was silent, looking out across John's front lawn. His shoulders slumped and his head bowed. "We lost a lot of good men, John. Very good men. One of us should have seen it coming."

John waited in silence.

"He had us pegged. Had anti-air protection. Suckered us right in. Ripped my guys apart before we knew what hit us."

"And him?" John asked.

"Nothin.' We trashed both of the boats. Chewed 'em up good. And no signs of anyone on 'em." Kerry rubbed his face with his right hand, sweat glistening on his temple. "I don't know. Maybe they saw us coming and jumped. Maybe a shark got 'em. Beats me." He turned back to face John. "Don't get me wrong. I'm glad we nailed sixteen, but I sure would feel a lot better about this if we'd plugged the dike completely."

"Tell me more about this Nick. Or whatever his name was. Give me some background." John got up and took Kerry's glass of iced tea to him, leaning against the window jamb near the shorter man.

"Ulrich was prior Air Force. Almost retired with honors. Super smart. Senior master sergeant. Got wrapped up in an ugly gambling and drinking thing at the end of an otherwise stellar career. Some say he was framed. Brilliant man, by all accounts. Savvy leader."

"It showed."

"Yeah."

"What else?"

"Prior Navy. Like you."

"I'm still *in* the Navy, thank you. Nothin' 'prior' about it," John said with a smile.

Kerry laughed. "So I heard, Captain." He punched John playfully in the left arm. "So he gets drummed out of the Air Force, a hair's breadth shy of a prison sentence, and drops off the radar. No records of him from that day forward. The last thing we could find on him was his passport passing through Heathrow Airport in London a few days after they stripped him of his uniform."

"Why the UK?"

"Nobody knows. Like I said. It was the last we saw of him until the attacks. Actually, the last until we picked him up working the net from Honduras. Until then, no one had any reason to track him . . . or care."

"What else?"

"We connected the dots three days ago," Kerry said, alternately looking at John, then back out the big window at the pre-sunset sky. "Wish I'd known earlier—lots earlier."

"Known what?"

"The guy was a professional *clown*," Kerry began.

"Clown?" John blurted out. "Like a *circus* clown?"

"Yeah. Don't underestimate him. We got a tip, on the night of the attack. He had this fascination for the circus, strange as it sounds. I've learned a lot about him in the last forty-eight hours."

"Go on," John said, shaking his head.

"Somehow—and we don't know how—he ends up in Russia. Not long after he got to London. Turns out he spoke the language —self-taught."

John nodded, waving him on.

"So he takes a job in Moscow at the State School of Circus and Variety Arts. The best clown school in the world, they say. Who'd have figured? He gets thrown out of the Air Force and follows his dream. Once we figured out this clown thing, our sources confirmed that he assumed a new identity. Worshiped this famous guy who died in '97, fella named Yuri Nikulin. The most celebrated clown in Russia. Ulrich works for three years at the school, tuning up his language skills and learning the clown craft from the masters. Next thing you know, he's an apprentice clown at the Circus-on-Fontanka, in St. Petersburg."

"Florida?" John asked, wide-eyed.

"No. Russia. Stay with me, John. Okay?"

"Gotcha."

"He works the circus for five years in St. Petersburg, then somehow gets pulled up to Moscow, to the big time. Nobody knows why, but it must have been good. Only the best end up there. At the Old Circus in Moscow, also known now as the Yuri Nikulin Circus. Named after his hero. Hence the handle 'Nick.' Who'd have figured this guy for a clown, you know? But don't sell him short. These clowns, they're acrobats, incredibly athletic. And he was one of the best. Even in his fifties. He spends two years in Moscow. Then—poof—he drops out of sight."

"And?"

"And, two years after that—boom. The attack."

Both men were silent for a time. John began to pace, arms crossed, his eyebrows furled. "In Russia, for ten years, fluent speaker, adopted country, mad at America, off the radar and new identity. Working nose to nose with reformed Communists. In Moscow and St. Petersburg. Then he disappears for two years and next thing we know, our space surveillance system and Washington transportation infrastructure disintegrate. That about cover it?" John asked, rubbing his chin in contemplation.

"Bingo. He's on the lam for a year after the attack, we shredded him—or lost him—three days ago, and the bad thing is . . . no one made the Russian connection until now." Kerry pointed at John. "So here I am, with my head in my hands, hoping you can help me out. Sounds crazy, but you did it before. Work your magic, Hawk."

Both men were silent for a time, staring at their drinks and each other.

"Don't beat yourself up, Kerry. It took a decade to catch bin Laden. So, what'd Ulrich do in the Nav'?" John asked, then drained his glass and set it down on a coaster.

The kitchen door slammed and John looked up to see Amy and the boys returning from the store. "We have a guest, Amy. Got a minute?" He waved at her from the den.

"Be right there," Amy called back, "soon as I shoo these wolves off our groceries!" John watched her grab the tea pitcher on her way, ever the perfect hostess.

"Hi. I'm Amy. You must be Terrance," she said as she proffered a refill of iced tea. "Would you like some more?"

"Yes, ma'am, I am—and yes, some more would be fine. It's a plea-sure—I mean, it's the first time I've met your husband, face to face. He's done a lot to help his country."

"I know," she said as she smiled at John. "And he's told me a lot about you. You've got a tough job, Mr. Kerry. We appreciate what you're doing."

He nodded. "Thanks, Amy. I'm sorry to barge in like this, with John going to quarantine soon and all."

"Please, don't worry about that. You and John have some impor-tant work to do. I understand." She refilled both glasses, and then hur-ried out of the room, leaving them alone.

Kerry watched her depart, then turned to the window. "I was mar-ried once. Wonderful woman." He put his hand in his pocket and pulled out his pocket watch, fondling it for a quiet moment. "You're a lucky man, John. Amy has to put up with a lot."

John nodded, his eyes fixed on Amy, working in the kitchen. "She's remarkable." He took a deep breath, then exhaled audibly and turned back to Kerry. "So, this Ulrich clown. What was his Navy background? And why'd he end up in the Air Force?"

"SEAL," Kerry said. "Ordnance technician. Good swimmer, incredible athlete. But he ruptured a membrane in his inner ear during a deep dive and came down with a vestibular disorder called Meniere's disease. From that point on he couldn't keep his lunch down in a black rubber boat. The SEALs sent him packing. I doubt he did much trapeze work in the circus."

"Don't be so sure. Amy had that disease once. You can reprogram your vestibular system and get over it," John said. "What about the rest of them?"

"The other three he got away with? None with any military background. Strong connections to mining and explosives, planes, or electronics. That kind of stuff. We're still working on it."

"SEAL?" John repeated the word and shook his head as he stared off beyond the window, breaking his eye contact with Kerry. At last he turned, speaking more rapidly. "Walk me through the escape again. Like you did on the phone last week." John set down the tea, walking to a side table to get a pad of paper from the drawer. "Draw it for me."

Kerry nodded and took the paper. He recounted the entire mission as he saw it from the gunship, with marks for the island, the hut, and the escaping boats headed north and south.

"Something I ought to know about, John? If there is, let's hear it."

"I think there's something. But run through it one more time — from the beginning. Show me the path of the boats, and your location in the airborne command post."

Kerry marked over his original sketch. "Two Cigarette boats at anchor. Four men ran into the water, fired 'em up, and headed west to sea. We were here, headed in to a point about ten kilometers from the island." He pointed west of the islands. "We came in closer later to waste the hut."

"Okay. Got that part. You know I've been there, right? Nicaragua? The Miskito Keys?" John asked, looking up to see if Kerry was surprised by that revelation.

"You're joking, right? A CIA analyst told me the same thing."

"No joke. Been lobster diving all around those islands. Probably visited that very hut. We used to swap our lobsters for magazines with an old man who lived in a shack on the largest island. Dove all over that area doing reef research — and I ate like a king." He pointed back to the paper. "Did the boats leave together?"

Kerry shook his head. "You amaze me," he said, as he pointed back to the sketch. "And yes, they did. Left together, about a hundred meters in trail, then they slowed and pulled alongside each other once they were a couple kilometers off the beach. Fifteen seconds later the boats turned, one headed north, the other south. Fast boats, man. Very fast. They outran my guys on the water."

John took the paper, orienting it so that the coast went north and south, then walked over to a bookshelf and pulled down an atlas. He thumbed to Central America and flopped the book open on the coffee table. "Come look at this a minute," he said, waving Kerry in his direction.

"You're on to something, Hawk. Spit it out."

"You told me about Ulrich a couple of weeks ago, but not the SEAL part. Did you ever record him speaking Russian during the surveillance, before you tried to pick him up?"

"We think so. But we only know what we picked up after we installed an Internet tap. He was all over the Net on Russian sites, mostly in Kazakhstan, and we picked up some voice chatter over IP. He definitely knew the language. None of what he said led us anywhere, though. And none of it gave away the clown connection. All we could make out was that he was moving military surplus. But none of it into or out of the U.S. He did a lot of work with Croatia."

John whistled low, shaking his head side to side.

"Speak to me," Kerry said, sitting down across from him.

John pointed at the map, at his old diving haunts. "I'd bet money he's alive. And long gone."

"Go on."

John pointed along the coast, drawing a line to the north from the Miskito Keys along Nicaragua, then around the bulge of the coast to the west toward Roatan. "Big undersea trench here. Good place to hide." He looked up at Kerry. "Your man got away. Underwater."

Kerry shook his head in silence.

"SEAL training, Kerry. Fast boat deployment. They roll off the side into the water while their skiff rips through enemy waters. With rebreathers and underwater scooters they can go miles undetected. Put a submarine in the mix, and they can join up through a dive bell on the hull. Slip away forever."

John thumbed through the atlas to Eastern Europe, and put a finger on the coast of Croatia. "Split," he said slowly, pointing to a coastal town by that name. "Used to be in Yugoslavia. Home to the Soviet Union's submarine reconditioning and resupply in the Mediterranean during the cold war." John drew his finger along the line of the eastern coast of the Adriatic, east of Italy, down into the Mediterranean.

"Split is a major shipbuilding port. If he was working the surplus market, I'd bet your man had him a diesel sub. How long were you watching his computer before he made the break for Nicaragua?"

"Less than a week."

"So he had what, a year and a half to work the system—arrange the deals—before you picked up his trail?"

"More than that. He had more than a decade. He was in Russia, remember?" Kerry said, pushing up from his seat and pacing about the room.

"Probably bought a boat off the Russians or the Croats. Or the Chinese—they bought a bunch of Kilos—Type 636—about ten years ago. Probably had the sub hanging out just off the coast. Track those Internet links back again, Kerry, and I'll bet one of them eventually connects you with Split and some logistic support for a 1980s era Soviet diesel sub."

Kerry stopped pacing, eyes locked with John's.

"Think about it," John said. "Where's he going in a Cigarette boat anyway? He apparently knew you were on to him, and surely he didn't think he was going to outrun an airplane, helicopters, and a superior military force. So why the fast boats?"

"Get off the island in a hurry . . . " Kerry said, his voice trailing off.

"Exactly. Then slow down, go feet-wet with his buddies, and send the Cigarette boats on opposite courses to draw your fire. The boats were probably autonomous like his 3/21 attack aircraft were. Except they were armed." John slammed the atlas shut. "But the bad guys weren't *on* the boats. That's why you never found them."

"Then where?"

"They made the slip. Had the sub waiting for them beneath the surface. While you were chasing their flotsam, they headed out to deeper waters, around to the north, into the trench, and poof . . . no more."

Kerry wandered toward the window. He turned, gesturing with his hands. "We had long-range video. We never saw any bodies coming off the boats."

"They slipped away on the far side from the plane. Even the tapes won't show it."

"Assumes they knew where the plane was," Kerry said.

"Stands to reason Ulrich knew you were coming after him, and figured you'd be orbiting over your forces, standing off the coast with the Navy. He went off the far side of the boats, to the east. Away from you."

Kerry nodded. "I've always suspected someone . . . or something . . . tipped them. So they might have been that smart."

"Not *might have been*. They *were* that smart."

"Granted. Then what?"

"Then they join up with the sub, using some kind of special hull access. Once they're in they blow it down, maybe decompress if the boat's below sixty meters. Then dry off and they're home free. Except—"

"More?"

"Except *we'd* know if they'd ever been there, and I can probably still pull that information. I might be wrong. Ulrich was a space guy. He had the clearances and he'd probably know what I know. Then—maybe he didn't. He's been out of the business for more than a decade."

"How? Know what?"

"Can't tell you. But if there was a sub in those waters, they had to communicate and navigate at some point. If they surfaced and radiated anything . . . and I mean *anything* . . . we have that electronic signal in a database somewhere. Your own ESM might have picked it up."

Kerry shook his head.

"Electronic Surveillance Measures. ESM. Every combat aircraft has it, and your special forces guys were loaded for bear. But the sub probably lay there for a day or more in wait, before you ever arrived. We'd need to find the historic signal data for that area." John flipped back to the map of Nicaragua.

"I'll bet we find the signal for a Russian Snoop Tray surface search radar sweeping the area a few days earlier, checking out the coastline and shipping traffic. Somewhere right around here." John pointed at the eastern coast of Nicaragua. "I'd also bet dollars to donuts that you have some more radar hits up here, or even past Roatan, a few days after the battle—like *today!*" He clapped his hands together. "Nearly four hundred kilometer range for a Granay class Kilo submarine at five kilometers per hour submerged." John pulled out his cell phone. "We need to make a call."

"To?"

"Can't tell you—"

"Or you'd have to kill me?"

"Exactly. But I know who to call. You just learn more about your friend's Russian connection. Incidentally, the Type 877 class is made in St. Petersburg, the same place where your buddy spent five years clowning around at Fontanka. I'll bet there's a clue waiting in St. Pete or Moscow that you haven't broken yet."

In silence, John traced the edge of Earth on the cover of the closed atlas with his index finger, then looked back up at Kerry, and planted his finger on the western coast of the African continent.

"Twelve thousand kilometer range, thirty kilometers per hour on snorkel—about sixteen days."

Kerry jumped up, pulling out his own cell phone. "He's still out there!"

"Bingo! If there *was* a sub—and he radiated *anything*—we can nail him for good. It's the quietest submarine on the planet. But once we know the sub's radar signature there's no place on the planet that he can hide . . . as long as he comes up for air and takes a peek around for surface traffic."

"He's gotta do that, right? Come up?" Kerry asked, holding his phone open, ready to dial.

"It depends. Some of the boats have been retrofitted to stay down a long time. Air Independent Propulsion, or AIP." John moved toward Kerry and put his right fist over his heart in a salute. "But I can promise you, Comrade—or my call sign isn't Hawk—eventually, he *will* come up. And when he does, we'll know it."

40

"CAPTAIN WELLS TOLD US you'd be arriving today, sir. He coordinated with the Bureau to get your clearances passed. Please, come in."

Lieutenant Commander Nancy Slagle escorted Kerry past two armed guards, placing her hand, then his, on a biometric scanner to swing the gate clear as they badged through the portal. Kerry followed, in awe of the security for this little-known corner of Maryland. *The National Maritime Intelligence Center.* Kerry read the sign and posters on the wall as he followed the lead of the redhead in a crisp white uniform. *Counter narcotics. Counterproliferation. Nuclear material monitoring. Counterterror. Antisubmarine warfare.*

His escort directed him down a long hall to a large door, scanning her hand and his to open the lock. Another guard reviewed his visitor badge as they entered a spacious computerized facility ringed with monitors that reminded him of a *Star Wars* version of a battle command center. The Bureau had nothing like this.

"Agent Kerry! Welcome! I'm Doctor Pestorius. We're glad you could come up so quickly." A tall, dark-haired man with a small medallion on his suit lapel met Kerry with a firm handshake.

"He's also Rear Admiral retired Pestorius," the Lieutenant Commander said, introducing the two men. "His doctorate is in computational fluid dynamics, but his expertise is in antisubmarine warfare. Our lab director, sir. You're in good hands." She saluted Kerry and dismissed herself.

"Thanks, Nancy. Bring us the latest intel summary on Kilo Niner Six Three, please."

"Yes, sir," she said as she left the room.

"Do you know John well?" the doctor asked as he showed Kerry a chair at the head of a long mahogany table in the midst of the control center.

"Until yesterday, only by phone. John was a big help in proving my hunch about 3/21."

"Domestic suspects?" the tall man asked, crossing his legs as he sat down.

"Yes, sir. At least, in the execution phase. No idea yet who's behind it."

"That is unfortunate," Dr. Pestorius said. "Citizen terrorists." He watched Kerry for a long moment, then continued. "So. John tells me that you might be able to help me find my good friend, Elias Ulrich."

Kerry's jaw dropped. "You know Ulrich?"

The doctor nodded, removing his glasses and placing them in his suit-coat pocket. "Until yesterday, not by that name . . . but yes, we know each other well—in an intelligence community sort of way. I've been searching for him—for Nikolai—for thirteen years."

"Incredible." Kerry put his hand to his forehead.

"Yes. It is. You have suddenly opened a door we thought we'd never find." Dr. Pestorius leaned back in his chair. "You are aware of the St. Petersburg connection, are you not?"

Kerry nodded. "Yeah. Nick was in the circus there."

"A very important location," the lab director said, punching a nearby keyboard to command the display of an intelligence briefing on the screen before them. He used a laser pointer to guide Kerry through the presentation. "The Admiralteiskiye Verfi shipyard in St. Petersburg is a former nuclear submarine production facility. They've built thirty-nine nuclear submarines, including Victor II and III class, which are very hard to find. I believe John's crew was the first to track a Victor III in the Mediterranean." Dr. Pestorius grinned. "Or, so he claimed the last time we rode together."

"Rode?" Kerry asked.

"Yes. We're both bicyclists. We find time to get together once a year for a two-day tour in the Shenandoah Mountains of Virginia. But back to the elusive Mr. Ulrich. The shipyard is also the production facility for a line of diesel submarines known as the Varshavyanka, otherwise known in NATO parlance as the 'Kilo.' The Russians are building them for the Chinese and Indian navies and are thus significantly tilting the balance of global power, though most of the free world is unaware of that fact."

"And Ulrich?"

"Ah yes — Nikolai. For years we knew there was an American in St. Petersburg, somehow aligned with the Verfi shipyard, helping them to locate and close on customers for their submarines. We know that there were additional submarines built that were never accounted for. The customer's code name was Nikolai — a hard name to pinpoint in Russia, like being named David or John here in the States. With your help, we now know who he is, and how he fits into this equation."

Kerry was dumbfounded. "You knew . . . for what, ten years—thirteen—that an American code named 'Nick' was in cahoots with the Russians? And now we know that your Nick and mine are one and the same?" Kerry's face went beet red. "Did you try to *find* him—before now?"

"We tried. For years. And to no avail. But you broke the code—or John did. Now we're back in the game."

"I don't see how," Kerry said, trying to keep his calm. "I thought we killed him. Although, John thinks he escaped and said that you could find him . . . if anyone could."

Dr. Pestorius smiled and pointed back to the screen at the front of the room, nodding to an enlisted man on his right. The screen came to life with a detailed map of the Caribbean. "John is correct. Elias Ulrich *did* survive. But we won't just help you find him . . . we intend to *follow* him." Dr. Pestorius used his laser pointer to illuminate an icon at the far right side of the map. "Because we know precisely where Ulrich is."

THURSDAY, JULY 26, 2012: COCOA BEACH, FLORIDA

"They let you out, just for me?"

John laughed and skipped a seashell across the flat water behind a wave as it receded from the beach. "Uh-huh. I pitched a fit and they threw me out of quarantine. For a few hours."

"You're teasing me," Amy said, pinching him on the side. He took off in a trot down the beach and she followed, both of them splashing in the low water.

"You're getting your shoes wet!" she cried out in the wind.

"Who cares?" John yelled back, as he reached for her hand and pulled her into the surf. They chased waves up and down the slope for half an hour, not saying anything, just romping in the water and enjoy-ing the evening. As the sun set behind the dunes, John pulled her up the beach. They fell exhausted on the sand, watching the darkening sky to the east.

"Thanks for the date, John. This is special." Amy rolled on to her left side to gaze at this man she would soon say goodbye to, headed to Mars and a destiny only he truly understood.

"You're welcome. Thank Marv, too. He gave us all the green light to play hooky one last time."

"I will." She began to trace the lines of his nose and chin with a salty finger. "A penny for your thoughts?"

John smiled, some sand falling from his face as the wrinkles of crow's-feet pushed the grit free. "Just a penny?"

"It's all I've got. My husband didn't leave me with any cash."

John rolled over and tickled her, Amy's screams of delight dying in the roar of the Atlantic wind. They fell back, sand coating both of their shirts.

"Okay. I was thinking about a buddy of mine, something he said."

"Who?" she asked, dribbling sand like an hourglass on a red, white, and blue embroidered "Epsilon" mission patch.

"Doesn't matter. But he was on this very beach, a few days before his own mission. Like us. His wife was strong—and godly—just like you."

"What did he say?" she asked, as the sand piled higher on his chest. The little mountain rose and fell gently as his breathing slowed.

"He talked about God's promise of protection. About how we're in His hands."

The wind whistled around them, disturbing the growing pile. She slowed the trickle, seeking to get the mound higher, as it pulsated below her hand.

"A penny for yours?" he asked.

"I was thinking of Maine. The day when you called from Athens. That was so long ago."

He nodded. "We're not here by accident, Amy. Whatever's ahead of us, it won't take God by surprise."

"I know. That's why I feel such peace."

He rolled over on to his right side, dumping the little sand pile as he raised his left hand to caress her cheek. "Come back here every so often, Amy—while I'm gone. Bring the kids. Throw shells in the ocean. Play in the sand. Remember tonight, okay?"

Amy nodded, unable to form the words she wanted to say, fearing she would lose all control. She had to hold together, for this moment, for herself—and for him.

"We'll come back here in eighteen months and celebrate. Promise me." John took her hand and squeezed it.

Amy nodded again, the lump in her throat sealing off the words she longed to speak. Her chin quivered as she struggled to hold her emotion in check. She watched the last rays of daylight twinkle in his eyes as she struggled to ask the one question she feared to have him answer. She couldn't break the moment, yet she dared not wonder for the next five hundred days what his response might have been. She forced her voice and it cracked. "Is this . . . the end, John?"

Her words were whisked away on the wind, yet burned into both of their hearts. He didn't speak for what seemed a long time.

"The end?" he asked. "No. I'll be back. You have to believe that."

"Hard as it is to understand, John, that's not what I meant."

He grimaced, and she knew the look.

"Do you mean, is this mission . . . The 'answer?' The 'call?'"

"That's exactly what I meant. Once we're back together, will you stop? Will you give it all up, for me . . . for the kids?"

John rolled onto his back, and put his hands under his head. "Are you asking me for a promise?" he asked after a long pause.

She shook her head, sand falling free from her long hair. "No. No promises. That wouldn't be fair. I'm just asking if you feel this is the calling that has driven you so hard for so long. Is this finally the end?"

John's eyes stared straight up into the gathering stars of the early evening. She watched him, unblinking.

"Maybe I'm asking *when*, John. *When* does God give you back to us? *When* does your calling and this force that compels you finally taper off? We want all of you . . . we *need* you. At home, and in one piece."

Pools formed at the edges of his eyes, and his chest rose and fell faster. His Adam's apple grew, like a lump of words stuck in his throat.

She put her hands to his face and pulled his gaze to hers. "Whatever the answer is, John, 'yes' or 'no,' you need to hear this. Where you go I will follow. Your people will be my people. If this is just one step of many, I'll walk the rest with you, with a supportive and rejoicing heart. But I need to know, right now. *Is this the end?*"

He rolled over and put his left hand on hers, squeezing it. The ponds fell from his eyes and joined her tears as they dropped into the sand below like wet sand lions eating their deepest pains.

John shook his head slowly, and her heart fell—yet rejoiced—all at once.

"No, Amy. My heart . . . and my prayers . . . tell me that there is more."

Deep pain seemed written in the wet wrinkles around his eyes. "I'm sorry. But that's what I feel . . . what God's Spirit seems to be sharing with me right now."

She sighed. She watched John for a long moment in the gathering dark, a gentle wind whirling her hair, some of the long tresses fluttering into his freshly trimmed flattop. Then a big smile creased her wet face, and she squeezed his hand harder. "Good," she said, the word erupting as if the emotional exertion of the past minutes were helping her get rid of a buried pain. "I'm *glad*."

"Glad?" he asked. "I don't understand." His forehead wrinkled in a puzzled expression, forming his distinctive single brow.

"Yes, *glad*. I trust your heart. I always have."

She pulled her hair out of his face, shaking her head to let the long strands blow behind her. His face was aglow with amazement. "Now I know that you'll be coming home." She tapped her index finger on his chest. "You're so compulsive about finishing a task that I know that you won't let anything stand in your way—as long as there's more to do." She pushed up and kissed him on the forehead, her right hand cupping his wet cheek.

"This is not the end . . . and that's all the encouragement I need to hang on. Forever."

41

"THEY'RE ABOVE US," **NICK** said with a whisper to the sonar operator. "I can feel it."

The young Russian sailor wagged his head, pointing to the jumble of green lines on the computer screen. "Nyet."

"Expand up this line. Right here," Nick commanded, pointing at a group of computer monitor traces that represented underwater sounds. The sailor complied, highlighting a faint squiggly line on the sonar screen.

A series of signals, representing noise transmitted into the water and clustering around sixty hertz, were instantly displayed on the sonar operator's video monitor.

"Bingo! U.S. propeller aircraft, multi-engine. Directly overhead." Nick turned to Tex, hanging close by, his hands wrapped around a bar in the overhead of the cramped diesel submarine. "Get word to Andraiev.

They're onto us. Probably an American P-3C—a submarine hunter."

"Got it," Tex said, and the tall man immediately headed aft toward the submarine's control room, in search of their Ukranian commander, Alexander Andraiev.

Nick turned to the weapon console operator. "Deploy the package now."

With a flurry of commands, Billy Carlisle launched a sleek black torpedo from the aft tubes with a barely audible *whoosh*.

Expelled behind the Russian Kilo-class diesel submarine, the cigar-shaped black vehicle turned north and began its distinct transmissions. Gently flooding the waters with a duplicate of the parent submarine's acoustic signature, the black fish hummed along into the distance, climbing slowly toward the surface.

Twenty minutes later, with an antenna deployed above the waves, the torpedo-like craft erected a Russian Snoop Tray radar mast to check for local shipping traffic and confirm its navigation plot. After two sweeps, the robot retracted the radar and plunged into the sea, headed north, and deep.

Nick watched the sonar display, tracking the bearing and amplitude on the sixty-hertz signal as it slowly diminished in intensity, departing in the direction of the submarine simulator's travel.

"Sonar shows the aircraft headed north, Alexander," Nick said to the bearded Russian to his left. "We heard the plane drop buoys in the path of the countermeasure, and they've got its track." Nick smiled. "They definitely took the bait."

"Da." The submarine commander watched the display a few more moments and then turned back toward the bridge of his vessel. "Thirty hours of air remain. We lie here twenty-four hours and wait. Come." He put out a cigarette as he left the sonar compartment, motioning at Nick to follow.

Nick patted the sonar operator on the back, and then pointed at Tex. "You two keep an eye on this. Any more lines pop up on the scope, you call."

"Got it," the tall man replied as he leaned over the Russian's shoulder, scanning the sonar signal waterfall displays with a practiced eye.

Behind him, the diving officer slowed the craft, settling gently to the ocean floor, one hundred meters below the surface, immersed in darkness and cold. The gentle thrum of the submarine grew silent.

SATURDAY, JULY 28, 2012: SUITLAND, MARYLAND

"Trust your instincts, Kerry," Dr. Pestorius said, shaking his head as he pored over a paper copy of a bathymetry chart for the eastern Caribbean Sea. "We have a signal at last—more evidence of our quarry. A submarine radar at that. But what does your gut tell you right now?"

Special Agent Kerry rubbed his face, trying to revive himself after six days of work in the operations center behind a bevy of guards and gates. He missed the sun and longed for the mountain air of Colorado. "My gut tells me—*Ulrich* tells me—that everything is not what it first appears."

"I like this Ulrich," Dr. Pestorius said, drawing out the name slowly. "And I would agree," he said as he turned to Lieutenant Commander Slagle. "Nancy? Pull the parameters on that latest Snoop Tray. Give me a fingerprint comparison."

She nodded and disappeared into an office on the edge of the room, emerging ten minutes later with two sheets of paper covered in a series of graphs.

"Not him." She said, frowning as she held up the first sheet. "It's a decoy. A sub simulator. We tracked it in 2009 off the coast of Split during sea trials. They made five of these, far as we know. This is the first time it's shown up deployed."

Dr. Pestorius shrugged and pointed at Kerry. "You see? You have excellent instincts, Agent Kerry. So, what now?"

Kerry shook his head. "Did you know it was a fake . . . are you just testing me?"

"You have excellent instincts, as I said. Continue, please."

Kerry stared at the bathymetry chart, a mysterious map of undersea geography that he'd never imagined. "Silent or not, Ulrich is cornered. He'd have a backup, some way to make the slip."

Dr. Pestorius nodded. "Good analysis. I agree. Nancy?"

Lieutenant Commander Slagle selected a new map display for the front screen, showing a series of ellipses overlaid on the Caribbean. Kerry now knew these were position estimates based on intercepted radar or radio transmissions.

"There are actually *two* Russian Kilo's in the Caribbean today," she said. "We have a track on the second, Kilo niner-six-zero here, north of the Netherland Antilles. Your hunch may yet prove to be correct, Agent Kerry. You should have been an intelligence analyst."

"Yes, he should," said Dr. Pestorius, smiling broadly, "and we'll soon have U.S. subs on the tails of both those boats. We're back in the game."

"You've got a call, John." Michelle waved him over to the central phone for the quarantine facility. "Didn't say who."

"Why someone's calling me on this line? I've got my cell," John said as he took the receiver. "This is John."

"It's Terrance Kerry. How are you?"

"Hey! I'm good. Two days to blastoff, two hundred more to Mars, and we're already going nuts locked up in here. How about you? Did you meet the Admiral?"

"That's why I'm calling." He paused. "You were right—again. Spot on, in fact. 'You know who' is alive and we're on his trail . . . thanks to you. I had to call and let you know before you left."

John was speechless. He lowered the phone for a second.

"You okay, John?" Michelle asked, standing nearby.

He nodded to her. "I—who'd have guessed?" he said into the phone. "Pestorius hit the jackpot, huh?"

"We're back in the hunt!"

John took a deep breath, his heart quickening. He'd been afraid this might come to pass. "Kerry. There's a new problem that you need to evaluate."

"*New* problem?"

"Do you remember our discussion last fall . . . three options, and the fourth one that was not good—the submarine launch?"

Kerry whistled in the background. "You don't mean?—"

"Remember you told me about his covert computer servers in Baikonur? That's a Russian Cosmodrome in Kazakhstan. A space port. If he's certifiably tied in with the Russians and a nuclear submarine pro-duction facility, then—oh brother—you need to tell the Admiral about Baikonur. Right now. He'll know how to proceed. Tell him about my theory, about the concept of a planned attack against the surveillance system, about secret orbits and possible space weapons—"

"John. This is an open line—"

"Tell him!"

Michelle stopped in her tracks as she poured a cup of coffee, staring at John, her mouth agape. John waved at her to go away.

"I will. But I've gotta go," Kerry said, the sound of a door slamming in the background. "You can blast off for Mars knowing that you might have broken the case of the century. There'll be an honorary badge at the Bureau waiting on you when you get back." The phone was silent for a moment. "Be safe, man. We need you."

"No," John said, shaking his head. "*You* be safe. You guys solve this thing, Kerry, and make sure there's a world waiting for me to come back to."

Michelle rolled her eyes as he caught her gaze. He shrugged as he hung up the phone. She walked over to him, John still holding the receiver where it lay in the phone's cradle. "Something we ought to know about?" she asked.

SUNDAY, JULY 29, 2012: NORTH OF SAINT-MARTIN ISLAND, NETHERLAND ANTILLES

"Make your depth forty meters," Alexander Andraiev said to his diving officer. The submarine commander turned to Nick. "Ready the dive bell. Is time."

Nick nodded, and waved to Tex and his other men, already dressed in wetsuits. They turned and headed aft in the submarine without a word.

Nick pointed to a paper map on the plotting table behind Alexander. "Be visible. Run the radar. Spend lots of time on snorkel. But don't hit port for at least two weeks. We'll need that long."

"Da."

A stout line connected the four men as they swam in single file, hearts racing, gulping precious recycled air, while they kicked in unison forty meters below the surface. The dark night covered them, with only a compass and an underwater beacon in each of their wrist controls to direct them. The silent rebreather systems let no bubbles float to the surface to give away their position. Behind them, Nick could feel the hum of the submarine as it moved off in the opposite direction, and ultimately, to the surface for precious air.

An hour later Nick slowed and flashed a dull light in the direction of his partners. They stopped kicking, pulling up next to him. He turned on his mask light, his face contorted under the mask and the pressure, with deep-set eyes that glowed like reptile orbs in the light of his yellow-green face light. Nick signaled with his hands, using fingers for code as he pointed to the beacon on his wrist, then down. They all nodded.

Nick pulled a flashlight from his belt, shining the torch straight down into the inky depths. Below the four men, stretching out twenty meters below and sixty meters beyond them, was the massive hulking body of a second Russian Kilo class diesel submarine, a sleek black sea monster. The submarine's sail towered up toward them. Nick could almost feel the beast alive below him, another familiar monster harkening back to the classified throat-slitting adventures of his Navy youth. He waved the torch toward his ashen companions, who were encountering, for the second time, a submarine at night deep in the ocean. Nick moved as if he had done this many times. He motioned to his men, and they started down, each lighting his own torch and careful to point lights down, in case someone was still pursuing them.

The Russian's sound-insulated black hull began to reflect a little of their light as the men swam down, reaching the sail fifty meters below the surface. Nick pulled himself deeper along the sail's ladder, his torch lighting a small pod-like structure on the hull aft of the sail. He tugged at the rope to alert his comrades, urging them on. Silently, the four made their way across the great blackness of the submarine, a sleeping leviathan seemingly unaware of their presence. Nick pointed to a hatch on the front of the pod, and Tex moved in, opening the seal with a quick twist of the locking mechanism. The four men disconnected themselves from their safety rope, entering the pod one at a time. Tex entered last, closing the watertight connection behind him. Water raced out of the enclosure as it pumped dry, and Nick's remaining crew decompressed in the wet but warm confines of their newest home. Two hours later, they were in dry clothes and inside yet another sub, chatting with the crew in Russian and some broken English.

The diesel submarine, now thirty years old and in the hands of its third owners since the Soviets, began to move ahead, accelerating to three knots as it slipped eastward toward the Atlantic.

Four hundred meters behind them, and far below in the cold deep, a much larger leviathan came to life.

"Chief of the Boat! Make turns for three knots and maintain trail at four hundred meters. Stay below the sound layer."

"Aye, aye, Skipper. Three knots, four hundred meter trail, below the layer."

"Sonar, Con."

"Sonar aye."

"Deploy the towed sonar array. Target is underway."

The Navy commander turned to his executive officer, standing near the periscope. "Get out a message, XO. Tell SUBLANT and Suitland that we're in trail on Kilo Niner-Six-Zero. Three knots, headed due east . . . and they've got passengers."

"Station is GO. Epsilon is GO. Endeavor is GO. Mission systems are GO. Countdown resuming at T minus two minutes and counting."

"This is it, guys," John Wells remarked, checking off the last of his system responsibilities on the digital checklist strapped to the sleeve of his space suit. "Five hundred days from now, we'll be dying to get out of these Gumby suits. Next stop, Epsilon—and our chariot to Mars."

"I'm ready to get out of 'em now. So let's blast out of here and go find us some aliens," Navy Captain Sean O'Brien joked, offering a gloved hand to John, who was seated to his left in the 'cave,' the windowless three-person crew position below the shuttle cockpit.

John returned the bulky space-suited handshake. "You go find 'em, big guy. I'm supposed to watch the house in orbit while you and Michelle do the dirty work on the planet."

"Fair enough. But don't accept any house guests while we're gone." Sean turned to his right and elbowed Michelle. "Ready for Mars, sweet thing?"

"'Mrs. Caskey' to you, mister, and don't you forget it," Michelle said with a wink as she clipped a checklist to her kneeboard. "I'm ready—aliens, rocks, and all."

Sean laughed. "I liked the title 'Chief Scientist' a lot better," he said as he adjusted his lip mike closer to his mouth. "Crew's ready, Launch Control. Lockin' 'em up now," he said into the tiny microphone. He thrust his arms straight out, both fists with a thumbs up, and then swung his arms playfully to each side, slamming back into the chests of his two orange-suited crewmates. "Time to button up, children. Say your prayers."

John chuckled and shook his head in wonder at his politically incorrect Mission Commander. Michelle's visor snapped shut just before he closed his own. The snap of her helmet was the last natural sound he would hear on Earth for months to come. He slowly dropped the visor and locked himself into the suit for the ride of his life. The first manned mission to Mars. The fulfillment of a lifetime of dreams and decades of inner longings. His suit was sealed.

Sean tapped his helmet with his right hand, and the others nodded, tapping their own, three sets of arms extended, thumbs up. "Locked and loaded," Sean said into his microphone. "Light the candle, boys and girls. We're ready to rock and roll."

One minute later, sparks flew below the massive rockets of Endeavor, setting the potent hydrogen and oxygen mix ablaze as the space shuttle main engines belched blue flame and clouds of water vapor. As the nozzles roared to life, the shuttle pitched forward ever so slightly, then backward. Three seconds later, the pair of solid rocket boosters exploded to life in a massive orange fireball and billowing clouds of vapor and smoke.

"We have ignition!" the voice of NASA intoned on television and radio around the Earth. "Liftoff of the Space Shuttle Endeavor. Headed to the space station and the Epsilon vehicle for America's first manned mission to Mars!"

Endeavor was on her way, her last flight ever into space.

The end of an era.

And a new beginning for the human race.

*Those who are wise will shine like the brightness of
the heavens, and those who lead many to righteousness,
like the stars for ever and ever.*
Daniel 12:3

1. John felt a strong calling "to make a difference," sensing that he was led to pursue selection as an astronaut.

   • Describe an experience that gave you an unquestionable sense that you were called to a goal or an action.

   • How can we cultivate the ability to hear God's call and understand His leading? Does God talk to us audibly? Why don't some of us hear Him?

   • When we fail to follow God's call, how does He work around us and continue to accomplish His purposes in the world? Does God ever change His mind? Do our actions change God's plans?

   • *Study opportunity:* How do we know God's will in our lives? Read *Experiencing God* by Henry Blackaby or *The Purpose-Driven Life* by Rick Warren. Each of these authors will help you understand God's purpose for your life.

2. John struggled with the decision to accept a possible nomination to the Mars mission. He felt caught between God's call and his commitment to Amy.

   • When we feel led, as John was, how do we know we are listening to God and not to our heart, our head, or our ego?

   • If you were faced with a dilemma in which you had to decide between God's calling and a God-given responsibility like marriage, how would you proceed?

   • Was John right or wrong to involve Amy in his decision about Mars crew selection? Should he have proceeded without her consent?

   • *Study opportunity:* Matthew 19:29 (NIV) states, "And everyone who has left houses or brothers or sisters or father or mother or children or fields for my sake will receive a hundred times as much and will inherit eternal life." Why would God call us away from family? Why do you think Jesus doesn't mention a wife or husband here?

3. Marv Booker asked John if he would have turned down the Mars assignment for Amy. John said *yes.*

- If God has given us clear direction (John's feeling led to become an astronaut), but we choose a different path because of marriage or family, have we failed God and His calling, or have we honored our God-given responsibilities?

- *Study opportunity:* In Matthew 4:19-22 Peter, James, and John are called from family to follow Jesus. Do you think this passage has application for John Wells' dilemma?

4. Michelle took a strong interest in John during their space station mission. John reacted abruptly when she persisted in drawing close and touching him. He said he did this to "put a hedge around his relationship" with his wife.

- Faced with a similar situation, perhaps involving a sexual temptation, what course of action would you take?

- Put yourself in Michelle's shoes. Do you think it was right or wrong for her to look to a "platonic" relationship with John to fill a need for companionship during a stressful mission?

- *Study opportunity:* 1 Corinthians 10:13 tells us, "No test or temptation that comes your way is beyond the course of what others have had to face. All you need to remember is that God will never let you down; he'll never let you be pushed past your limit; he'll always be there to help you come through it" (*The Message*). How do you apply this passage to issues of sexual temptation? Does this passage mean that we can bear any burden or temptation, no matter how difficult?

5. A central theme of this novel involves credible evidence of the existence of intelligent alien life.

   • What do you believe about the possibility of life on another planet? Can you think of passages in the Bible that address this?

   • If there was intelligent alien life on Mars, would it pose a challenge to your faith? How so?

   • Michelle asked John, "What about the aliens? Did Jesus die for their sins, too?" How would you answer her?

   • *Study opportunity:* Genesis 2:1 states, "Thus the heavens and the earth were completed in their vast array" (NIV). *The Message* says it this way: "Heaven and Earth were finished, down to the last detail." What do "the heavens" include? Does your interpretation of Genesis allow for alien life forms?

6. John shares his faith with Michelle, with his father, and with Special Agent Kerry.

   • What form of evangelism does John employ with each of these people? Relational? Confrontational? Intellectual? Was he effective in his witness?

   • *Study opportunity:* Read *About My Father's Business* by Regi Campbell or participate in a group study such as *Becoming a Contagious Christian* by Bill Hybels. Learn to share your faith in a variety of situations.

Meet the Author
Austin W. Boyd

Tell us about your first book. Why astronauts, aliens, and terrorism?

This was my first novel, but it was not my first book. I self-published a poetry anthology in 1978 when I graduated from Rice University. After my degree in Physical Education—I was a distance runner at Rice—I pursued a master's degree in spacecraft systems engineering. That was a challenging educational leap—and a fun one. The creative side of me and my technical bent combined naturally to lead to fiction about technology. But there's more. I spent thirty-two years pursuing my dream to be an astronaut. As a Navy pilot, flying in three wars and doing flight test work, then with four Navy space assignments designing satellite communication systems, working in space surveillance, and building covert devices to chase terrorists—I invested my entire career in an effort to become an astronaut. Some would say that I wrote from what I know. But *The Evidence* is not a biography. Absolutely not. However, it does draw on much of my experiences, things I can speak about with credibility and passion.

Tell us more about your dream—to be an astronaut.

When I was twelve I felt a strong pull toward astronaut and I put everything I had into my dream. I worked hard in school, won a full scholarship to Rice, made it through flight training, then did everything I could as a Navy pilot and space engineer to get selected for astronaut. NASA takes applications every two years, although there were some off years with the Challenger disaster. I applied eight times—the most of any officer in the Navy, I've been told—and I got very close. I was a

Navy finalist four times, and once I made it all the way to Astronaut Candidate finalist, with an interview in Houston in the summer of 1994. I interviewed the same year that Rick Husband did. He was the commander of the Columbia mission, and our life stories have many common elements. His wife's book, *High Calling,* does a remarkable job of capturing the stresses and dreams of anyone who pursues astronaut selection. My wife, Cindy, put up with an enormous amount of that stress enduring eight applications and years of separation while I was deployed overseas or working long hours. After fifteen homes in twenty years, the pressure manifested itself in her as medical problems, and we felt it was finally time to stop the great chase. I retired from the Navy and decided to write about life as an astronaut, drawing on my experiences. So, in a way, I'm headed to space in a vicarious way—through John Wells.

What's coming next in your writing?

Writing is a passion of mine, but it's still an avocation. My job eats up my days. Writing is a 5 a.m. and weekend activity. I wrote two more novels in the Mars Hill Classified trilogy. The second book wraps up many of the story lines from the first book, and a third novel will bring John's life full circle. My passion for those books, and more to come, is to write in such a way that I wrap an issue inside an exciting tale. I feel strongly about the need for us to look at the technical world that we live in and give thought to how God would have us respond to modern challenges from a biblical perspective. What's the implication, from a spiritual point of view, of everything from cell phones to cloning? I want to inspire readers to give technology issues some deep thought in the context of their faith. If I can engage them in a story line—get folks emotionally involved in an issue—perhaps I can accomplish the goal of stimulating people to think about the spiritual implications of a new technology or a technical issue. And do that in a fun way. For example, medical implants, like pacemakers, are remarkable, often life-saving inventions. But what's the spiritual repercussion of implanted memory devices that give you instant recall of the Bible and the encyclopedia? Is that good—or bad? So, that's what's next in my writing. Fiction that makes you ask "What if?"

You have John Wells being approached, perhaps romantically, by his co-astronaut, Michelle. How does that reflect your experience as a Navy pilot?

There is an old saying in the Navy that goes like this: "What goes on deployment stays on deployment." That old saw is meant to cover a multitude of mistakes, all of them revolving around the tendency of men and women to err when placed under extraordinary stress, far from home for long periods of time and in mixed-gender settings. What happens when you are gone from home is intended to remain a squadron secret, letting the failures and excesses of deployment life remain unspoken in order to preserve marriages and relationships.

In my experience, men and women on extended deployment often failed to recognize the enormous pressures they were enduring in the midst of military action and isolation. When they paired up for solace and friendship, seeking a consoling face in the midst of loneliness or wartime stress, they often found themselves giving each other the intimate support they both craved when far from home and spouse. Neither person would have fallen into that trap overtly—seeking to stray and break their vows—but they got there because they didn't build defensive walls around their relationships. Unless you've been there, you can't imagine the incredible stress of isolation, wartime action, or long deployments when surrounded by available partners. You have to actively avoid those situations that could lead to mistakes, even when it makes you unpopular. That's what John Wells tries to do, and succeeds.

Do you believe there's a chance for a woman to lead a trip to Mars, or is the space culture still so oriented to male astronauts that this will not happen?

From a numbers perspective, there are more men than women in the astronaut corps. On that basis, it's likely that the mission commander would be a man. The key question is whether our culture would embrace a woman leader for a mission of that import. Americans say that we're ready for a woman leader of a high-profile mission, and sometimes we follow through on that commitment. Eileen Collins, the commander of the "return to flight" Shuttle mission, is a good example. I think there's a chance of a woman commanding a trip to Mars, but it probably won't be the first trip. Whoever goes will need to be a strong leader, a good listener, and a peacemaker.

There are some excellent NASA and scientific studies that discuss what you need for a long-duration mission, such as going to Mars. Those studies emphasize that NASA can't ignore the influence of our sexual nature. Some studies recommend that we send a mixed crew, preferably married couples. "Pair bonded couples," as those studies call them, preferably mature couples in their fifties and with women beyond the age of menses, would have worked through those issues in marriage and life that would make them most adaptable to long-term stress and internal conflict. The question is, if we send "pair bonded couples," can we have the mission commander be one of the wives? That would be historic. But I think it could happen.

What parting words can you share with us to help us understand you better?

In March 2005, after my agent had engaged the interest of several publishers for this book, I was in shock—overwhelmed by the sudden transformation from nonstop rejection notices to enthusiastic competing publishers. I went out early one morning in Santa Cruz, California, to hike a nature trail to a small chapel deep in the redwoods at Mount Hermon. In prayer in that forest chapel, I asked God "Why me? Why this sudden interest in my book?" I felt a clear reply to my prayer and that message stunned me. His words to me were these: "This is what I spent forty years preparing you to do. It's time."

My parting words are that God needed four decades to do His work in me, to prepare me, to place me on the path to astronaut, Navy pilot, author, marketeer, and engineer, that I might write about all these things one day in a way that could inspire others.

When your days seem dark and the future is uncertain, be like the scarecrow in *The Wizard of Oz:* Stuff the straw back in your chest, paste on a smile, and keep on plugging in the face of daunting challenge. Remember that God has a marvelous plan for your life. He will reveal His plan in time, and accomplish a great work in you.

THE PROOF

 BOOK TWO

1

SIMON FLINCHED AS THE roar and snap of igniting solid rocket boosters boomed across Cape Canaveral. Alone behind a line of tall bleachers, the nine-year-old glanced at the Space Shuttle as it soared skyward, momentarily diverted from the mysterious wave of swaying reeds in a nearby marsh.

"T plus thirty, passing ten thousand feet," a voice boomed from big speakers in front of the people in the bleachers: his mother, uncle, and hundreds of strangers—important people, he'd been told. Simon watched for a moment, then jogged on toward the fascinating swamp.

Something large was moving in the marsh. As he ran closer, he could see a line of tall cattail stalks waving, probably pushed aside by some giant water creature swimming past. *Alligators!* Simon dashed to the water's edge, pulled off his shoes and socks, and stepped without hesitation into the black water. Sinking knee deep into muck, he crept between sharp blades of saw grass into the bog.

✦

"Endeavor, you're GO at throttle-up," NASA's flight controller announced, his words amplified over the huge speakers before the VIP stands. Robert cringed.

"Roger. GO at throttle-up," the Shuttle commander replied.

Dr. Robert Kanewski, chief scientist for the robotic Mars Rover mission, held his breath as he watched the early morning launch. This was the moment when, twenty-six years earlier, Mission Commander Dick Scobee spoke Challenger's last words. Robert envisioned the pilot advancing the engines to maximum thrust. The deafening rumble and crackle of solid rocket boosters shook Robert's insides, but Endeavor's O-rings held one last time. Robert sighed with relief, reveling in the awesome power of the launch. Endeavor was on her way, carrying a crew of seven, including three astronauts headed to a new commercial space station and then on to Mars. Their mission: to confirm what his own robotic Rover had discovered only days earlier—irrefutable evidence of intelligent alien life on the Red Planet.

The winged spaceship arced majestically to the northeast, her long white plume like a massive stack of cotton balls reaching up to the sun.

"SRBs separating at this time," the voice of NASA announced over the speaker.

Moments later, Robert saw the reusable boosters split off to either side of the vehicle, their fall to the ocean retarded by parachutes. There would be no need to recover these boosters; Endeavor was the last of her kind. This was the Shuttle program's final mission.

Simon waded up to his waist in smelly water, heading toward the splashes and rustles in the reeds just ahead. He fondled a hank of bailing twine in his submerged pocket, brought all the way from the farm in Minnesota for this special day. He pulled it free, wrapping the cord around his hand just as his hero would. Now he waited, heart pounding, hoping the line was long enough. Favorite episodes of *Crocodile Hunter* raced through his head. No one would make fun of him again, not after today.

Moments later, the tall cattails parted ahead of him. Simon caught sight of the creature—and screamed.

Robert's pulse raced for minutes after the eye-watering launch of the first manned mission to Mars. He imagined the crew—including three people he'd helped train—heading to the interplanetary craft, Epsilon, a brilliant white cylindrical spacecraft docked to a new commercial space station in equatorial orbit. For the next 470 days, Epsilon would be the home of three modern Magellans headed across the solar system to investigate evidence of alien life. His own robotic exploration of Mars, history-making though it was, seemed pale in comparison to this magnificent venture.

"Robert? Have you seen Simon?" asked a freckled woman to his left, interrupting his daydream. Barbara, his sister. "He was playing under the stands a minute ago . . ."

Robert shook his head, frustrated that she'd broken his concentration. She stood and pushed past him, hurrying up the bleachers against the flow of the departing crowd. He turned to watch her scan the sea of people. The last time he'd seen his nephew was before the launch, at least fifteen minutes ago.

"Are you sure, Barbara? I mean, that it was just a *minute* ago?" he asked, huffing to the top of the aluminum stands to join her.

"Simon!" she yelled.

Robert's annoyance grew; his wandering nephew was nowhere to be seen. Then he spotted two shoes on the grass near a large wetlands area, about thirty meters away. In a flash, Robert forgot all the previous lost-child episodes, his only thought of Simon—of his vivid imagination and his passion for reptiles. He dashed down the stands, yelling over his shoulder. "The marsh!"

Behind him he could hear Barbara's feet pounding down the metal stairs in frantic pursuit.

The creature pushed through a clump of cattails into the open. It was a towering silver spider-like thing, with eight gleaming jointed legs that emerged from an egg-shaped body and descended into the moss green waters. Some manner of head rose from the front of the egg, like a football on the end of a silver snake-like hose. The head, barely hidden by the tall cattails, had one large eye and no mouth that Simon could see. The head descended to face him.

Simon couldn't move, his legs frozen in sucking black goo. His hands, shoulders, and knees shook out of control. A second scream lodged in his throat.

A moment later, other reeds parted to the right and left of the metal spider. There were three of them. He squeezed the braided twine in his right hand with all the force he could muster. He refused to run.

Simon gritted his teeth, pushed sweaty hair off his forehead, and bent to grab his right knee, his arm immersed to the shoulder. He pulled hard and freed his foot but lost his balance and fell face first into slime. *Mom's gonna be mad,* he thought. He regained his balance and moved within reach of the creature's closest leg, his heart pounding in his ears.

He leaned left and right, trying to see around the massive silver thing. *Maybe it* is *a spider from space,* he thought, remembering the stunning images of two spiders pursuing the American rover on Mars only a few days before. *Or maybe there's an alien inside a ship that's* built *like a spider.* Either way, his excitement and curiosity barely overcame his burning desire to turn and run.

The head thing followed his every movement, then looked to the left and right at the other silver spiders. Simon heard a noise, like a high-pitched cry in the distance, but he couldn't make it out. The other creatures heard it too, and all three heads elevated to the top of the cattail stalks, looking to his right.

Simon shook so hard that he could barely breathe. He forced himself to calm down, then extended his left arm, palm out. He reached up to touch what looked like a jointed aluminum bamboo pole, one of eight, that extended in a gentle arc from the creature's body. The leg was cool. As he touched it, Simon could feel the silver thing hum.

The spider didn't seem to like his touch; it retreated beyond his grasp, four long legs on each side pulling free of the muck in quick succession with a *shlop* sound. Simon waded forward, let one end of the cord fall loose in the water, and cinched it to the closest leg.

This is no alligator . . . and even if it was, 'gators only eat when they're hungry, he remembered. Memories of his Australian hero whipping ropes about snapping reptile jaws emboldened him as Simon tightened his first knot.

Robert reached the marsh first. He raced past a neat pile of shoes and socks and stumbled headlong into the slimy bayou. "Simon!" he yelled for the third time. "Answer me!" Stinging blades ripped at his bare arms as he pushed through clumps of saw grass, eyes darting as he searched for the boy.

"Over here!" he heard from somewhere to his right. *Simon's voice!*

"Simon!" Robert screamed again, stumbling through a thick

mound of weeds. His shoes were sucked off his feet in the black ooze as he pushed through dense water lilies in the direction of the boy's voice. He could hear Barbara hit the water about ten meters behind him.

"Uncle Robert!" he heard, just ahead of him. "I've got one! Come see!"

✳

Robert stood aghast, unsteady in the muck five meters from his tiny nephew, gasping for air, sweat sheeting off his face. Simon slogged slowly toward him, a short hank of braided twine cinched around the mud-drenched leg of a three-meter-tall silver tarantula that followed the boy's lead. Behind it, another two moved through the muck, their jointed silver legs making a *shlop-shlop-shlop* sound as twenty-four appendages slid in and out of the marsh mud. The three moved forward single file at the speed of Simon's proud progress through the green and black water.

Robert fought to get a full breath. The closer they came, the more his chest constricted. Barbara stumbled into him from behind, pressing through the last clump of weeds and nearly bowling him over. She fell face first into the green water. Robert helped his sister to her feet as she spat mud and gasped at the sight of her son with his bizarre captives.

"Simon!" Robert commanded, "Stop now. Let them go."

Barbara whimpered behind him. He gripped her hand hard to hold her back.

"I caught some Martians!" Simon said with a huge grin as he led the ominous trio.

"Simon!" Barbara screamed and pulled harder at Robert, as though pleading with him to let her go to her son. He relented, and the two struggled to free their feet of the mud, then moved toward the boy.

One silent minute later, Barbara stooped in slime-covered water, sinking to her knees at the base of the lead spider to take her son in her arms. He handed the twine lasso proudly to his uncle and hugged his mom.

Robert looked up at the stationary spiders ahead of him, their heads moving about crazily on long slender necks. One peered above the weeds in the direction of the bleachers, and another looked back along their line of advance. The lead creature lowered its head to confront him, one unblinking eye the only feature on its "face."

Robert pulled Barbara up from the dank water. "Move back," he said, motioning toward the shore behind them. She nodded in silence. Mother and son slogged a retreat to safety.

Robert waited. He could hear Barbara pulling Simon through the swamp, thrashing their way through tall reeds. "Uncle Robert!" Simon called. But Robert was alone now. He'd lived this moment remotely two weeks ago with Rover, his marvelous robot one hundred and fifty million kilometers from Earth. Rover had been cornered on Mars by two of these creatures; Robert faced three.

"Run!" Barbara urged from a distance.

Run? Not a chance. He stood still, grasping an insane hope that these creatures would behave like those on Mars. Peacefully.

He didn't have to wait long. "Claws!" Half a minute later, Simon yelled from somewhere behind. A pair of snapping pliers-like grapples on long appendages emerged from the belly of the lead alien, just as Robert and his colleagues had witnessed two weeks before in startling images from Mars.

Once fully extended, the claws coiled upward to the underside of the craft and reached inside the muddy pod—just like on Mars—and pulled an iridescent golden orb from its belly. It reached both flexible arms across the water and presented the polished sphere without hesitation. Robert extended his own arms, his pulse pounding in his ears. The alien seemed to be waiting on Robert's next move. Again, just like on Mars.

He took one step forward, Barbara's soft cries the only other sound in the wetlands. His hands trembled, poised at the edge but not touching the shiny grapefruit-sized offering. This was an exact duplicate of the Martian greeting nearly every human being in the modern world had seen at least once — many a hundred times — on the television in the past fifteen days.

A sudden pain stabbed his chest. *What's happening?* He ignored the sensation, his whole will focused on the historic importance of this moment.

Swallowing his fears, Robert clasped the sides of the offering. As soon as he grasped it, the orb transformed to a brilliant blue, a hue so intense that he turned his head to shield his eyes. The alien released its grip, backing away. Slowly, with the gift safe in Robert's hands, the searing blue light paled to a gentle azure glow.

The spiders crept backward a few meters, and all three heads again snaked to the top of the cattails. A piercing whine from the lead alien was followed by five loud tones in short succession, one each from the two spiders behind the leader and three more from somewhere deeper in the marsh. Then, with a soft *whoosh*, each of the spiders began to power up as though for flight.

Cattails and saw grass blew wildly around Robert as the propulsive blast of the aliens flattened weeds and sprayed water like the rotor downwash of a helicopter. Robert shielded his face with his right arm as the spiders rose, slipping their long tendrils free of the dark bog. In the distance, he could see three more spiders rise above the vegetation.

He wanted to watch it all, but chest cramps doubled him over. He clutched the sphere tight in his right hand. He couldn't breathe. Craning his neck, he looked up one more time, cringing from the pain he could no longer ignore. The alien craft rose in a triangle formation, the lead one followed by its two partner spiders and three more from deeper within the swamp flying behind them—1-2-3, pointed like a dart straight up into the sky.

A searing pain brought him to his knees. The blue orb slipped from his grasp and sank slowly in the murky water as Robert crumpled, chest deep. A hot spike seemed to drive itself through his left shoulder, numbing his left arm, and he fell forward. He heard Barbara scream once more as he gasped for air, then sank beneath the green scum.

"Welcome back," Barbara said, squeezing Robert's hand half an hour later. He lay immobile on a stretcher at the edge of the marsh. Emergency medical technicians lifted the gurney and began to roll it away.

"Barbara?" Robert whispered.

"I'm here," she said, trying to hurry along with the EMTs. "We almost lost you."

"My heart?"

She nodded. "Simon ran for help. I held you out of the water." She shivered, still shocked by how close they'd come to losing him. "He saved your life."

"I'm proud of him," he whispered. "Roped some aliens, too." He winced and squeezed her hand. "Must tell you . . . something," he said, struggling to speak as the EMT locked the gurney into the floor of the ambulance and hooked Robert up to a portable EKG.

"Be quiet, Robert. Save your strength. We have that blue ball they gave you. It's safe. Some NASA folks found it." Barbara returned his squeeze. "You made history today—*again*." Her tears fell on her brother's shoulder.

"Listen! Must tell Scott O'Grady . . . at my lab . . . no one else."

She nodded.

"They *spoke* . . . to me." She saw him glance at the EMT, as though waiting while the technician moved to the back to close the doors.

"The *aliens*?" she asked.

He nodded; she felt his hand tremble in hers. He motioned with his head for her to lean closer as the van started its diesel motor. "These words. Repeat them . . . to Scott."

He whispered into her ear. Barbara felt her skin go cold—then the EMT hurried her out the side door of the ambulance.

Robert leaned back, relieved. "Be sure to thank Simon."

She wiped her wet eyes and waved in silent reply as the door closed and the vehicle rolled away.

Robert's whispered message gnawed at her as she knelt beside her wet son and pulled him close. She'd always denied that aliens existed, certain that her brother's recent Martian discoveries were the result of someone's cruel hoax. Yet she'd seen the aliens today with her own eyes. Simon had delivered them to her. The proof.

And now her brother's desperate whisper had, in the course of only a few minutes, shredded her deep conviction that life had been created only on Earth—and validated the beliefs of eccentric groups that stood for everything she opposed. She wanted with all her heart to forget this message that testified against the very foundations of her faith—

We are many. Do not fear. We are the Father Race.

AUSTIN BOYD IS AN award-winning novelist who writes about faith issues related to technology, and spiritual allegories that represent a fresh approach to Christian fiction. He creates stories that encourage readers to wrestle with dilemmas of faith through what he calls "a novel approach to truth." Austin is a Christy Gold Medal finalist (*The Proof,* 2007) and winner of multiple writing honors, including the Mount Hermon Christian Writers' "Pacesetter Award."

Austin writes from his experience as a decorated Navy pilot, spacecraft engineer, and as an astronaut candidate finalist. He and his wife Cindy are the parents of four children and live in America's "Rocket City," Huntsville, Alabama, where he serves as the Senior Vice President of a product engineering company that supports NASA, the Department of Defense, and commercial entrepreneurs.

Austin's creative talents include inspirational fiction, poetry, and finely crafted reproduction colonial furniture. In addition to his writing, he is active outdoors as an avid archer, cyclist, and hiker. He serves Huntsville's First Baptist Church and his community as an advocate for crisis pregnancy centers, and as a speaker on issues of lifestyle evangelism through a popular series entitled "Understanding Islam."

Learn more about the author at www.austinboyd.com and www.amgpublishers.com

LOOK FOR THE NEXT 2 TITLES IN THE Mars Hill Classified SERIES BY AUSTIN BOYD.

The Proof

ISBN: 978-0-89957-829-3

Navy astronaut John Wells leads NASA's manned mission to Mars to investigate signs of intelligent life. At the pinnacle of a lifelong quest to conquer space and safely returned from Mars, John gains his life but must give up that thing he has always treasured most. This second novel in the series was a finalist for the Christy Gold Medal in fiction in 2007.

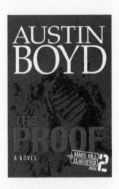

The Return

ISBN: 978-0-89957-830-9

John Wells accepts the call to return to the Red Planet a second time. But this time he goes to the surface to explore the planet, not simply spend thirty days in orbit. Can he reach out to those he has discovered? Faced with immense personal loss, can he forgive? Why did God call him to this place, to grievous loss, and then force him to confront his tormentors face to face? The alien trilogy of Mars Hill Classified comes to a surprising close.

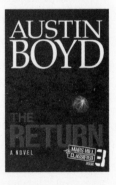

Visit your local Christian bookstore, call AMG at 1-800-266-4977, or log on to www.AMGPublishers.com to purchase.

Living Ink Books
An Imprint of AMG Publishers